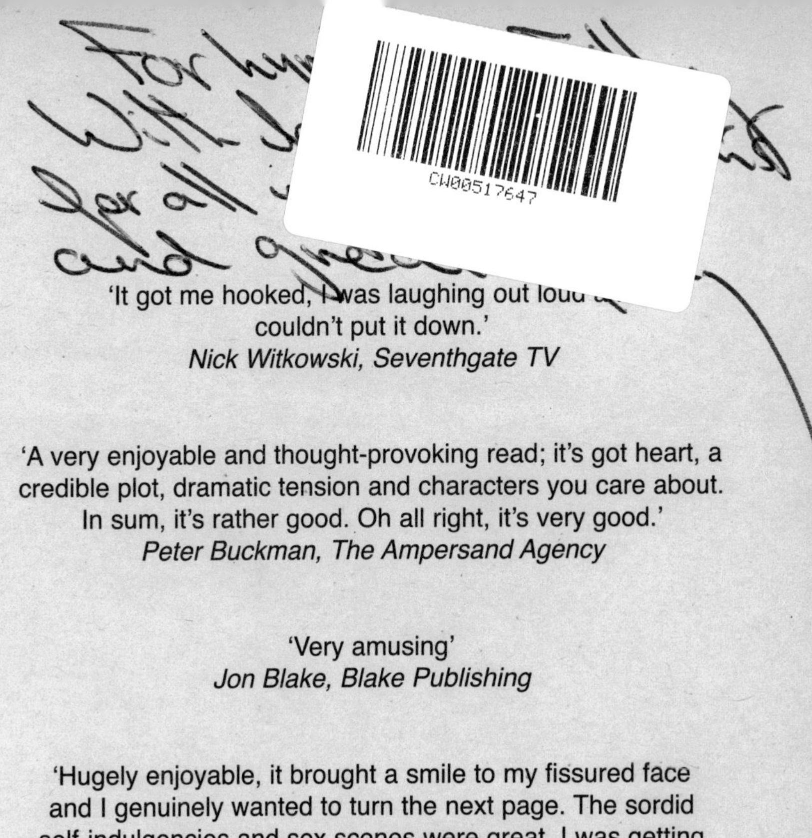

'It got me hooked, I was laughing out loud and
couldn't put it down.'
Nick Witkowski, Seventhgate TV

'A very enjoyable and thought-provoking read; it's got heart, a credible plot, dramatic tension and characters you care about. In sum, it's rather good. Oh all right, it's very good.'
Peter Buckman, The Ampersand Agency

'Very amusing'
Jon Blake, Blake Publishing

'Hugely enjoyable, it brought a smile to my fissured face and I genuinely wanted to turn the next page. The sordid self-indulgencies and sex scenes were great, I was getting quite hot under the condom in places.'
Ian Forth, Professor of Linguistics & Literature, University of Wales

hope that it's not
as rude as they
say it is.
Big Kisses

ABOUT THE AUTHOR

Geoff Baker was born in Lyme Regis in 1956. Leaving Lyme in 1974 he became a Fleet Street journalist and then switched, by fluke, from being showbusiness editor of the *Daily Star* into rock music PR. He represented Oasis, The Beatles and the teen band Purplemelon but was best known for the fifteen years he spent as the PR of Linda and Paul McCartney.

After leaving the publicity pond he became an impoverished writer, working on Rock Bottom for four years in between bouts of severe depression. Rock Bottom is the first of a number of titles to be published by Ragabond Press.

First published in Great Britain in 2011 by Ragabond Press

ISBN 978-0-9567729-0-9

Typeset in Times New Roman
Printed and bound by CPI Bookmarque Ltd

PUBLISHER'S NOTE
This is a work of fiction. Names, characters, places and incidents are
the products of the author's imagination.

Ragabond Press
www.ragabondpress.com
info@ragabondpress.com

AUTHOR'S THANKS

I send my thanks and love to these wonderful people, without whom this book would not exist:

Jill Newton, my editor and muse, quite simply for bringing it all together, sculpting, inspiring, tirelessly supporting and making it happen (although there was nothing at all simple about any of that) and for being brilliant.

Nick Witkowski, Ian Forth, Lea Hurst, Sarah MacLennan, Sue Ziebland, Elisabeth Nord and Amanda Baker for test-reading and suggestions, and Clare Smith for her patient and diligent proof-reading.

Alex MacLennan and Justin Tunstall for publishing advice and mateship.

Geoff Fisher at CPI for his patience and publishing expertise.

Peter Buckman for first suggesting the novel, signing me up as my literary agent and sacking me just as it was finished.

Paul McCartney, for good times and for giving this book his green light.

Barrie Marshall, Margo Buchanan, Ken Lennox and Tracks for their great kindness.

Robbie Montgomery for being there.

Pip Evans, for giving me my best job in journalism.

Kevin O'Sullivan, Tony Purnell, Roger Taverner, Pat Hill, Lester Middlehurst, Baz Bamigboye, Pat Codd, Stafford Hildred, Michael Burke, Ivan Waterman, Henrietta Knight, Pauline Wallin, Lesley Ann Jones and Sarah Bond for being the finest of Fleet Street hack packs.

Bernard Doherty, Joe Dera, Christian Down, Elizabeth Freund, Fiona Hurry, Nikki Turner, Julia Smith, Mika El Baz and Jane Sen for teaching me the honest art of rock PR.

Shelagh Jones, Emma Sutton, Laura Gross, Cathy Hawkes, Neil Aspinall, Derek Taylor, Bill Porricelli, Richard Ogden, Paul Winn Lilian Marshall and Alan Crowder for teaching me about the music business.

Hundreds of stars and reporters worldwide for letting me witness how they worked. Hundreds of thousands of Beatles-related concert goers, for turning me on to the psyche of fandom.

Amanda and our treasured children Jessie, Emily, Nicky and Robbie, for their love.

And Bob Marley's gardener for the seed.

DEDICATION

To Mum and Dad for their love,
and to all who suffer from the black dog
that is so difficult to understand.

GEOFF BAKER

ROCK BOTTOM

RAGABOND PRESS

IAN TAYLOR
BIOGRAPHY

1949 Nov 28th Ian is found in a baby basket on the steps of the Birmingham Children's Hospital. Nurses estimate the child is between two and three days old. A note inside the basket reads '*His name is Ian Taylor and he is special.*'

1960 Following failed placements with a series of foster parents, Ian is convicted of stealing a motorbike and is sentenced to six months at a juvenile detention centre in Dudley, West Midlands. There he makes his first electric guitar and teaches himself to play.

1961 Ian wins a charity-sponsored scholarship to King Edward's School, Birmingham, where he excels in English and Art. Despite possessing perfect pitch, he is thrown out of the school choir for smoking in chapel.

1963 Ian forms his first band, The Teddy Boys, with schoolmates John 'Dick' Jackson, Micky Grigson, Dan Fisher and Archie Wendles-Mellor. Ian writes his first song, *You Don't Get It.*

1964 April 10th, The Teddy Boys give their first public performance, at the Handsworth YMCA, to a crowd of 34. Their performance wins them a Sunday night residency.

1965 Ian leaves school with 10 'O'-levels and enrols at the Birmingham College of Art with John (now 'Jack' Jackson). On July 30th at Digbeth Studios The Teddy Boys cut their first record, the Taylor-Jackson composition, *Flower Queenie,* making three copies of which two were later stolen. After a row over musical direction, Ian and Jack quit The Teddy Boys and form Taylspin with Wim Rogers, Roy Adams and Eileen Lore. With a growing following in the West Midlands, Taylspin is signed to the BPA label.

1966 Taylspin's single *Love You Girl* is No.1 in 18 countries. The band's first album, *Don't Ask Your Mother*, tops the charts in both the UK and US. Taylspin tours North America and is named new band of the year by *Billboard.*

1967 During the band's second US tour Ian is arrested in Pittsburgh and Los Angeles at demonstrations against the Vietnam War and is subsequently investigated by the FBI on suspicion of funding underground anti-war movements. Taylspin's second album, *Exhibit A*, tops seven million sales worldwide. US radio stations ban the Taylspin single *J. Edgar's Secret.*

1968 Taylspin rocks the music world with the release of the anti-war album *Grey Rose.* The highly-controversial and limited-edition record tops critics' polls around the globe as album of the year, despite the band's self-imposed ban on its live performance. Ian is fined £3,000 by a London court for possessing cannabis. After paying the fine in ten shilling notes Ian leaves England to live with the heiress and feminist poet Marcelle Du Pont on a hashish farm in North Africa, where he builds a studio to record an album of Algerian choirs.

1971 Taylspin shocks their detractors with the worldwide success of their fourth album *Thank Christ For The Cong*, which achieves triple-platinum sales in the US and tops the UK album charts for 10 weeks. The 18-month *'Cong'* world tour sets a new record as the highest-grossing ever, despite death threats and riotous protests at concerts by opponents of the peace movement. Taylspin's Christmas single, *I Don't Want To Die Before Frosty*, is the UK No.1.

1975 Ian's self-directed film of Moroccan brothels, *Mustafa's Donkey,* wins the prize for best documentary at the Cannes Film Festival but is banned by censors in the UK, US and 80 other countries. Following a libel action, Ian makes a substantial out-of-court payment to three British Members of Parliament filmed in the documentary without their permission. Taylspin's greatest hits album, *You've Already Got This,* tops the album charts in the UK and US. A North American theatre tour to promote the album is marred when 45 fans are hospitalised in New York and 57 crushed in San Francisco at stampedes for tickets.

1976 Citing 'musical, ethical, mystical, sexual, pharmaceutical and shoe-size differences' Ian stuns fans around the globe by announcing the break-up of Taylspin and his own retirement from the music industry. At a press conference in Amsterdam to announce the split, Ian and long-time writing partner Jack Jackson engage in a punch-up after Ian reveals that he has bought sole rights to all of Taylspin's music publishing.

1980 After his secret two-year sojourn touring Britain in a canal boat is revealed in a Sunday newspaper, Ian buys a stately home in Wiltshire and announces plans to turn it into a tai chi centre and spiritual retreat under the direction of his girlfriend, the Hong Kong TV presenter Wendy Zhu. Ian is fined £5,000 for possession of cocaine.

1984 Ian returns to the music business with the acclaimed release of his first solo album, the nod to his Motown influences *It Has to Bop.* The album reaches No.1 on both sides of the Atlantic. A range of organic preserves from his country estate, *Jam Jam,* goes on sale in British supermarkets, with all profits going to Barnardo's children's charity.

1986 Ian performs his first concerts in 11 years on a worldwide solo tour, selling out every gig in 55 cities and releasing a documentary movie of the trek directed by a 16-year-old art student.

1987 Ian announces his second retirement from the music business.

1990 Ian announces his return to the music business with the release of a critically well-received country album *Hello Cowboy*. In support of Amnesty International he attempts to mount an impromptu concert in Shanghai but is deported by the authorities.

1994 B PA's release of Taylspin's second greatest hits album, *You've Already Got This Too*, sells five million copies.

1997 Ian breaks both legs in a collision with paparazzi while snowboarding in Aspen.

1999 Ian is sued for $75 million damages by a fan, citing unfair discrimination, when it is announced that all 4,000 tickets for a Colorado Nursing Federation benefit concert will only be available to people in wheelchairs.

2002 Ian is arrested in Milan after threatening a photographer with a flick-knife.

2004 After secretly paying for the life-saving treatment of a nine-year-old child with leukaemia in New York, Ian is charged with assaulting a photographer whilst visiting the child in a private ward. The charges are dropped following huge public outcry.

2005 Ian makes an unannounced appearance at Glastonbury, backed by a 200-strong gospel choir and ending a festival-stopping set with a 12-minute version of *Give Peace A Chance.*

2007 A solo album of previously-unreleased Taylspin songs, *The Label Twisted My Arm Guys,* peaks at No.3 in the UK charts and No.7 in the US.
2008 Publishers in London announce a $9 million deal with Ian to write his autobiography.

2009 Ian launches his own range of menswear for an Italian fashion label.

2010 A South Korean car company unveils the Ian Taylor 'Eco Minx' at the Paris Motor Show.

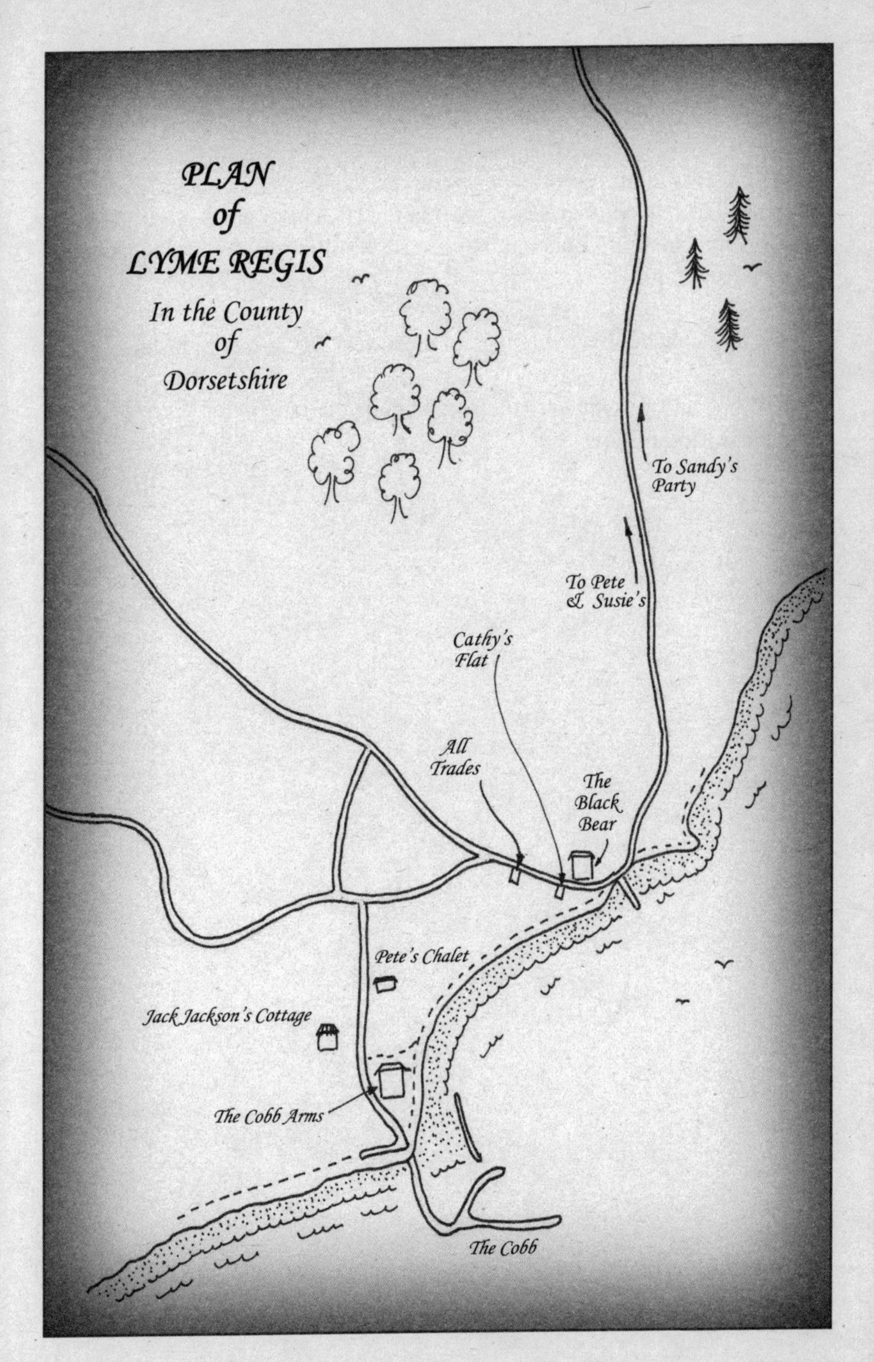
PLAN
of
LYME REGIS
In the County
of
Dorsetshire
To Sandy's
Party
To Pete
& Susie's
Cathy's
Flat
All
Trades
The
Black
Bear
Pete's Chalet
Jack Jackson's Cottage
The Cobb Arms
The Cobb

CHAPTER 1

The manager in sole charge of the opulent career of one of Britain's most enduringly-idolised rock stars looked at the envelope that his uninvited guest had placed on the restaurant table beside his glass of Chablis.

Billy Vernon was nonchalant about the intrusion on his private time. With his left hand he continued to fork lobster into his large mouth as he kept his right hand beneath the table, between the parted thighs of his young blonde companion, whose nose was clearly running.

'What's this?' said Vernon, poking at the envelope with the fork.

'My results from the pox doctor?'

The blonde tittered but their guest retained the grim expression that Vernon had noted when he had walked purposefully into the New York restaurant seconds before.

'Or is it Sam's fee, Peter? In which case looks a little thin, doesn't it?'

The girl giggled again and ostentatiously dabbed her nose with a white damask napkin as she widened her legs further to accommodate more of Vernon's shuffling fingers.

'I think you should look at that alone,' said Peter Forth as he wondered how long it would be until he was asked to pull up a chair. Not wanting any interruptions, he went to turn off his mobile and saw three bloody messages to ring his wife at home in the middle of her night. He turned it off anyway.

'What do you mean?' said Vernon.

Peter indicated the girl but Vernon ignored the insinuation for privacy. Grinning, he put his fork down on the side of his plate and reached for the envelope. Immediately, Peter put his hand down over Vernon's and held it there.

'Really. Alone. It's not a laugh, Billy.'

'Don't be ridiculous,' said Vernon, still smiling as he retrieved his right hand from under the table. He wiped his fingers surreptitiously on the tablecloth then tore open the envelope.

'I wouldn't...' warned Peter, but Vernon continued to ignore him.

'I'll just take a peek, Pete; Sam here can shut her eyes. Can't you Sam?'

The girl simpered, and Peter thought that he remembered seeing her in the office of the record company's marketing department. He wondered if she actually worked there or whether she was one of the consultants claimed on expenses as flowers and wine, the usual record company codeword for the coterie of hookers that they kept on retainers.

He watched Vernon make a pantomime display of gingerly pulling a photograph from the envelope and, without looking at it properly, holding it close to his face so that the girl could not see it. There was silence at the table and then everybody dining at the chic and expensive brasserie was interrupted by a yell of, 'Fucking hell!' as Billy Vernon leapt to his feet, briefly exposing to the restaurant the flash of his member, which Sam had been fondling through his open flies beneath the table.

Peter had pulled a fifty-dollar bill out of his pocket before a flustered waiter appeared wide-eyed at their table.

'Go away,' said Peter, palming the waiter the note. Then he leant over and put his face close to Sam's red-lipped gape.

'Do you work for the label?' he said evenly. She nodded nervously.

'Good. Well then fuck off before I make sure you don't.'

The girl fidgeted with her dress below the table and, once decently rearranged, stood and walked huffily out of the room. Peter slipped into her seat and looked at Vernon, who was seated again now, holding his bald, florid head in his hands and staring at the photograph in despair.

'Tell me this is a fake, Peter,' said Vernon, gulping at his glass.

'Well it doesn't look like it, I admit. And unless I took it to a lab I couldn't be sure. But it's not real anyway, is it? I mean, it can't be. It's Ian for God's sake.'

'Shit,' said Vernon.

'What do you mean?' said Peter.

'Where did you get it?'

'Bizarrely, it just came in my post at the office,' said Peter. 'There was a note, claiming to be from some big fan who says he doesn't want to ruin Ian's reputation. Why are you getting so stressed?'

'How much does he want for it?' said Vernon, looking stern.

'He doesn't mention money. The note just says he wants to do us a favour – and he wants to meet with Ian.'

'Let me see it,' said Vernon.

Peter took a smaller envelope from the breast pocket of his black suit and passed it to Vernon, who snatched it and took out a plain piece of white paper with a few lines of typing at the top. Vernon scanned it, then looked back at the photograph with a face darkening with anger, pointing to the second figure in the photograph.

'Who's that?' he said.

'I don't know,' said Peter, confused by Vernon's intensity.

'Have you made copies of this?'

'No, that's the only print.'

'But how… where… how did he shoot this? Where was it taken? How did a bloody photographer get in this position?'

'It's not the photographer's position that bothers me,' said Peter, politely asking a waiter for a large Scotch. 'It's the position of Ian's head that would spell the end of a brand as we know it. If that was real it'd trash the comeback you keep talking about.'

'Just a bit,' said Vernon.

'But it's not real, is it? It can't be real, can it?' said Peter, cynically.

Vernon grimaced as he looked again at the picture. There was no doubting that there was the head of Ian Taylor in the groin of a naked anonymous man, and there was no doubt either that if this was circulated on the Net then Ian Taylor's forty-year reign as rock's most eligible ladies' man would be somewhat in question.

'I don't suppose there's any up side to it?' ventured Peter.

'Upside?' snorted Vernon. 'Well what do you think, Pete? What exactly is the upside of the housewives' heart throb getting caught with some bloke's dick in his mouth? I'm sorry, I must have missed that particular silver lining in my excitement at having my life utterly ruined here. Silly me.'

'I just meant…'

'Meant what? Tell me, what is the up side of this wonderful study? That we'll sell more albums in Old Compton Street?'

'Billy, it's a fake. It has to be. And, Christ, even if it's not, it's not illegal. Who gives a flying fuck in this day and age? I don't think even the newspapers are bothered anymore,' said Peter.

'Are you mad? The newspapers would have him for hypocrisy; they'd fucking love it.'

'Bloody hell, Bill, if I'd have known you were going to take it this seriously I'd never have shown you. It's only some geek's prank. I only thought you should see it because it appears so convincing.'

Vernon sighed heavily and thought in silence for some moments.

'It possibly is real, Pete,' he said at last.

'You're fucking joking.'

'I wish.'

'What? How? Are you sure? Bloody hell. Oh, for fuck's sake.'

'I know, bit of a turn up isn't it?' said Vernon grimly.

'Jesus. Is he still? I mean, fuck! Ian's gay?'

'Keep your fucking voice down,' said Vernon. 'Anyway he's not, he's bi.'

'How come that I didn't know?'

'Because I can't afford the risk that you wouldn't leak it when you're pissed.'

'Why would I do that? I'd be creating a publicity nightmare for myself,' said Peter indignantly.

'Look,' said Vernon wearily, 'we've spent millions keeping this quiet over the years. Why else do you think all those rumours began about other members of Taylspin being on the turn? Who do you think started that gossip?'

'Why?'

'Because years of clandestine market research has clearly shown that women would not buy albums of Ian's love songs if they thought that the sweetheart he was singing about was some pert-bottomed boy who delivers his pizza.'

'Are you saying that all that stuff about the drummer and their promoter was made up?' said Peter, appalled.

Vernon nodded.

'But that guy killed himself, the drummer.'

'I know. I was at his funeral.'

'But he killed himself because he couldn't handle people thinking he was gay. Are you saying that was set-up to deflect attention from Ian?'

'All I'm saying,' said Vernon as he helped himself to a gulp of the Scotch that the waiter had brought for Peter, 'is that he was only the drummer; he couldn't write songs. He didn't matter.'

'But he killed himself!'

Vernon eyed him evenly.

'Peter, Peter. There's a frog and a drummer standing on the side of the road, both trying to hitch a ride. Who do you pick up? The frog because the frog's on his way to a gig. Drummers are replaceable. Ian Taylors are not. Too much money rests on him.'

'That's disgusting.'

'Oh, and I suppose what you do for a living is not? Fuck off,' spat Vernon, who was now studying the photograph again.

'When exactly was this taken do you think?' said the worried manager.

'I'm not sure, I'm not used to seeing him in that sort of pose. It's obviously a copy of the original and Ian's obviously younger; his hair's darker, not that that means much. Don't know; I'd say mid-seventies. It would help if he had clothes on.'

'It would help if he wasn't sucking a dick,' said Vernon, who was re-reading the note.

'It says the photographer is dead,' said Peter, pointing to the note.

'I can read that,' snapped Vernon. 'Not that it means it's true.'

'So what do you want me to do?' said Peter as he poured Vernon some more Chablis from the expensive bottle in the ice bucket to keep him away from his Scotch.

'Find them, obviously. Find out who sent it and fuck them.'

'How?'

'Jesus Christ, talk about keeping a dog and barking yourself. I don't fucking know. Get a private investigator, I don't know…'

'I suppose we could always ask Ian if he remembers who took it?' said Peter without thinking clearly.

'Yeah, that's a good idea,' said Vernon sarcastically. 'Just slip it into the pile of new handout pics that you said you want him to approve. See if he notices.'

'Actually,' said Peter, 'I suppose all that I have to do is wait.'

'How's that work, then?'

'Well, whoever sent it isn't just going to leave it at that. They'll be in touch again. You can bet on it.'

'You've got a lot of experience of blackmail, have you?'

'Nobody's just going to send you that and never contact you again, are they?'

'Not unless they really hate you,' said Vernon grimly, 'which, knowing our game, limits the suspects to just about everybody we've ever dealt with.'

'No, whoever it is will come back to us,' said Peter.

'So that's the damage limitation strategy is it, then? You're just going to wait?'

'No, I'm going to make a real fake of it.'

'What?'

'I'm going to make it look like it's a fake. Cut the head off and re-photo it or something; Photoshop it. I don't know. I need to get it treated to make it look like it's been doctored. Just in case it does get to *The Sun*. So I can lie and dismiss it as an Internet prank.'

'Makes sense; assume the worst,' agreed Vernon. 'In which case, I need you to think about how to best re-represent our Ian as the notoriously heterosexual stud that the world loves him to be. Now, of all bloody times, he needs to be seen to be doing some serious shagging.'

'Are you going to tell Ian?'

‘Unless you’d like to do the honours. Which I wouldn’t recommend,’ said Vernon, looking worried again. ‘Anyway, fuck off now and let me think. Oh, and you can pay for that Scotch on the way out. I’m not funding your addictions, as I’ve told you before.’

As Peter left the table, Billy Vernon read the note again. He smirked at the irony of the phrasing:

Dear Ian,
This came into my hand. Hopefully we can prevent any ugliness if you and I can meet to chat. I have something very important to tell you. I don’t want to go to the papers because I don’t want to hurt you because I love you. But there are things you should know.
A Big Fan

PS: The person who took this picture is dead, so don’t worry.

Thanks for the reassurance, thought Vernon, but I’ll worry until I can see you dead too.

CHAPTER 2

Ian Taylor lay in bed pretending to be asleep and wondered just how long exactly it was going to take for the young man dozing beside him to wake and realise that his role was to burrow under the duvet and wake him up with the expert application of fellatio. The lad's place was not, he noted irritably as he glanced at his watch, still to be sleeping for an hour after he – the actual bloody star around here – was awake and requiring attention.

Not for the first time in recent years, Taylor noted that groupies weren't what they used to be. For starters, his groupies of choice had changed sex now. Back in the Seventies he had almost always boned girls; but that was because someone had advised him that a pretence of rampant heterosexuality would result in better album sales than if the never-married songwriter came out about the gayness that only the very few close to him suspected.

For a moment Taylor mused on a whim to complain about the lethargy of the modern starfucker in his next interview, but he rejected the idea because the press would get it wrong, and the story would come out looking as if he was some sad old git. He hated that almost as much as he resented the fact that women didn't fling themselves onto their knees before him anymore. These days they just asked for a picture for their grandchildren.

He slid his eyes over to look at the tangle of dark curly hair on the pillow beside him. He estimated that the boy was about twenty, a third his age, and he had a hunch that when he did wake up he was going to be one of those who expected him to be nice to him just because he had offered Taylor repeated use of both of his puckered apertures throughout most of the night. On the other hand, the lad was a very expensive rent boy and it was surprising that he was so unprofessional.

Taylor wondered whether this Daniel, or whatever he called himself, was going to be one of those boys who latched onto his entourage during the day of promotion ahead, which he already regretted allowing his manager to talk him into. He hoped that Daniel was not going to act over-familiar with him just because he had had his penis in his arse. He had known that type before, the kind who thought themselves entitled to greet him with a world-informing peck on the cheek simply because he had spent the night licking him all over.

Taylor looked at his watch again and decided to give the boy five more minutes to get over his narcolepsy and get his act together down there. After that he would belt out of bed in a dark, muttering sulk contrived to impress upon the lad the feeling that he should get the fuck out of his room for his unspecified wrong-doing.

As he waited he mulled over what he could remember of his schedule. Radio interviews all morning and then that bloody signing session at lunchtime. Talking of radio, he realised that although he had been half-listening to WRBQ for all of the sixty minutes since his erection had woken him up, he had still to hear anybody mention on air the fact that he was staging an album-signing appearance for the first time in his career. He'd have a good moan about that to his record label. Not that it would do the slightest bit of good, he knew that. Nobody wanted to take responsibility for anything in record companies anymore, not since they had been taken over by the sort of corporate people who got scared by the rumblings of their own stomachs.

He could mention it to Pete and that would get something done; but only after Peter had first stuttered a fit of contrite shame at his failure to ensure that it hadn't been done properly already.

Taylor knew that this in-store album-signing was a shit idea and he had said as much to his alleged team of squabbling advisers when they had trotted out for him their spectacularly tedious and safe plan of how to resurrect some interest in the single that he had watched fall thirty places in the Billboard Hot 100 last week. He had said then that if it was such a wonderful strategy, how was it that he had not entertained it for the past forty years? But he saw on their scared little faces that they did not understand his logic, so he had stopped complaining and contented himself instead with making his displeasure felt by glowering and refusing to sign any promo copies for the store's staff.

He noticed that his manhood, which had been magnificent a little while ago, was now attempting a disappearing act of its own and that pissed him off too. Of course he could just roll the boy over onto his belly and start rogering him from behind; as the paying star around here he would be perfectly entitled to do so. But that was no fun, he wanted the boy to want him or at least pretend to, not the other way around; it was boringly usual to be allowed what he asked for.

For a while Taylor pondered about the gap in the chain of command around him. Take this album-signing horror, for instance. As far as he was concerned, he didn't want to do it, so how come that he was? How the fuck had that happened? And why was it that his idea of performing the single over and over again with a band on the back of a flat-bed truck had been rejected? Because the Stones and U2 had done it, they said. So?

Anyway, he knew that this 'it's been done' argument was a ruse and the real truth that nobody around him wanted to admit was that it wasn't allowed; the city authorities wouldn't permit it on account of noise pollution or some such politically correct snivelling. Taylor wondered if anything was allowed in New York anymore, since various conservative powers had conspired to turn the city that never slept into the town that drank warm milk before saying its prayers at bedtime.

He began to wonder if the boy beside him was actually dead. He recalled that the lad had taken a great deal of his cocaine last night; maybe he'd gone and done a bloody Entwistle on him. Tentatively he took his right hand away from playing with himself and touched the small of the kid's back. He was too warm to be dead; which was a shame because that meant that Taylor had to face the fact that Daniel was not now brushing his teeth with his penis just because he didn't want to.

He got out of bed and walked naked through the suite. As usual it was cluttered with baskets of bloody fruit and champagne from idiot general managers who did not realise that very rich men such as he were not in the slightest bit impressed by having free groceries given to them.

He walked over to the full-length mirror that ran down the face of the antique wardrobe and studied himself. For a man of his age, his stomach was pretty flat. Well, flattish. Either way, he decided, he could benefit by losing a few pounds; he'd get the office to book him in for another session of the liposuction that was so much less sweat than all that buggering around on a rowing machine.

He walked into the bathroom to consult another mirror because the light was more flattering, but he still looked nothing like the face that appeared on his album covers. As he ran the hot tap so he could shave, Taylor considered the advantages of having cosmetic surgery. Although it was as affordable to him as buying a bag of popcorn, he was reluctant to do it because he knew that a facial refurbishment would prompt the newspapers to unleash another round of potshots at his vanity which would just cause him embarrassment in restaurants when diners strained their necks to try spot the scars.

As he pulled the wet razor through the foam on the parts of his face that were not covered by his blonde moustache and goatee beard, he winced as he regarded the folds that never used to be there making grey shadows below his eyes. He noticed, too, that his cheeks had become puffier than his 'improved' publicity photos would have people believe. Maybe, he mused, he should just stop worrying about his increasingly craggy looks and just record a country album.

He looked at his Cartier again and determined that as there was no time now for Daniel to wake and be any fun it was time for him to go. He walked back into the bedroom, drew $7,000 from his wallet, the going rate for total discretion, and swatted the notes gently against the rent boy's face, waking him.

'Can you leave, please? I have a meeting. Thanks for your inattention,' he said, huffily.

He went back to the living area of his suite and called room service to order two large pots of Turkish coffee, no milk, scrambled eggs, bacon and a large Bloody Mary.

'Make that a large jug of Bloody Mary,' he added, 'and a small jar of multivitamins. Oh, and some Rizlas.'

Taylor put on a bath robe and turned his attention to his favourite Perez Hilton TV show chuckling along to the stream of irreverence until, fifteen minutes later, the security guard knocked on his door and announced his breakfast tray, brought in by an unnecessary number of stewards augmented by the hotel's general manager. Taylor was relieved to see that the platoon was coincidentally accompanied by the early arrival of Billy Vernon.

'Look after that, Bill, would you?' said Taylor.

As Vernon dealt with the tips, Taylor peeked into his bedroom and was pleased to see Daniel disappearing into the corridor through the suite's other door. Satisfied that he was now alone with his manager, he returned to the lounge.

'So, what's up?' he said curtly as he began to pick at his eggs.

'Well, the good news is that the label is hugely excited about the Rose release and they're going to throw everything behind the promotion,' said Vernon cheerily.

'What's the promo budget?' said Taylor, pouring himself coffee.

'Worldwide, it'll be six million,' beamed Vernon.

'Dollars?'

'Pounds.'

'Hmm,' said Taylor, knowing it to be too early in the meeting for him to reveal any sign of pleasure. 'And what's the bad news?'

'Well, there's no real bad news as such. I mean, it depends on your view. It actually may be nothing...'

'Gob it out,' said Taylor.

'Umm... I met up with Peter...'

'I'm pleased for you. Is he still wanting me to go to that Vanity Fair do? Because he can fuck off if he does.'

'Err... no, he's accepted that you're going to be ill that day. No, it's a little more personal than that...'

'If he's still asking if I can go to the mayor's wife's lunch, the answer remains 'No',' said Taylor. 'I'm not in the business of impressing her salon of house-trained do-gooders and I couldn't give a fuck about the cause. What is the cause, by the way?'

'It's a benevolent fund for injured ski instructors.'

'Birthday parties for toy boys you mean,' observed Taylor. "No' is the final answer.'

'Fine,' said Vernon, who felt that he was sweating. 'I'm afraid Peter's concerns are somewhat more serious…'

'Get on with it…'

'Umm… he has reason to believe that… err… that… you are err… in danger of being… umm… outed.'

Taylor frowned and proceeded to drink the Bloody Mary. When he had emptied the glass, he filled it again from the jug and drank half of the second glass too. He lit a cigarette, stood up and began pacing the room.

'What do you mean? Actually, fuck it, I know what you mean. Why is he saying that? How does he even know? Who fucking told him? Who else knows about this? What've you said?'

'I've said nothing,' said Vernon defensively. 'Pete received a photograph…'

'Of me and a guy?'

Vernon nodded grimly.

'Me and a guy getting it on?'

Vernon nodded again.

'I take it this photo no longer exists, you've destroyed it?'

'And the photographer is dead…' said Vernon, seizing the opportunity to spin the truth.

'I don't want to know,' Taylor cut in, 'but I presume that you and the publicity department are worried that if the public knows I've been touching rock bottom then I'm, basically, fucked?'

'Basically, Ian.'

'Hmm. Well… on the one hand I'm tempted to say so what? Big deal. Oo-er matron. Does it matter?'

'Pete feels it might matter to some of your fans,' said Vernon, confused by the calm defiance which he had not expected.

'By which he means what?'

'Our sales in the Mid-West could be affected. And in the South. The sort of people who voted for Bush could get uptight and could stop buying your albums.'

'I'm not sure I want idiots buying my albums anyway,' said Taylor. 'In fact we should have a sticker made up for the Rose covers saying 'Not for sale to minors and bigots.' Hmm… what does our Pete suggest?'

'He was wondering if you could get yourself photographed with more women…'

'I don't know, Billy. Would that be enough? I mean, we can all name the so-called studs who disguise their queeny secrets in the much-publicised company of slappers. I'm not sure I can be arsed to pretend I'm Don Juan any more. Let me think about it. Thank you, Billy.'

Taylor walked to the door and opened it. Vernon rose and blinked, astounded by his employer's lack of hysterics. As he shut the door behind him he heard the crash of glass smashing against the wall of Taylor's suite. He wondered if it was difficult to remove the stain of tomato juice.

CHAPTER 3

Peter Forth was padding around the kitchen of his home in Dorset at seven in the morning in a foul mood for three reasons. The first was because Susie had yet again rejected his attempt to roll over to her side of their bed to try to give her a rude awakening, mumbling that she would rather have tea and toast, two slices.

The second was because he was exhausted after drinking on the plane back from New York. But the hangover from that was nothing compared to the fucking mind-splitting migraine he was getting from the third reason; worrying that every phone call might be a press request for a comment on Gaylorgate, as he knew they would call it.

As usual, Peter was torn by his bigamous attempts to maintain his marriage while indulging the mistress that was his job, so when he heard a telephone ring in his office, he forgot about the toast and rushed to answer it with an adulterer's enthusiasm.

The ringing ended before he could pick it up and there was no message. He dialled 1471 and was told, 'You were called today at seven nineteen hours, the caller withheld their number.'

Peter did not like the sound of that. A journalist would have left a message or would have immediately rung his mobile. But his mobile wasn't ringing. That meant it was work ringing but, as Ian Taylor's office didn't open for almost another two hours, it seemed more likely that Taylor himself was calling, having probably read something about himself in a gossip column which he would demand to be retracted.

Peter tensed; he hated the sort of call he was now expecting, in which Taylor would order him to ring up an editor and threaten legal action unless there was a printed apology for a small gossip fiction that he had built a gym at home to get his weight down.

What Peter especially disliked was hearing the editor's disbelief at the sheer pettiness of his client. Although, usually, the alleged wrong would be righted simply out of respect for one of Britain's most treasured stars, Taylor still maintained his constant whingeing about the press to the press.

For years he had wanted to shout at Taylor, 'Don't you get it? If you're nice to the press they will be nice to you. You can't bully these people because newspapers always have the last word. And in your case, that word is frequently becoming dickhead!'

But you didn't shout down Ian Taylor. Nobody had shouted down Ian Taylor for forty years, because if you tried it, he just screamed even louder. Peter admired the effectiveness of this approach – it was an extension of a child's tantrum – no one could fail to capitulate to the screeched demands of the increasingly hysterical pop star who wanted his own way; you gave in just to shut him up.

Embittered by what he calculated to be the toll on his nervous system of being nanny to a multi-millionaire, Peter walked back into the kitchen and unthinkingly swore as he stumbled over the cat that was dashing to escape a water blaster attack from his five-year-old, Tommy.

'Bloody fucking cat!' said Peter, at once wishing he had not as he felt Susie's blue eyes salvo disapproval at him.

'It's not the cat. It's Tommy. Tell him off for once,' said Susie in the headmistressey voice that she reserved exclusively for conversation with her husband.

'And can you not swear, please? Mrs Aplin is complaining that Tommy is picking up your language.'

'What do you mean, my language?' Peter lobbed back, ignoring her jibe at his lack of attention.

'You know what I mean,' said Susie dismissively as she turned away from him with a plate of Marmite toast she had made for their seven-year-old, Henry.

'I do not know what you mean at all,' said Peter, the anger at her rejection in the bedroom earlier now finding an outlet. 'What do you mean, my language?'

'It's too early for this,' said Susie, wearily. 'You know what I mean.'

Peter did know. He knew that although it was barely breakfast time he had already lost his second battle of the day and his third – trying to make excuses for journalists whilst getting shrieked at by Ian Taylor – was about to begin its lurch into similar defeat. He felt picked on and his resentment made him depressed.

'Get off!'

Peter turned to see Henry swatting his little brother away from his toast.

'Get off! It's mine! Get your own!' Tommy's eyes began to well up and, instinctively, Peter took his side.

'It's alright; Daddy'll get you some toast, darling. What do you want on it?'

'I hate Henry! He's horrible to me!' whined Tommy as he deliberately kicked his brother's chair.

'You don't hate him,' Peter soothed. 'Don't do that… Tommy! Stop kicking Henry's chair.'

'I'm not.'

'You are! Stop it… Look, never mind… what do you want on your toast?'

'Nothing. I hate toast.'

Peter busied himself with finding the Marmite and the olive oil-based spread which he claimed should be re-named *I Can't Believe I Am Eating This Crap*. Susie, who had made her usual immediate exit as Peter had once again commandeered her role, walked back into the kitchen from the sitting room. A flash of black leg from under her blue silk dressing gown seized his attention.

'Are you wearing stockings?' Peter asked, incredulously.

'Are you making the tea as well now?' said Susie without even looking at him.

'No… um… Who wants tea?'

'I would and so will Henry. Tommy? Tommy, Daddy wants to know if you would like a cup of tea?'

Their youngest son just scowled at her as Peter methodically made a pot of tea whilst taking furtive glances at Susie's legs. He could see the black nylon toes… And she had eye shadow on. Quite a lot of eye shadow, in fact.

'I said are you wearing stockings?'

'You bought them for me,' said Susie with an air of attributing blame.

'But you never wear them,' Peter replied whilst wishing that this was not happening in front of the children.

'That is so untrue, you just don't notice…'

'I bloody well do notice!' Peter protested. 'And I know for a fact that you have never gone out in stockings before. You told me you hated wearing stockings; you said it looks cheap.'

'Will you make your mind up? You keep saying you want me to wear stockings – and these are not stockings, by the way, they are hold-ups – and then, when I do, I get a hard time about it.'

'I am not giving you a hard time. I'm just amazed, that's all… Are you going out?'

'Obviously.'

'Who with?'

'I'm going to take Kevin into Dorchester, for the market. Is that a problem? Then we'll have lunch in Nellie's and I think he said something about wanting to pop in on Jack Jackson later… He wants to see him about something to do with a photograph, I don't know.'

Too much information, thought Peter as his stomach sent him that signal he had known since childhood; the mangling feeling that was as if something had bored into his guts, which came when his instincts knew that very bad things were going to happen.

He considered; Kevin was a family friend and it was usual that the pair of them should go off for the day in order to shop and generally bitch about what an unreasonable bastard Peter was. Nothing to worry about there.

But Jack Jackson…

Peter had been worrying about Jack bloody Jackson. Ever since he had moved near to Peter in Lyme Regis a few months back, Peter had been suspicious of the bloke. Of course, it was very weird that Jackson had been in the band, Taylspin, which had been fronted by Peter's boss. And, although that link provided an initial point of conversation, the fact that Taylor and Jackson had spectacularly fallen out decades ago made contact with the guy awkward for Peter. His discomfort had increased as Susie had begun to pay an excessive amount of interest in visiting the small camera shop and gallery that Jackson had opened in Lyme in his retirement incarnation as a photographer.

Susie went upstairs to their bedroom and Peter followed her. As always, the bed was still unmade. As Susie ignored it and sat at her dressing table Peter picked up the duvet from the white wood floor and shook it out onto the bed, covering it with the expensive dark red Persian throw, as Susie got dressed.

She opened her wardrobe and paused thoughtfully, then chose a mid-length black dress and stepped into it the legs that Peter found so erotic in their black, lace-topped hold-ups. No knickers, Peter noticed with growing horror.

'You're not wearing any knickers,' said Peter, instantly appalled to hearing himself sound like her mother.

'I never wear knickers…'

'But you never wear a dress either… you've never worn a dress with stockings or stay-ups or whatever they're called and no knickers…'

Susie looked at him with an expression that Peter was alarmed to read was one of patronising contempt. She sighed in that 'Oh-for-God's-sake' way that she used when she wanted to belittle him which, to Peter, seemed to be most of the time these days.

'Look… if it's such a big deal for you, I'll wear knickers. Although I think you're being rather hypocritical – you don't wear pants and I don't think that means you go around flashing your cock at anybody…'

'What do you mean? Are you planning on flashing your cun…?'

'Oh for Christ's sake!' Susie exploded with an anger that Peter took to be tactically evasive. 'Did I say that? That's just your sick bloody mind always suspecting the worst of everybody.'

She shoved past Peter and pulled open her underwear drawer. 'If it'll stop all this bollocks, I'll wear knickers,' she said as she put on a pastel orange thong that matched, Peter noted, her bra.

Great, thought Peter, matching undies, that makes it worse; now she's even more appealing and she knows that. He considered whether he had just been set up.

'Happy now?' Susie sneered as she faced him, her dress hitched up over her hips, making an erotic pose in stockings that led up to her lace thong through which he could see her crew-cut bush.

'Susie…' he faltered.

'What! What's the matter? Oh dear, is this turning you on?'

'Forget it, just fucking forget it,' said Peter as he left the bedroom, punching the door.

CHAPTER 4

Peter clomped noisily down the stairs, retrieved the pile of newspapers from the kitchen table and returned to his office, slamming the door shut. Methodically, he read the nationals in the order in which he most expected to find something that would upset him, *Sun, Mail, Star, Mirror, Sport, Express* and then the broadsheets.

He had done with *The Times* and *Telegraph* and had just turned to the *Guardian* when he realised what the problem *du jour* would be about. There, slightly off-centre across four columns and five inches deep on the front page of the *Guardian* was a photograph of a man on the cover of the new issue of *Saga*, the magazine for pensioners. The man was Ian Taylor. Above the picture a helpful sub had put a three-deck headline which read, 'Taylor Now Grandma's Fave'.

Peter looked at the photograph and winced. He knew immediately that it was not an approved studio shot; it was a blow-up of Taylor singing on stage and he looked, well, old. The hair around his ears was prominently grey, his bearded jowls sagged into the collar of his shirt, the many lines around his blue eyes were evident and his thick-lipped mouth was set in such a way that it seemed as if he had forgotten to put his teeth in.

Peter was confused; what was Ian doing on the cover of *Saga*? There had been no recent interview with *Saga*; in fact he had never done an interview with *Saga*. He read the story and the full horror of the events became clear.

The *Guardian* reported that Taylor, once the slim-hipped idol of the teenagers of the Love Generation, had been voted the musician most popular with *Saga's* readers, or 'the rocking-chair rollers' as the *Guardian* had dubbed them. Apparently he had pipped Cliff Richard and Tom Jones to win the accolade which, Peter knew, Taylor would be less pleased to hear than being told that he had leprosy.

Now Peter knew why his office telephone had rung so early. Taylor wouldn't have read the newspapers by then, but he may well have caught an item in the review of the day's press that ran around that time on the breakfast television channel that Taylor liked to watch in his hot-tub. Either that or some well-wishing member of his feral family had phoned to say sorry to bother him, dear, but he was in the papers, looking awfully old – always a great opener.

Whatever the ifs and probablys, Peter knew that a Mossad Doorbell – a massive explosion of Taylor's fury that came your way without warning – was on its way. The door to his office opened and Susie stood there with Tommy and Henry. The youngest boy walked in and kissed his father on the lips.

'Love you, Daddy,' he said.

'I love you too, sweetheart,' said Peter, meaning it.

Henry entered and kissed him, turning his cheek as he did so. 'Bye, darling. Love you,' said Peter.

He looked up to meet Susie's stare. Although she said nothing, he noticed no obvious scorn on her now.

'Sorry,' he said holding up the *Guardian*. 'I'm in big trouble... bad story in the papers.'

'Surprise surprise,' said Susie, coldly. 'Why don't you just tell that git to bugger off?'

'Err...'

'I haven't got time for this; I've got to get the kids to school. I'll see you later.'

Peter watched as his family trooped off through the garden and he heard Tommy ask, 'What's a git?' Sadness came over him as he felt distant and detached from the three people who should have been the most important in his world but weren't, because Peter preferred reputation to affection.

The telephone rang again and Peter flinched. He lifted the receiver and was immediately relieved to hear Billy Vernon, not Taylor, say, 'Have you read the fucking *Guardian* yet?'

Peter looked at his watch. It was early for Vernon to be ringing which meant that Taylor had probably called him first, doubtless in a fury about this story and expecting that his songs would now be featured in stair-lift commercials.

'Hello? I said…'

'Yeah, I've read it,' said Peter. 'Has he seen it?'

'You could say that.'

'And?'

'What do you mean, and? You know the rules; he is fucking furious. It's all 'How did this happen?' Now I have to find out and do him a report. By the way, any more contact from our blackmailer?'

'Not yet. What's his problem with the *Guardian* piece, Billy?'

'His problem? What's his fucking problem? Have you read the story, Pete? Are we talking about the same thing? Today's *Guardian*? The front fucking page? His problem is that he doesn't want to be seen to be the new pin-up of the sort of people who wet themselves!'

'But it was a poll! We can't control polls. We can't dictate who is allowed to like him.'

'You know the rule; he has to have control. We should have known that this was happening…'

'How the fuck were we meant to have known?'

'The *Guardian* should have warned you before it appeared. You should have known from your mates at *Saga*.'

'I don't have any mates at *Saga*. *Saga* is not the sort of magazine I usually deal with; you know that.'

'What I know is an irrelevance. The point is that Ian is very pissed off that a national newspaper is saying that he's the heart-throb of people with liver spots.'

'He's got liver spots,' said Peter indignantly.

'Get real, Pete; he's woken up to learn that the media world is now officially declaring him to be old. Old is worse than being dead. Ian doesn't do old; he doesn't want to be seen as old, he wants the MTV crowd.'

'The MTV crowd doesn't know who he is,' said Peter coolly. 'Anyway, he is old; but that's why he's considered to be cool. Not because he's old, but because he doesn't look or act like people of his age. He is defying age and still rocking. If he was thirty years younger, what he's doing now wouldn't be such a big deal.'

'What are you saying?' said Vernon, calming down for a moment.

'I'm saying his fucking age works to his advantage. If he weren't as old as he is, the music he is making now would mean fuck all. He's well regarded because nobody expects him to be up to it. He should promote flying in the face of his age, not hide it away.'

'You've never quite understood rock stars, have you Pete?'

'What do you mean?'

'You've never understood why rock stars do it, why they fight to be famous.'

'For the money and recognition, I guess,' muttered Peter.

'Have you taken an idiot pill this morning? If you're famous you want to advertise your fame to everybody else in the rich club. You do that by the trimmings, the Roller, the jet, the big house and your birds. You want to shove your fame in the face of your peers, I'm more successful than you, look at my trimmings.'

'So?'

'So good headlines are the best trimmings of all. And that's not getting on the front page of the house magazine for the fucking deaf, looking like you've just been embalmed!'

'Don't shout at me, Billy, I didn't place it.'

'Look,' said Vernon, calming down, 'you know he wants to be Peter Pan, he wants to appeal to the young…'

'Doesn't he have any mirrors in his house?'

'Peter! We're talking about the guy who wrote "Grey Rose"! All these young fucking bands say that album was their biggest influence. He wants to be in that gang and not in their grandmothers' fucking bingo team. Anyway, I've got him screaming like a nuthouse patient for a full report, so how did this fucking happen? He says he's never done an interview for *Saga*.'

'He hasn't. It reads to me like some of the quotes were lifted from the *Rolling Stone* interview and repackaged by a freelancer for *Saga*. Bill, why don't I just ring him up and tell him all this?'

'He doesn't want to speak to you right now, I wouldn't go there.'

'Why not? I didn't write this fucking story. It doesn't say by Peter Forth on the front of the *Guardian*. Why am I to blame?'

'Because you didn't tell him it was happening…'

'I didn't know it was happening. How the fuck am I meant to know what is going to appear in every bloody publication on the planet? I can't police the world. And I come back to the fact that I don't think this is a bad thing for Ian. Old age is about compromise. This story is saying is that Ian is leading a whole generation into a new spirit of being uncompromising, of bucking the trend – actually it's very rock and roll. It's the whole point of rock and roll; that you don't play by the accepted rules. Ian is, by example, helping old people to grow young again.'

'That's good… helping them to grow young again; yeah, he'll like that. Good one.'

'I didn't invent it.'

'What do you mean?'

'It's a line from a Springsteen song.'

'Yeah, well he probably doesn't know anybody else's songs so let's keep that quiet. So, what am I telling him, that you think this article is good?'

'If it's looked at in the right way, yes.'

'You can spin this, right?'

'Of course, it's a piece of piss.'

'I'll call you back.'

'Err… Billy, that other matter, the photo…'

'I can't even think about that now. I'll talk to you later about it,' said Vernon and he rang off.

Peter felt exhausted. It was too early to reasonably demand him to perform mental gymnastics. He found a bottle of Coke, poured himself a pint of it and lit yet another cigarette. He logged onto the Net and checked the Press Association's site.

As he'd expected, PA had already lifted and was running its own, now-exaggerated version of the story: *Ian Taylor No.1 in Care Homes*. Fantastic, thought Peter, almost lighting another cigarette as he waited for the phone to ring again.

He wondered whether Vernon would relay any of his points to

Taylor and then realised that probably he would not. DFA – Don't Fucking Argue, just keep him happy – was the mantra of Taylor's team, no matter how psychologically bloating the consequences. No wonder Elvis ended up choking to death on the results of always getting his own way, he thought, as he lit another cigarette.

CHAPTER 5

Peter thought that he would put his new publicity instructions on the back burner as they were absurd and the blackmail photo business was more urgent. He was just preparing an email to Vernon explaining this when he noticed Susie walking up the garden path.

She was talking on her mobile phone and Peter watched as she stood still beside the hammock that he never used, laughing at what the caller had said to her. She was late forties but passed for younger because of her doll-like face and tall, taut body which she kept toned by a sparrow's diet and a daily session at the gym.

Her short, black hair added an androgeny to her sex appeal but that was balanced by her long legs, large breasts and all-year spray tan which, Peter thought, was an odd, almost bimbo-like affectation for a self-employed country accountant who spent most of her days advising late-paying farmers how to apply for grants.

Despite her coldness towards him, Peter loved Susie. He admired her wit and intelligence and he felt guilty that his uncontrollable depression, drinking and drug taking had alienated her. He also pitied himself because, although it was debatable whether she still loved him, it was beyond dispute that she had certainly ceased to like him.

Susie finished her call with what, Peter noted, appeared to be a rather lascivious giggle and then opened the door to his office.

'Phooo! It's smokey in here,' she said with a smile.

It was the unexpected sight of the smile that prevented Peter from backlashing some caustic comment about it being his office and he did not care about the tobacco fumes. As ever, he responded eagerly to any sign of a temporary truce in their five-year post-natal war.

He looked up into her eyes, immediately assessing the size of the pupils as he had once read that dilation revealed attraction. His stare moved down to the line of her dress to where it ended just above her black-nyloned knees and her long leather boots.

'What?' said Susie, with a pointed little laugh.

'Nothing,' said Peter. 'You look nice.'

Susie let the compliment hang in the air as she reached out and combed her fingers into the back of his hair that had not yet been brushed.

'I'm sorry I was grumpy this morning,' she said in a slower, lower tone than Peter had heard for a week. 'I'm probably getting PMT; I'm feeling a bit out of it, that's usually a sign.'

'It's allowed,' said Peter, his instincts rising that, bizarrely, she was going coming on to him.

'You were up early, what are you working on?'

Peter decided not to detail the problems he was having with Vernon and Taylor, as he knew that Susie held in contempt his obsessive fretting over his job. He knew that what she most hated was that he rarely stood up to Taylor. He was never sure whether she most despised him for his cowardice, or Taylor for his bullying.

'I'm trying to write this bloody book I keep on about,' he invented.

'How far have you got?' said Susie with what Peter believed to be genuine interest.

'I've only done the first paragraph.'

'What does it say?'

'It starts with a BJ,' said Peter, dropping into the playful, childlike code that they used whenever they discussed sex without arguing about it.

'You can't begin a book with a BJ,' said Susie and, as she was laughing in a way that Peter interpreted to be somewhat saucily, he resisted the instinct to snap, 'How many books have you written?'.'

'Actually, it's not a bad idea. Look at this,' said Peter as he pulled from beneath his pile of notes and ideas for the novel a page torn from The Sunday Telegraph which read 'Explicit Sex Now Used to Lure Young Women Readers… publishers are abandoning romance and tall, dark handsome strangers with a spate of graphic books aimed at the *Sex and the City* generation.'

'It says that publishers have been looking for what they call 'literary porn' for a long time,' said Peter, précising for her. 'There's a new market for it.'

'Well, you should be good at that; you love porn,' said Susie, still smiling.

'I know,' said Peter, honestly. 'But for some reason I've got a block about it, I can't describe it properly. The BJ.'

Susie chuckled and Peter felt, but did not follow, an urge to push his hand up her dress and massage her through her knickers.

'Well you've had enough of them; I would have thought you could describe that with your eyes closed.'

Peter wanted to argue that, actually, he had not had anything like enough, or even anything approaching enough, but there was a knowing weight in her words that he read as flirting. He could not recall the last time that they had flirted. He shifted his bottom in his chair as he felt his worn jeans tighten at the crutch.

'Yeah, you would have thought so, but I've got a complete block, I just can't picture it. I just can't get the kind of detail into my head, writing from memory…'

Peter stopped explaining himself and looked up at Susie, who was grinning. He believed that the flashing light in her eyes, the pupils of which were now definitely dilated, indicated that she took his comments as the hint he had intended them to be.

Still standing just behind him, Susie began rubbing the back of his neck with the fingers of her left hand and then scrunched his hair as she gripped it gently in a fist. He felt her lips brush the nape of his neck and then she began to lick it as Peter's penis reacted.

'Maybe…' Susie murmured, but the air of sexual promise that now charged the air was interrupted by the sudden roar of a lawn mower fired up by the gardener, who had arrived at the bottom of the garden to give it its weekly maintenance.

'Maybe what?' said Peter, sounding a little too irritated at the gardener's ignorant intrusion.

Susie resumed licking the back of his neck. She took her time, seeming to relish turning him on. She moved her head so that her wet tongue could encircle lobe of his right ear and then whispered into it, 'Maybe I should refresh your memory… and you can take notes while I'm doing it.'

'But Gerry's in the garden…' said Peter and immediately hoped that he had not jarred the rhythm of the seduction by his minor protest. He was relieved to feel Susie was licking his neck again.

'Gerry can't see anything if you're sitting at your desk,' said Susie.

'But I am sitting at my desk.'

'He can't see if I just sneak underneath it… move your chair back a bit.'

Peter pushed his chair back by three feet. Susie brushed by him and, as he rode his hand up under her dress to try reach the cool, smooth skin of her thighs above her hold-ups, she crouched down into the space beneath his desk and knelt between his opened legs.

'You carry on with your work,' she teased as she rubbed his testicles through his jeans. 'Don't mind me… have you got your notebook ready?'

As she lowered her head she thought how effortless it was for a woman to get her own way when she wanted to wrong-foot her man.

CHAPTER 6

'Ugh!' thought Susie as she crawled out on her hands and knees from beneath Peter's desk. Without saying a word or giving much more than a glance at the figure of her husband sitting splay-legged in his seat with his already-shrunken member shining in its icing of saliva and semen, she stood and straightened her dress.

She was irritated to see that by smoothing the line of her black agnès b she had smeared it with the stuff that had clung to her fingers and which the fabric instantly absorbed. Sighing heavily, she left the office and strode into the kitchen wondering which particular Stain Devil the manufacturers recommended for removing slut spills.

She lent over the sink and spat vehemently into it, then swilled her mouth under the running tap and spat again. Taking a clean tea towel from a drawer, she dampened it and dabbed at the stain, which only made it darker. Fuck, she thought. If it shows, it will be a talking point for later; which could prove interesting…

Susie climbed the stairs to the bathroom and shuddered again as her mind skimmed over what she had just done. She reached for the Listerine, poured a cup and swilled and gargled for more than a minute. She knew that she wouldn't want cock breath today.

Wiping her mouth on a towel, Susie examined her lips in the bathroom mirror. She had read that a consequence of giving fellatio was a slight bruising and swelling of the lips. Hers did appear to be slightly more swollen now and she smirked at the irony of her husband's penis working as a fluffing tool for what she might allow to happen later.

She had no particular desire to let anything happen later, but as Peter's insane jealousies had already convinced him that something had happened when actually they hadn't, she really had nothing to lose. Except, of course, a clear conscience, but she wasn't bothered about that.

Susie thought about Pete and how transparent he was. As soon as he had mentioned his alleged writer's block with his damn book, she knew what he was angling for, even if he didn't. Three minutes of jaw ache with a bit of deliberate moaning thrown in and she could pretty much depend on getting anything she wanted from him which, in this case, was to stop him pestering her with suspicions.

She had long ago given up feeling pity for Peter. He had lost his right to her sympathy when he replaced her in his life with his nervous scampering to attend to the complaints and whims of the other man in their relationship, Ian Taylor. Susie knew she could endure all the times Taylor took Peter away from her and twice as many times again if only, just once, Pete would acknowledge that the man was, at times, a manipulative, selfish, power-mad shithead. But Pete would not. Even to her. He was grotesquely loyal to Taylor, rejecting any criticism of him.

All that she ever wanted, she mused, was for Pete, just once in his bloody life, to admit that Taylor was not his God. And it wasn't because she thought the man wasn't talented; she, like most of the rest of the world, accepted that he was and, judging from the many times that she'd met him, could be a very nice bloke, quite a sexy, flirtatious and yet feminine bloke, actually, whom she would not be averse to pleasuring. No, Susie could see why Pete adored Taylor; it was just that, as a woman, she wished that Pete adored her the same way.

On the rare occasions when she had mentioned this, Pete would fly into some frenetic pronouncement of his love for her that involved anguished apologies and the promises of change, which were reassuring. But those, and the expensive gifts that Pete regularly bought her, never quite compensated for the fact that, as Pete's wife, she was jealous. She envied Taylor having Pete's utterly selfless love, and she hated Peter for not seeing that Taylor neither knew nor cared that he mattered so much to Pete.

Now in the throes of her final checklist before leaving to see Jack, she reached her hand between her legs and touched the crotch of her thong. Damn! It was wet. Susie couldn't decide whether it was the anticipation that had lubricated her, or whether it was the turn-on of the power that a blow job gave her. Either way, she had no intention of going out moist.

Quickly, before Pete recovered sufficiently to come upstairs and maul her with questions, she pulled off the damp thong and kicked it out of sight beneath the bed. She slipped off her dress and removed the orange matching bra. Kicking the bra under the bed too, she pulled open her underwear drawer and chose a sheer black bra that Pete had brought back from Victoria's Secret in Chicago. Black looked better, she reasoned, and besides the bra revealed her hardening nipples through its fine net. Rummaging rapidly, she selected a tiny black G-string to complete the look.

She pursed her lips as she daubed them with a new stick of scarlet lipstick that she had bought after reading in Cosmopolitan that men were attracted to a cosmetically painted mouth because the sight subliminally resembled an aroused vagina.

Susie had long ago calculated that there was a stack of love crimes for which Pete owed her more than apologies: his four affairs, which he excused as merely sexual, his frequent use of hookers when away on work and his flirting with the nanny, whom she'd later sacked.

When, she wondered bitterly, had been the last time they had gone out to a party when she had not been jittery with trepidation that he would embarrass her by some loud-mouthed display of adolescent buffoonery that he ridiculously excused as, 'being upbeat is part of my job.' Susie had detailed memories of every evening that Pete had spoiled by his gigantic indulgence of intoxicating substances, always leaving her feeling sick with shame as he reached the inevitable collapse.

In the early days of their spitfire relationship she had so wanted old school friends to see Pete at his scintillating wittiest, when he could reign in a room full of laughter. She had so wanted the others to see her man on the top form he achieved just by being himself, and she had always prayed before a party that Pete would make others like him and admire her choice. Instead, she left the evenings aware of the pity in the eyes of those who hugged her goodbye as Pete babbled the repetitive and earnest nonsense that a gram of cocaine had brought to his brain.

As she checked her make-up, Susie reflected on the many periods when Pete had stopped drinking. Eighteen months, he'd lasted once, propelled by the sheer force of his belligerent willpower. She had adored him then; his sparkiness was so captivating. But then some crisis at work would turn him into the Anti-Pete seeking strength in a bottle and the spiral of furious arguments, irrational accusations and childish self-pity would start all over again. She hated the fact that Ian Taylor had put her husband in such a state of pathetic and perpetual anxiety that both she and Pete had each submitted to counselling and courses of anti-depressants in their desperate attempts to cope with the pressure caused by his fear of getting pulverized for saying the wrong thing to the press, who constantly called with no regard for the hour.

As she reflected that she had never witnessed anyone so regularly roughed up by the put-downs of their employer, Susie began to feel sorry for Pete. He didn't actually deserve what she was doing to him and she realized it was wrong. But, she rationalized, she would only ever have this one life and she had already distilled the excitement of enough of it by marrying a moody child with a problem with addictions.

So, as it was her life and nobody else's, Susie persuaded herself that she felt no guilt at all.

CHAPTER 7

There were three telephones on the ink-stained schoolmaster's desk that Peter had years ago pulled out of a skip because it had the space to hold all the clutter of pens, note books, various cigarette lighters and the empty cigarette packets on which he had scribbled what had seemed to be good ideas at the time.

The white telephone on the left was for incoming calls. The black one beside it was for Peter to call out. And the cream telephone at the top right corner was Ian Taylor's hotline. It was the cream phone that began to ring now.

The alarm that the sound caused in Peter could not have been greater had he installed an air raid siren in place of the phone. With his right hand he grabbed a notebook, flipped to a clean page and pushed the computer keyboard away from him to create more space. With his left hand he picked up the phone as he forced a surprised tone into his voice as he said 'Hi, Ian.'

'Hah! Had you going there,' said Billy Vernon, now sounding much more chirpy than he had earlier.

'Billy!' said Peter, annoyed at the prank. 'Can you not do that? Where are you? I'll phone you back.'

'Why?' said Vernon, who appeared to be relishing Peter's unease. 'What's the matter with this line?'

'It's Ian's line, as you bloody well know. If he calls and it's engaged there will be a witch hunt over who's had the audacity to jam his line. Let me call you back.'

'He won't call,' said Vernon with the air of smug authority that people adopted when they were acting as Taylor's chosen messenger. 'He's with his personal trainer.'

'Yeah, but as you know, 'Billy said…' is not a legitimate excuse. Let me phone you back,' said Peter, putting down the receiver of the hot line and dialling the number of Vernon's mobile on his black phone. The line rang once and Vernon answered.

'Hang on,' he said, and Peter thought he detected the sound of a sniff that hadn't been there when they had talked earlier. Peter heard Vernon issuing off-phone instructions in the bellicose tone that he took with almost everybody except Ian Taylor.

'Yeah... espresso. Yeah, double. Yeah, a large one, right? And gimme a receipt for that. Receipt... can I have a receipt? Yeah for the coffee, what the fuck else would I want it for?'

There was the sniff again, thought Peter. He looked at the Longines watch that he had bought on a flight to New York years before British Airways had got hip to passengers using over-the-limit credit cards that couldn't be authenticated at thirty thousand feet. The dial said it was twenty five to ten. A bit early Billy, Peter felt, for cocaine.

'OK,' said Vernon at last. 'Got your pen?'

'Go on,' said Peter. He spoke placidly; partly because he did not want Vernon to hear in his voice any of the anxiety that was now rising in anticipation of Taylor's latest dictat, and partly because he knew that sounding calm would irritate Vernon whom, Peter knew, would be getting increasingly jumpy once the espresso's caffeine gave an over-drive hit to the coke.

'OK... right... oh yeah... He wants you get him on a kids' news show.'

'What for?'

'Just write this down, will you? He wants you to call up these people, the BBC and all that, you're to use those dimwits at the record label if you want to, and get him on whatever is, like, the highest rated kids show...'

'Does he mean MTV news or news with proper news in it?' Peter interrupted with increasing defiance.

'I don't know, MTV, VH1, that's your bag,' said Vernon, wanting to finish passing the orders.

'VH1 is watched by businessmen wanting to drown out the sound of the hookers in their hotel rooms,' said Peter.

'I thought VH1 was big,' said Vernon, sounding confused.

'Not outside America. Over here it means fuck all.'

'But it's on Sky! I get it on Sky.'

'So is QVC.'

'What's the matter with QVC? I watch QVC.'

'QVC's great,' said Peter laconically, 'If you want to appeal to an audience of geriatrics.'

'He doesn't want fucking geriatrics!' Vernon exploded. 'That's the fucking point! He's really fucked off with all your fucking old dinner ladies.'

'What do you mean, 'my dinner ladies'?' said Peter.

'All your fucking Saga pals, all those toothless fuckers who show their age by hoarding dirty washing-up water…'

'Do what?' said Peter, genuinely interested in this observation.

'Dirty washing-up water; old people hoard it. You and I let it run out of the sink when we've washed-up. Old people fucking keep it, all grey and tepid, in case they need to wash something else up later.'

'Billy,' said Peter, feeling the need to guide him back to reality, 'what does he want? Just tell me what he wants.'

'I'm fucking trying to, but you keep interrupting.'

'Sorry,' said Peter, pleased to have unsettled Vernon's obsequious acceptance of anything Ian Taylor told him.

'Look,' said Vernon, who was now sniffing like a schoolboy on a February morning, 'what he wants is for his fucking press officer, which is you, to get onto the BBC or whoever and get him on a show that kids watch.'

'Why?'

'Does it fucking matter?'

'They are going to ask me why he wants to come on their show; what he wants to talk about.'

'He wants to go on a kids' show because he wants to deflect this bloody news story that has got him pegged as the idol of people who smell of piss,' said Vernon with characteristic brutality. 'Oddly enough, he's not thrilled about that; so he wants to be seen with a load of kids.'

Peter was ruefully experienced in coping with Taylor's knee-jerk ideas for instant publicity. Invariably they backfired and then he got shouted later at for allowing Taylor to have had his own way.

'Billy,' said Peter patiently, 'this is a really crap idea.'

'It's not my idea! Call him up and tell him that.'

'OK, what's the number of his trainer?'

'Look,' said Vernon, plaintively, 'can't you just do your job?'

'I am doing my job. I'm doing my job by not agreeing with a crap idea. If he goes on television with a bunch of kids everyone will know what he is trying to do and instead of looking all hip and cool, he'll look like he's trying. And anyone who is seen to be trying just looks a berk,' explained Peter.

'But he looks a berk with all this fucking Saga business,' said Vernon.

'Says who?'

'He fucking says so. He's really fucking pissed off about this.'

'Yes, but I'm saying that if Ian reacts to the Saga poll story, especially if he reacts petulantly, he'll just make the story bigger because Ian reacting to anything is a bigger story. Plus, if he is so concerned about not looking old, the last place he actually wants to be is on children's television.'

'But he wants to.'

'I know he wants to but it won't work for him because kids are just going to think, 'Who's that old twat?' He'd make his age more apparent.'

'So I've got to get back to him and tell him that Pete says if he goes on BBC people will say he's an old twat. Great.'

'No. What I am saying is that if he goes on children's news or MTV or Children in Fucking Need at the moment, anybody – whoever is interviewing him – will ask him about this Saga story. Whether he likes it or not, they will ask him to comment. And that makes it a bigger story, even if he refuses to comment.'

'He won't talk about it,' said Vernon, gruffly.

'Well then he'll definitely fan the flames of the fire he wants to put out,' argued Peter. 'If Ian goes on a kids' news show, a propos absolutely fuck-all, and then refuses to discuss the one story that people are currently linking him with, he-will-get-fucked.'

'Fuck off, Pete,' said Vernon. 'Anyway, who says he has nothing to talk about?'

'Sorry?' said Peter, genuinely wrong-footed.

'If you'd actually ever let anybody finish before jumping on your high fucking horse, you'd see the bigger picture. He said that he wants you to get him on some kids' news show – oh, and if there are any kids around him they've all got to be ugly kids...'

'Ugly kids? Why ugly kids?' said Peter, unsure that he actually wanted to hear what he suspected was certain to be insanity.

'Ugly kids because he's also worked out that anyone of his age on a kids' show will look older – you're not the only one who went to school. But if you've got ugly kids around him then at least he will look better,' said Vernon with such an air of acceptance that Peter wanted to hit him.

'Did he say that?' said Peter, horrified. 'Can you imagine how long it would take for somebody at the BBC to phone up the whole of Fleet Street if I call them up and say Ian will only appear with an audience of deformed children'

'I said ugly. Nobody said anything about them having to be deformed,' said Vernon, bleakly.

'Ugly, deformed, spotty, it doesn't fucking matter if they've all got two fucking heads and ginger beards!' Peter shouted, 'If anybody ever heard that he is that bothered by how he looks, then he is finished. Is he hell-bent on self-destruction?'

'OK,' said Vernon in agreement. 'Forget the kids.'

'Forget all the kids or just the ugly ones?'

'Forget the uglies. As I keep trying to say, get a TV interview organised, on a kids' TV show and he'll go on and talk about his gig...'

'What gig?' asked Peter, at last hoping to learn something worth knowing.

'You see, you don't know everything,' said Vernon, who had started to sniff again. 'He wants to kill all this appealing to the oldies crap by giving the press a bigger story...'

'That's always his style,' agreed Peter.

'Yeah, so he's going to do this gig, and he's going to perform Grey Rose.'

'What?'

'He's going to play Grey Rose. Live. At a gig.'

'What, the track?'

'All of it,' said Vernon, who was enjoying breaking this part of Taylor's instructions.

'All of Grey Rose?' said Peter. 'Bloody hell, that's a story.'

'Yeah,' said Vernon. 'He said you'd think that. Anyway, there's a meeting about it at three at the office. I'll see you there. Any news on the other photo business?'

'Not yet. I've photoshopped the pic to make it look a bit iffy. Have you told Ian about it yet?'

'Yeah. I'll talk to you later,' said Vernon and rang off.

CHAPTER 8

Peter lit another cigarette. He saw there was a new message on his mobile that he hadn't noticed before. He played it back and recognized the voice of an Ian Taylor fan whom he believed to be insane and trouble.

'Hi Pete, it's Catherine Hornby… I need you to talk to me. I've had it with hearing nothing. I don't care anymore about not rocking the boat. You can tell Mr Taylor that I'm thinking of getting a lawyer to sue him for paternity. He owes me! And whether you want to answer me or not, Pete, I'll find a way to get to him. I'm not a fool Pete. Call me!'

Wonderful, thought Peter, it was bad enough that Ian was going to get gleefully exposed at any moment by the redtop newspapers as King Gay; now nutters claiming to be his bastard bloody children wanted to join in ruining the parade. Maybe that would be a good defence, he mused sarcastically, producing a deranged fan as amazingly convenient proof of Ian's doubted sexuality.

Peter wrote down the gist of Catherine Hornby's ranting. He was surprised to hear from her as he believed that he had scared her away a year before with threats of sectioning so savage that she was crying when he had last yelled at her for calling his voicemail with a barrage of threats against Taylor.

The calls were always made when he was sleeping and only once had he managed actually to speak to the woman to try to discover the nature of her problem. On that occasion he had initially spoken softly, reasonably and, so she obviously thought, sympathetically.

By giving her the impression that he had the slightest interest in her predicament he had heard her claim that she had been told by her mother on her deathbed that she was Taylor's illegitimate daughter, the result of a one-night, wham-bam-thank you fan during one of his rock tours.

Such a conception was, Peter rationalized, entirely possible. Taylor had regularly boasted during his media interviews that over the decades he had played, laid, rolled and seeded the field to Bill Wyman's legendary level of 'more than 1,000 girls' and his former roadies had admitted to Peter that Taylor had to have a body in bed with him every night on every tour, or else he would be overcome by shaking fits.

Peter had once worked out the maths of Taylor's years on the road and, given the likelihood that not every teenage girl was on the pill, it was probably the case that there were sons and daughters of Taylor out there who had grown up to be the cashier at a supermarket check-out with a face that reminded everybody of someone famous.

He wondered which type of fit would best represent how Billy Vernon would take the news that just as his artist was about to re-launch himself off the back of his own reputation as the ideal man, skeletons would be competing in the cupboard to expose him, paradoxically, as both a closet queen and a fugitive father.

Shit, thought Peter and he turned to reading his e-mails in the hope that one would read, 'message from a blackmailer'. But instead his inbox just bobbed up a couple of interview requests from Canada, three miracle methods of getting a mule-length penis and a rather polite note from a Lyme Regis band called Tundra Pox, who were asking if they could talk to him about publicity and getting known.

More fool you, he thought.

CHAPTER 9

Putting her husband's histrionic anxieties completely out of her mind, Susie Forth drove her old Renault away from their home through the winding back lanes towards Lyme Regis. After she had driven for a few minutes, she pulled in at a lay-by where parked vehicles were hidden from the road by a hedge and tall trees. She felt as if she was in a dream, as if this was not really happening, when she fumbled through her handbag, found her mobile and dialled the number of Jack Jackson.

In her head she had already rehearsed, dozens of times, the way she would add a saucy huskiness to her voice when he answered and she would say 'Hel-lo Jack' in a sort of purr which would infuse the three syllables with a dark, sexual intent. But his line was engaged, and that so threw her that she had to have a cigarette while she waited to compose herself again into the vamp that she was not entirely confident of being.

As she smoked, she wondered whether she was deluding herself that Jackson actually wanted her, a married mother of two connected, through Pete, to his ex-best mate. Susie had no interest in photography, nor in the gossip that this Jackson was 'a right flirt' until she had been driving up Broad Street one morning and had seen a tall, raffish-looking man with broad shoulders and a cute backside opening the photo shop.

He had grinned at her as he had caught her staring and, in his wolf-like smile, she had seen a desire that she had not known since her husband effectively dumped her to give his all his time and attention to Ian Taylor.

She grinned at the memory of that encounter, and of subsequent ones when she visited the shop on the pretext of buying something. The fact that Pete had shouted at her about 'consorting with the enemy' naturally made her encounters with Jackson all the more appealing.

Susie ferreted through her handbag again to find the packet of mints to mask the tobacco on her breath. She took two, then redialled his number.

'Hell-lo, how are you?' he said and his recognition surprised her and again dashed her plans to talk how she imagined a vamp might sound.

'Er… um…' faltered Susie.

'Where are you?' he said.

'I'm at home,' she said, wondering why on earth she had said that.

'Whereabouts at home?' he continued.

'Umm… we live just outside Charmouth.'

He laughed affectionately, and she noticed herself relaxing back into the car seat.

'No… I mean where are you at home? In what room? What are you doing?'

Susie understood now and she willingly joined the role-play.

'Hmmm,' she said in the alluring tone with which she had intended to start the conversation, 'I'm in my bedroom.'

'Are you now? Are you dressed?'

Susie got the picture.

'Hmm, sort of,' she said. 'I'm getting dressed…'

'How far have you got?'

'Oo, just the basics… my undies… and my stockings.'

'Stockings eh?' he said with evident relish. 'Are you planning something special?'

'That depends,' she said, knowing full well that 'that depends' in this context pretty much meant, 'Do you fancy a fuck?'

His next remark threw Susie from the reverie of deep-tongue snogging that she was already imagining.

'Are you dressing up for your husband?'

'What?' she could not help herself snapping.

'I just wondered if you were going out somewhere special together, seeing as you're in stockings.'

'Huh!' she snorted. 'Pete thinks I'm wearing stockings in order to see another man. It's been a sore point here this morning.'

'And are you?'

'Am I what?'

'In stockings for another lucky man?'

Susie caught hold of the 'lucky'.

'Could be,' she hinted, cutely.

'Mmmm,' said Jackson in a low murmur. 'What else are you planning on wearing for him?'

'Oo, anything he likes, really. I'm not sure what he likes, though. I've not known him long... what do you think a guy might like?'

Susie could not believe she had added the codicil. She felt wanton. Wanton and wanting now.

'I think a guy likes to be surprised,' he said.

'Do you? Do you like to be surprised?'

'I love it,' he said, tellingly.

'Well, you never know what...'

'Might develop,' he said, chuckling again.

'Hmmm,' she teased. And then, having made the point, she playfully changed tack a little.

'What are you doing?' said Susie. 'Are you busy?'

Not realising that she was assessing his availability, he replied honestly. 'Not really. I'm working on a new idea I've got for some pictures but... well, they're a bit rude, actually.'

'Rude's good.'

'Is it?' he laughed.

'Yeah, rude sells, doesn't it? Everyone likes a bit of rude.'

'Do they?'

'Yeah,' she giggled.

'How rude do they like it?'

'Depends.'

'On what?'

'Umm... the mood you're in.'

'The mood to be rude?'

'Yeah.' Another giggle. She paused and waited to see if he would bite.

'What sort of mood are you in, Suze?'

Bingo!

'Hmm… I might pop by later…'

'Good…'

'…and show you…'

'Great!'

'…what I think of your new pictures, of course.'

'Of course. What time?'

'What time do you close?'

'Around six, but come when you like.'

'Oh, I always do,' she said, huskily again.

She ended the call and looked at herself in the rear-view mirror. She saw that she looked flushed and she grinned at the unfamiliar feeling. She wished now that Kevin wouldn't be chaperoning her but she felt confident that she could escape his scrutiny for the a few moments that would be all she would need to leave Jack in no uncertainty about the purpose of future rendezvous.

CHAPTER 10

Peter drove the hour-long route to Taunton railway station. Finding a space to park was, as ever, a problem because of the plethora of Saabs and BMWs left there earlier by the commuting class who thought little of paying a mortgage for a return to London Paddington. Peter charged the ticket to his Visa hoping, as the bored ticket-seller ran it through her machine, that the transaction would not fail and humiliate him again.

As always, when the train arrived, he looked for the very front seat in the front carriage knowing that most people's fears of surviving train crashes would ensure that the seat was empty. It was, and Peter slumped into it and worried about how long it would be until he heard from the blackmailer again.

Peter turned his mobile off. Over the years he had sensed too many ears alerted by the words 'Ian' and 'Taylor' spoken in the same minute. He put his ticket on the table in front of him so that the guard would not disturb him, shut his eyes, leant his head against the window and tried to sleep despite the juddering vibrations.

Some while later the train's sudden braking woke him from a nightmare in which a ginger male TV presenter was attempting to fellate Ian Taylor during a live televised children's carol service as Billy Vernon held Peter back from stopping the interview.

Shaken by the emotions of the dream, Peter blinked himself back to reality as the guard announced that the train was now entering Paddington. He walked across the main platform concourse and queued at the taxi rank behind about twenty people who had just arrived at Paddington on the Heathrow Express. He noticed that the tags on their luggage indicated that they had flown in from New York. Their dress code of high-waisted, stonewashed jeans over screamingly clean, white trainers confirmed his suspicions that either these were Americans, or else a bunch of Brits who had got dressed in the dark.

Peter lit a Marlboro, blew the smoke ostentatiously out through his nose and then waited.

'What the h…'

'Oh for Gadddd's sake!'

Peter knew his smoking would upset the Americans; that was why he'd lit up. Ever since New York's puritanical mayors had banned Peter and anybody else from smoking in public, Peter had made a point of smoking everywhere in public in London whenever he detected an American. He realised that his retaliation was petty but he didn't care, for it was one of Peter's principles that you should always fight against bullies, even if it gave you lung disease. He continued to smoke the cigarette, wondering if any of the Yanks would reveal their characteristic bluntness by complaining about how he chose to conduct his private life in his own country.

'Hey, fella…'

Peter turned to gaze at the twenty-stone man. He smiled and said in a ludicrously polite tone, 'May I assist you, sir?'

'Uh, hey… can you smoke in the street here?' asked the tourist.

'You most certainly can,' said Peter. 'Would you like a cigarette?' Peter took the Marlboro soft pack from the inside pocket of his pin-striped grey linen Boss jacket and offered it to the fat man.

'Hey! No… er… no, thanks. It's… er… kinda unusual for us to see people smoking, you know. We're from the States,' said the man.

'Oh!' said Peter. 'How strange.' He examined the cigarette packet in his hand and added, 'These are made in America, apparently… by a chap called, ummm, Philip Morris. I believe that he's American too. Do you know him?'

The American's eyes narrowed and closely examined Peter's still-smiling face for any sign of threat. Not reading it right, he continued his protest.

'You see, in the States now, we've kind of quit smoking…'

'Oh, really?' said Peter with mock fascination. 'So now you've got to dump your excess stock over here, I suppose?'

'No, no... er,' said the fat man who was now showing signs of agitation, 'it's just with the whole cancer thing...'

'Oh yes,' said Peter sympathetically. 'That's been going around, hasn't it?'

'Secondary cancer!' said a tall thin woman whose hair appeared to have been highlighted with toilet bleach. 'Smokers give it to nannn-smokers.'

'I don't believe that it is infectious, madam,' said Peter, enjoying himself.

'Hey!' said the fat man who had finally detected Peter's insolence. 'It's just that we're not used to seeing people smoke anymore. It's an American thing, you know, healthy living and all of that...'

'So I can see,' said Peter, looking the obese man up and down in a way that even he thought was pushing it too far. 'Excuse me, I believe that is your taxi behind you.'

Distracted from their debate by the waiting cab, the Americans bustled with their massive suitcases, attempting to load them into the back of the vehicle as Peter stepped away towards the taxi behind it.

He directed the driver to a red brick building off the Edgware Road in the centre of New Arabia. Here, amid the Gucci blonde wives who lunched daily on gossip and talk of new shoes and the sauntering Arabs tripping over the hems of their robes, was the home of Taylor's company, the Taylor Music Corporation.

Peter instructed the cab driver to drop him off at the junction with the Bayswater Road so that he could enjoy another cigarette on the short walk to the office. He paid and excessively tipped the cabbie with all the change he had in his pocket, keen to get rid of the coins that spoiled the line of his suit.

Peter was lighting the cigarette when a scruffy street-sleeper in his thirties shuffled up to stand too close to him and asked for spare change.

'Sorry, mate, I've just given it all to that cab,' said Peter honestly. He watched the tramp's eyes dart to his cigarette, so he added, 'Do want a fag?'

'Fantastic!' exclaimed the beggar. 'You won't give me no money, but you'll give me cancer!'

'Are you American?' asked Peter as he walked away.

The facade of the Taylor Music Corporation gave no indication that the three-storey building was the hub of the business of a rock musician. The premises had once been a hairdressers and Taylor had retained the gaudy purple exterior and its whitewashed front window.

Peter pressed the buzzer and waited for the voice of receptionist Sandra Knowles to say 'TMC.'

'It's Pete,' he said and the lock on the door was released.

Peter walked the short length of a low-ceilinged corridor that was decorated with dozens of framed platinum, gold and silver discs. He stopped at the black doors of the elevator and tapped in the security code that activated the lift. The lift arrived and the doors opened, revealing a red-velvet-lined interior over which a dozen more gold and platinum discs were mounted. Four speakers set in the ceiling carried the sound of Grey Rose in the style of Musak, recorded by a symphony orchestra at the cost of £93,000, just because it amused Taylor to have a lift that played elevator versions of his music.

Peter pressed the button for the first floor and, for the five hundredth time, endured the several seconds of piped pop that was amusing only the first time you heard it. The lift stopped and Peter walked out into a small black reception area which was entirely unfurnished apart from a school desk. Seated behind the desk in a huge, high-backed chair was Sandra Knowles, a slim, sexy woman with blonde shoulder-length hair in her mid-twenties. Like all of TMC's female staff, she wore a uniform of four-inch black stilettos, dark nylons and a grey, long-sleeved Prada dress that stopped five inches above the knee. Pinned to the dress above her left breast was a silver brooch fashioned in the form of an italic 'TM'.

Sandra gave Peter a smile that filled her blue eyes and said, 'Hello, stranger.'

Peter leant over to Sandra and kissed her on the lips. She tilted her head back to receive it more obviously. Peter put his mouth gently to her ear and whispered, 'Didn't your school do the pep-talk about snogging strangers?'

'I never paid attention, I'm afraid,' murmured Sandra as she arched her back suggestively and parted her knees a little.

'No fanny flirting today, Mrs Knowles; I'm late,' he said, smiling.

'I know,' said Sandra. 'Billy's already rung down twice to ask where you are, the git. I wanted to tell him to fuck himself.'

'I expect that what he really wants is to fuck you,' said Peter.

'Everybody wants to fuck me, hon,' said Sandra, grinning at that truth. 'By the way, nobody's meant to know this so you owe me for telling you, but Ian's joining your meeting later.'

'Why is nobody meant to know?' said Peter.

'You know what it's like, Pete; nobody's meant to know anything about our Ian.'

'Thanks, I owe you,' said Peter and he leant over kissed her parted lips again. He looked up at the CCTV camera, gave a wink at its lens, then ran up the steel escalator to the floor above and knocked at the door of the boardroom. There was no answer from the other side of the door. Peter counted to ten and then knocked again. He counted to five and the door was abruptly pulled open by Billy Vernon.

'Where the fuck have you been; and why are you knocking?' said Vernon.

CHAPTER 11

'I wouldn't want to walk on anything uninvited, Billy,' said Peter, smiling. 'You know that it's rude to listen at doors to people talking behind your back.'

Peter heard giggling behind Vernon. He looked over the manager's short frame and smiled at the faces he recognised; Jill Brown, PA to Ian Taylor, early fifties, witty, plump and so pretty that Peter regularly mock-vowed to give up all to marry her. She smiled at Peter and wagged her finger in feigned admonishment at the taunting of Vernon that Peter knew she relished. Like Sandra, Jill wore the stipulated uniform but she had lowered the hem to the knee as a minor protest against the psychology behind the prescribed dressing-up.

Next to Jill sat Alfred Keating, the bald marketing chief from Ian Taylor's British record company, BPA. Alf was the only member of the original Grey Rose promotions team who was still employed by British Phonographic Artists. Taylor insisted that Alf continued to work on all his musical projects because of his unrivalled knowledge. Keating respected Taylor for his pedigree but disliked him for his tantrums.

Peter walked over to Keating and shook his hand, then leaned over and kissed Jill on the cheek which she offered him. He then made individual greetings to the others assembled; Polly Dunn, BPA's product manager, and Klive Whicker, the gay PR from the label who gave his hand a gentle extra squeeze when he shook it. He sat at the spare seat at the head of the table, poured himself a coffee from the large pot that was already almost empty and reached for his cigarettes before Jill's frown reminded him that she hated the smell.

'So,' said Peter, 'What's it all about?'

'We all know why we're here,' Vernon butted in.

'I don't,' said Peter. 'I don't know why I've been here for the past five years.'

‘Don’t start,’ warned Vernon. ‘Our governor has decided that he finally wants to do what he said he never would, perform the whole of Grey Rose at one very exclusive concert. It will be one-night-only, never to be repeated and he wants it to be world news. Obviously our man is his own man and will make up his own mind, but we are here to give our advice.’

‘Which will be ignored,’ said Peter.

‘Not necessarily,’ said Vernon, patiently. ‘Ian has said that he is very open to the opinions of the team on this one.’

‘Who are the team?’ persisted Peter, belligerently.

‘You’re looking at it,’ said Vernon. ‘Stop pissing about, Pete, this is serious. OK, first item, where should we hold the gig?’

‘The Hundred Club?’ suggested Keating, nominating the tiny basement venue below London’s Oxford Street .

‘Too small,’ said Peter. ‘You’d only have enough room for the press, the punters would never get in.’

‘ Earls Court?’ said Whicker. ‘He’d fill that easily.’

‘Yes, but it’s a bit of a barn,’ noted Jill. ‘It’s not exactly intimate in there.’

‘Does it have to be intimate?’ asked Polly Dunn.

‘That’s what he wants, apparently,’ Jill replied.

‘It has to be somewhere that kids will go,’ said Vernon, volunteering a little more of the clauses and codicils that Taylor had dictated to him earlier.

‘Why?’ said Peter.

‘Because the gig will be the launch of a remastered, special anniversary edition of Grey Rose and we want to sell records.’

‘So what’s that got to do with appealing to kids?’ retorted Peter.

‘Kids buy albums,’ said Vernon, dismissively.

‘Not Ian’s albums they don’t,’ said Peter, authoritatively. ‘If we want to have a hit we’ve got to stop this ridiculous pandering to the youth market.’

‘But surely the youth market is the music market?’ suggested Jill, tentatively.

‘No, not in Ian’s case. Not in the case of his peers either. Did you see the last Stones’ tour? Most of the guys in that crowd were wearing their shirts outside their jeans.'

'What the hell does that mean?' said Vernon.

'It means that they've all got too fat to be able to tuck them in. The kids of the sixties aren't kids any longer but they behave and think like they still are. We are the forever young mob; constantly scrambling for excuses to keep feeling like that. And one of those ways is to keep buying music,' said Peter, didactically.

'Every generation buys music,' muttered Vernon.

'Sure!' said Peter. 'But music is more important to our generation, it's the toy of our time. And if you're talking album sales, that's our generation. Kids now download the odd track of ours from the internet but have far more gadgets competing for their attention. Our music is only a part of their world now. Whereas for us, it was all of our world.'

'And your elusive point is?' said Jill, irritated by Peter's platitudes.

'My point is that we are in the music business. We are not in the kids business. We should promote and market and publicise what we're doing to the demographic that will be most receptive to what we are selling. And that is not kids. So aim your publicity at the dads.'

'Like your friends at *Saga*,' said Vernon, spitefully.

'Billy,' started Peter, angry now. 'As I have been saying to you all fucking day, the *Saga* thing had nothing to do with me. But you're wrong to dismiss *Saga*. Eighty per cent of the wealth in this country is created by the over-45s. All of these pot-bellied blokes are running around with shitloads of money.'

He listened with feigned interest as Alf Keating outlined the record company's proposal. Keating detailed the story of Grey Rose. Released in 1968 by Taylspin, Ian Taylor's seminal band of the sixties, Grey Rose was immediately hailed as messianic by the critics. *The Times* called the 60-minute record 'rock and roll's finest hour'.

Years ahead of its or any time, Grey Rose predicted punk rock with the rasp of buzz-saw guitars throughout its ten tracks, but – unlike punk – the songs were made of melodies sweeter and more instantly memorable than anyone other than The Beatles was creating at the time. In the forty years since its release, Grey Rose had rarely failed to be in the top ten of polls of the best British rock album of all time.

But, unlike Revolver or London Calling or any other classic Brit album, Grey Rose was also special because very few people owned it. At the time of its release, Taylor was busy with his 'white period', as he dubbed his cocaine addiction, and the skewed common sense that resulted from that habit had persuaded him only to allow the album to be released as a strictly limited edition. So limited, that only 500,000 were ever pressed by BPA.

Taylor had further insisted at the time that the record was only to be sold in the UK. Predictably, the record had become one of the most sought-after albums of all time. Mint editions could easily command bids in excess of $1,000 on eBay and its rarity was made the greater by the fact that, for forty years, Taylor had refused every plea to allow BPA to press more copies.

Grey Rose had created both Taylor's legend and controversy. Taylspin had split up acrimoniously after Taylor – who had written all the songs and retained sole publishing rights – refused his bandmates' begging to re-release the album and thereby earn them a decent pension. Only once had Ian Taylor ever sung any song from the album in public and that was when he arrived, unannounced and uninvited, to sing the title track unaccompanied at the funeral of Taylspin's drummer William 'Wim' Rogers.

Somehow – and Peter had never worked out how, as Taylor's personal security had searched mourners for recording devices with offensive thoroughness – a bootleg existed of that lone performance. Peter still grimaced at the memory of the publicity firestorm he had fought at the time when the breakfast jock on Swindon's previously unknown commercial station, Radio SWN, had threatened to play the bootlegged track on his show. As the DJ, Steve Smythe, courted national and international publicity by stringing out a five-day countdown to the broadcast, Taylor had retaliated by buying the radio station, closing it down and sacking all the staff. His press statement at the time, 'Mr Taylor said today,

'I couldn't give a toss',' had not won him great support.

Peter was nudged from his reflections as he heard Alf Keating say, 'and we will be pressing ten million worldwide…'

'How many?' said Peter, genuinely astounded.

'Ten million,' said Keating. 'That's initially. The marketing bods say the research indicates that it could eventually go on to out-sell The Eagles' Best of.'

'So,' said Jill Brown, moving the discussion on, 'Ian wants to promote the re-release of the album with one show, right? But we still haven't agreed which venue to recommend.'

'I don't think it matters,' said Klive Whicker. 'The tickets will sell out in less than an hour even if he performs it in Hyde Park.'

'If this really is a once-in-a-lifetime experience, we should design it as such,' said Peter. 'So we need to find somewhere so exclusive that just being there doubles its whole uniqueness. People are going to die to get tickets for this one: we really need to pump up their blood by staging it some place the whole world will want to get into.'

'Such as?' said Vernon.

'I'm thinking,' said Peter.

'You know the American label will want it in the States,' said Keating. 'It's his biggest market and all that.'

'The American label can piss off,' said Peter. 'This has nothing to do with them and, for once, they can't bully their way in.'

'What do you mean?' asked Polly Dunn. 'Our American sales far exceed…'

'I know,' said Peter. 'But Grey Rose was not released in the States in '68 as Ian's personal protest against America's involvement in the Vietnam War. It would be a monstrous hypocrisy to perform it for the first time in the country that the album was dedicated against, especially now we're at war again. The gig has to be here, where he lives. Where he wrote it.'

The meeting fell silent for a moment.

'Westminster Abbey,' said Peter abruptly.

'Where?' said Vernon, Polly and Keating together.

'Westminster Abbey,' Peter repeated with conviction.

'But it's rock and roll,' said Jill, protesting. 'Westminster Abbey is a place of worship, they'd never agree to it. Royalty gets married in Westminster Abbey; people sing hymns there, not rock songs. It's completely inappropriate!'

'Actually,' said Peter, 'it's not.'

'Oh for God's sake' exclaimed Vernon, ignoring the office rule and lighting a cigarette to calm his indignation.

'You're mad' said Keating.

'Fucking bonkers,' said Vernon, blowing smoke all around and not caring. 'Have you started taking drugs again?'

Peter looked down at his black sneakers and concentrated until the uproar abated. 'Listen,' he said. 'Just listen for a moment. Westminster Abbey is a British institution. So is Ian Taylor. Nobody gets to sing rock and roll in Westminster Abbey. So Ian's getting what nobody else can get; and we know we like that. But more than that, Westminster Abbey is a place of peace. Grey Rose is an album that is all about peace. It was written as the anthem for the peace movement. It's the one album that is seen to speak to all nations who are otherwise beheading or vapourising each other. It was launched against the Vietnam War, an American war that the world thought was wrong…'

'So?' said Vernon.

'So nothing has changed. We've still got the fucking Americans going around the world bombing wherever they feel like it. We've still got war and now we're fucking in it as well. The point about Grey Rose wasn't just that it was anti-Vietnam, it was – and is – anti all war. Its point is as pertinent today as it was in the sixties. It still holds up.'

'What has that got to do with the Abbey?' said Vernon.

'If we present Grey Rose in a place of peace it will re-send the whole message because it's as relevant now as it was then. It will give us the spin of uniting Ian's sixties generation, who were anti-war, along with their kids – these fucking kids that are apparently so important to the label and to him – and motivate these politically-indolent kids of today to become as anti-war as we were…'

'You mea…' butted in Polly.

'What I mean is that by presenting Grey Rose as the perennial flower of peace, it's no longer some retro gig like The Shadows getting back together at the Bournemouth Winter Gardens.'

'Fucking hippy bullshit,' said Vernon.

'Is it?' said a voice that everybody in the room recognized at once.

Peter and all around the table looked in astonishment at the elevator from which Ian Taylor had emerged.

'Is it bullshit, Billy,' said Taylor in his soft Birmingham accent. 'What's a better message, Billy? Pete's right; nothing's changed and so we've got to keep on trying to change it. And besides, I like 'the perennial flower of peace'.'

Vernon started to bluster, a panic that became greater as he realized that his cigarette was still burning. Peter was impressed that Vernon crushed it in his fist without wincing.

'I… I… just meant…' he began.

'What?' said Taylor and Peter noticed that his eyes were black with the Great White look that he adopted whenever he went on attack.

'But the Church wouldn't like it, Ian,' Billy squirmed.

'The Church would like money,' said Taylor. 'Imagine their cut of the rights to a global satellite broadcast? Besides, how does the message of Grey Rose differ from the message of peace be with you? That's what they say in every church at the blessing, isn't it? We'd just be adding a twelve-bar to peace be with you.' The hymns of the old ages were only the rock songs of their time.'

'That's the press release, Ian,' said Whicker enthusiastically, making Vernon scowl because he would have liked to have said that.

CHAPTER 12

Ian Taylor threw his feet up onto the antique table after sitting in the chair which Vernon had vacated at just a glare from him. He stretched his long, jean-clad legs, yawned, then picked at his teeth as if nobody was present. Scratching at his dyed-blonde hair, which was streaked to blend with the spreading grey of his beard, he shifted his shrewd glance over to Peter.

'You're a bit outspoken today, Mr Forth,' he said, coolly. 'What was all that you said? Kids don't like me, I ignore your advice and you don't know why you work here? Hmm. Good to know.'

Peter was about to begin stammering an explanation but Taylor raised his voice to cut off any intervention.

'Good to know… Still, s'pose it saves me all that time reading the transcripts of the bugs on your phones at home.'

Taylor smiled thinly but his eyes stayed bleak. Although Polly giggled at the jibe, Peter was not convinced that he was joking; long ago he had realized that Taylor made his most serious points in jest. The meeting was still silent after the shock of Taylor revealing his presence. As always when the great star entered a room, confidence was crushed. Peter knew that Taylor knew that and, like a dog, the singer sniffed at the room for fear to exploit. He had read dozens of articles commenting on how Taylor's presence electrified a room, but he knew it wasn't that which made the atmosphere charged; it was his history that did it, the confusion caused by not knowing quite how to react when a legend was sitting there behaving, apparently, as normally as the next man; only the next man was close to cowering.

'I don't mind if you smoke, Billy,' said Taylor.

'Oh… err… thanks, boss,' said Vernon. 'But I thought this was a non-smoking…'

'It is,' said Taylor, 'but not because I said so. I couldn't give a fuck if you get cancer. Smoke if you want.'

'No, I'm fine thanks, boss,' said Vernon, lying.

'As you like,' said Taylor, who was scanning the table to see if anybody had bothered to make a pot of the Turkish coffee that he preferred when the distinctive ping of Peter's Zippo cut the silence. Taylor and the others looked over to see Peter ostentatiously drawing on a cigarette. Peter held Taylor's eye.

'Want one?' he asked, offering the packet.

Taylor smirked with the mix of anger and admiration with which he reacted to displays of open defiance.

'Good old Pete, can't take him anywhere as usual,' he deadpanned.

Polly giggled again but Peter saw the 'I'll deal with you later' look in Taylor's eyes.

'Soooo,' said Taylor, rearranging his feet on the table, 'it sounds like nobody has a problem with re-releasing the Rose. Huh?'

'Great idea,' said Keating.

'Inspired,' said Vernon.

Everybody else nodded. Taylor glanced at Peter and cocked his left eyebrow to indicate he wanted his opinion.

'It'll be big,' said Peter, smiling.

'Good,' said Taylor. 'And everybody's cool with a gig, yeah?'

Again everyone nodded their approval.

'So, anybody got a better idea than Pete's thing about doing it in the Abbey?' asked Taylor, as if he was quizzing a Latin class on their knowledge of verbs.

Nobody spoke. Keating and Whicker looked intently at the notepads on the table in front of them.

'Billy?' said Taylor.

'Yes boss?'

Taylor sighed impatiently. 'Do you have a better idea than Westminster Abbey?'

'No,' said Vernon. 'I think it's great.'

'That wasn't what you said just now,' said Taylor, evenly. 'I thought you said Pete was on drugs…'

'Pete is always on drugs,' said Jill, throwing Vernon a lifeline that made everyone laugh.

'OK,' resumed Taylor, 'if we do the Abbey, what coverage will we get out of it?'

'We should get all the main news bulletins,' said Whicker. 'BBC, ITN, Sky, Channel 4 News... It depends on how many interviews you'd be prepared to do.'

'What if I don't want to do any interviews?'

'Err… they should still cover it, it's a big story,' said Whicker.

'OK,' said Taylor. 'I really want this to be big news. So let's say it again – what sort of coverage will I get if I do the Rose in Westminster Abbey? Pete?'

'Well, to be honest…' began Peter.

'I'd rather you lied to me,' said Taylor archly.

Peter grinned.

'OK… If you do a live broadcast of the gig you'll get a lot of news bulletins leading up to it on the channel that buys the rights. Announcing the gig at the Abbey will make a big story with all the music mags. The broadsheets will run it, probably on the line of how much money you'll make from the album. The *Independent* will probably drum up the peace protest line, as will the *Guardian*, because they're anti-war…'

'Isn't everybody anti-war?' said Taylor, genuinely.

'Not all of the tabs,' said Peter. 'Some will take Billy's 'hippy bullshit' line; possibly asking our boys what they think of you making some peace protest. I wouldn't be surprised if one or two try to piss on the story by tracking down the band and asking if they've been asked to do the gig… err… I don't know what you think about doing it with the band…'

'Go on,' said Taylor, giving nothing away.

'If we want to ensure mass newspaper coverage, we need to come up with some scam that will interest that huge section of society who wouldn't even want a ticket – the young and the thick – because they are too young or too thick to appreciate the history and occasion of the gig. But this is not about selling tickets. This is about attracting the constant attention of the tabloids as they drive the respectable media. If we get them behind it, then the gig becomes a big event.'

‘So how do you do that?’ said Vernon. Peter noticed that he said ‘you’ and not ‘we’. As ever, he thought, Billy would never sign up for responsibility because with that went the risk of blame.

‘We need to involve the young,’ said Peter. ‘I know that I’ve been saying that they don’t buy the majority of our records but the tabs court the young and we need to get the tabloids’ attention. And to do that we have to compete with these new so-called celebrities and their stunts. We have to out-stunt them.’

‘Competitions are good,’ said Polly. ‘We could provide the *Sun* with tickets to give away to their readers.’

‘It’s not enough,’ said Peter.

‘What about win a job at the gig?’ suggested Vernon.

‘Win what job? Win your job?’ said Taylor, who was still cross about being called a fucking hippy.

‘Err… no, I meant something safe, something controllable. Like working with Pete,’ spluttered Vernon.

‘Pete is not controllable,’ said Taylor, grinning.

‘What about win tickets for a meet and greet with a photo with you?’ said Polly to Taylor .

‘Could do,’ considered Taylor. ‘It’s a bit tame, though. I mean nobody’s going to hold their front page just for a snap of me with some fat girl from Bradford. Judging by what Peter is saying, it has to be sexier.’

‘What if we fixed it so that the winner was like one of those FHM High Street Honeys?’ suggested Whicker.

‘What are high street honeys?’ said Jill.

‘Basically a bunch of birds you’d want to shag,’ said Peter. ‘Well, not you, Jill. Girls that Billy would want to shag. They’re the next crop of instant celebrities.’

‘I would not!’ protested Vernon.

‘Yes, you fucking…’ argued Peter.

‘I would,’ said Taylor and everybody laughed as the tension was eased.

‘Actually,’ Taylor continued. ‘What about that? Fucking? As every celeb story in the papers is now linked to sex, why don’t we go for that? I’m going to be performing the Rose and we all know

'Come to Daddy's on it, the song about a singer who fucks his fan. So why not actually enact that as part of the gig? Seriously. That's what the new decadence demands isn't it, Pete? That's what the readers and viewers want – a new Gomorrah for t'morra. The press laughs at us lot because they think we're old and conservative. Fuck it! They want to be shocked? Let's really fucking show them who can shock around here. There's your competition – win a shag. That should get us some coverage.'

'What?' said Keating, horrified.

'Some lucky punter can win my cock,' said Taylor, looking at Peter. 'And you better make sure she's one of these bloody honeys.'

'You're not serious?' said Jill, appalled.

'Billy?' said Taylor, ignoring her.

'Yeah, I love it, boss. Buy a ticket, win a shag. Fucking great!' said Vernon.

'Billy!' said Jill.

'Relax, Jill. Purchase is not compulsory,' laughed Taylor.

'But the newspapers will go mad!' argued Jill. 'The *Daily Mail* will have a field day.'

'I know,' said Taylor, smiling. 'So will the rest of them. There will be questions in Parliament about my propriety. All the TV news will report the controversy. I can hear it now…'

Peter warmed to the theme, 'It'll be rock star Ian Taylor has caused outrage with a live sex contest for his controversial peace concert at Westminster Abbey'. Ha! The Archbishop of Canterbury will condemn it, of course.'

'Yeah,' said Taylor, Tory MPs will start jumping up and down. They'll try to ban me from using the Abbey. There will be fucking TV crews and paparazzi outside my home all night, waiting for a comment. Brilliant. It'll be huge.'

'What if a bloke wins?' said Keating, naively.

'Then you can shag him,' said Taylor. 'Good point, though. We'll have to put in a clause that only pretty women can enter. That should piss off the politically correct mob. I love it. I could get sued by the Equal Opportunities Commission for refusing to shag a guy. How many more headlines would that get you, Pete?'

‘They’re not my headlines,’ said Peter. ‘Nobody’s writing about me.’

‘You know what I mean,’ said Taylor, for a moment ignoring everybody else in the room. ‘You love all that scamming stuff, frothing up the papers with the expectation that you seed. You live for all that; you’re a headline junkie. Along with all your other bloody addictions.’

Peter considered the sad truth in this. Taylor was right; his entire happiness was now entirely dependent upon his job. If Ian Taylor was getting great press, he, Peter, was elated. If the articles and profiles and interviews were knocking and hostile, then Peter felt as though it was his fault. Never mind fame by association, Peter now lived so vicariously that his had become life by association. But it did allow him the money to buy drugs whenever he felt like it, so that was OK.

He was brought back from his reverie by the awareness that everybody else was now getting to their feet and Taylor was saying, ‘but let’s all keep this quiet because I’ve not made my mind up about any of it yet. But, good start, guys. Pete?’

‘Yes, Ian.’

‘Can I have a word?’

Vernon took this as a sign to dawdle in the hope that he too would be invited to remain. As the others made their moves to shake Taylor’s hand and exclaim banal good wishes like ‘this will be great,’ Vernon busied himself with appearing to have mislaid something in his briefcase.

‘What’ve you lost, Billy?’ said Taylor, knowingly.

‘Er… nothing, Ian.’

‘Do you need to see me?’

‘Errr…’

‘I’ll catch you upstairs, then, in my office. I just need a moment with Pete. If you don’t mind,’ said Taylor .

Vernon shuffled to the lift and pressed the button to retrieve the elevator. Although Peter was himself curious whether the tête-à-tête was going to be about that photo business he willed himself not to mention it unless Taylor raised the subject. Finally, after Vernon had entered the lift, and after Taylor had checked that it actually had moved to another floor, he turned to Peter.

Peter fidgeted with his cigarette packet and pulled open its lid. 'Want one?' he said.

'No, ta,' said Taylor, who occasionally would share a cigarette or a joint when there wasn't an audience who would gossip about it.

'So, do you think this shagging thing is a good idea?' he asked.

'Good?' said Peter.

'Don't get cute, Pete. Doing 'Come to Daddy' for real. Do we need it?'

'Well you're not actually going to do it, are you?' said the PR, horrified at the prospective nightmare publicity that would cause.

'I don't know. It'd be fucking horrible, shagging in public. Even behind closed doors you'd feel the whole world would be watching…'

'Which they would.'

'Yeah, right. Anyway, I don't need some slag selling a story that I haven't got a dick like Lenny Kravitz.'

'So why don't we just drop it?' said Peter, earnestly. 'As you say, do we need it? I mean, you're doing a gig for the first time in history of the best fucking album ever made. Maybe you're bringing the band back for it, I don't know. You're doing it in Westminster Abbey and the whole peace thing about the gig is going to really piss off the Americans anyway.'

'I know, I know,' said Taylor. 'But there's a part of me that really wants to just fucking stick it to those fuckers. Really fucking shock them for once and for all.'

'Which fuckers?'

'Fucking Fleet Street with its sanctimonious standards of filling up their pages with sex and tits on the one side and then getting all ooo-er on the other about anyone actually having sex.'

'Well, if you're not intending to do it, we can't announce it and have some sort of competition because everyone's so fucking litigious these days someone would win and then sue us for breach of contract,' said Peter seriously.

'I know,' sighed Taylor. 'Ridiculous, isn't it?'

He went silent and stared at the carpet. Peter waited until he looked up again.

'Are you alright?' he asked sincerely.

'Not really. I'm fucked off. What I really want is to give up having to compete; waking up every morning feeling like I'm getting judged by people who couldn't write a bloody nursery rhyme, who'll piss on me because my new songs might not be in the same key as my old stuff. I hate being fucking judged all the time. Nobody else gets judged in public just for the crime of fucking being. I don't want to get a fucking reputation for fucking fans, like that's the only way I can get in the papers. It's so fucking shallow, but that's the way it's gone now… What the fuck's it all about?'

'Ian…?' he began.

'What?'

'Why do you want to do this, this whole thing with the Rose? I mean, obviously it will get you shed-loads of attention and the album will go to number one, but what's it for? Is it to make the anti-war call again? I'm only asking 'cos the press are going to ask me.'

'Let me tell you how it works,' said Taylor, who was now pacing the room and not looking Peter in the eye. 'It's all about being remembered. I'm not going to last forever. To tell you the truth, I'm surprised I've lasted this long. But you can make the songs last, if they're any good. And if your songs last after you do, then you'll be pretty well remembered… My point with all of this Rose revival, this second bloom, is that I want to do the definitive follow that.'

'I'm not with you.'

'When we started off in the sixties, playing R&B in little pubs and working men's clubs in Aston, hoping that maybe we just might get picked up by some little jazz label, you were always looking to do some amazing set that the other bands wouldn't want to follow. You wanted to get to be so bloody good that none of the others would fancy even trying to match you, so you'd nudge your way up to the top of the bill. Until we had our first hit, in '66, we were like fifth on the bill. But because 'Love You Girl' was such a big hit, nobody wanted to go on after us because they couldn't top the reaction, so we got shoved up the bill. And that's where you always want to be, top of the bill. If you're good, you don't wanna follow anyone. And now, even though you've got all these bands calling themselves the new Beatles or the new Stones, the new best things all over the place, I still want to be up there doing something that'll make other bands think 'We're not fucking following that!'

Peter said nothing; he knew there was more to come.

'Nobody goes into this business to be the runner-up,' Taylor resumed. 'I certainly didn't. You don't want to be on any inside pages, you wanna be on the front fucking page. Fuck what they write about you inside, so long as your mug's looking out of the newsstand. So that's why I don't want the announcement of doing the Rose at the Abbey to trickle out like some pissy little mention in *Bizarre*. I want to be on the Six O'Clock News with this one. But in a cool way.'

'It's easy, all we have to do is to get Polly and Klive...'

'Who's Klive?'

'The PR who was sitting here.'

'Is he gay?'

'Why do you ask?'

Peter realised too late the implications of what he had said and started to blush. He wondered again whether Vernon had told Taylor about the photo business yet and that made him blush even deeper; and then deeper still as he realized that Taylor had sensed the permutations of his gaffe.

'What?' snapped Taylor.

'I... err... I just meant what was it about him that made you think he's gay, because I was thinking that too. Anyway...'

'Do you have a problem with gays?'

'Well hardly...' Peter could not stop himself saying.

'What do you mean, hardly?

'Well, nothing really... I meant... you can't work in this business if you're going to get weird about things like that,' said Peter honestly. 'I mean, it's not us who are anti-gay. It's the fucking newspapers and uptight macho men who wouldn't understand sexuality if it fucked them in the arse… I mean… oh shit.'

'Nice analogy,' said Taylor warmly. 'Good to know, Peter. You were saying…?'

'What?' said Peter.

'You were saying Polly and Klive and…'

'We just have to get one of them to tip off a couple of tabs that you're thinking about fucking a fan as a peace protest inside Westminster Abbey.'

'And then the *Sun* phones you and what do you say?'

'I say that, strictly off the record, you are thinking about performing the Rose but nothing is agreed yet, there's no date for the gig yet and that if people are saying that you're going to enact Come to Daddy as part of it, well that's just speculation. The whole planet will just explode with supposition.'

Peter was excited now. It was ideal publicity, controversial without commitment. Ian was not saying he would be having live sex during a rock show on sacred ground and, as long as neither he nor Peter confirmed anything, the press could jump to as many conclusions as they liked.

'So I don't actually have to shag anyone?' said Taylor, grinning.

'You can shag whoever you want,' said Peter. 'I'm just saying that you're not under any obligation to tell anyone that you're going to.'

'The tickets to the gig will sell in minutes,' said Taylor.

'If we can persuade the dean or the abbot or whoever that this whole sex thing in the press is just tabloid nonsense.'

'Will they believe us?' Taylor wasn't sure.

'Who's the Church going to think is most likely to be lying, you or the *Sun*?'

'Us, probably,' grinned Taylor.

'Fine, but nobody will know whether we are lying right up until the night. Even I won't know until the night, will I?'

'Good point,' said Taylor. 'OK, nobody is to know about this conversation. This is just between you and me. There's probably going to be quite a bit of 'just between you and me' coming up. Keep it to yourself and make up something else for Billy, he'll be beside himself by now.'

As they took the elevator to Taylor's private suite and office on the top floor, Peter wanted to know what counted as quite a bit but he didn't dare ask because Taylor had started humming along to his bloody musak.

CHAPTER 13

Taylor's private floor was furnished in the style of a mogul palace with trimmings of Arabian brothel. Crimson, purple and orange silks hung the full length of the walls. Over the silks were fixed more than a dozen antique mirrors from Maharashtra.

Large outdoor joss sticks burned in brass holders twenty-four hours a day, frequently provoking choking fits among those unused to the atmosphere. A scarlet Steinway grand piano occupied the far corner of the large room. To the right of the piano lay stacks of gold-embroidered cushions upon which Taylor liked to slump, while holding business meetings with visitors who were ushered towards their choice of four vast damask upholstered armchairs. In the centre of the room, at a large circular desk made from the wheel of a watermill from Hyderabad, sat Jill Brown. On her desktop was only a pad and pencil, a laptop computer and ten telephones – a direct line to Taylor's home in upstate New York, another to his mansion in Wiltshire, another to his London flat, another to his shoreline villa on Lake Garda, another linked to his Bentley, Ferrari, Range Rover and Jeep, another to the office switchboard and the last, an unlisted outside line.

As Taylor and Peter entered, causing the five Siamese cats that lounged there to raise their heads idly, Jill was saying, 'Yes… yes… uh-huh… yes… yes…' into the mouthpiece of the outside line. As Taylor was right next to him, Peter deduced that she was not conducting a typical conversation with her employer so was therefore probably telephone bidding to Christie's.

'Right,' said Taylor. 'You go and keep Billy happy, spin some yarn. I'll be through in a minute. I just want to see how much I get my tank for.'

'Your what?' said Peter.

'I'm buying a tank, some Russian thing; I might arrive at the Abbey in it.'

Peter went to find Billy. There, pacing the room that was

furnished only by four Victorian chaises longues set in a square in the centre, he found Vernon smoking whilst shouting into his mobile phone.

'I don't give a fuck,' said Vernon, typically. 'What? What? Listen you fucking little fuck, this is what Ian fucking Taylor wants and what Ian Taylor wants, you will fucking do. If it weren't for Ian Taylor you wouldn't even have a fucking record company. Just fucking do it.'

'Problem?' said Peter as Vernon ended his call abruptly.

'Fucking BPA twats,' said Vernon, as if the exclamation alone explained all. 'Did he mention the, err, you know?'

'No. What about the BPA twats?'

'Saying they think that the approach to Westminster Abbey should come from us, like it's our idea.'

'But it is our idea.'

'I know. Your idea, in fact. Yet another brainwave from the ideas officer. Only you're not going to get the credit on this one. Ian is going to want it to look like it's their idea and he is accepting their request to perform.'

'When did he say that?' said Peter.

'He didn't. But I know that he will. It looks better if it seems like it's the record company who has come up with this whole idea of finally performing the Rose…'

'Why?'

'So that we can, or you can brief the press on the fact that Ian didn't want to do it.'

'Why?'

'So that Ian can explain at his press conference or whatever that he refused the label at first and has only agreed because he feels that the anti-war message of the album now needs to be heard again.'

'Is he going to donate the profits from ten million sales to the Red Cross?' asked Peter provocatively.

'Why the fuck would he want to do that?'

'Because if we're going to bang that John and Yoko drum, the papers will ask whether Ian's going to give any money to the peace movement.'

'Tell them to fuck off.' said Vernon. He mused for a moment.

'He's doing the gig for peace, he'll be getting all this publicity that will put peace back into people's minds. That's his contribution. Without his gig there wouldn't be much of a peace movement.'

'I think the concept was invented a bit before the Rose,' said Peter. 'Ian doesn't hold the world exclusive on wanting peace.'

'How much would we have to donate?' said Vernon anxiously.

'A million would be good.'

'Dollars?'

'Quid,' said Peter.

'Are you fucking mad? Who is going to tell him he has to give away a million pounds? He's not going to do that. He'd rather call off the whole thing than pay to perform,' ranted Vernon.

'He'd hardly be paying. Ten million albums, call it seven million to be safe. What's eight per cent of seven million sales?'

'How the hell should I know?' said Vernon, irritated, as Peter began jotting figures on a notebook he had taken from his briefcase.

'It's a fuckload of dollars.'

'Plus his cut of the tickets,' said Vernon. 'Plus TV rights and a DVD deal and merchandising. You're probably looking at the best part of twenty million bucks, all in.'

'Which means that he can afford to give one million to charity,' argued Peter.

'Well you can suggest it. I already had a bollocking this morning about sending a bike up to St Albans because he wanted to see right away some proofs that I'd forgotten I'd left at home. Apparently I'm to pay the three hundred quid for that.'

'It won't cost him a penny,' said Peter. 'If he gives the money to charity it's entirely tax deductible. In effect, he'll have personally given fuck all.'

Peter watched Vernon think on that and he knew that he would later suggest the tax dodge to Taylor as his own idea. He knew too that Vernon would instruct him to reveal that Taylor had made 'a seven-figure donation' because that could imply that he had given away as much as nine times what Peter was suggesting.

'Anyway, what the fuck are we going to do about the band?' said Vernon.

'Good point, Billy,' they heard Taylor say. 'What about the band?'

'Are you going to use them for the gig?' asked Peter, already dreading the potential disaster looming ahead.

'Ah yes, the good old band,' said Taylor, sneering. 'Where are all the guys these days? I believe you have a report for me on that, Billy. Let's have it.'

Vernon produced a clipboard onto which was attached a typed report that Peter, reading from the corner of his eye, saw was headed 'Security Trust International'. Vernon began to read the report of the band members' current whereabouts.

'Well, Wim Rogers is dead,' he said, robotically.

'That's a good start for a band reunion,' said Taylor, sarcastically. 'And I already knew that, you twat. So we'll need a drummer. Who's good now?'

Vernon looked flustered, as he did not like to make suggestions unless he had been advised on his opinion first.

'Err... these sort of guys, the guys who did the report, er... they don't really do that,' he said.

'Do what?' snapped Taylor.

'Er... they're not the sort of people who know about drummers,' squirmed Vernon.

'This gets better and better,' said Taylor, unsmiling. 'Anyone else dead?' said Taylor, moving on.

Vernon returned to his report and read aloud and verbatim.

'Er... Roy Andrew Adams. Aged fifty seven. Currently living in Little Venice. Married to Annie. Three kids. Mistress's name is Kirsti Ericsson, twenty five-year-old Norwegian model based in London with The Zeek Agency. One-time smackhead, now in recovery. Does a bit of coke...'

'Who does?' interrupted Taylor.

'Sorry?' said Vernon, confused.

'Who is doing coke? Roy or his Scandinavian shag?'

'Oh, sorry, they mean Roy Adams... er... does a bit of coke.'

'Lucky him,' said Taylor, irritated.

'He was last interviewed in November in *GQ* when he was reported as saying that he rarely played bass anymore…' read Vernon.

'Great,' said Taylor.

'…But he apparently claimed that making Grey Rose was the best thing he ever did…'

'He did fuck all. I had to overdub most of his bloody parts,' grumbled Taylor.

'…and that is apparently his eternal regret – his words, eternal regret – it's his eternal regret that he never got to play it live…'

'Because I sacked him.'

'Err… yeah, that's what he said. Apparently.'

'I know,' said Taylor. 'I read the article. The little shit called me a control freak. It's fucking great, isn't it; I'm a fucking freak just because I asked him to do something as complicated as play in the same key as the rest of the band. OK, so what else is new in the wonderful world of Taylspin? Go on, Billy. What's Legs Galore up to?'

'Who?' said Vernon.

'Easy Eileen,' said Taylor, referring to Taylspin's backing singer, his former lover Eileen Lore.

'Oh, right,' said Vernon, catching on and considering his report. 'Umm. Now living in Beverly Hills with a twenty two-year-old guitarist, one Mikey Max. In and out of rehab. Still on the coke but attending NA. Was down on her luck but came into a packet when Capitol released 'Sod's Lore's Greatest Hits' last year. Still selling out the smaller arenas. She's writing a new album and possibly touring next year.'

'Has she still got The Chuffer in her road crew?' asked Taylor lazily.

'Sorry? The what?' said Vernon, frantically looking through his report.

'The Chuffer,' instructed Taylor. 'That's what they used to call the guy we employed to blow Charlie up her snatch…'

'Sorry?' said Vernon, aghast.

'Haven't you heard of The Chuffer? Oh, this is great. Dear old Eileen got so strung out on the marching powder that she couldn't sing without it. Which was OK when she was in the studio but it presented a bit of a problem when she was on the road. This is fucking wild. She couldn't snort it off the amps like anybody else would do because too much gear had fucked her nose…'

Taylor was laughing now, revelling in the excesses of the Taylspin era. 'Ha. So she worked out that as coke works on any membrane, she could take it up her quim. But it was a bit of a problem stuffing half a gram of toxic tampon up herself whilst singing at the Staples Center. So she devises this scam where we got a fucking tent put up just offstage with this roadie sitting in it with a pile of coke and a peashooter.'

Peter knew the story, but he was amused to watch Vernon become increasingly agog as he heard it for the first time.

'So… so…' Taylor continued, giggling, 'so every time that dear old Eileen wants a buzz during the gig, she nips off into the tent during a guitar solo or at the end of the song. She spreads 'em and this roadie blows the equivalent of a few lines up her chuff. It's true. And he became known as The Chuffer. That's all he did on tour. 'Hello, what's your job, then?' 'Oh, I blow coke up Eileen Lore's snatch.' Brilliant.'

'Is that for real?' said Vernon.

'Totally,' said Taylor. 'We've got to get Eileen back. Just so that I can meet the fucking Chuffer again. I want to try it on her myself.'

Peter stayed silent as he knew that Taylor's mood was about to turn black at any moment.

'And finally,' Vernon read from his notes, 'there's Jack Jackson…'

Here we go, thought Peter.

'Who?' said Taylor.

Vernon's bafflement could not have been greater had Taylor queried the identity of Eric Clapton. 'Jack… Jack Jack-son?' he stammered. 'Your guitar man?'

'Guitar man!' sneered Taylor. 'Oh yes, the fucking guitar man. Mr Fucking Telecaster his fucking self. What about him?'

'Sorry?' said Vernon .

'For what?' bullied Taylor.

'Err… you asked me to do a report on, err… what the band is doing… Jack Jackson… he's the only one we haven't mentioned.'

'And I fucking wish you hadn't mentioned him,' said Taylor as he became increasingly surly.

'But how…?' Vernon began, poleaxed by Taylor's characteristic contradictions. Peter decided to throw Vernon a line.

'He's a photographer now,' he interrupted. 'He lives near me in Dorset. He's got a camera shop in Lyme…'

'How d'you fucking know all this?' snapped Taylor.

'He's retired,' continued Peter.

'Retired? Fucking over the hill, more like,' ranted Taylor.

'He still plays. A bit,' said Peter tentatively. 'He did a gig a few weeks back in a pub down there. Playing with Robbie Earle.'

'Huh,' said Taylor.

Peter decided to push it. If Taylspin were to reform, Taylor would need Jack Jackson. Nobody else could replicate the sound of the band so there would no point reforming Taylspin without him. So even though, personally, he wanted the man to die hideously for what he was doing with Susie, professionally Peter knew that Jackson mattered. So he stuck his neck out.

'They were brilliant,' he said.

'Who were?' said Taylor grumpily.

'Robbie and Jack. They were really fucking good.'

'How the fuck do you know?'

'Well, I live down there,' said Peter, knowing that his employer of many years could not reasonably be expected to pay any attention to the life that his staff had beyond his demands of them.

'So?'

'I saw 'em,' said Peter. 'Robbie's a brilliant player.'

'He's good,' Taylor conceded, reluctantly. 'He probably carried Jack. I bet Jack's amp wasn't even plugged in.'

Peter leaned forward and looked Taylor in the eye.

'Jack was really good, Ian,' he said softly.

'Well, yeah,' butted in Vernon, sensing the mood. 'But like not as good as when he played with you, boss.'

'How the fuck do you know?' Taylor exploded. 'Were you fucking there as well?'

'Err... no. I... um... just heard,' said Vernon .

'Heard where? On the fucking Nine O'Clock News? And finally... Jack is back...'

'I told him,' said Peter.

'Oh great! So you're doing my fucking rhythm guitarist's publicity now, are you?' Taylor was getting furious; his eyes were going black.

'He asked about you,' said Peter.

'What?'

'Robbie introduced us. Said I worked with you...'

'For me,' corrected Taylor .

'He spoke well of you.'

'What? Who did?'

' Jackson. He said he admired you because you had never sold out.'

Peter watched Taylor consider this unexpected news.

'Did he actually say that, or is that your interpretation; you fucking spinning it again?'

'He said, verbatim, 'What's he up to these days?' I told him you were working on your book and he said, word for word, 'Ian's alright. He's a grumpy sod and he tries too hard. But I admire him because he has never sold out'.'

'What else did he say?' said Taylor, sourly.

'He said he wanted a large vodka and tonic.'

'Oh, so he's still a pisshead, then. You two should get on well.'

Peter was about to lose his patience and say 'Actually, I think we would, because he's not fucking insane like you,' but he backed off because he watched a calm suddenly come over Taylor.

'He's right,' said Taylor, who appeared to be talking to himself. 'I haven't sold out. I never sold out. That was the whole thing about the Rose, that's why it all fucked up, because I wouldn't sell out. I wouldn't back down and give in to all those fucking record company twats who just wanted to make money. They couldn't dig that the Rose was a fucking protest album. The best fucking protest album ever made. But Jack dug it. He knew it was us against the bastards…'

'It still is,' said Peter.

'What?'

'It's still you guys against the bastards. Vietnam, Afghanistan. Nothing's changed, Ian. The Rose is as relevant now as it ever was.'

'He's right, man,' said Taylor, addressing Vernon, who was relieved to hear the word 'man' as its familiarity indicated the storm had passed. 'He's fucking right. The Rose is as much now as it was then. We've got to fucking do this gig, you know, we've got to fucking stick it to 'em again. Fuck the fucking record company with their fucking oh, we don't want to upset anybody snivelling shit. We gotta do this guys. And, you know what? If me and Jack do it together then they'll really take notice this time. We gotta do it, babe.'

Having swung from being a twat to a babe in less than five minutes, Vernon grinned. 'Yeah, man,' he said, awkwardly.

CHAPTER 14

Peter was sitting in the back of a taxi on his way back to Paddington station when a ping announced a new text. He checked it absent-mindedly and was startled to see a message saying *Re the b-j pic, we should talk.*

Peter knew he should alert Vernon but the ambulance chaser in him wanted the glory himself, so he rang the number. The line rang twice and a woman answered.

'Mr Forth, I presume. Hello.'

Peter had not expected to hear a woman's voice, nor had he expected what sounded like an attractive, young woman's voice, with the hint of a giggle in it.

'Hello,' said Peter, unsure of how to proceed.

'You've seen the picture?' she said.

'Yes,' said Peter.

'Do you know who I am?'

'No,' said Peter honestly. 'And I suppose that you're not going to tell me either.'

'Oh, I'm quite happy to tell you,' said the woman brightly. 'In fact, you already know me.'

'Really?' said Peter, surprised that this blackmail business did not seem to be half as demanding as TV dramas made it out to be.

'Cathy Hornby.'

'Oh. You're the…'

'Yes.'

'Sorry,' said Peter, 'I'm confused…'

'I can hear that.' She giggled.

'I mean… err… Sorry, Cathy. Right. You're the one who reckons that Ian is your father…'

'That's right.'

'And your Mum met him after a gig?'

'Uh-huh. And she slept with Ian and they made me…'

'But you're now saying you're also the one who sent us that, err…'

'Porn shot?'

'Well, yeah. I don't quite under…'

'My mother took the photograph,' explained Catherine. 'It was a rock and roll night. You know that shit.'

'And the other guy?'

'A friend of my mother. He's dead too. AIDS. My Mum had cancer.'

'I'm sorry,' said Peter reflexively.

'Look,' she began firmly. 'You're obviously not very good at this. I don't mean to be rude but you sound very unsure of how to play it. So may I suggest that we meet up? It'd be cheaper than doing my 'This is Your Life' on your mobile.'

'Fine,' said Peter, thinking this is easy.

'What are you doing later?'

'Well, the thing is I… err… I don't live in London. I live in…'

'Dorset. I know,' said Catherine brightly.

'Do you? Well, then you'll know that it's bloody miles away. Shall we meet in town? I mean, are you here?'

'No, I'm in Dorset,' she said with another giggle that Peter was alarmed to note he was finding uncomfortably attractive.

'Are you? Whereabouts?'

'In Lyme. I've got a flat in Broad Street. I thought that would make it easier to meet with you.'

'Bloody hell,' said Peter.

'So what are you doing later, Mr Forth?'

'Never mind me. I mean I'll drop everything, obviously.'

'Did you have plans?'

'Only a meeting, but I can get out of that.'

'Is that a meeting-meeting or an AA meeting?' she asked nicely.

'How the fucking hell did you know that?' exclaimed Peter, causing the taxi driver to eye him in his rear-view mirror.

'You're not very difficult to stalk, Peter. Where are you going, Bridport?'

'Yes, but…'

'I'll meet you there. I'll find out the time, although it's usually eight isn't it? I'll see you at the meeting and then we can chat over a drink afterwards.'

She rang off. Over a drink afterwards, thought Peter. After an AA meeting? He was intrigued by her frivolity and he wondered if she was as attractive as she sounded.

He was about to call Vernon enthusiastically to say that he'd found the blackmailer but he remembered the pitfalls of raising false hopes: Vernon would call Taylor and say he'd found her and then, if she didn't turn up, Peter would get a huge bollocking.

As the taxi dropped him at the station Peter hoped that she wasn't attractive. He had an unprofessional weakness for attractive fans and he didn't want it to complicate matters when they turned her over to the cops or the nuthouse for blackmail and harassment.

CHAPTER 15

Catherine Hornby stepped out of the corner shower in her small bathroom and pulled the only towel she owned from the rail. As her slender body dripped onto the torn linoleum, she rubbed herself down and reviewed her all-over electric suntan in the mirror. 'Well I'd shag you,' she said to herself as she turned this way and that, pleased to see in the reflection that her bottom showed no sign of sagging. She posed a little longer for her own pleasure; nice slim waist, comely hips and breasts that were neat, rather than voluptuous. The contrast of her bronze skin against the lone white triangle left by her G-string in the tanning booth made her appear more shimmering and, now that she had shaved her legs, more youthful. She only frowned when she regarded the clump of dark hair between her thighs. That looked a tad too bushy for the task in her head so she reached for the Femishave and pruned her pubic hair until she was satisfied that she could just make out the suggestion of the lips of her outer labia through the thinned thatch.

She towelled her dark, shoulder-length straight hair, finished drying herself and began methodically to apply musk-scented body lotion, taking particular care to rub a generous blob into the cleft in the cheeks of her taut backside. The body lotion had cost Catherine far more than she had haggled for during her last trip in Casablanca, but it was laced with pure Arabian civet and, therefore, always achieved its purpose as it made its wearer reek of sex.

She left the bathroom and sauntered around the living area of the rented one-bedroom flat, humming along to Al Green's 'Let's Get Married' that played on the battered boombox. She walked to the clotheshorse on which her underwear was drying in front of a two-bar electric fire and picked off a white thong that had flat chrome studs sewn into its front. She put on the thong and strapped herself into a plain black Wonderbra and began thinking about Peter Forth. Catherine knew a lot about Peter Forth. She mused that she probably knew more about him than his wife Susan, forty-eight years old and known as Susie. She knew the make and registration of both his cars, his home telephone number and his mobile number. She knew where his sons went to school. She knew that he did not exercise, that he smoked a lot and that he drank too much of pretty much anything he was offered.

But Catherine knew about far more than Peter's suspected alcoholism. She knew his every weakness – his insecurity, his unprofessionalism, his mental instability – all of which she would exploit in order to get close to him and achieve her goal.

Catherine knew all of Peter's Achilles heels; booze, cocaine, marijuana, pathological insecurity, a drama queen's ability to throw a tantrum, a liking for the casual sex available to members of a rock-star's entourage, an over-sized ego, an inflated sense of his own importance and an addiction to the coat-tails of fame. In fact Catherine knew that, had it not been for his complete lack of any musical talent, Peter had most of the personality defects needed to make him a damn good rock star.

Well, that was his problem. Her problem was to try to set up her Plan B, the Jack Jackson safety net in case Forth turned out to be the prick he sounded like on the phone - which was why she was now dressing in a preposterously short skirt and black leather thigh-boots and was renting this dive of a bed-sit in Lyme Regis.

She had come to the Dorset seaside town not only because this was where Peter lived with Susie. There was another player in her plan who lived here too; a player whom she'd noticed Susie had started to toy with and he, too, might be useful to get her close to Ian Taylor.

For weeks now she had watched Susie, following her around the town, parking close when she picked her boys up from school. And, suspiciously, she had seen Susie paying a lot of interest in Jackson's photo shop. Now she wanted to know what Susie was up to. Was her focus on the hunk behind the cameras? Catherine needed to ensure that Susie was no threat to her plans.

Pulling on a black gypsy blouse that made the best of her cleavage, she went to do her make-up in the unhelpful light of her bathroom's one bulb. Realising that her outfit would bellow 'tart!' at passers-by, she buttoned a thin raincoat over her leggy look.

Catherine left her flat and began to climb Lyme's steep high street, at the top of which was All Trades, the small gallery and photographic supplies shop that Jackson ran next to the cinema. She brushed aside the beaded curtain that hung outside the door and walked in. The small shop was empty apart from the lank-haired teenage assistant who looked up truculently from reading Bliss on a stool behind a glass display cabinet. Catherine returned the glare with a friendly smile.

'Hello again,' she trilled cheerily. 'Seems like I just can't keep away.'

The teenager grunted and continued to stare.

'Do you have anything new in?' enquired Catherine, dancing her eyes over the sepia prints about which she had faked enthusiasm the week before.

'Nope,' said the girl. 'Dunno, really.'

'Well, it's all very nice, but...

'Humph,' said the girl, returning to her tales of pubescent drama.

'I don't suppose Jack's in, is he?' Catherine asked casually. She noticed that a protective, almost possessive look came into the teenager's eyes and Catherine wondered whether Jackson, rumoured to be the new resident ravisher, was having sex with her in addition to the three married women he was locally said to be rutting.

She regarded the girl again; she was barely seventeen. No, she decided, too young even for satyr Jack. He was probably just letting her suck him off.

'He's working,' said the girl, guardedly.

'Oh. Is he? Is he working here?'

'Upstairs,' said the girl.

'Do you think I could see him?' said Catherine. 'You see I want to buy another of these wonderful pictures but I need his advice first. His expert advice,' she added, to let the girl know that she was evidently incapable of providing anything of the sort.

'He don't like to be interrupted when he's working,' said the girl.

‘Oh I do understand,’ said Catherine, smiling again. ‘Could you just give him a shout and tell him that Catherine Hornby would like a quick word? If you don’t mind.’

The girl scowled and picked up the telephone that connected the shop with the flat above. Jackson answered almost immediately.

‘There’s a woman down here wanting you. Called Horn,’ said the girl.

‘Bee,’ said Catherine. ‘Catherine Horn-by.’

The girl grunted and ended the call.

‘Said he’ll be down,’ she said. ‘But there’s nothing new leastways.’

Catherine ignored her and concentrated surreptitiously on checking her make-up in a mirrored crucifix whilst wondering who bought such tat.

‘Hello again,’ boomed a loud voice behind her.

Catherine turned demurely and looked up at the six foot two inch, unshaven and grinning Jackson.

‘Oh, hello Jack. I’m so sorry to butt in on your work like this.’ Catherine extended her hand and was pleased that he held it for just a little longer than was necessary to acknowledge a reintroduction. The assistant noticed that too and defensively got up off her stool.

‘She’s looking for something new,’ she said, brusquely. ‘I’ve told her there ain’t nothing.’

‘Oh really?’ said Jack, still grinning broadly and not letting his eyes stray from Catherine’s face. ‘Er, have you had a look out the back?’

The girl attempted to say ‘I’ve already told her there’s nothing n…’ but Catherine snapped, ‘No, I haven’t,’ with a smile over the girl’s protest.

‘Well, let’s go and have a look, then,’ said Jackson .

‘Yes, let’s,’ said Catherine for the benefit of the girl, who scowled as Catherine followed Jackson through the shop and down a short passageway to a damp-smelling room where some two dozen prints were hanging on the whitewashed stone walls.

As Catherine walked the few yards that were enough to command some privacy from her adolescent rival, she quickly unbuttoned her raincoat but held it closed together with her hand.

'This is where we keep the wilder stuff,' said Jackson with another characteristically self-mocking guffaw.

Catherine scanned the little gallery. Whereas the shop had featured Jackson's studies of local scenery and the shoreline, here were hanging abstract images printed in angry reds and vivid greens. Unlike the tourist pleasers at the front of the shop, a large number of these works featured big-breasted women.

'Aaah,' said Catherine, lingeringly. 'From the Tate to the Teat.'

Jackson roared with laughter.

'The Teat Gallery. Excellent. I must use that.'

Catherine was pleased. To emphasise her conquest but disguise it as submission, she took her hand away from holding her raincoat together as she appeared to stare intently at one of the more obviously mammary abstracts. From her peripheral vision she was aware that Jackson's eyes were set on the bosom that had been revealed as the raincoat fell back.

'Who models for you?' she said, still studying the nude.

'Oh, you know, anyone who fancies it, really,' said Jackson. 'I'll take anyone I can get my hands on.'

Catherine turned to face him, widening her stance slightly but significantly as she did so.

'There must be a queue then,' she grinned.

Jackson returned her lascivious look and held it long enough for his smile to be telling too, sensing the heaviness in the room and subliminally aware of her musk.

'Were you expecting rain?' he said.

Catherine instantly realised the now-or-never chance and she took it.

'I never know when I'll get wet,' she purred meaningfully, leaving her mouth just a little open as she finished the sentence. She was about to add another atomic hint to the conversation when a voice called his name from the shop and she watched alarm leap onto his face.

'Oh, there you are,' said the voice, which was Susie's.

It took all of an instant for Susie to read the scene; the panic in

Jackson's widened eyes, this unknown woman's blatantly provocative pose, the boots, the micro-skirt, a very dense atmosphere and a peculiar trace of something in the air that smelt like sex.

Catherine made her own instinctive assessment of Susie's assumed position. She had barged in with the confident air of almost owning Jackson, which was odd. Catherine saw the surprise on Susie's face change tellingly to suspicion before she camouflaged it with a smile. She's pretty, close-up, thought Catherine, pretty but surely a little too Max Mara for a bohemian such as Jackson?

Susie felt herself being surveyed by this, this… what was she? A rock chick? More like a cock chick, she thought huffily. She had never seen boots like that anywhere off a poster for Barbarella. Rather common, she thought. But sexy, though. As sexy as hell. And she could see that Jack thought so, which was troubling.

Susie was preparing to extend her hand to introduce herself, when Kevin blustered into the now-uncomfortably-crowded room and pricked the brooding silence.

'Oh, an orgy. How fab!' he exclaimed, eyeing up Jackson even more lasciviously than the women. 'You are popular, Jack. Tell me, do you brew your own testosterone?'

Jackson grinned and was about to reply when Kevin theatrically sniffed at the air around the musk-oiled Catherine.

'What is that pong?' he hammed. 'It smells like snatch.'

'Kevin!' scolded Susie instinctively whilst thinking actually, that's exactly what it smells like – what's been going on here, then? Catherine was astonished to feel herself blushing, her embarrassment made all the worse when she saw Susie notice her state. She awkwardly pulled her raincoat to – and saw Susie clock that as well – and was about to flee in a wave of excuses when Susie's reluctant good manners changed the subject.

'Susie Forth,' said Susie, offering her hand and adding, 'this is Kevin. Ignore him, he is a complete tart.'

'Ooo,' said Kevin, 'Pots, black and kettles, Suze.'

'Catherine Hornby,' said Catherine, briefly shaking her hand before offering hers to Kevin.

'And you are?' said Susie to Jackson with a coquettish grin that she made especially for Catherine's benefit.

'Captain Cock, by the look of things,' muttered Kevin. 'Is this the audition for the groupies?'

Jackson watched as Susie now blushed. She caught his eye and he could have sworn she appeared to twinkle. What was all that about? Catherine sensed the twinkle too and regrouped her assertiveness.

'Jack was showing me his other collection,' said Catherine, gesturing towards the abstract nudes. 'I was just asking him who his models were?'

'Chesty Morgan and Dolly Parton, I'd say,' said Kevin, glancing at the pictures. 'Tell me, Jack, are you sponsored by the Milk Marketing Board?'

'I'm really sorry about him,' she apologised, genuinely. 'We don't want to interrupt. Kevin wants to buy some pictures before I take him back to his asylum. But, look, you were here first. We can come back another day, we don't live far.'

'Well I'm just down the street,' replied Catherine, watching Susie's eyes to see if that titbit would trouble her.

'Really?' said Susie smiling, but thinking shit!

'Really?' said Jackson, making Susie think shit, shit, shit!

'I've got a flat above the charity shop,' said Catherine matter-of-factly, delighted to be letting Jackson know where to find her.

'We're neighbours,' said Jackson as Susie fumed.

'I'll pop round for a bowl of sugar,' Catherine flirted, to piss off Susie.

'We should go,' said Susie, feeling forlorn and wretched.

'No, it's fine,' said Catherine. 'Really. I can come back at any time. Or you can pop in, Jack. If you're passing… as you say, we're neighbours.'

Noticing that this had pissed Susie off, she deliberately added, 'I hope you're good neighbour, Jack… Actually, I bet you're very good… Anyway, nice to meet you Susie. Kevin. I hope to see you again.'

Susie, who was now reeling, watched in horror as Catherine let her coat fall open again and, instead of shaking Jackson's hand, the bitch seemed to just take it and give it a little squeeze.

Catherine walked away briskly, thinking Shit! Problem.

'Who is she?' said Susie once she was confident that the cow had left the shop.

'I don't really know,' said Jackson, honestly. 'She came in the shop the other day and bought one of my pictures. I didn't know her name until just now.'

'That's what all the boys say,' chipped in Kevin, who had finished studying all the works on the walls. 'These are very nice, Jack, but all of this tittage isn't really me. Do you have anything else? Anything a little less udder-like.'

'There's all the seashore stuff in the shop,' said Jackson. 'Lobster pots and beach huts. Trawlers, seamen, that sort of stuff.'

'Darling, I don't need your pictures to help to decorate my home with semen,' camped Kevin and brayed with laughter.

'The only other stuff is upstairs,' said Jackson. He hesitated. 'It's er, a new idea I'm working on. Called Florotica.'

'Florotica!' said Kevin. 'It sounds divine. Let's go and have a butcher's. And I'd just die for a cup of tea.'

'Fine. Let's go up. The door's open,' said Jackson, indicating that Kevin should lead the way back out to the front of the shop where the stairs lay to his flat above. They passed the scowling assistant, who gave Susie an 'I hope you die' glare, which Susie met with a smug smile that replied, 'Fuck off, child.'

Susie followed Kevin and, as she reached the first step of the stairs, she surreptitiously pulled at her dress so that she raised the hem by a good three inches and held it there in her hand. Calculatingly, she climbed the stairs four steps in front of Jackson, so that his eye-level would be directly in line with her bottom pressed against the tightened dress. She hoped that this exercise would give him a good look at the outline of her thong and possibly the hint of the top of her stockings.

The atmosphere of Catherine's musk was affecting Susie as she felt a glow spread between her legs and up through her belly to her breasts. She stepped into the living room of the flat and let her dress drop to its normal length again.

Kevin flounced over to the two large sofas that were covered in ornate Indian throws and set at right angles to each other, flumping down onto one of them and loudly commending Jackson's taste in décor: Afghan rugs on the wooden floor, dozens of little candles across the mantelpiece above the old iron fireplace, Moroccan lamps with shades of stretched and red-dyed goatskin in the corners of the room and joss-sticks sending out thin serpents of scented smoke.

'Hmm,' said Kevin, approvingly. 'Very Tunisian whorehouse.'

Susie walked over to the antique Bengal table upon which Jackson had untidily laid out several pencil sketches and almost-completed studies of what, at first glance, appeared to be flowers. She studied the pictures and realised from their titles that they were not quite what they seemed. The picture of tulips, for instance, was titled 'twolips' and as she looked into it she saw that at its centre of its petals, above the sepal, was the now-becoming-obvious detail of female labia, curling towards to a clitoris in the general area of the stigma.

'This is clever,' said Susie earnestly, holding up the picture. 'Is this your florwhatica thing?'

'Florotica,' corrected Jackson, grinning shyly. 'Yeah, I'm still sort of not there with it yet; I'm sketching ideas for a session.'

'Ooo,' shrilled Kevin. 'Let's have a look.'

Susie passed the painting to Kevin, who scrutinised it with pained bewilderment.

'But it's just a… Oh-my-God! Ugh, it's vile,' shrieked Kevin.

'I like it,' said Susie.

'You would, love,' said Kevin. 'Your taste has always tended more towards the Moaning Lisa. It's horrid, Jack. I can't buy this sort of thing; people would think I'm straight.'

'What about this, then?' said Susie, holding up another, ostensibly of a bunch of bluebells.

'What's that?' said Kevin.

'It's titled 'Blue Bellends',' said Susie, grinning. 'This is much more you, Kevvie.'

'Ooo, sounds promising,' said Kevin as he leapt off the sofa and snatched it from her hand. Now that he knew what he was looking for, genital shapes hidden among traditional flora, he caught on more quickly.

'I love it. I love it!' he said as he identified the tips of penises that the bluebells developed into at the base of their petals.

'They're not really right yet,' said Jackson, 'I'm still playing with them.'

'Ooo, I'd like to play with this, lover,' flirted Kevin. He brushed past Susie and made towards the other prints on the table. 'Out of the way, you old mare. Let me have a look at the rest of it.'

'Tea?' said Jackson, pleased at the uncritical reaction.

'One sugar,' said Kevin over her shoulder as he hunched over a pile of sketches.

Jackson looked at Susie.

'Tea?'

'I'll help you,' she replied, smiling.

They stepped into the narrow kitchen that ran alongside the width of the living room. As Jackson filled the kettle and found the teapot, Susie sat on a high stool at the other end of the galley, with her back to the window.

'They're really very good,' she said to Jackson's back as he hunted for Earl Grey teabags in the shelves above the sink.

'Thanks,' said Jackson. 'I kind of think they might work. I'm not sure where the market is, though.'

'I'm sure loads of people would buy them. They're very rude, but it's not obvious.'

'Maybe,' said Jackson, still ferreting in the shelves, now looking for biscuits. 'They're not easy to get looking right. I've sort of been copying from textbooks, but the illustrations are a bit flat and medical. I need to get more life into them.'

Susie felt the semi-sickening glow of excitement flood through her again as she realised her blatant opportunity to make her case.

'You need a real-life model,' she said, flatly.

'Exactly, said Jackson. 'And they are hard to fi...'

His words evaporated as he turned to take in the unexpected sight before him. Susie had raised her booted heels onto the top rung of the stool, hitched up her dress and parted her knees to present him with the overt display of herself. She looked him straight in the eye and grinned.

'Oh! My!' came the sound of Kevin from the other room, startling Susie into tugging down her dress and closing her legs again.

As Kevin's cackling indicated he was absorbed in Jackson's sketchbook, Jack moved across the room to stand directly before Susie. He reached up and ran a forefinger down her cheek. Susie quivered and opened her mouth, parted her knees again.

In a moment his mouth was over hers, grinding his lips into her. Susie sucked at his tongue, relishing the tang of his saliva and licking with abandon and as she felt his hand thrust into her crotch and rub against her already-sodden underwear.

'Oh God,' said Susie as she felt a wave gather uncontrollably inside her. She pushed her pelvis against him as she moved her hand down to his flies. She moaned softly, spreading her thighs further, her stomach tightening.

Fuck, thought Susie, coming quickly, this is the sexiest man alive.

'Has it boiled yet,' came Kevin's shout from the living room.

'Just a bit,' muttered Susie as Jackson quickly moved away and zipped up his flies.

'Do you want biscuits?' Susie called to Kevin, hoping that he had been too absorbed in the pictures to have picked up any tell-tale sounds that may have carried into the living room over the noise of the kettle boiling.

Soundlessly, Jackson passed her a plate of biscuits and she took them through.

'I hope those are ginger nuts. I do like to nibble ginger nuts,' said Kevin, as he disturbed Susie by studying her with what she uncomfortably felt was too much of a knowing air.

'They're chocolate nobs,' said Susie. 'I'm sure you're familiar with gobbling those.'

‘Get you,’ said Kevin and Susie detected a stern edge to his voice that hadn’t been there before. Worried, she looked down at her dress in case it was stained with any give-away signs. There were none, but she still felt uneasy.

‘You’re flushed,’ said Kevin staring at her accusingly.

‘I do feel it’s a little warm,’ she blustered.

‘It’s not warm in the slightest,’ Kevin continued to taunt. ‘What’s that rash on your chest?’

Susie was horrified to hear that her body was telling tales of her post-orgasmic state and she was just about to rush to the toilet on the edge of tears, when Jackson stepped into the room and disturbed the inquisition.

‘Have you found anything you like, Kevin?’ he said evenly.

Kevin shot Susie another look of disapproval and then dropped the matter. He looked down at the pile of sketches and took one from it.

‘God knows why, but I quite like this. It’s sort of Daliesque, in a vulgar way,’ he said, holding up a half-painted sketch entitled ‘Pussy Willow’ that depicted a tree with various vulvas growing from its branches.

‘Oh yeah,’ said Jackson with forced cheerfulness. ‘I thought of calling that one ‘Sex Doesn’t Grow on Trees’.’

‘But then I suppose you discovered that, for you, it plainly does,’ said Kevin spitefully as he looked tellingly from Jackson to Susie again.

‘Is that the only one?’ said Susie, who had sat on a sofa but then immediately stood up again, fearful that she might leave a telltale damp patch.

‘Obviously, I like the bluebells too,’ snorted Kevin. ‘So, Jack, how much do you want for them?’

‘They’re not for sale,’ said Jackson. ‘They’re just sketches for the photographs I want to create.’

‘What?’ said Kevin with annoyance.

‘They’re not for sale until they’re finished. But if you want them you can give me a small deposit.’

‘Hmm,’ said Kevin. ‘That’s usually what I say. OK. Now

where's my cheque book?' As he rummaged in his leather shoulder bag, Susie watched him and determined that he was definitely very irritated. Shit, she thought, shit, shit, shit.

'I must have left it in your car,' said Kevin, walking over to the table and picking up Susie's keys. 'I'll just go and get it.' As he walked towards the door he turned and looked at Susie.

'Be good,' he said with a smile that Susie felt was almost a sneer.

As soon as she heard the front door close, Susie sat down on the sofa and held her head in her hands. 'He knows,' she said, panicking. 'I can see it in his face. He bloody knows.'

'Knows what?' said Jackson, dully.

'That! That! That what just went on! He knows! Oh God.'

Jackson squatted down beside her and put his hand on the top of her knee, an action that relaxed Susie's panic and caused a very slight shudder of excitement again.

'He knows nothing that cannot be easily denied,' said Jackson reassuringly. 'It's very difficult for anyone to prove anything if you just keep on denying it.'

'Oh God,' said Susie and she felt his hand moving up her thigh again at the same time as Jackson leaned up and nuzzled at the back of her neck. She didn't resist either advance.

'Anyway,' murmured Jackson, 'we're not done yet.'

Susie pulled away from him and grinned.

'Listen, you,' she mock-scolded, 'I am not doing anything else! He could walk back in at any moment.'

'He hasn't got a key, he'll have to ring the bell,' said Jackson softly, rubbing his fingers lightly towards the top of her stockings as she parted her legs a little to allow him.

'I don't care!' said Susie but his kissing smothered her protests.

'Do you think your husband suspects?' whispered Jackson moments later.

'Probably,' murmured Susie.

Alarmed at her matter-of-fact tone, Jackson stopped groping and pulled himself back from her.

'Are you serious?' he said and she was disappointed to hear panic in his voice. 'I bloody hope not. I've heard about him. I don't want him around here, raging.'

Susie moved closer to him. She took his hand in hers and positioned it back between her legs. She put her face against his and brushed his cheek with her open mouth.

'Don't worry,' she said, huskily. 'Pete will be too busy pleasing the real love of his life, your old mate.'

She caressed his groin with her hand again to emphasise her point and they began to kiss again. Immediately, his fingers were inside her thong and she bucked against them as another orgasm grew and then spread over her. Panting, she struggled to undo his straining flies as the doorbell rang announcing Kevin's return. Pecking her affectionately and grinning, Jackson rose, did up his flies and went to let him in as Susie re-centred her thong and pulled her dress down.

Kevin blustered into the living room, complaining that he couldn't find his cheque book, not that he'd have been able to have found a elephant, because of the state that Susie's car was in. He searched his bag again and, finding nothing, slumped dejectedly on a sofa.

'It's OK,' said Jackson, 'I don't need a cheque, Kevin. I'll keep them for you.'

'Oh thanks for telling me now,' camped Kevin, 'I've only just trekked halfway to bloody Weymouth.'

'Sorry,' said Jackson. Susie grinned and Kevin spied it.

'Never mind, I suppose at least this gooseberry gave you two an opportunity to fecundate.'

'Kevin!' objected Susie.

'Don't Kevin me, dear. Sitting there all covered in your sex hives.'

Susie was relieved to see that he was grinning and relishing, as usual, the sound of himself being shocking.

'I don't know what you mean,' she said, her own grin widening.

'Hmm, I'm sure,' he huffed. 'Right, madam, if you've quite finished whatever it is that you are obviously up to, I think we should go. And wipe your grin off first, you slag, or else the teenage dirtbag downstairs will have your eyes out.'

Susie exchanged a complicit smile with Jackson, which Kevin noticed.

'You two should have cold showers,' he admonished. 'For God's sake, woman! I can't be doing with all this promiscuity. Anyone would think you're in the music business.'

Kevin surprised Jackson with a kiss goodbye. Susie followed suit, with a demure peck on his cheek.

'I'll give you a call,' she said.

They walked down to the shop and said goodbye to the teenage assistant, who grunted 'yeah' and gave Susie a look of contempt. Susie smiled back, feeling like top dog and not caring if it showed. She was still grinning as they reached the car and had to go through her usual pantomime of searching her Lulu Guinness bag for her keys.

'By the way,' said Kevin after emitting a series of tuts at Susie's characteristic incompetence at finding anything she ever kept in her bag. 'If I were you I'd have a good bath before Pete gets home. You pong.'

CHAPTER 16

It had been a while since Peter had last visited AA but on entering the Quaker's Hall his only trepidation was about that awful friendliness that he knew he'd have to meet, when stalwarts of the fellowship looked up and greeted him with that hello, how've you been? which he, spitefully, found ridiculous as he thought that his mere presence in hall of drunks should be answer enough.

He took a chair in the corner, as always as far away as possible from where anything like involvement might be expected of him. He noticed that a 'No Smoking' sign had been erected since his last visit, which figured; even addicts had to be healthy these days.

After nodding to a couple of faces whose crimson complexions he remembered, he sat and studied his fingernails in an attempt to appear to look down and dejected, whereas in fact he was just trying to avoid anybody talking tedious bollocks to him.

More people entered the hall and, when there were around a dozen present a voice said, 'Welcome, everyone, to this meeting of Alcoholics Anonymous. My name is Tony and I'm an alcoholic.'

As the rest of the room chanted, 'Hello Tony' like a primary school class welcoming a new teacher, Peter looked up at last and saw that Tony was a handsome, smiley man with black hair, aged around forty. Peter scanned the room for a face that he guessed could be Catherine's and immediately found himself staring into the attractive eyes of a woman in her thirties with shoulder-length straight dark hair and a compact cleavage partially-contained inside a black gypsy-style blouse worn outside a short skirt and black boots.

Peter thought he caught the briefest of winks flit from her before she looked away. He hoped that she was her but he suspected that, knowing his luck, Catherine would turn out to be the lank-haired skeletal woman in cheap clothes seated beside her, or else was the plump redhead at the front of the room who hadn't stopped fidgeting with her rosary.

Peter heard Tony proclaim a warm welcome to some new faces here tonight. There was a silence, and Peter knew from previous meetings that the new faces were meant to fill this pause by saying 'Hello, I'm Peter and I'm an alcoholic,' but he just glowered at the floor, filling the room with the air of his refusal to play by the rules. The silence was broken by a low, husky voice which he recognized from her calls.

'I'm Catherine and… I… err… yes, I guess I am an alcoholic… I mean, at least I hope I'm an alcoholic, otherwise I'm in the wrong place. And my story is…'

Peter liked her. I hope I'm an alcoholic? Excellent. Sexy, though. Fuck.

As others in the room looked distinctly uncomfortable with Catherine straying from the traditional introduction, Peter registered his immediate approval of such seditious behaviour by sitting up straight and grinning at her.

He listened, absorbed, as Catherine told how her mother had had her when she was twenty and how she had grown up never knowing who her father was. Her mother had always kept this a dark secret, as if she was ashamed, and how she'd started drinking to numb the memory of her unspoken past.

She told how she had run away from home at the age of seventeen, how drink confused her judgment, and how she slept with dozens of men, looking for kindness from each one and willing to trade sex in repeated attempts to try persuade them to love her. She'd tried her hand at acting, but was never taken seriously as a drink could always lure her onto the casting couch. She'd tried nursing, but was fired after helping herself to the drugs cabinet and then she just drifted, prostituting her prettiness to make men look after her, growing to hate herself for it and drinking more to try to blot out her awareness of her own failure.

It was not a story that Peter had never heard before, as the main ingredients of low self-esteem and a longing to be loved were pretty much essential to the story of any alcoholic, but he liked the way she told it, more laconic and self-deprecating than the usual I was lost but now I'm found bollocks that most people intoned when talking of their life as a hopeless wretch.

Love it, thought Peter. Personally, he liked her because she appeared to echo his point on alcoholism, which was not that it was the disease that most AA members conveniently told themselves that they suffered from, but that heavy drinking was, in fact, a perfectly reasonable response to a totally shitty life which you knew that only luck could have made better, but hadn't.

The meeting wound up after Catherine's share had been added to by confessions from people whom Peter found to be utterly tedious. Then the hat was passed and, as always, Peter ostentatiously put a twenty pound note into it figuring that although it looked flashy, it also helped. The room then fell into silence before they recited in unison the alcoholics' Serenity Prayer.

'God grant me the serenity to accept the things I cannot change, the courage to change the things I can and the wisdom to know the difference,' they chanted.

Eyes closed, Peter reflected that the mantra was an excellent philosophy worthy of Plato and wasted on drunks. For a moment he considered what he could change and then decisively vibed himself up back to work.

He walked across the floor to Catherine and held out his hand.

'Peter,' he said. 'You know the other bit. I thought your share was great; lovely and honest.'

'Thank you,' she said, still smiling. They hovered there for a moment, not talking, as Peter pretended he was as damaged as he took her to be.

'Look, I'm sorry,' said Peter who had detected others watching them begin to mentally mate, 'but I really need a cigarette. I've got to go outside.'

'Me too,' he was delighted to hear her say.

'Why didn't you talk in there?' she said once Peter had located a shop entrance that was sufficiently distant from the gaze of those that he did not want as friends.

'What do you mean?' he said, lighting her cigarette with his Zippo and noting how she needlessly cupped his hand as he did so.

'I would have thought you would have a lot to say, with all the worries on your plate,' she said, exhaling smoke from her mouth and inhaling it up her nose in a way that Peter found very attractive.

'Sorry?'

'Well, for starters you must be going insane wondering what I'm up to.'

'Is this a set-up for a newspaper,' said Peter, suspiciously.

'No, no newspapers. Not yet, anyway. Don't frown. You frown too much. I was watching you scowling in there, I'd say you could easily be the arrogant cunt that the other fans say you are.'

'You're a bit forward, aren't you?' said Peter, grinning as he enjoyed this audacity.

'Oh, I can be a lot more forward than this,' she twinkled. 'Do you want to go for a drink?'

'We've just come out of a bloody AA meeting,' he laughed.

'Oh I know, but it's just like a Catholic going to confession isn't it? We've done our good bit for the day and now we can play again. I want a drink as we have much to discuss, Mr Forth.'

They walked to a pub and, having asked what he was having, said that she, too, would have a large vodka. Peter bought the drinks and, on returning from the bar, saw that she had found them a small booth at the back of the lounge. They sat opposite each other and clinked glasses across a narrow table as she smiled and said that she didn't mind at all, after he apologised for touching her knee with his.

'So, tough day, eh?' she said.

'You don't hang about, do you?' he grinned.

'Well, I figure that, as you already know so much about me, especially about my drink and drugs and sexual history, there's not a lot of point to us going through all of that what's your favourite band stuff. Anyway, I already know that.'

'I bet you bloody don't, actually,' said Peter.

'Oh dear,' she grinned, teasing him. 'He's really upset you, hasn't he?'

'Do you mean Ian?'

'Is anybody else capable of upsetting the laid-back Peter Forth?'

'Laid-back? Who says that I'm laid-back?'

'That's what the newspapers always call you. Taylor's laid-back spokesman said... We fans quite like it, actually.'

'Good,' said Peter without interest, 'So, Catherine, what's the deal? You give me the pictures and the negs, I'll take you to Ian and you guys can sort out whatever you have to say to each other.'

'You're very calm,' she observed, gazing at him in a way that Peter would have said was 'dreamily' if it had been anyone else that she was looking at.

'What do you mean?'

'Well, I must represent at least two publicity nightmares to you, my parentage and the don't-speak-with-your-mouth-full shot, and you haven't started threatening me with lawyers, or whatever it is that you usually scare people with.'

'I don't know what you want yet,' said Peter evenly.

She offered to buy another round and, when she returned with the vodkas, she changed the subject. Peter went along with her shift to keep her sweet.

'How long have you been going to AA?' she asked.

'Off and on, about ten years. More off than on, though.'

'Do you go to NA too?'

'Narcotics Anonymous? Why, do you think I should? You're very informed, Ms Hornby.'

'Cathy,' she offered.

'The truth is that there isn't an NA branch around here and besides, I don't have a problem with drugs. I have a problem with people who have a problem with drugs.'

She grinned. 'So, is there an SA around here that I could go to?'

'Sexaholics? I'm surprised that someone like you would need to go to SA.'

'What do you mean someone like me?' said Catherine, still smiling but with a steeliness in her eyes.

'Well, you know,' said Peter, feeling awkward now. 'I mean... well, you're very attractive. I wouldn't have thought that somebody who is as stunning as you needs to find self-regard through sex.'

'What, you think that only ugly people are addicted to sex? As I was hinting in the meeting, sex is my real addiction. If I'm in bed with someone, doing something that is really turning them on, then I get the buzz. You must know the buzz, you're an addict. It doesn't matter what we're addicted to as long as we get the buzz.'

'Yeah,' said Peter, thinking that he wished he had not been getting pissed, as he had work to do. 'I've often been to AA meetings stone cold sober but with the best part of half a gram stuck up my nose. What I meant was I wouldn't have thought that somebody looking like you would need to look for men. I mean, every man in this bar clocked you as soon as we walked in.'

'I know,' said Catherine honestly, 'but are any of them good in bed? That's the problem; if you're a sexaholic, you want to have really good sex.'

'What do you call good sex?' said Peter, who was pretty sure that it was her leg, and not the table's, which was now pressing against his.

'Just complete rutting,' said Catherine, who emphasised her point – needlessly, Peter thought – by widening her eyes and licking her lips. 'Doing anything, just anything for the sheer thrill of the dirtiness.'

'Is that the kick, the dirtiness?' said Peter, who was genuinely interested in the root of addiction. 'Is that it, doing something that you feel is actually wrong? Is it the being bad that's so good?'

'Yeah. You'll do anything to get turned on. Anything. Blokes. Gangs of blokes. Women. I've fucked all sorts.'

'Really?' said Peter, seeing his cue, 'So now you want to fuck Ian Taylor?'

She gave a small, wry laugh in response to his sudden cold tone and sipped her drink, watching him over the rim of the glass.

'Hardly. He's my father,' she said, smiling.

'I meant fuck Ian over.'

'No,' she said softly, 'I don't want to hurt him at all.'

'So what's with the photograph and all that stuff on my answerphone about going to the papers? What do you want?'

'Are you going to tell him if I tell you?'

'Yes,' Peter lied.

'Liar.'

'Pardon?'

'You'll tell Billy Vernon and then you two will sit with a lawyer and try to get me sectioned. Or you'll have me charged with blackmail.'

'What's to stop us?' said Peter with a smile.

'Nothing, nothing at all. But the minute that anybody gets heavy with me, that photo goes out to the agencies.'

'Which ones?' said Peter. 'Actually, it doesn't matter, our lawyers know them all and one call will sort it.'

'You can't stop multiple uploads to the Net with an injunction. My lawyer has a key to a security box. If I don't make a weekly check-call, he will open the box and follow the instructions that will spell hell for you guys. By the time you're hip to it, the planet will know Ian's secret. Don't waste your time being dutiful, Peter, this is well outside the usual publicity box.'

'OK, now you listen to me', he said, just stopping himself adding bitch. 'This is the oldest game in the fucking book. I've got a fucking stack of files on people who reckon Ian's their father. Every PR of every star has them and so have the newspapers. And you know what? We and the press just ignore them, because you are all fucking nutters.'

'How many of these nutters have a picture of their Dad having sex with another bloke?' she said, smiling still.

'OK,' Peter conceded. 'What do you want?'

'I want Ian to acknowledge me as his daughter.'

'Forget it. He won't do it.'

'Why not?'

'Well, A, because he doesn't know whether you are…'

'Well that's easily proved…'

'And, B, because it would open up all the floodgates to all the other nu…'

'Don't call me a nutter!' she sparked and Peter saw violence in her eyes.

'I was going to say nurslings,' he said.

'No you weren't. Will you please stop lying to me? I'm not lying to you. Why don't you try telling me the truth? This is not one of your press conferences.'

'Sorry,' said Peter, furious that she should know anything about the press conferences from which he insisted all fans were barred. 'Why do you want him to acknowledge you? Is this some debt that you feel you owe to your mother?'

'No. He's rich and I've had a shit life. If he accepts me as his daughter, I'll have a better one. It's as simple as that.'

'In exchange for the picture we could give you enough money to start a better life,' said Peter.

'I know. Buy me off. Pay me hugely to go away. I've thought of that. But then I'd be denying the fact that I am his daughter. And I am. It seems only fair that he should accept his parental responsibilities like any other father.'

'And you think he'll want to know?' Peter said harshly.

'Yes, I do,' she said evenly.

'So what's the problem?'

'The problem is the same for me as it is for any fan, getting to him so that I can convince him. You know better than I do that nobody who you lot think might upset him is allowed anywhere near him.'

'Where did you hear that?'

'Don't play games, Peter, you're crap at it. I know how it works, nobody presents him with anything that's controversial in case he reacts by ripping the presenter's head off.'

'So why do you think that I would volunteer for decapitation? I presume that's what you want, for me to be your presenter?'

'It is,' she confirmed, smiling.

'So why should I do that if – and it is an if – if I feel that he may, in some way, not be entirely ecstatic to hear this news?'

'Because long-lost daughter is a much better story for you than long-hidden homo and because you know that, if that photograph goes public, your life will become crap as you fail to suppress it.'

Peter took another gulp of vodka.

'You appear to be ignoring a rather salient point,' he said. 'I don't know that you're Ian's daughter at all. I'm prepared to accept that the bloody photograph is real, but, as I've said, you well may be not. I'm hardly going to go to Ian with a story that some addict told me in a pub.'

'A DNA test would prove it,' said Catherine flatly.

'Why me? Why don't you contact Billy? He's his manager, not me. I do publicity, luv, not paternity.'

'Vernon hasn't got the balls.'

Oh, and I have?'

'I think so, I'll know later for sure.'

'What?' asked Peter, thrown by what he thought was the whiff of a come-on.

'You'll see,' she said and changed the subject back to bartering. 'Look, it's very simple. You can refuse me my audience with Ian and within a few days rock's most eligible bachelor, as you call him, will have his bachelor status thoroughly and explicitly confirmed. Which means that armies of media will camp at Ian's door and you will be yelled at until you manage to make them go away. Which you never will.'

'Or?'

'Or we do the test.'

'What if the test says you're not his daughter?'

'It won't.'

'How can you be so sure?'

'Because I am his daughter.'

'OK,' said Peter as he began his gambit with a lie, 'I'll take you to Ian, but first I'm going to need all the pictures, the name of your brief and I'll need you to sign a legal undertaking.'

'And as soon as I do that you'll have me busted. Fuck off,' she said.

'Not at all,' said Peter, lying. 'You can have your lawyer present if you like. Sign and then I'll take you to Ian. He's much nicer than me. Don't worry.'

'Sorry Peter, but I'm not that thick; if you want the pictures then I have to see Ian first. Let's have another drink.'

Peter let her buy another round while he mused on the problems. He could drive her to meet Ian, or at least Vernon, in the morning, once he had the photographs. Or maybe he should call Billy for instructions? He couldn't think clearly, the vodka was taking effect and now she was returning from the bar with more of it.

'Have you decided?' she said, smiling at him with odd familiarity.

'No.'

'Let me tempt you,' said Catherine, reaching out to stroke the back of his hand.

'Sorry but… no way,' he said firmly as he pulled his hand away.

'Oh, I think I can,' she said, her eyes dancing as her hands went beneath the table to find his leg again.

'Forget it.'

'Oh, you will,' she said with complete confidence.

'Why do say that?'

'I've seen a like mind, Peter. I think you're just as into sex as I am.'

'I can assure you I'm not,' he protested, feeling stolid.

'Prove it.'

'I am proving it.'

'Prove it outside.'

'No. Fuck off, we don't fuck fans.'

'Come on, Peter. Can you imagine? Doing it with a girl who'll do anything? Let me persuade you…'

'No. I'm married. No.'

'But you're interested, I can tell…'

'No!'

'I'm wearing stockings…'

'Good for you.'

'And suspenders…'

'Well done.'

'I'll sit on your face.'

'It's very kind of you to offer, but…'

'I want to lick your balls…'

'Cathy! Catherine… for God's sake. Stop. OK. Let me make a call to Billy.'

Peter was annoyed to see that his surrender made no difference to her advance. Her eyes seemed glazed now, her lips were parted far too voluptuously and for a moment he thought that any minute he was going to wake up in sheets made sticky by his own wet dream.

'Never mind that now. I want to fuck you.'

'So you keep on implying…sorry, no.'

'Really?' she said, her eyes widening with surprise.

'Really.'

'OK,' she said simply and she rose from the table, picked up her glass and shocked him by throwing its contents in his face.

She walked out of the bar as everybody else turned to stare at Peter, who pulled a smirk that made him appear even more stupid. He ignored their chuckling and drew more attention to himself by trying to dry his face on his shirt sleeve.

After minutes that seemed like hours, he left the bar and walked to the car park. He was nearing his Volvo when his mobile rang. The number was withheld, like most calls from newspapers.

'Hello, Peter Forth,' he said.

'Hello Peter Forth,' said her voice, which was lower and purring now. 'Look behind you.'

Peter turned and saw that Catherine had emerged from behind a VW, but now she was just in her underwear. She was grinning at him. Peter was pissed off. He looked around, fearing that somebody would see. It was not her striptease that concerned him, it was the precaution in the back of his mind that she might be Catherine Hornby-Taylor and then what would the neighbours think?

'What the hell are you doing? Where are your clothes? Get dressed, for God's sake! No, just get in my car. Bloody hell, you're insane!'

'Not really,' said Catherine, nonchalantly opening the front passenger door of Peter's Volvo. 'I just need to catch a bit more of your attention.'

'Well, you've done that,' said Peter, still looking around to see if anybody was watching. 'Where are your fucking clothes?'

'In my bag.'

'Well, put them on. Please, get dressed.'

'Only if we can talk some more.'

'Fine, fine. Talk all you like. But get dressed first. Please.'

She quickly pulled on her skirt, smiling to herself as Peter sat smoking a cigarette and still looking around carefully. When she had buttoned up her shirt, he started the car.

'Is this the way you always negotiate?' he muttered crossly.

'What do you mean?'

'I mean acting hysterically, going over the top to make your point. You remind me of your fa...'

'My father! You were going to say I remind you of my father! So you do believe me.'

'Look, all I believe is that you're a bleeding nutter,' he said cuttingly. 'I think you're out to lunch, luv. I've dealt with your lot before, remember.'

'By my lot, I take it that you mean fans of Ian's?'

'Obviously.'

'All of whom you think are mad?'

'Some.'

'Why do you treat Ian's fans with such contempt? You seem to hate the very people who buy his records. Without them, you'd be out of a job.'

'Roll on that day,' said Peter.

'Do you want to know what I think?'

'No.'

'I think that you hate fans because you are a fan, but you don't want to admit it because fans are normal people and you don't want to be a normal person. You want to be a star.'

'Bollocks,' said Peter, upended by her accuracy.

'I think you love all that fame by association. You love all the hubbub of the crowds and the TV cameras; it's exhilarating, heady and it makes you feel important, even though it's not for you. You fear the fans because you don't want people, or rather, Ian, to see that you're actually one of them and impressed by it all. So you act all aloof to the glamour, like you're above it, and you make a point of hating the fans, because if you're seen as a fan it's not cool. And being cool is the drug for Peter, isn't it?'

‘Fuck off.’

‘I’ve got it,’ she said excitedly, ‘You may be addicted to alcohol, but you’re more addicted to rock and roll.’

‘Fans can be obsessed and that can be dangerous,’ said Peter, ignoring her assessment, ‘If fans were safe and cuddly, why would artists employ so much security?’

‘Because it makes them look more important, you twat.’

‘Look, I don’t want to talk about this. This is not why I’m here,’ Peter dodged.

‘Where are we going, by the way?’

‘I presumed you wanted a lift home. You said you’re staying in Broad Street.’

‘I don’t want to go home yet; let’s go to the beach,’ she suggested.

‘What? This isn’t a fucking date, you know.’

‘Isn’t it?’ she said and he fell silent, intimidated again.

CHAPTER 17

Despite his protests, when they reached Lyme Peter drove up Broad Street without stopping and then down the steep Cobb Road to the beach. Local knowledge and an awareness that a lot of people late-walking their dogs might recognize him made him park several hundred yards away from the three busy pubs that faced The Cobb.

'Shall we walk?' she said.

'I'm not going to another pub. I know people around here,' he insisted.

'It's a lovely night, let's walk around The Cobb.'

'I'm too local to be doing the Meryl Streep number,' he grumbled. 'That's just for the grocks.'

'Grocks?'

'Grockles. Tourists. They like to hang out on the end of the Cobb posing in their pashminas.'

'Oh come on, it's romantic,' she laughed, getting out of the car.

'Why the hell should we be doing anything romantic? This isn't meant to be romantic. This is work.'

'Come on, stop acting like you're dead. Live a bit; it's alright, it won't kill you,' she said smiling widely at him.

'You're bloody incredible,' he said, sounding exasperated.

'Thank you,' she said, playfully.

They walked to The Cobb and took the steps to the high Victoria Wall that defended the moored sailing boats and dinghies against the occasionally destructive waves.

'It's cold,' she said as an onshore gust from the west billowed against them.

'Not if you're properly dressed,' he said cuttingly.

'You could keep me warm, you know,' she teased.

'I could also throw you into the sea. Don't push your luck.'

'Would you do that to me?' she asked seriously.

'It'd be one way around the problem, wouldn't it? You could

slip; people have done before.'

'You're forgetting that, if anything happens to me, my lawyer will open the box.'

'I haven't forgotten, and it's because I haven't forgotten that you're not over that edge,' he said, pointing to the choppy sea, twenty feet below the wall.

They walked to the end of The Cobb. She was openly shivering in the breeze that was picking up as the skies grew darker. But Peter felt that she was too much of a liability for him to start getting gallant.

'Tell me about your mother. Why did she tell you about this Ian business?' he said.

'She told me because she was dying. I don't believe people lie to their children when they die.'

'How do you know? Have you tried it?' he said cruelly.

'My mother loved me. She was not a mad fan, as you call them. She was a teacher, at a college. She was bright, not deluded.'

'She was deluded enough to have you.'

'What the fuck do you mean by that?'

'I mean she didn't abort you, but if she was so remarkably intelligent she must have known that Ian wasn't going to marry some shag in the night.'

'You are a bastard, aren't you? No wonder he employs you.'

Peter let it pass; there was no point in disputing the truth.

'Had she ever mentioned it before she was dying, the Ian thing?'

'I wasn't brought up in a house full of Ian Taylor posters, if that's what you mean. We didn't go to his gigs and hang out at the stage door making pleading noises, buy all his albums. No, she never mentioned it.'

'Which is why you believe it?'

'Partly. But mainly because she wouldn't lie to me, not when there was no opportunity of saying I was only joking later. It would have been heartless and pointless to say it if it wasn't true.'

'Why did she tell you, then?'

'Because she loved me, idiot. Because she was dying. Because it was the end, there was no point in not telling me.'

'Except that by doing so she lumbered you with a fucking great hang-up for the rest of your life,' he observed.

'Maybe she thought there was a chance that Ian might look after me.'

'She didn't know him very well, then, did she?'

'She only had sex with him that one night.'

'So how did the photograph happen? How did she get hold of that? What did she do, buy it at a fan convention?'

Catherine spun round from looking out at the waves and faced him angrily. 'I've already told you, she wasn't a fan. I wish you'd stop it.'

'Stop what?'

'Having a go at me. She had the photograph because she took it. She was in the room. The guy who... he was a friend of hers, a gay guy. They met Ian in a bar, they were all staying at the same hotel. He, Ian, liked them; they were bright, interesting. Not fawning…'

'And because he wanted company, like he always does, he asked them up to his room,' Peter filled in.

'Yeah.'

'And they all got stoned…'

'And drunk…'

'And stuff happened.'

'Yes.'

'Hmm,' mused Peter, considering the story to be entirely possible. 'Tell me, did she say whether Ian saw her take the picture?'

'I don't know, no; she didn't say. Why? Does it matter?'

'Not to you, no,' said Peter. 'But if he was aware of the existence of a photograph he must have been bricking it that one day it'd come out.'

'So all you need to do is to show him the picture and it'll cast him back to that night,' Catherine urged.

'Hang on,' said Peter coolly. 'The photograph, if it is real, just proves that Ian was, on one occasion only, one occasion when he was by your own admission out of his mind, tempted to experiment a bit. It doesn't prove that you are his daughter. Anybody could have banged-up your mother for all I know.'

'But, as I said, DNA would prove it.'

'And as I have said, fuck off with expecting me to help you until you give me the picture and sign the legals.'

'Fine,' said Catherine and she turned away from watching the sea and began walking back along the harbour wall.

'Where are you going?' he yelled after her. She stopped and faced him. He saw that her eyes were cold now.

'I'm going to call my lawyer and tell him to write to Ian and send him a copy of the photo.'

'We'll intercept it, it will never get to him.'

'Maybe. Maybe not. You certainly won't intercept all the copies to the picture agencies and the uploads to every fan site.'

'We'll just explain you away as a nutter,' he threatened.

'Maybe you will. And you can explain away the note at the same time.'

'What note?' said Peter, feeling uneasy.

'The note that my lawyer will also put out with the picture. The note that says all of this shit publicity could have been avoided because I told you the truth, but you refused to give Ian the information because you were drunk, abusive and threatening.'

'What? So you're blackmailing me now? You fucking bitch!'

'I'm not blackmailing you at all. I'm just saying that if you won't tell Ian something that may be of considerable significance to him, I think he deserves to know that you've held back information. You're playing God with his life.'

'Catherine, I will take you to Ian, as I keep fucking saying, once I have the pictures and an agreement,' said Peter.

'And as I keep saying, Peter, I don't trust you. So either we do it on my terms or he and the world will see that all the bad publicity he'll get is your fault because you decided not to tell him things that he should know.'

'Hang on, hang on,' said Peter, grabbing her arm to stop her walking away.

'Changing your tune?' she mocked, grinning at him in triumph.

'Shit! Look, can we talk about this some more?'

She smiled and put her arm in his. He did not resist and they walked back towards where the car was parked. Before they got to it, Peter diverted them to a row of empty beach huts that faced onto the sea and away from curious eyes.

'Let's just sit down for a moment and think about this,' he said.

'Have you got a joint?' said Catherine, sitting close against him.

'I can roll one,' he replied, reaching into his jacket pocket for Rizla papers and the plastic-wrapped eighth of grass that he almost always carried.

As he began the manufacturing, the breeze increased, so he had to ask her to cup her hands around his to prevent the weed blowing away. When that failed to be a sufficient windbreak, she pushed her body closer to him, shielding him. He felt her small breasts flattening against his arm. When the joint was rolled, albeit badly, he noticed that she did not move away from him again.

They smoked it together in silence, passing it each time that the other had taken three or four puffs. He was surprised how effortless it had become for them to act intimately and was alarmed that it seemed comfortable.

'Great,' he said sarcastically after they had finished smoking.

'What?'

'Well, I'm pissed and very stoned now. I can't drive.'

'We can wait. It will pass, you'll be OK,' she reassured softly.

'I'm fine. I'm as high as a pig. I feel great, I just can't drive. But that's OK because I, a married man with children, am sitting here stoned and snuggling up with the daughter of Ian Taylor who wants to provide photographic evidence to the planet that he is an occasional bender. Great. Everything's fine.'

'You forgot to mention that we've also just been to AA together,' giggled Catherine. 'The papers would want that in the story.'

'What would Daddy say?' Peter spluttered, giggling uncontrollably.

'Dunno. But you'd have to be the one to ask him for that quote for the papers. You're the bloody press officer,' she laughed.

'Shit,' said Peter as the reality of his situation surfaced along with a horrible sensation of feeling trapped. 'Shit; I'm buggered.'

'You'll be OK,' she murmured, stroking his cheek gently with her forefinger.

'How the hell did I get into this?'

'A PR man who cared not wisely but too well,' she said softly. 'So you may as well throw it all to the Indian wind now.'

'Do I have anything left?'

'Only your long-preserved professional virginity.'

He looked at her closely. She was gorgeous, fantastic eyes, deep and seeing.

'Forget it,' he said. 'We don't fuck fans and I can't have sex with Ian Taylor's daughter. I just can't.'

'So you won't have sex with me because you believe I'm his daughter and he'd go mad?'

'Something like that. But I'm not saying that you are his daughter.'

'But by not fucking me, you are.'

'What?'

'You won't fuck me because I may be his daughter. Therefore the only way to prove that you don't believe I'm his daughter is to have sex with me,' she said, smiling at him as she lay back and hitched up her skirt to reveal her underwear again.

'Oh for fuck's sake,' Peter sighed.

'I've had more charming acceptances,' said Catherine as she gently pulled him towards her.

CHAPTER 18

It was late when Catherine unlocked the door to her flat and emptied a carrier bag of her quick shop around the 24-hour store onto the only table: onions, tinned tomatoes, ricotta, penne and two bottles of Frascati. With a little tomato paste, some oregano and Parmesan from the fridge she'd soon have a rather authentic Italian supper to share with herself whilst checking her Facebook.

She unzipped her boots and kicked them off and thought about Peter. He had been an easy pull and, despite his uncertain fumbling, the experience had not been unpleasant. It had all been over much faster than a girl might hope, but that was OK; her vibrator would finish what he had almost started.

Catherine considered that she might like him; he was cute in an uncley sort of way, and she could see that he might almost be interesting if he didn't always act as if he was trying for Academy Award for best victim. If anyone should win an Oscar, she reflected, it should be her for her performance in front of all those bleeding hearts at the AA meeting. The act had gone well, and Peter was far too easy to fool. He was compromised now, enough to make him worry and, therefore, make more mistakes.

Catherine switched her thoughts to Jackson. He would be another effortless pull and she knew that she could call his shop, have a brief conversation and easily be fucking him within fifteen minutes from now. But she was tired, and entertaining Jack's inflated ego would be as exhausting as accommodating his legendary penis.

She was amused that Peter's wife was so blatantly possessive of her secret shag. Susie bloody Forth: who'd have thought she had it in her? She didn't particularly like what she had seen of Susie but she wasn't going to look a gift whore in the mouth; Susie's philandering could be something else to exploit when the time was right for a little marriage-wrecking.

As it was now apparent that Susie wanted to be top dog in the battle to be Jackson's bitch, Catherine considered it wouldn't be wise to allow that liaison to develop too far; she didn't want Susie to make Jackson too happy because that would leave him less vulnerable if she needed his involvement in her plan. She decided that she had better make a move there soon, just in case Suze was any good in the sack, as she needed Jackson to be hungry.

Catherine exchanged the new bottle of Frascati for the one already opened and chilled in the fridge. She poured herself a tumbler of wine and thought back over what she knew of Susie: attractive, middle-aged, probably bored, and scornful of being second choice to the seductress that was Peter's job; excited by the adrenalin of a taboo encounter but not so crazy to cheat to the point of separation.

She sat down on the uncomfortable sofa and turned on the television but didn't take in whatever was flickering on the screen. Finishing her glass and pouring herself another, she went into her tiny kitchen and began to make her pasta supper. She had made the sauce and was just dribbling olive oil into the water boiling for the pasta when a buzzer loudly announced that somebody was at her front door.

'Fuck,' she thought, 'I bet that that will be Mr Jackson.'

She went to the mirror and ruffled her hair to make it look tousled, pulling at it to form a bit of a fringe. She briefly considered the boots, but then hid them behind the sofa, undoing another button of her gypsy blouse. Feeling more comfortably bohemian, as the buzzer sounded again she went downstairs and looked through the spy-hole in the door. Her suspicions were right, but with affected surprise, she opened the door and batted her eyes at him.

'Jack! What a pleasure. Missing me already?'

Jackson coughed nervously and she smelt drink on his breath.

'I was, as they say, just passing,' he said as he held up a bottle of red wine. 'I thought maybe you'd enjoy a welcome to the neighbourhood.'

Catherine looked at the bottle.

'Oh, Australian. What a shame,' she said.

‘Sorry?’

‘Don’t worry, it’s just that we’re having Italian.’

‘We?’

‘I thought you might pop round,’ she lied. ‘Please, come up.’

He followed her into the flat. She took his suede jacket, poured him an even larger tumbler of the Frascati and shooed him into lighting candles on the table and setting their places. An hour later and a second bottle was almost empty. Catherine was pretending to bask in his compliments about her cooking whilst filing in her memory the few personal details about his time with Ian Taylor that she had picked out of the usual swapping of birthplaces, schooldays, broken romances and what new bands they liked.

Tactically, she laughed at all of his jokes and looked him in the eye a lot and, after he had finished his second serving of pasta, as she reached to clear his plate away she leaned over to give him an eyeful of bosom.

‘That was fantastic,’ said Jackson honestly, meaning the food.

‘Ooo, thank you,’ said Catherine coquettishly as she took the plates out to the kitchen.

‘Do you want a cigarette break before we think of anything else to eat?’ she flirted as she returned with his bottle of red.

‘I don’t smoke but please, go ahead,’ he said.

‘Do you smoke smoke?’ said Catherine, indicating the small cube of plastic-wrapped hashish that she had placed on the table with a packet of Rizla.

‘Not really, hash sends me to sleep these days,’ said Jackson.

‘That’s a shame, I’m running out. I thought you might be able to suggest a source, being a rocker and all that.’

‘No, not me. Although I hear that Peter Forth’s your man for that. He’s the weekend rock and roller around here.’

‘Peter?’ said Catherine with mock ignorance.

‘Susie’s husband. The woman you met in the shop today. He’s sort of in the music business; he works for my old mucca.’

‘Really? What’s he like?’

‘Forth? I don’t really know him but from what Susie says he’s one of life’s tortured souls…’

‘I meant Taylor.’

‘Oh, Ian. Umm… I’ll tell you when I know you better; I don’t really like talking about him. It tends to piss me off.’

Sensing a lull in the atmosphere, Catherine decided to change the subject. ‘You’re not very good at this, are you?’ she said smiling as she reached over the table and squeezed his hand.

‘What do you mean?’ he said, almost offended.

‘Well, you and I sniff around each other in your shop like a couple of dogs. Then you come around here on a pretend whim. I make us dinner, we’ve each drunk a bottle of wine and now we’re both ever-so-obviously calculating the chances of going to bed,’ said Catherine matter-of-factly but smiling wide.

‘Are we?’ said Jackson, grinning.

‘Yes,’ said Catherine flatly. ‘Why else would you come calling so late?’

‘So… err… are you saying we’re going to…?’

‘It’s not entirely out of the question,’ she grinned.

‘Excellent.’

‘But I’m afraid we’re going to have to tie a knot in it.’

‘Sorry?’ he said, his face falling.

She moved closer to him, widened her eyes and hoped that somehow her point would find a way through his evident inebriation.

‘I’m so flattered,’ she lied. ‘But if I’m going to get laid by the real talent in Taylspin, I want to have longer than what is left of this night to enjoy it.’

‘Is this a brush-off?’ he said, a little huffily.

‘No, it’s setting a date. Now be a good boy and let me go to bed and dream about all the wild things I am going to do to you.’

‘Nothing on account, I suppose?’ Jackson attempted as he walked unsteadily to the door.

‘Only my promise,’ she said, kissing him slowly and thinking, *‘Who the fuck do you think I am, a groupie?’*

CHAPTER 19

Peter had just got home and he was already imagining all sorts of threats to his position caused by having sex with Catherine.

He realised, gloomily, that he had just broken every rule. Sleeping with a fan was never done as it could provide a conduit to an inner sanctum that was traditionally closed to any artist's most-fervent supporters. Sleeping with the boss's daughter, if she was, was bad news whatever your employment. And sleeping with somebody who had already highlighted her likelihood of selling her story to the newspapers was an exceptionally stupid move, especially for a PR.

Only after he had fretted himself through all the permutations of how his behaviour was a betrayal of his work responsibilities did Peter consider that it was also a betrayal of his marriage.

That realisation set him off on another tangent of despair; what if she became pregnant? What if she gave him a disease? What if he then gave Susie a disease? What if she told Susie about their few moist minutes, which he had been married for long enough to know would have been unsatisfying for her?

But he put Susie from his mind as he rang Vernon.

'Sorry it's late, I've found our blackmailer,' said Peter.

'Fantastic,' said Vernon. 'Good boy. Mail me his details now and I'll get him nicked. You've got the pix?'

'It's a she. She won't let me have them. She doesn't trust us not to have her arrested or sectioned.'

'Sectioned? Why the fuck would we want her sectioned?'

'She's a fan. She's called Catherine Hornby.'

'I don't give a fuck what she's called,' said Vernon, 'and not all our fans are insane, Peter. Mail me where the cops can get her.'

'She's got back-up, Billy.'

'What do you mean? I'm not getting a good feeling off you here.'

'She says if she gets lifted, her lawyer puts the picture out.'

'Ah,' said Vernon.

'She could be bluffing but she strikes me as quite smart. I don't know if we should take the risk. That's why I was calling. What do you want me to do?'

'Shit. Let me speak to Ian. I'll call you in the morning,' said Vernon and he rang off.

Peter couldn't sleep yet. He checked his email and pondered for a while over yet another polite request from bloody Tundra Pox, the local band who kept writing to say that they honestly did have the money to hire him 'to help us make the big time'. Peter decided that the next time they wrote he would tell them to change their bloody name as pox of any description had never looked good on a T-shirt. Still restless, he wandered into the utility room where he kept the tattered trunk which held his several hundred vinyl albums. As he had long ago lost the key he prised open the lock with a screwdriver. He flipped through the stack of LPs that once had thrilled him; 'Selling England by the Pound', 'Born to Run', 'High Tide and Green Grass', 'Taste Live at the Isle of Wight', 'Fleetwood Mac's Live Blues Jam at Chess' and there it was, 'Grey Rose'.

The sleeve was dog-eared now; scuffed from years of handling in bedrooms where it was passed between squatting friends in awed admiration. Peter had been thirteen years old when Grey Rose was released. He had read about it on the front page of *Sounds* and he still remembered the headline ' Taylor Makes Miracle!'. The music mag's worshipping reaction to the record was typical of the critics of the time.

He looked more closely at the sleeve and admired the simplicity of its design; a battleship-grey background with a darker grey rose in bloom embossed upon it. It was the grey of the mud of the wartime trenches, the pundits had claimed at the time. It was the bleak grey of humanity's future they said; the colourlessness of ordinary life.

Both the front and back outer sleeve of the album had no text. Neither the album title nor the band's names were on it. The only words appeared when you opened the cover. On the left hand side in large grey lettering over a wash of lighter grey was Edmund Burke's quote, 'All that is necessary for evil to triumph is for good men to do nothing.'

Peter smiled inside as he remembered copying the thousands of others kids who had stencilled that, often misspelling neccesary, onto the back of their Levi jackets in black felt tip.

On the right hand side of the inner sleeve were the song lyrics. Peter's eye flicked to 'Come to Daddy' and he read on.

You want this, baby, a shot of this fame?
You want the candy? To play in the game?
You say you're different,
I bet you suck just the same
Come to Daddy.

You look much older now the light's gone dim
In boots and mini with that black leather trim
But are you ready
To be loving my sin?
Come with Daddy

Taste Daddy's sugar
Open up and enjoy
I'm your rock idol
Learn to lick on this boy
Taste Daddy's sugar
Just take it like that
I'm your sugar Daddy
Rip your nails in my back

You smell like a teen queen
Now you're getting wet
Here come greet my pal
You'll be glad that you've met
Our backstage all access
Will freak you, I bet
Come for Daddy

Close the door now we've finished,
We don't want you here
But first go and pour me a new can of beer
The way that we took you
Don't make us no queer
And don't tell your Daddy

Peter remembered the arguments that had erupted in his and many other British homes in the summer of '68 when the release of 'Come to Daddy' had outraged the national press and a proposal to jail Taylor for obscenity received the backing of 82 Members of Parliament in their letter to The Times.

Taylor had fled his London home to hole up in Morocco while his lawyers argued that the lyrics were oblique and that obscenity could not be implied. Homosexual lobbies harangued Taylor for 'the pejorative use of queer' and their anger was matched by the NSPCC, parents' groups and the then-new feminists.

In a spectacular move of self-destruction, Taylor had responded to his lynch mob with a press release pointing to the 'more crucial message of pacifism that pervades the album as a whole', unfortunately adding 'but those who are offended by the song should please feel free to send me pictures of their daughters'.

Peter heard a familiar engine outside and looked out of the window to see Susie returning from her book club. Sexy, he thought as he watched her lock the car. But the thought of sex refreshed his guilt and he felt wretched again. He walked out of the utility room and met her in the kitchen.

'You're late,' he said, sounding possessive.

Susie did not want to stand close to him in case she smelled of Jack. On her way back from her book club she had seen him swaying up Broad Street and had pulled up to say 'Hi, I can't stop'. But as he had been insistently horny they had gone back to his place for a very fast fuck in the hall. Now she wanted to tell Peter, actually, dear, she was late because she'd been shagged so sore that when she did attempt to drive home her post-coital dizziness had sent her off in entirely the wrong direction as she fuzzily wondered if she'd ever walk properly again. But instead she said 'Oh, I thought you'd be in bed. Sorry, it over-ran. My fault, I talked too much. We were doing Hardy, we get so absorbed.'

Peter watched her with a feigned air of indifference. He noticed that her hair had been recently brushed and, unless Revlon had invented Hammerite cosmetics, her lipstick had been recently reapplied.

'I'm tired, I think I'll have a quick shower,' said Susie airily.

'Bit late, isn't it? If you're tired why not go straight to bed?' goaded Peter, his intuition now on full alert.

'Did you pay the babysitter?'

'Yes.'

'Are you in a bad mood?' said Susie, tactically trying to reverse this inquiry.

'By the way, how was Jackson earlier?' countered Peter, dodging her trick.

'Fine. Good. Kevin and I didn't see him for long,' lied Susie.

Peter wanted to pursue this, but he sensed that it would only start a lot of shouting and he couldn't cope with that right now.

'What've you got that out for?' said Susie, indicating the Grey Rose vinyl that he held.

Tactic two, thought Peter, changing the subject.

'Oh, it's just work.'

'Oh God! He's not releasing the Rose again, is he?' said Susie with typical disdain.

'I can't say,' said Peter. 'I'm not allowed to talk about it.'

Susie stared at him with contempt. They both knew that he told her pretty much everything about his work and was forever sharing secrets.

'Suit yourself,' she said.

'He's going to perform it. For the first time. In Westminster Abbey.'

'I shouldn't imagine that anyone will be interested in that old hat,' said Susie coldly.

'Are you fucking mad?' reacted Peter, instantly regretting that she had effortlessly pushed him into his usual role of defending Ian Taylor's stardom and, he realized, therefore side-stepping the

Jackson matter.

'Nobody cares,' she goaded.

'The papers will care! It's a huge story.'

'If you say so. But I don't think normal people care. Who is Ian Taylor anyway? People only like him because he was in Taylspin.'

'He's reforming Taylspin,' said Peter pompously.

'I don't think Jack knows that. Anyway, I thought they were mostly dead.'

'Only Wim Rogers is dead, the others…'

'Well as long as we don't have to go.'

Peter failed to see the trap again.

'Of course I'll have to go!' he said in the sort of tone that implied he wanted to add you fucking idiot to the sentence.

'Another missed weekend, then. Well this time you can explain it to the kids.'

'Hang on, hang on,' stalled Peter, getting a grip. 'This is ridiculous, you come home and I ask how was Jack and we get into an argument.'

'This isn't an argument.'

'Of course it's a fucking argument, it's how we communicate these days.'

Susie gave him a look that he took to confirm that she despised him.

'Look… I'm sorry,' he began. 'I've had a hard day. I missed you and…'

'Well done, Pete. You always have to ruin it, don't you?'

Feeling massive relief that she had managed to wrong foot him, Susie went upstairs to the bathroom. Part of her wanted him to storm after her, demand answers and fuck her hard like Jack had deliciously just done. But, she sneered, bugger Pete, he had brought this on himself.

She ran the shower and sat on the toilet for a pee. She glanced down at her thong and, curious, stepped out of it and held it up to her nose. Bloody hell, even Pete couldn't have been fooled into thinking that smell was anything other than grounds for separating. She looked for her mobile so that she could text Jack. He'd never believe she'd got away with it. Damn, she realized it was in her handbag in the kitchen. It would look far too obvious if she went down and retrieved it now. Besides, Pete was probably going through it.

Which he was. And he was confused as to why Susie, who was a strictly-no-sweets person, had a half-eaten packet of mints in her bag. Gingerly, he took her mobile and scrolled down to the recent calls list. Deleted, all of them. He felt his fears punch him again in the stomach. Peter replaced the phone and the mints and went to the open door to smoke another joint.

Ten minutes later he heard Susie coming down the stairs, her hair in a towel and a robe around her. She walked straight past him, saying nothing and carrying a hair-drier into the sitting room.

Peter's instinct whacked him yet again. He dawdled in the kitchen, pretending to be reading a magazine, until he heard the drier start up. Quietly but swiftly, he went upstairs to the bathroom. If she'd been having sex…

Susie's dress lay on the floor. Peter picked it up and shook it, but nothing fell out. He took the lid off the washing basket and looked in. There on the top of the pile were her stockings and a black bra. A black bra? But no knickers.

Peter stepped out onto the landing to check that the noise of the hair-drier still indicated that Susie was busy. Satisfied that she was, he darted back into the bathroom and very carefully began to delve into the dirty laundry looking for what, he sadly noted, might later be called evidence.

He didn't want to find it, and he was just about to replace all the clothes he had disturbed when he saw an edge of black lace peeking out from the pocket of a pair of Susie's jeans at almost the bottom of the basket. Feeling as if he was now in a dream and not sure if that was due to the effects of the marijuana or the surrealism of his horror, Peter pulled the thong from the pocket, completely aware of the connotations of it being so thoughtfully hidden.

He lifted the thong to his face, sniffed and then examined the sodden gusset. He replaced the thong and went to bed, furious that Susie took him for a fool.

CHAPTER 20

When Peter went into his office the next morning, his first action was to double the dose of his tranquilizers. He felt he would need the extra sedation in order to try to tolerate the madness that now filled every pore of his life. He felt almost relieved when the telephone rang and the interruption diverted him from thinking about hanging himself.

'Hello?' said Peter weakly.

'Hmm. Rough night?' said Billy Vernon and Peter wondered how it was that Billy always seemed to know that. Did he have the house bugged as well as the phones? He quickly pulled himself together.

'Nah, just late. What does he want to do about his blackmailing daughter?'

'I haven't talked to him about it yet, he sounded a bit grouchy. Anyway, he wants a press release off you by lunchtime, and a strategy plan for the press campaign for Rose.'

'There is no strategy,' said Peter belligerently.

'What do you mean?'

'We don't need a strategy. Our strategy will be to put on crash helmets and cower with our hands over our ears whilst the press, the Church, Members of Parliament, the White House and every welfare group in Europe bombs us to fuck with outrage and indignation,' predicted Peter.

'And we get to sell millions of albums,' added Vernon.

'And we get to sell millions of albums, because we really need the money. Even though we won't get any of it.'

'Pete, it's just a job,' said Vernon, comfortingly. 'Anyway, who says everyone will get upset?'

'Billy!' said Peter. 'You say you want a release, but have you any idea what the actual story is going to be?'

'Ian Taylor is performing Grey Rose for the first time ever.'

'Not exactly, Billy. The story is that Britain's biggest rock star has shocked just about fucking everybody by announcing he is to fuck a teenager by the fucking altar where royalty get married in order to make a protest for peace!'

'I wouldn't write fucking altar if I was you,' placated Vernon.

'You know what I mean,' Peter replied wearily. 'Anyway, when does he want this release to go out?'

'I don't know, why don't you call him?'

'It's a bit early…'

'He wants you to call him,' said Vernon, explaining why he was phoning so early.

'Did you say he's grouchy?' asked Peter warily.

'It's fine. He wants to talk to you. Don't mention the blackmailer. Unless he does, in which case don't mention that you mentioned her to me.'

'I'll call you back,' said Peter, ending the call, reaching for the hot line and punching the autodial for Ian Taylor's Wiltshire home.

'Hello?' said the famous Brummie burr after the phone had rung only once.

'Hi Ian, it's Peter Forth,' said Peter politely.

'Yeah, thanks for calling,' said Taylor, confounding Peter with an unexpected warmth. 'We need to get this story about the Rose out. In fact I was kind of hoping that you'd have had it ready already…'

'Err… I've got it written in my head,' said Peter truthfully.

'In other words, 'no',' said Taylor, and Peter sensed it was going to be one of those conversations. 'OK, never mind. The thing is… I don't want this to rebound on me…'

Then don't do it, thought Peter. But instead he said, 'What do you mean?'

'I don't want any shit press on this. I want this to be expertly handled, nice and smoothly in a professional manner. I don't want to wake up tomorrow with fucking TV crews outside my house.'

You said you did…

'Err… I think you might get that, Ian. I think that when this breaks, everybody will be chasing it. It's a big story.'

'Well, good,' said Taylor contradictorily. 'OK, but keep it straight. Don't try and get clever with it. We don't need any of your spin with this one, none of that sensationalism. Keep it dignified.'

Dignifiied?

'OK.'

'And maybe write it like it's coming from the record company. Don't put your name on the top of it because then it looks as if it's coming from me. I don't want people to think I'm blowing my own trumpet...'

God forbid.

'Sure.'

'But I don't want it issued by the record company. In fact, don't even tell them we're putting out a release from them.'

That's nice.

'OK. I'll get on with it now,' said Peter. 'I'll email it over to you when it's done, so you can make any changes.'

'Good. Bye.'

Shit!

Realising that he had forgotten something that he considered important Peter rang Taylor again.

'What?' said Taylor in the sullen way that he announced his immediate irritation.

'One thing before I write this. Should I say that you're reforming the band?'

'What do you mean?'

'Well, are you going to contact the band before we say...'

'What the fuck has that got to do with you?'

'Sorry,' said Peter, 'I just thought that maybe you'd want to talk to the band before they read that you're reforming...'

'Are you my manager now?' said Taylor, pronouncing 'manager' with the same distain that others would use to say 'Nazi'.

'Err...'

'Just write the fucking release,' said the voice of reason and he put the phone down as Peter blustered, 'Yes, but, do you want me to mention the ba...?'

Ignoring a rise in his blood pressure that his doctor had already expressed concern about, Peter turned on his laptop and began to write the words that he instinctively felt would herald the start of very bad things indeed.

Ian Taylor is to reform Taylspin and perform Grey Rose live for the very first time in the 40-year history of rock's most seminal album. Organisers of the unexpected concert are aiming to stage it in Westminster Abbey on Armistice Day...

Peter knew that nobody had even suggested a date but it was a good idea, especially if it appeared to be Ian Taylor's idea.

The date has been chosen especially by Ian Taylor in order to endorse the anti-war message of Grey Rose, which was originally recorded in 1968 as a protest against the Vietnam War.

No, not 'endorse', Peter thought; 'reiterate', that's better.

Ian Taylor said today, 'The message of Grey Rose needs to be heard as clearly now as it ever was. I will reunite Taylspin for this concert, which will be filmed and broadcast on television around the world.

Peter continued to type, inventing that an international search, apparently, was now on for a new drummer, that the label would be re-releasing the album in conjunction with the gig, that a spokesman for the label said something that he had not actually said or known that he would be saying and then he wrote the line that he hoped would make Kevin O'Mara sit up at the *Daily Mirror*.

A BPA spokesman said, 'It is hoped that this unique staging of Grey Rose will be performed as close as possible to the script for the original concept for the album in the sixties.'

Peter finished writing the press release and checked it for spelling. Deliberately, he deleted 'Westminster' and retyped it as 'Wesminster', knowing that it was best to provide at least one mistake in order for Ian to satisfy his inclination to correct anybody about anything, otherwise he would start looking for changes that Peter didn't want made.

He realised that the release failed to mention that this was the first time that the Dean of the Abbey would have heard of any such concert, but that was unimportant because his hunch was that the Abbey would say 'no way' anyway, so that he could put out another release saying that Taylor had been banned by the Church.

He checked his watch. Ian should still be at home, probably shouting down the phone to his office by now that someone had forgotten to replace the empty bottle of HP Sauce again and how the fuck was he supposed to enjoy his bacon and eggs without it.

Peter emailed the proposed press release to Taylor's home and decided to have some breakfast himself, knowing that it would be a little while before he was phoned back to be told that even a child of eight should be able to spell Westminster properly. But then the phone rang and it was Billy Vernon again.

'Have you…?'

'I've written the release and sent it over to him,' Peter confirmed.

'Did you send that strategy over as well?' asked Vernon nervously.

'No.'

'Why not?'

'Because as I said, Billy, there is no strategy of any great note. It will be a snowball job once the release hits the wires.'

'That easy, huh?' said Vernon, relishing the firestorm.

'Well it's not exactly hard to get the attention of a celebrity-obsessed media by revealing that Ian is refusing to deny plans to globally televise scenes of him shagging a girl inside Westminster Abbey,' said Peter, cynically.

'How do you think they'll angle it?' asked Vernon naively.

'Angle it, Billy? Fucking angle it? There is only one angle, Bill, and that is a story that begins with the words, 'Church leaders have condemned plans by the pop singer Ian Taylor to…'. That'll be the first story. By News at Ten I expect we'll have graduated to, 'MPs have joined the Church and family groups in condemning…'. By breakfast time it'll be, 'The rock star Ian Taylor has refused to react to a furious backlash that has met his plans to…'

'Good' said Vernon.

'That's not even the start of it, Billy. All the camera crews will be outside his house doing live pieces to camera that will begin 'Behind me is the home of controversial rock star Ian Taylor…'.'

'He won't like that,' said Vernon, who was now sounding worried. 'He said he doesn't want anybody outside his house.'

'Billy! I've already fucking told him that the crews will stake out his place. He knows that. You watch. Around eleven on the morning of the second day of this hell, he'll come out of the house and get into a ruck with the snappers. He'll have security down there acting like they own the fucking pavement; there'll be cameras flying and punches thrown and Ian will be in the thick of it waving a fucking Peace sign and saying he just wants to sing to stop the war. Bish, bosh, front page news and great television footage of what they will report as ugly scenes.'

'And Ian will fucking love it,' said Vernon.

'Why will he love it?'

'Pete, this whole thing has nothing to do with Grey Rose or campaigning against any war. This is some pantomime from hell, which Ian has very cleverly dreamt up in order to protect himself. He knows that his new stuff is not a patch on his old stuff. So if he concentrates on new songs he'll just get pretty much ignored.'

'Worse than the pox in our game.'

'But Ian's seen what's coming. I think he's planning on baling out with the definitive follow that – the biggest bang in showbusiness.'

So he's seeding that line to everybody, thought Peter, as his hotline began to ring.

'Hang on, Bill,' said Peter, 'it's him.'

He put the receiver down on his desk so that Vernon could hear at least his part of the conversation.

Peter took the call and was surprised to hear not tones of irritation but Jill Brown's elegant Englishness instead.

'Hello, dear. Sorry to call you on the hotline; you were engaged. I expect it's Billy, isn't it?'

'Yeah, he's holding on,' said Peter, always impressed by Jill's understanding.

'I won't keep you long. Your lord and master is a little bothered by your incapacity to spell Westminster. He wants to know when your birthday is, so that he can buy you a dictionary. I expect that was one of your deliberate mistakes, wasn't it?'

'You taught me, Jilly,' said Peter, adoringly.

'Yes, well I didn't say as much to him. Anyway, apparently you are to consider yourself in the corner wearing the dunce's hat. And, apart from your appalling transgression of literacy, he says that the rest of the release is fine…'

Peter ended the call, picked up Vernon on the other line and told him he would call him back later. Now the release was approved he needed to act quickly and not trust to the luck of the story just leaking out.

CHAPTER 21

Although he had promised Ian Taylor that he wouldn't spin this story Peter knew that he had to assist its birth. He reasoned that he could always apologise later.

Kevin O'Mara was at his desk at the *Daily Mirror* when Peter rang his mobile. They exchanged cynicisms expressing their mutual disbelief of the various alleged exclusives in the day's editions before Peter listened to O'Mara deplore the lack of proper stories.

'Hey,' said Peter when they had finished discussing the sexual merits of a well-known breakfast television presenter, 'do you know it's the birthday of Grey Rose coming up?'

'Don't tell me – BPA's remastering it and putting it out again at last.'

'Yeah.'

'That's not a bad story,' said O'Mara in a tone that implied it was not a particularly good story either. 'How many are they pressing this time?'

'Ten million,' said Peter.

'Really? Fuck. Are you sure?'

'Really. But it gets better,' said Peter, who wanted his friend to have the satisfaction of guessing the story himself.

'He's not bloody doing it at last, is he? Fuck me, and all those years of denying he'd ever play it.'

'He's going to perform it for one night only and never again. In Westminster Abbey.'

'Westmin... Why's he doing it there? Is he getting the band together again? I thought they didn't talk.'

'They don't even exchange Christmas cards,' said Peter, continuing to drip information. 'But they'll do it because they'll earn a fuck load of money. It's going to be televised live around the planet. Millions of viewers, apparently.'

'Can we say it'll be bigger than Live Aid?'

'You can say it; it won't be true but you can say all of that shit. I thought this would be up your street, given The Mirror's anti-war stance. He's going to stage it as one big fuck-off-America peace gig, that's why he's chosen Westminster Abbey, tomb of the unknown soldier and all that. Oh, and the gig is going to be on Armistice Day.'

'So it's rock star Ian Taylor is finally to perform his legendary anti-war concert to spearhead a worldwide call to America to stop the bombing?' said O'Mara.

'Something like that,' said Peter. 'Or maybe Brit popper Ian Taylor has declared rock and roll war on America.'

'Have we got this to ourselves?'

'The record company just wanted the *Sun* to have it,' Peter lied. 'But I'm telling you as a mate. Anyway, the *Sun* won't go on the anti-war line.'

Peter waited for a moment. He still wanted O'Mara to work it out for himself. Which he did.

'Hang on, wasn't there some shit in the sixties about this? Didn't your man plan a gig before but it got called off because of some sex row involving groupies?'

Now we're off, thought Peter.

'It wasn't a gig,' said Peter, taking his time because he knew that O'Mara would now be taking notes. 'It was an idea for a film. Ian wanted to do Grey Rose like The Who did 'Tommy', with all the songs acted out. But it got scrapped because there was an almighty fucking row over Ian's claims that the film had to be real and so…'

'Was it that 'Come to Daddy' track?' said O'Mara. 'Everyone went fucking mad because Taylor was saying that a groupie…'

'A teenage groupie,' offered Peter.

'Yeah, that's right. He got clobbered for wanting to shag somebody playing a teenage fan,' recalled O'Mara.

'Actually, he wanted the fan to be a real fan, not an actress,' Peter supplied as he continued to pour petrol onto the flame of the story.

'Hang about,' said O'Mara, realising that he was now set to be writing the next splash of his newspaper. 'Are you telling me that

Ian Taylor is going to fuck a teenage fan? Are you on the piss, Pete?'

'Look at the lyrics of the song,' replied Peter.

'Storm over rock star jailbait sex in abbey shocker,' roared O'Mara, self-mockingly. 'Are you serious? This is a bloody good yarn.'

O'Mara's use of 'jailbait' set off an alarm in Peter. He made a note of the word on the pad in front of him and ringed it. He knew he would have to sort that out. But any clarification now would ruin the story, so he said nothing.

'But he'll get arrested,' said O'Mara, having a similar thought.

'For what?' said Peter.

'For having under-age sex. In the song the girl is under age. He'd be sent down.'

'I'm not saying he's shagging anyone,' said Peter uneasily.

'What do you mean? Is this just a scam?'

'No. If you ask me, on the record as the spokesman, whether Ian Taylor is planning to have sex as part of this production I will have to refuse to confirm or deny that. I will have to point you to the line in the press release which says, err, what does it say? Got your pen?'

'I'm taping the call.'

'Good. OK. It says... a record company spokesman said – quotes – it is hoped that this unique staging of Grey Rose will be performed as closely as possible to the script for the original concept for the album in the sixties.'

'As possible to the what?' said O'Mara, taking notes as he didn't trust the telephone taping device to work properly.

'To the script for the original concept for the album in the sixties.'

'...album in the sixties. OK. And what's your official quote?'

'I don't have one,' said Peter. 'I can't be quoted because this release isn't going out until tomorrow, via PA. We are not having this call.'

'But I need to say something.'

'You can say that an aide of Ian Taylor – and for fuck's sake don't name me – refused to confirm or deny plans for the production.'

'Yeah, OK, that'll do,' said O'Mara. 'Look, it's editor's conference in a minute and this is going to shake things up. I'll call you back after that. This is just for us and the *Sun*?'

'Uh-huh.'

'You know they'll go after him over the under-age sex?'

'Yeah,' said Peter, 'I'm thinking about that. Between you and me I don't think Ian's thought that out fully. In fact, fuck it, Kev, I'm not going to get messed up with cops and the NSPCC. Say a close insider said that any girl who may be considered for the part will have to be aged over sixteen. Can you make that point?'

'Aren't we losing some of the story if you say that?'

'Hardly!' said Peter, 'You've still got Ian Taylor set to shag a girl in Westminster Abbey during a live TV broadcast. I don't think the fact that the girl could be sixteen or seventeen puts this story anywhere near the ballpark of respectability. I don't fucking care as long as she's not under age.'

'Can we say that Taylor has backed off from shock original plans?'

'No, don't have him backing off anything. He'll go fucking mental if anyone says he's backing off. No, say… err… just say that the girl would have be over sixteen. In fact, don't even mention the underage thing at all. I don't want to go there.'

'Probably wise,' agreed O'Mara. 'My editor won't be exactly thrilled if we're seen to be aiding and abetting some sort of paedo pop stunt. OK, look, I'll ring you later.'

Job done, thought Peter. But now he was worried about how Taylor would react when he discovered that his publicist had intervened. He hoped that Taylor would see the wisdom of his intervention, but he also knew that Taylor tended to get most infuriated when he was corrected.

He lit another cigarette and checked his emails, feeling like he was on a treadmill that never, ever altered; fag, email, worry, fag, phone call, fag, earful, fag, email, worry, fag, press call, lie, fag, email, more tranquilizers, fag.

CHAPTER 22

The next morning Peter collected the pile of national newspapers and took them into the kitchen, rifling through them to find the *Sun* and the *Daily Mirror*. Their front pages told him it would be a good idea to go back upstairs and pinch a couple of the Valium that Susie was given for PMS but which, each month, she forgot to take. Peter prescribed himself ten milligrams and then went back downstairs to look at the newspapers again.

Shit, he thought.

The *Mirror* was reporting it straight enough. IAN TAYLOR IN CHURCH SEX SHOCK ran the three-deck headline on the front page. Peter considered that this was fair, it was pretty much what Taylor wanted, although he would have preferred the first two words to have been ROCK LEGEND.

The *Sun* typically pushed the story a little more with its splash – ROCK STAR PLANS ABBEY TEEN SHAG.

Peter had not told the *Sun* that Taylor would be involved in enacting the controversial song, so somebody in Wapping had read the cuttings. He worried for a moment that if that was the case, maybe a smart-eyed sub had also unearthed the original controversy of the girl being under age in the song. He hoped not, and a quick scan of the story placated him.

His blood pressure was almost beginning to calm when he turned to the *Daily Mail* and was horrified to see an ancient-looking Taylor photographed next to a huge-lettered headline that said simply, 'ROCK'S DIRTY OLD MAN!'

Oh my fucking Christ.

Peter could not immediately decide whether it was the 'dirty' or the 'old' that Taylor would most object to. He suspected that it would probably be the latter word, but he rapidly revised that opinion when, as instructed by the *Mail's* 'The Full Shocking Story – pages 4 & 5', he flipped to a spread above which ran the headline

IS IAN TAYLOR THE BIGGEST PERV IN POP?

Hoping that, if he looked away, the story would miraculously disappear, Peter turned back to the front page and read that, 'Aging rock star Ian Taylor was last night condemned as 'a dirty old man' over his plans to try to resurrect his flagging career by appearing in a live sex show inside Westminster Abbey.'

Peter felt like vomiting. He lit another cigarette and then attempted to rationalise the *Mail's* stance, defensively rehearsing what he would say when the call came that began with the words whose fucking idea was this?

Their story was legitimate; Ian was not young anymore, he was planning to depict a song that involved sexual acts, apparently an MP had called him a dirty old man, well, that was to be reasonably expected, and Ian did want it all to take place at the Abbey. But aging star and flagging career? Did the *Mail* not know that this would turn 'the biggest perv in pop' into the biggest beast in Armageddon?

The biggest perv in pop? Oh for fuck's sake.

Peter braced himself and went into his office. Each of the three telephones on his desk blinked red message lights at him. Predictably, that included the message alert on Ian's hot line.

As if in a dream, Peter sat in his chair, took a blank piece of paper and began to work out how much money he had left in the bank. Probably just a couple of thousand. But he was due to invoice for the last four weeks' work, so that would take it up to around ten grand. He could live on ten grand for a few months until he'd finished his novel. And after that failed, he reflected, he could get a job driving a van.

Wearily, Peter pressed the play button on the answer machine on the Taylor hot line. He was not surprised to hear a furious voice saying 'phone me fucking back!'

Peter called Susie's mobile instead. Typically it rang several times before she answered, sounding flustered.

'It's me. Where are you?' he said evenly.

'Outside the village shop. Can't it wait? I'll be back in a minute.'

'I'm going to get fired.'

'What, again?' sneered Susie.

'No, really,' said Peter miserably. 'I thought you should know before it happens.'

'Pete. I can't wait for you to be fired. Bloody hooray! Maybe then we'll all be able to start living again and not have to go creeping around worrying that somebody might upset Ian fucking Taylor.'

'I'll see you in a minute,' said Peter and rang off.

As he did so, Taylor's hot line began to ring.

Peter lifted the receiver and heard Taylor say, 'What the fuck is going on?'

'Err…'

'Have you seen the fucking papers! The biggest fucking perv in fucking pop! What the fuck is that about? Eh? How the fuck did this fucking shit happen?'

'Err…'

'I'll fucking tell you how it happened. It fucking happened because, once a-fucking-gain you didn't do what I fucking told you! I fucking said put out the press release. I didn't fucking say anything about tipping off your fucking mates at the fucking *Mail*…'

'I didn't tip them off,' Peter managed to blurt.

'Didn't tip them off? So how the fuck did this story happen, then? Don't fucking tell me you didn't fucking call them. I fucking know what you're like…'

'I didn't.'

'Well then how the fuck did they get this story? Fucking tell me that.'

'They lifted it from the first edition of The Sun…'

'And how did the fucking *Sun* get hold of it? You fucking told them.'

'Well, yes, it was leaked…'

'Did I fucking tell you to tell the *Sun*? And the fucking *Mirror*! Did I? Did I fucking tell you to fucking tell anyone?'

'You said to put out the release…'

'Yeah,' Taylor 's voice calmed for a moment that Peter knew

would not last for long. 'I said to put out the release. To the Press Association. That was what we agreed. Break it in a dignified way and then see what happened.'

Peter wanted to tell Taylor that it wouldn't have made any difference when or how the *Mail* first learnt of the story, but the Valium wasn't helping his concentration. Ian had wanted a storm of publicity, he had made jokes about the likely furore when they had first discussed it, he had approved the press release, which essentially announced the same story that had so outraged the *Mail*, so what was his problem now?

As if reading his mind, Taylor began to rant again.

'Do you know what has really fucking pissed me off? Why I am so fucking angry with you? I don't give a flying fuck about what some jumped-up rentaquote MP says about me. I think it's fucking rich been called a fucking pervert by some public-school Tory prick, and I shall probably fucking say so. But I'm really pissed off with you because you don't fucking do what you're fucking told!'

Peter stayed silent, accepting the truth.

'What is it with you? Do you think you know better than me? Because you fucking don't! I've been dealing with the fucking press all of my life. I fucking know how they fucking think and how to play them. I don't need your fucking advice! I know, man, I fucking know. But, oh no, you always have to know fucking better! You're fucking out there knowing better, fucking everything up because you always fucking know fucking better! And I'm fucked off with it. You think you're the fucking boss! You think you call the shots! Well, you fucking don't! You've got to fucking learn to do just what other people fucking tell you. If I want you to fucking think for yourself, I'll fucking tell you.'

Another of his telephones began to ring.

'Do you want to fucking get that?' snarled Taylor .

'It'll be the press,' said Peter.

'Of course it'll be the fucking press! It will probably be the fucking press who are now camped outside my fucking house, the one thing that you fucking know I don't fucking like! Fucking answer it!' he ordered.

Presuming that this meant Taylor wanted to hang on the line and listen to how his publicist would deal with the enquiry, Peter dispiritedly picked up the other call and attempted to put a bright edge into his voice.

'Hello? Oh, hi,' he said as he heard Mike Stone from the Press Association announce himself.

'Errr… yeah, so I see,' said Peter as Stone commented that 'his boy' was causing 'something of a press storm' today.

Peter chuckled as Stone added, 'So how is the biggest perv in pop this morning?' and then wished he hadn't laughed as he realised that Taylor would be straining to hear his every response.

'I think you will find that the label will be shortly issuing a press release about the production,' said Peter buoyantly.

'What?'

'Oh yes,' continued Peter. 'The proper story is all contained in the press release. I have no comment to make.'

'What are you on about? I said, 'How is Ian taking all of this?' said Stone, confused.

'Exactly,' said Peter. 'That's right, 1968.'

'What?' said Stone, who had been a friend of Peter's since their days on Fleet Street a decade ago.

'Yeah. I agree,' said Peter. 'I think it will be the gig of the century.'

'What the fu… hang about. Pete, can't you talk?'

'Precisely,' said Peter.

'Is there someone in your office?'

'No, I don't think so. I have heard of nobody phoning to complain,' continued Peter.

'Nobody pho… Is someone on another line?'

'Yes, that's true,' said Peter.

'Is it another journo?'

'No.'

'Your office?'

'No, I think it is much more significant than that.'

'Fuck!' exclaimed Stone. 'He's on the other line?'

'Uh-huh.'

'Is he seething?'

'Um-hum.'

'Do you want to phone me back in a minute? By the way, don't worry; the label's already let us know on the quiet who's behind all of this. I heard about the meeting at Taylor's gaff. I'll speak to you later. Good luck with the perv.'

'Thank you, yes, just phone the BPA press office. Goodbye,' said Peter, now speaking only to the ether.

He picked up the other phone, leaving the receiver off the hook of his incoming line to avoid other interruptions.

'What is more significant?' said Taylor as Peter knew that he would.

'That was PA. They were saying that the performance of Grey Rose should be a bigger deal than Brian Wilson's Smile show.'

'I should fucking think so too,' said Taylor with typical charity. 'Who said it'd be the gig of the century?'

'PA. The Press Association. That was Mike Stone, you know him. He said the show will be a huge hit,' Peter lied.

'So what fucking line is PA taking on all of this?'

'Well, I don't know if you heard but I said he'd have to get the release from the record label. I'm not commenting.'

'Good. Is he important?'

'Who?' said Peter. 'Mike?'

'The PA bloke.'

'Well, yeah. I mean it's the PA; their stuff goes to every newspaper and TV and radio station in the country. And they're picked up for abroad by Reuters and AP. That's why we said to give them the story first.'

'Which you fucked right up by deciding on a better idea,' Taylor reminded him. 'So if I talk to this Mike bloke I suppose I could clean up some of the fucking mess that you've caused.'

'Well, yeah; he'd love it,' said Peter.

'What's his number?'

Peter recited the number of the Press Association showbusiness desk. He was about to suggest that he called Stone first, but Taylor had abruptly rung off.

Peter grabbed his mobile, sped through the contacts and hit the dial button to call Mike Stone's mobile. Stone answered immediately.

'Mike, it's me,' said Peter and he heard a phone begin to ring in Stone's office. 'Don't answer that for a second...'

'What? Why?'

'It's Ian calling you.'

'What?'

'It's fucking Ian! Look, pick it up but tell him to hold on. Don't ask who's speaking.'

He heard the ringing stop and Stone say, 'Could you hang on just one moment, please,' before coming back to Peter.

'Listen,' said Peter, thinking quickly, 'he's going to give you an interview. Probably his only interview. Do us a favour, butter him up. Tell him this whole thing about the Rose is a great idea. Tell him it'll be huge. Go on the anti-war line first. For God's sake don't go in on that pervert line because he'll just ring off.'

'Gotcha,' said Stone and ended the call.

While he waited for Taylor to complete the interview and then probably phone him back to fire him, Peter rang Taylor's office and asked to speak to Jill Brown.

'Hello you,' said Taylor's personal assistant, cheerily. 'What's new in the wonderful world of depravity?'

'Oh God,' groaned Peter, 'don't you start. I've already had him on for a bollocking on the disastrous consequences of me of thinking like a PR.'

'Thought you might.'

'Why are you sounding so happy about it? I'm going to get sacked over this.'

'No. You won't,' said Jill in her sensible, soothing tone. 'He brought this on himself. I was in that meeting too, remember. He wanted all of this. He approved your press release. Unfortunately your stories appeared on a day when he is in a particularly vile mood.'

'Why's that?' asked Peter.

'Oh, the usual thing; hangover. Don't worry, once again you've got him the attention that he wanted. I think it's all hideous but he'll love it when he calms down.'

'If he calms down,' said Peter, 'I've never heard anybody swear like he just did.'

'Yes, well swearing is his métier,' said Jill. 'Anyway, consider yourself fortunate that you aren't having to search London's finer emporiums for rear-view sunglasses.'

'Pardon?'

'He's bothered because he thinks people are sniggering about him behind his back...' said Jill, who viewed Taylor as an insufferable toddler with permanent temper tantrums.

'Which they are.'

'Quite. So now muggins here has got to find some ophthalmic engineer who can construct for him a pair of shades with a tiny flip-up wing mirror on the side, so that he can see what people are doing when his back is turned...'

Peter was not surprised.

'Are you still with us or have you topped yourself already?' he heard Jill say.

'Sorry,' he said. 'I...'

Peter stopped as Taylor 's hotline began to ring again.

'Good luck. Don't worry,' said Jill and she put her phone down. Peter picked up the hotline and said hello.

'Hi,' said Taylor so curtly that he managed to make the word sound less than monosyllabic. 'So I spoke to your mate...'

'Great!' said Peter and hated himself for gushing.

'Yeah, well I think I've sorted out all of your fucking mess now...'

Taylor paused and Peter presumed it was because he was expected to say, 'thank you'. He said nothing.

'Are you there?' said Taylor, immediately annoyed at his publicist's insolent refusal to grovel.

'Yeah. Sorry, I'm listening. You spoke to Mike...' said Peter and thinking don't push it, 'I bet he was blown away that you called.'That's it, stroke the ego.

'Yeah, well I suppose he was. Yeah, I suppose it's not every day the likes of him would get me phoning him out of the blue. I didn't think of that. Maybe you should have warned him.'

'Oh, he's a professional. He'll have dealt with it,' said Peter patronisingly.

'Yeah. Well, as I say the thing is I turned it around for you.'

For me?

'I got him going on the whole peace thing behind the gig, like we said. I hit out at the Yanks for bombing the fuck out of everyone whose ass they just fancy roasting, and I told him that was why I'm doing the gig, to keep making the protest for peace like we did in the sixties. And I said that was why I'm having to sensationalise this gig with the sex, I've got to make it controversial that way I'll get people's attention for the main message – which is stop the fucking war.'

'That's clever,' said Peter, meaning it. 'That's actually a really good line. I like that.'

'Yeah,' said Taylor, sounding pleased with the approbation. 'Yeah, well, as I say, man, I know how to do this press shit. And I'll tell you what – and you should have thought about this, but luckily I did – Mick…'

Mick?

'….Mick the PA bloke was saying that some people thought the chick in the abbey was going to be like a fucking teenager, 'cos back in the sixties there was like some talk of that shit with the film that never fucking happened. I thought hang on, times have changed, so I fucking stamped on that one. I told him no way, man, I don't want to make it with some teen chick. Well, I do, but that's like between me and you. I told him we'd be looking for like a bit of an older girl, in her twenties at least. I think that's alright, don't you?'

'I think it's spot on,' said Peter, truthfully and relieved.

'I mean now we've got all these great headlines…'

These great headlines that were fucking shit a little while ago?

'…and now, like, it's a big fucking story that the press has just blown out of proportion, now we've got everybody's attention I can come out with the real story, that we're doing this for peace, and now everyone will listen to that more than they would if we hadn't got in the *Sun* and the *Mirror*. So I think that this is working out well.'

'Did he ask much about the sex line?' asked Peter.

'Not a lot. I told him there's sex and fucking going on in theatres and cinemas all over London, within yards of Westminster Abbey, so what we're talking about doing is just what people in the theatre are doing anyway. They did it in *Oh! Calcutta!* years ago. I told him, it's not like we're inventing nudity and sex here. We're just doing what all the other arts are doing, I read the other day that they had sex stuff in opera now. I told him, the only difference is that they're doing it for art and we're doing it for peace. There's no other difference, there's sex in shows all over fucking London.'

The only marginal difference being that traditionally not a lot of it goes on in Westminster Abbey.

'That's a good take,' said Peter, 'doing this in the name of peace. It harks back to John and Yoko's bed-ins.'

'Exactly,' said Taylor, loving the comparison. 'I tell you man, you'd have been proud of me, your mate said what did I say to, like, these MPs and stuff who said this was obscene. I said, what is the greatest obscenity – sex or war? 'Cos it's fucking war, man. It's fucking war every fucking time.'

'Sounds like a great interview. It'll be all over the shop by lunchtime, it'll probably be on the BBC mid-day news,' said Peter honestly.

'Yeah? Well check it out. Let me know. OK? And on what I was saying before, listen man you really have got to let me be the one who calls the shots with this shit. I fucking know what I'm doing.'

'I know.'

'Yeah, well. Never mind, it sounds like this is going to work, so that's good. And I've saved your arse…'

'Thank you.' Peter felt he had to say it this time.

'It's OK, man. Cool. Right, now I suppose I had better inform this band of mine about this gig they're gonna be doing. Speak to you later.'

Taylor rang off. Peter sat back in his chair, lit another cigarette and felt knots of anxiety unravel as relief oozed through his body. As always, his elation was not caused by doing a good job, it was the result of escaping a telling off by not doing a bad one. Fear was the spur that motivated all who worked in Taylor's empire, fear of being scolded, just as it had been at school.

Now that Taylor was unlikely to split his ears and crack his spirit again today, Peter resumed his work and began making a list of those who had left messages on his answerphone demanding confirmation or comment on the storm.

His mobile started ringing; Peter looked at the screen and saw that it was Vernon calling.

'Don't you start,' said Peter as he answered.

'Start? Oh, Ian,' said Vernon. 'Was he boiling? He was insane with vulgarity when he got me.'

'Just a bit,' said Peter sardonically. 'I've just had him on again; he seems calmer now, not so many fucking fuckings.'

'Don't worry about it, the label is delighted. We've just saved them a million on pre-promoing the album. And of course for our other purposes, all of this moral hysteria is ideal.'

'What do you mean?' said Peter.

'That photograph, Peter. Painting Ian as this shagmeister nicely smokescreens any suggestion that he's a dung-puncher.'

'Maybe,' said Peter cautiously, 'but for some all of that would fit with his new image as an alleged pervert. Did you mention the blackmailer?'

'I judged that he's not in the mood for that,' said Vernon sighing. 'If it was important he'd have mentioned it.'

'But it is important, fucking important. What do you want me to do with her?'

'Stall her. Keep her sweet.'

'How sweet?'

'Well I'm not saying you can fuck her. We have to bear in mind at least the slight possibility that she is his kid, in which case you shafting her would send him mental. You haven't, have you?'

'What?'

'Had her?'

'Hardly. How do you want me to stall her?'

'Lie, Pete,' said Vernon, 'that's what you're good at. Tell her Ian is not contactable, he's gone to ground because of all the press stuff. Tell her whatever you have to but make sure you get those bloody pictures.'

'OK, but she's clever, this one. We can't con her too far.'

'Just keep her hanging on until I can talk to Ian. For all we know he may pay her to go away.'

'I don't think that would work, mate. She's determined.'

'Well then you be more determined. Convince her it'll work out fine. You've got to con her into trusting you. You can do that, Pete, you're the great liar.'

Vernon rang off and Peter felt wretched again.

CHAPTER 23

Catherine couldn't believe what she was hearing. In her eagerness to hear it better, she knocked over a full cup of coffee as she reached to turn up the volume on the radio. The coffee was spreading across the table, making the morning's post sodden and brown but she let it, not wanting to break her concentration on what the news reporter was saying.

As the pool of liquid reached the edge of the table and started to drip down onto the newly-ironed clothes that she had piled on a chair, she just sat there and watched it ruin her morning's work.

She had lurched for the volume control as soon as she had heard the newscaster of the eleven o'clock bulletin say *'Top stories on the hour – the latest on the Ian Taylor sex scandal...'* and now she was transfixed as she heard the newsman say they were now going over live to Tim Marshall outside the rock star's home.

'Yes... well the breaking news just reported by the Press Association is that Ian Taylor has defended his controversial plan to include live sex scenes in the first-ever live performance of his classic Grey Rose album inside Westminster Abbey.

'Taylor has confirmed that he will press ahead with his move to perform the sixties' anthems in the Abbey – and that this one-in-a-lifetime production will include a performance of the scandal song 'Come to Daddy', during which the rock legend will have actual sex on stage.

'MPs have condemned Taylor's plans, calling them pornographic and, although there has been no word yet from Church authorities, Taylor says the sex show will go on. The sixty-year-old star says he is making his provocative stand because, as he puts it, it will make a sex-obsessed media pay attention to what he contends is the main anti-war message of the album which is now set to be performed live for the first time in its colourful history.

'Taylor said he hopes that his show, inside one of Britain's

premier churches, will make people think about what he calls 'the true obscenity' which, he says is not the sex scenes in Grey Rose but the war in Afghanistan.

'But pundits expect him to meet strong resistance to the concert from not only our own Government, but also from the White House, neither of whom will want this planned performance to become the world focus of the growing anti-war movement.

'Although there has been no word yet from Downing Street, there is mounting pressure from back-bench MPs who are already calling on the Prime Minister to ask the Church to ban the concert on the grounds of obscenity.

'By the way, Trevor, Taylor did clear up some of the controversy surrounding the performance of his 'Come to Daddy' song. Press reports today suggested that Taylor was looking for a teenage fan to play this much-disputed role and, of course it is partly this youth aspect that has caused so much of the row. But Taylor dismissed suggestions that the girl will be a teenager. He said he was not looking to, as he put it, 'fill the part with jailbait' and that he and promoters of his highly-controversial concert were now looking for a more mature woman to play the role. Back to you, Trevor, in the studio.'

The newscaster said, '*And now in the City, where shares have this morning crashed for the ninth day running...*' but Catherine was no longer listening.

She sat watching the dripping coffee make stains in a white skirt of thin linen that she had only recently bought because it was so see-through. She made no move to mop the spill. Instead she reached for her tobacco and rolling papers. It was a few moments before she saw that her hands were shaking so much that she had spilt the tobacco and was rolling up only thin air.

Catherine had been waiting for an opportunity like this for years, waiting for Taylor to be up to his neck in controversy, stressed, not thinking straight and therefore vulnerable. But even at her most deranged she had never imagined that it might actually become this easy to fulfill her promise to her mother. Fate, she thought, had given her a way to avenge her mother for all those heartbroken letters that had never been answered. Now she knew how to nail Ian Taylor to a tree if he did not accept her.

She smiled at the thought of how she could accomplish the fall of Ian Taylor if he tried to dodge his responsibility. She relished the picture of him huddled alone in his vast home, stripped of his standing, vilified by the media that once fêted him and nobody wanting to buy any of the albums of that sordid old sod, as people would call him.

It was going to be so easy to achieve, if he refused to do what she wanted. She found her mobile and called Peter. It was time to start playing mind games.

'Forth,' he said, sounding exasperated. She could hear other telephones ringing around him.

'Hello, lover,' she purred.

'What? Oh… look, Cathy, not now. This is not a great time,' said Peter as yet another journalist left a message pleading for a call back.

'It is for me,' she said. 'It's a great time.'

'Fine, but your concerns are not my biggest priority today, I'm afraid.'

'Well, they should be,' she said, adding a little ice to her tone.

'What do you mean?'

'Your man's hot now, isn't he? All the newspapers must be going crazy looking for a new line. I should imagine they'd just combust with joy if I told them that the so-called biggest perv in pop is also as bent as a nine-bob note.'

'Oh God,' said Peter miserably. 'OK, what do you want?'

'I want to see you.'

'I can't. Really. The phones are melting; can't you hear them?'

'Surely you can spare half an hour; it could be a Taylor family matter,' she teased.

'Don't make jokes. OK, I'll meet you. Where and when?'

'Say in an hour. At my flat. It's above…'

'I know where it is,' said Peter and he rang off and took another of the endless press calls.

CHAPTER 24

Spying from the kitchen window that her husband was obviously busy in his office, Susie rang Jackson's mobile.

'Hello?'

'Hi, it's me,' said Susie, sweetly.

'Hello you,' chuckled Jackson. 'What are you up to?'

'I was wondering if you were around today, maybe lunchtime?'

'I could be… what did you have in mind?' he replied lasciviously.

'I thought I might pop up and see you at the flat and, um, maybe work on a few ideas for that modelling thing we were talking about.'

'What thing would that be, then?' teased Jackson.

'You know, posing for you,' she giggled.

'What do you mean, work on ideas?'

'Look,' said Susie a little curtly as she feared Peter could come in and interrupt them at any moment, 'are you up for it or not?'

'I'd love to see you,' answered Jackson suggestively.

'OK, well I'll pop by later. Oh, by the way, that woman I met in your shop last week, Catherine something, I thought she mentioned something about posing too,' Susie fished.

'So?'

'Well, don't take her up on it. It's my assignment. You won't be disappointed.'

Susie rang off. She went to the kitchen window and looked through to check that Peter was still in his office. As usual, he had the phone to his ear and was gesticulating wildly. Not sacked yet, then, she thought, so that was another of his 'cry wolf' alarms.

CHAPTER 25

Peter was cross because Jill Brown had phoned him to say that Ian had decided that he would do an interview with BBC Radio 4's *Today* programme, but he didn't fancy their suggestion of a live debate with the American ambassador, which was apparently a bloody stupid idea, and instead he wanted to argue against somebody of lighter weight and Peter was to get the Archbishop of Canterbury on the show.

Peter had explained to Jill that the Archbishop of Canterbury had declared no opinion on Taylor's Westminster Abbey stunt and besides, as he was neither pro the war nor American, what was the point of asking him to fill the role of arguing against Ian? Jill had said she completely agreed but, 'DFA; that's what he wants.'

Peter saw no merit in informing the BBC that Ian Taylor was too daunted to take on the US ambassador, and he had no intention of phoning the press office at Lambeth Palace to ask if the Right Very Reverend, or whatever one called him, would mind going on radio pretending to be both an advocate of genocide and a little bit thick. He also knew there was no point trying to explain any of this over the phone to Taylor, because he would just say 'So?' or 'Find me somebody who can do your job properly.' So he wrote an e-mail to the singer, belligerently spelling it all out in simple sentences more appropriate for a pre-school class. He sent the explanation and lit another cigarette while he waited for the call to come via Jill to announce that he was incompetent.

As he knew that the petulant star would then sneeringly enquire what Peter thought was a better idea, he called the *Today* office and said that if Ian was to appear on the show answering his critics, why didn't they invite on the programme one of those MPs who had called him a pervert?

His telephone rang and it was Jill again, now saying that Ian wanted assurances about doing the *Today* show.

'What assurances does he want?' asked Peter warily.

'He wants the interview taped and put on a five-second delay.'

'I've already organised that,' said Peter peevishly. 'What else does he want?'

'Nobody is to ask him for any autographs while he is at the BBC. He doesn't want to pose for any photographs with anybody. He wants a supply of hot, Turkish coffee in the Green Room and no other guests are to be allowed in there while he is using it, but he wants Billy, not you, to organise all of this with the Beeb, because he said that you won't do it properly because you'll think he's being unreasonable.'

'Anything else?'

'Err, yes. He wants you to get on to the fan clubs and organise fans to phone in to the BBC and protest against anything that is said against him. And by the way, he doesn't want the Archbishop of Canterbury talking against him now. You're to get *Today* to get on one of the MPs who had a go at him in the *Daily Mail*.'

'I've already done that too,' said Peter. 'Just as a matter of interest, why did he veto the Archbishop of Canterbury?'

'Ian thinks that he might be too clever.'

'Jesus fucking Christ!' said Peter. 'I dread to ask what else.'

'And he wants his slot on the programme to last for a guaranteed fifteen minutes.'

'I'm going back on heavy trank,' said Peter in disgust. There was a bleep in the earpiece of his telephone.

'Jill, I'd better go, I've got a call coming through. It's probably Billy.'

'Good luck,' said Jill, pityingly.

Peter could tell that Billy Vernon was very upset because when the manager began to speak he did so via a gymnastic manipulation of nose and throat which enabled him to both sniff and cough at almost the same time.

The sniffing signified that Vernon had just taken a stiffening snort of cocaine, the coughing betrayed his natural nervousness at the list of new problems *du jour* that Ian Taylor had given him.

'How the fuck am I meant to arrange any of this? Who is this

Rupert Rees? Whose fucking idea was this?' said Vernon, predictably.

Partly because he liked Vernon, and partly because he was relieved that it was Vernon, and not him, who had been passed the poisoned chalice, Peter calmed him down.

He explained that Rupert Rees, the right-wing Tory MP who had condemned Taylor in The Daily Mail, was already in the bag for the Today show. He gave Vernon the direct line of the programme and the name of the researcher who would forward Rees's details. He advised Vernon to speak to the same person about getting hooked up with Today's editor.

'Thanks,' sniffled Vernon, 'but what about getting Come to bloody Daddy played? I thought it had been banned. The BBC's not going to play a fucking porno record at eight in the morning.'

'You don't need them to,' said Peter calmly. 'We'll get Today just to play a snatch of it, get them to say it's an exclusive, first-ever listen on air, but then have them fade it out and say something like, 'Unfortunately we are not permitted to play any more of the song because of the controversy now raging again over its lyrics,' and that would cue up their intro to interviewing Ian.'

'But what if he starts ranting about wanting to hear the rest of it?' said Vernon nervously.

'He won't. Ian is far too well media-mannered to rant on air.'

'You reckon?' said Vernon, still unconvinced.

'Definitely,' Peter assured him, 'It makes sense. If Radio fucking 4 plays the whole song, where's the controversy about it? We need to maintain the controversy.'

Peter ended the call and lit a cigarette. He really did not want to have to get up early tomorrow morning and drive to London for three hours just to baby-sit Ian at the BBC for all of fifteen minutes. But he knew he had to because that was the job, it was just like being in the army but with longer hair.

He felt flat and he wanted a Scotch and a line of nose whisky but he had to be what he imagined was meant by 'professional'. So he let the phones keep ringing and went to see Catherine Hornby instead.

CHAPTER 26

After Jackson welcomed Susie back into the flat above his shop with a kiss that lacked tongue, she was further surprised to find him edgy and a little irritable.

'Anything the matter?' she said, smiling as she flopped down onto his sofa, the action billowing the long black skirt that she had chosen to wear because it would allow her to be easily accessed.

'Do you know Billy Vernon?' said Jackson, grumpily.

'Of course.'

'I've just had him on the phone. Ian's putting the band together and he wants me to do this Grey Rose gig.'

'Well, that's been on the radio. It was in the papers this morning. Pete's going mental trying to deal with the press on it.'

'Exactly,' said Jackson, crossly.

'I'm not with you.'

'It's been in the bloody papers and all over the TV news and only now, hours after the rest of the world has been told about it, does bloody Ian decide that it might be nice to tell the band about it.'

'Oh dear,' said Susie, forcing her smile. 'Well come and sit by me and I'll take your mind off it.'

'Yeah, yeah, in a minute,' said Jackson dismissively. 'Sorry, but I've got to think about this first.'

'What do you mean?'

'Billy's saying Ian wants to offer me a lot of bread…'

'That's good.'

'You don't understand…'

'Try me,' she said, keeping her patience.

'I don't want to play with Ian again. I hate all of that reunion shite.'

'So don't do it,' said Susie simply. 'Come over here and play with me instead.'

'But it's a lot of bread.'

'So take the money and do the gig. Do you need the money?'

'Anybody needs this sort of money.'

'So what's your problem?'

Jackson glared at her. It was a look that she had seen before, the same look that Peter pulled when he imagined he was talking to an idiot. She was surprised to see it on Jackson .

'My problem is that if I do the gig then people will say I'm selling out. I vowed never to work with him again after he broke up the band.'

'Which people will say you're selling out?'

'The press; well, the music press anyway.'

'Do they matter?'

'Of course they fucking matter! Hasn't that dickhead of a husband taught you anything?'

Susie stiffened; she had not expected this side of him. She had endured too much of this from Peter, that was why she was in Jackson's flat after all. But she did not react, because she was horny for him. So she tried to change the subject back to what she had been waiting for.

'Have you got your camera? Because I haven't got my knickers,' she smouldered.

'What?' said Jackson, preoccupied.

Susie hitched up her skirt to reveal her boots and stockings again. She began to open her legs.

'What are you doing?' said Jackson irritably.

'I thought…'

'Yeah. Well, please don't. The situation's changed. I need to think a bit first.'

'What do you mean, changed?' snapped Susie, embarrassed by his lack of interest and flaring at last.

'Sorry,' he said, not meaning it. 'But work comes first.'

Susie began to seethe. She couldn't believe it. Just like Pete, just like bloody everyone, here was yet another bloody man who wanted to put her in line behind the massively-important priority that was Ian Taylor.

'What did you say?' she asked evenly.

'What? Look, I've got to get back to Billy. Ian wants a decision, apparently.'

'Can't it wait for half an hour?' she pouted, pulling her skirt up a little more.

'What? No. He's waiting for me to call back or they're going to ask Clapton. Sorry, you're going to have to wait. I've got to sort this out.'

'Ohhh,' said Susie in a silly schoolgirl voice as she lay back on the sofa and revealed that she had not been fibbing about the knickers. He looked at her, looked at it, then lit a cigarette instead.

'Nice,' said Jackson, 'but if you want some more of the other night you're going to have to wait, luv. Although if you're desperate, there's a cucumber in the fridge.'

It wasn't the lewdness of his suggestion that enraged Susie, it was the 'luv' that infuriated her, the 'luv' with all of its rock and roll assumption that not only was it her place to wait but also that she would do so.

'Stick it up your arse!' she yelled as she flounced out of the flat, humiliated.

CHAPTER 27

One hundred yards further down the hill, Peter was waiting for Catherine to answer his knock at her door. When she did, she saw immediately that he was plainly very agitated. She leaned forward to kiss him on the lips but he turned his head so that her welcome just brushed his cheek.

'Oo, I can tell that someone's not going to be any fun today,' she pouted playfully.

'I'm not here for fun, Catherine,' said Peter grumpily as he followed her up the stairs and into her flat.

'Coffee?' she offered as he lit himself a cigarette.

'I haven't got time. Just tell me what you want.'

'You already know what I want. I told you on the phone.'

Peter looked at her incredulously.

'You said you wanted to see me.'

'That's right,' she smiled.

'And that's it?'

'What do you mean?' she asked, still smiling.

'I mean is that all that you wanted? Just to fucking see me? You don't have anything important to tell me, you just want to see me?'

'What's wrong with that?'

'Are you spectacularly stupid?' shouted Peter, lighting a cigarette.

'I don't understand. And please don't yell, Peter, you're not at work now.'

'You daft bitch!' he yelled. 'I'm always at work; I never do anything but bloody work. And just now I'm having the PR equivalent of Pearl fucking Harbour, a fact that should be obvious to the biggest of idiots. But you call me away from fire-fighting because you just want to fucking see me?'

'Yes,' she said, holding his glare but feigning alarm at his lack of control.

Peter dropped his cigarette onto the worn carpet and stubbed it out with the toe of his shoe. Catherine said nothing.

'You're a fucking nutter!' he spat.

'Please don't call me that, Peter. I just thought…'

'No,' Peter interrupted as all of his problems burst with his temper. 'No, you didn't think at all. You called me over here at a time when I shouldn't be leaving my desk even for a fucking piss, and it's just because you want to see me. Un-fucking-believable.'

'I thought you might want to see me, Peter,' she said calmly. 'I didn't realize it would be such a disruption for you.'

'Did I sound like I wanted to see you when you rang? Why the fuck would I want to see you, or fucking anybody, at the moment? Catherine, I'm not having fun here.'

'I thought…'

'What?' he yelled.

'After what we did… our chat on the beach… I thought… I thought I'd found a kindred spirit, that's all.'

'But I'm meant to be working, you insane moron! I'm meant to be doing my job, not popping in for fucking coffee with bloody soulmates or even fucking nutters. I don't do coffee. I don't do hello how are you? I'm not fucking interested in how anybody is.'

'But on the beach…'

'We fucked, luv. We just fucked. There's no bond between us, we just fucked. It means no more to me than blowing my fucking nose. I thought you were the sex addict. I thought you said fucking meant fuck all!'

Peter was so angry about everything. He could feel himself losing all professionalism and he did not care.

'What, nothing?' she whispered.

'Fuck. All. Ziltch. Nothing more than taking a piss. Jesus! No wonder you're so fucked-up by your dying fucking mother. You've inherited her stupidity. You think that because we shagged there's some form of fucking commitment involved. Like I owe you, like Ian owes you. You're owed fuck all. It was just a shag. Like your mother fucking Ian. Just a shag, not a basis for a bloody relationship.'

'But…'

'You know what? You say you're not but you're just like the other fucking fans. You think that the tiniest of communications with you is tantamount to a declaration of affection. You think that we fucking care what you think. We don't care. We don't care if you drop dead tomorrow. It doesn't matter a fuck to us; we just move on. That's what we do.'

'I thought you liked me…'

'Where did you get that idea from? Did I say I liked you? Did Ian tell your idiot mother that he liked her? Liking has got nothing to do with it. We don't have to like people we fuck.'

There was an urgent knocking at her door. A voice from outside it said, 'Catherine, it's Jenny from upstairs. Is everything alright?'

Peter opened the door that led onto the landing between the flats. A plump woman in her fifties was standing there, her mouth open in surprise.

'Fuck off, you nosy bitch!' he yelled and slammed the door on her.

'That was my neigh…' began Catherine, indignantly.

'I don't fucking care!' shouted Peter. 'I don't care if she's the fucking police. I don't care about anything to do with you! Fuck off out of my life. Fuck off out of Ian's life. You're like fucking flies, you lovefans; grasping, clinging, leeching, fucking losers.'

'Peter for Christ's sake, calm down! I'm sorry you're having a crap day; I'm sure it's vile but, look… OK, the truth is I need your help.'

'What sort of fucking help now?' he railed, lighting another cigarette.

'I need some money. My savings have nearly run out and I'm behind on the rent of this place. I only need a bit.'

'So get a bloody job'.

'Doing what, Pete? There are no jobs. C'mon, don't you think you owe me just a little?'

'Owe you? Owe you for what? That shag? Bloody hell, I didn't know you were charging for it!' he ranted.

'I'll pay you back. Look on it as an investment in my silence.

I'm sure that Susie…'

'Oh I get it,' he sneered. 'Back to your blackmail game, are we?'

'I'll go to the papers if this is your attitude,' she threatened, angry now. 'The photograph… they'll give me some money.'

'Fuck your fucking photograph. Shove it up your arse. Take it to the papers. Go on. See how far you get with your sentimental bullying. Go on, try it. We'll lock you up in so many injunctions, you'll die in court of old age.'

'I will.'

'Good! Then I look forward to wrecking your fucking life. I'm a PR, you twat; I spin things and smear people. I'll make you look such a money-grabbing whore that nobody will believe you. Who do you think the papers will side with, some whimpering little bastard tart on the make or a national fucking icon?'

'But I'm his daughter, you bastard. I really am.'

'Not unless it suits us, you're not,' snarled Peter and he walked out of the flat, glaring at the neighbour who was still standing shocked on the landing.

'Fuck you!' he heard Catherine spit behind him. As he walked down the stairs Peter realized that he had blown it all now.

CHAPTER 28

Peter returned to his car and began to drive north to Wiltshire. As he drove, he called Jill Brown and asked her to contact Taylor and tell him that his PR was en route to his home, where he needed to see him in private to discuss a very personal matter.

'I don't want to know,' said Jill when Peter had started to explain. 'Be aware that you may not get a very friendly reception, he said he only wanted to be disturbed today if it was vital. Billy's already annoyed him by insisting on a meeting for the new album artwork.'

'So Billy's there?' said Peter, glad there would be a witness to his showdown.

'He will be,' said Jill. 'But he – and now you – will have to wait until Ian's done his important business.'

'Which is what?'

'He's making a presentation of a special birthday gift to one of his gardeners who's twenty-one today.'

'He's doing what?'

'Don't ask,' sighed Jill. 'You'll see.'

Ninety minutes later Peter could tell that he was nearing Taylor's country home because the hedges of the winding lanes near Marlborough gave way to a nine-foot brick wall on which signs saying 'PRIVATE KEEP OUT' were mounted every fifty yards. Peter noticed that somebody had sprayed 'PONCE!' on one of them.

Rose Hall was a 30-bedroom mansion in the Vale of Pewsey that was originally built as a rural retreat for Charles II. The 800-acre estate included lakes, waterfalls, fountains, woods and huge rolling lawns. It was also equipped with indoor and outdoor pools, four tennis courts, a nine-hole golf course, stables for fifteen horses, a go-kart track, and a 500-seat amphitheatre that had been hacked into one of the chalk hills. Taylor had bought the stately pile in 1970 for £5 million and had since spent five times as much modernising it and installing security devices.

Taylor retained a full-time staff of 30 people to run the hall and the estate, including a 12-man security unit of former Marines. Like his staff at his London office, everybody was attractive and wore the grey uniform.

After Peter had presented his ID to a guard on the gatehouse that was manned by three men rumoured at the office to be illegally armed, he was waved on up the long gravel drive that was flanked by rose bushes. As he parked next to Billy Vernon's company BMW another guard came from the hall to escort him.

'The guv'nor is out on the lawn, doing this birthday thing,' said the guard, who was receiving instructions through a tiny earpiece.

'What is this birthday thing, Jack?'

'Do you know Sam, one of the gardeners?'

Peter shook his head.

'He's a bit of a pet of the guv's. Ian's having a special present flown in for him.'

'Flown in?'

'A chopper's bringing it. Any moment, actually. You're to watch and wait until the presentation's over.'

'What's the chopper delivering?'

'I'm not meant to say, but seeing as it's you, it's a bike.'

'A what?'

'A scrambler. Sam's into bikes. Ian's bought him a new Moto-X thing and he's having it delivered by chopper.'

'Bit elaborate, isn't it?' said Peter.

'That's nothing. The plan is for the chopper to sweep in low over the lawn with the bike hanging off it on a cable with a fucking great blue ribbon around it. Ian's organised it personally.'

Peter followed him around the side of the house and saw that, gathered on the lawn, resting after shooting clays were Taylor, Billy Vernon, Taylor's butler Morris and about a dozen very thin and very beautiful models with their musician partners. Everybody was drinking champagne and eating birthday cake served by two waitresses in preposterously short skirts.

Peter noted that Taylor had his arm around the shoulder of a tall Latin-looking young man in a checked shirt and tight jeans.

'Who's the cowboy?' said Peter.

'That's Sam,' said the guard.

'They're friendly,' Peter noted.

'You should see the CCTV tapes,' said the guard with a grin.

Suddenly a rocket, ignited by Morris, marooned into the air and exploded. Peter presumed that this was a signal for the helicopter and as he looked towards the tall trees that ringed the far end of the lawn a black Lynx came into sight. Peter looked for its supposed load but could see nothing hanging beneath it.

'Shit,' said the guard and he muttered, 'this is Jack, the bloody bike's missing,' into the microphone attached to his lapel.

Peter watched as the chopper swooped up the lawn and hovered near the birthday party, a steel hawser hanging from it but no motorcycle attached to its swaying end. The helicopter landed on the lawn and Peter saw Taylor walk purposely towards it. The pilot opened the door to his canopy and as the rotor blades slowed and then stopped Peter could hear Taylor yelling.

'Oops,' said Peter, smiling.

'Must have clipped the trees and got knocked off,' surmised the guard. 'We said that would happen, but the guv knew better.'

'Doesn't he always?' said Peter as he walked towards a worried-looking Billy Vernon.

'Trouble, Bill?' said Peter as they shook hands.

'You could say that. Glad I'm not that guy,' said Vernon, pointing to the pilot who was now waving his arms to defend himself from Taylor threatening him with a shotgun.

'It's not my fault,' Peter heard the pilot protest.

'What's going on, Morris?' said Peter as the grim-faced butler walked towards him.

'Ah, Mr Forth, sir, very good to see you again. It appears that we have suffered a calamity. Mr Taylor is somewhat displeased.'

'What's he doing with that gun?'

'I believe, sir, that he is encouraging the pilot to summon a replacement machine.'

'Is it loaded?' said Peter.

'Yes, sir,' said Morris.

Peter nodded to the butler and sauntered nearer to where Taylor was berating the unfortunate pilot.

'You keep saying it fell off, I can fucking see that. And I'm saying get another one!' Taylor was shouting.

'I'll have to go back to my base and tell my boss,' said the pilot.

'You're not fucking going anywhere, mate,' menaced Taylor. 'Phone your boss and tell him he's fucked up. Tell him I've got a fucking gun on you. Tell him I want another bike on another fucking chopper and tell him if I don't see it in an hour, you're all fucked.' Taylor noticed Peter and glared at him.

'What do you want?'

'I asked the office to ring you earlier. I need a word, in private. When you're free,' said Peter, smiling.

'Well according to this useless cunt, I've got at least an hour until anybody can pull their bloody finger out,' snarled Taylor. 'Hang on a minute, I've got to sort something. Morris!'

The butler was at his side immediately. Taylor took his arm and led him out of earshot of the helicopter pilot, who was frantically complaining into his mobile, 'I'm not joking; he's got a fucking gun. He's mad!'

'Take them to the pool and keep the champers coming,' Taylor was instructing the butler. 'Get the best charlie from the safe and give 'em a load of that. And rig up a film for them; show 'em that porn thing we shot of those models in Ibiza. They can enjoy themselves spotting their mates. And don't let any of the faggots monopolise Sam.'

As the butler led the guests away into the house, Taylor indicated that Peter and Vernon should follow him on a stroll down towards the lake.

'So what's so fucking private and special?' said Taylor .

'Umm… I believe Billy's mentioned a photo to you, a picture that was sent to the office in New York?' Peter began delicately.

'The knob and gob shot? Yeah. So what?'

So what? Oh God, thought Peter, he's going to be Captain

Bravado.

'Err… the person who sent the photo was threatening to go to the papers with it.'

'Good. Let him. I look forward to them trying to get a blowjob on the cover of the *Independent*. They could re-name themselves The Indebendent for the occasion,' said Taylor, chuckling bitterly.

'Umm… sorry but I thought you wanted this picture stopped,' said Peter, glancing at Vernon who looked away sheepishly.

'You mean Billy wants it stopped. Bad for my image. Go on.'

'Well, I've found the person who sent the picture,' said Peter, feeling deflated.

'And? What's he want? Money?'

'Err, no; not exactly.'

'Well what does he want? Exactly?'

'It's a girl. Well, a woman. She's called Catherine Hornby. Mid-thirties. Very pretty. She's a fan.'

'And? Get to the fucking point. Where is she?'

'In Lyme Regis at the moment, she's….'

'That's where you live, isn't it?'

'Yeah. Err… she's…'

'Why's she living there?' Taylor interrupted again.

'It's a long story,' Peter said unwisely.

'No. It's my long story. The story is about me, not you. I'm the one in the picture. I'm the one who's going to be in the papers. This isn't about your record sales. So fucking tell me what you know.'

Peter took a deep breath and looked to Vernon for support. Vernon looked away again.

'She's living in Lyme because she wanted to try get close to me in order to try get to you. Her mother took the photo and…'

'I know who took the picture,' Taylor revealed. 'I was fucking there, remember? The bird dared me to do it, you don't forget posing for a shot like that. She had great tits. So you're saying this is her daughter?'

'Yeah.'

'And where's she, the mother?'

'She's dead. She left Catherine the photo.'

'Oh, I see. Like a family fucking heirloom to flog when she got broke,' said Taylor, still sounding bitter. 'How much does this bird want for it?'

'Um... she doesn't.'

'What?'

'She doesn't want any money,' said Peter.

'What does she want, then?'

'She wants to meet you.'

'Jesus fucking Christ!' exploded Taylor. 'All this fucking fuss over a bloody meet and greet. Fuck me, what a palaver. You say she's pretty, what else do you know about her?'

'Umm... she's had a bit of a rough life, a lot of bad scenes with blokes. Possibly an alcoholic. She's smart. And funny. Very likeable, really. Articulate, dresses well, impish humour. She's...'

'How come you know she's impish? How close did you get to her?'

'Well, I didn't...' Peter began. 'I mean, I did, but she got close to me. She sort of tracked me down, came on to me.'

'Have you given her one?'

'Umm...'

'Well, fuck it, that's your problem,' dismissed Taylor. 'I haven't got time for this. OK, so she's got the photo, you know where she is, she wants to meet me for some reason and, I take it, in return she'll give us the pic. Yeah?'

'Yeah,' said Peter uncertainly, 'but...'

'But what?'

'She claims that she's your daughter.'

'You've shagged my daughter?' Taylor looked more furious than Peter had feared.

'You've shagged my fucking daughter? You? I don't fucking believe it! Who the fuck do you think you are? You've fucked my fucking daughter? My own kid? Fuck you, man!'

'It wasn't like that,' Peter protested, confused that Taylor was accepting his surprise fatherhood a bit bloody suddenly.

'Who the fuck do you think you are? I'm going mad. My own people tell me they've found me a daughter I didn't know I had and they've fucked her for good measure? My own fucking people? Fucking hell.'

'I didn't…'

'Didn't what? Didn't know? Didn't she tell you first? Or do you just shag people on sight and then find out who they are?'

'I didn't believe her!' Peter protested. 'I still don't. It's the old fan's trick; they never turn out to be who they claim they are.'

'So because of this overwhelming evidence of past statistics, which again I probably know a lot more about than you do, you decided to bone her just for what, good luck?

'Fucking hell! Not only do you know that shagging fans is forbidden, you decide that maybe she's not a fan, maybe she's Ian's daughter, so then you shag her. You're fucking incredible.'

'I was stoned,' Peter finally spat out.

'Oh. What a surprise. Well, that makes it all OK then. Tell me, did you think that blessing her with the attention of your fantastic knob was going to prevent her going to the papers? Was that some clever PR plan?'

'She wasn't just going to the papers with the photograph. She was also threatening to go to the papers with the story that's she's your kid. I was playing for time,' argued Peter, looking again at the shuffling Vernon.

'And you thought that shagging her would help a negotiation? You're a fucking idiot. How do you know that I don't want a kid? I might be delighted, as far as you know. I might have always wanted a kid. Still might.'

'Do you?' said Peter earnestly.

'It's none of your fucking business. Show me her picture.'

'Sorry?' said Peter woodenly.

'Her fucking photograph! Show me what she looks like. I want to see if there's a similarity, what she's like. Go on.'

'I haven't got a photograph,' said Peter, looking at the floor.

'What?'

'I didn't think to take her picture…'

'But you thought enough to fuck her, Jesus! OK, OK, calm down, Ian. Ommmm. Deep breath… Right, does either of you completely crap cunts know where she… what's she called again?'

'Catherine,' said Peter and Vernon simultaneously.

'Catherine,' said Taylor softly to himself. 'Cathy. Cath. Katy… Lovely name. OK, where is she now?'

Vernon looked at Peter as if they were playing pass the parcel and the music had stopped.

'Umm…' said Peter.

'If you tell me that you don't know or, I will personally shoot you in the balls and everybody here will testify that it was an accident,' threatened Taylor.

'Err….'

'So I advise you not to answer, not to say another fucking word and to get the fuck out of my sight. Find her and bring her to me. Now fuck off.'

CHAPTER 29

Billy Vernon watched Peter's car drive away down the long private lane that led back to the main road. Judging by the speed that it was moving, he could tell that Peter was furious and he expected to have to spend time later listening to him offer to resign. Vernon turned back to Taylor and was astonished to see his face wet with tears.

'Are you alright?' he said unhelpfully, instantly regretting the idiocy of his question. Taylor ignored him; he appeared to be attempting to catch his breath amid great gulps of grief.

'Here,' said Vernon as he offered Taylor a handkerchief. Taylor ignored it; instead his legs bent and he fell into a kneeling position on the lawn, sobbing, with his head bent onto his chest like a man in his last minutes before execution.

As he knelt there mewling, Vernon wondered whether this response was part of the 'dope rage' that Jill had told him she was worried about with Ian; the over-reactive histrionics that she claimed was a psychosis brought about by smoking too much marijuana.

Vernon thought he would have the lawyers look into the official medical status of this dope rage and have it included among all the other ailments which their insurers accepted as justifiable reasons for the sudden cancellation of Ian's commitments. He was startled from his machinations by an anguished whimper.

'A little girl…' Taylor wept. 'My little girl…'

'Well, yes; if she is your…'

'Don't you dare say that,' snapped Taylor without looking up. 'Don't. Just don't.'

'I just meant…'

'Sit down,' said Taylor. 'Sit by me. It's OK, it's only grass.'

Wondering whether he could claim the dry-cleaning on expenses, Vernon sat down uncomfortably. Taylor's hand found his and gripped it. Vernon recoiled as if he was about to be raped.

'Do you know why I'm upset?' sniffed Taylor thickly, ignoring Vernon's telling shudder and wiping his nose and eyes at last with the handkerchief.

'You have every right to be. Peter's behaviour is shocking; he's out of control,' said Vernon.

'It's got nothing to do with him. I'm crying with relief, mate. I've been so fucking lonely; you have no idea how fucking isolating this game can be. You can't share it around because people take advantage and nick more than they should. It's only blood that you know won't rip you off. And I've never had any blood before.'

'You're not alone, Ian. There's lots of us who are always here for you,' said Vernon gently.

'Would you still be if I didn't pay you?' replied Taylor succinctly. 'Would anybody like me if I wasn't so fucking rich?'

Vernon thought this was not the time to say, 'Pete would,' so he kept quiet and reflected on Taylor's life.

As everybody knew, he had been abandoned by his mother when he was only a few days old, left in a carrycot in the reception hall of Birmingham Children's Hospital. Taylor had never met either his mother or his father and had grown up as a street-fighting delinquent whom his many foster-parents had since described as a complicated kid who violently rejected all attempts at affection.

'You think I'm mad, don't you?' said Taylor suddenly.

'Of course not,' lied Vernon.

'Liar. Of course you think I'm mad. Everybody I know thinks I'm mad. I can see it in their eyes; they either avoid me as if I'm rabid, or they agree with anything I say in the same way as people talk to a retarded child. Pete's even told me I'm mad.'

'When did he say that?'

'One night, when we were out of it. He said that I had no comprehension of his reality.'

'The cheeky git…'

'It's alright,' sniffled Taylor, 'because he also said that there was no such thing as madness, there were only different degrees of normality. I've always remembered that.'

'What do you want to do about the girl?' said Vernon, thinking it wise to get off the questionable wisdom of Peter's take on normality.

'Her name is Katy…'

'You mean Catherine...' corrected Vernon before he could stop himself.

'I believe that a father gets to name his own child, Billy.'

'Of course. Sorry. Really, I'm sorry.'

'Find her, Billy. Find her and bring her to me. I need… what do I need? I need the anchorage of someone who doesn't want anything from me. I could trust somebody like that.'

'Of course,' said Vernon, who doubted that she would want nothing from him, and felt that the loose cannon of an honest opinion was the last thing he wanted Taylor to have.

CHAPTER 30

As Pete set off from home at four in the morning to meet Billy and Ian at the BBC, he was worried; Catherine had taken none of his calls and hadn't called him back, despite his many messages. She hadn't answered the door at her flat and had disappeared. For all Pete knew, she could be hidden away in a hotel, reciting her story to a reporter.

He steered the Volvo through a succession of shortcuts near Regent's Park and approached Broadcasting House from the north. He reflected that the only benefit of taking this run was that at least there were empty spaces by the parking meters, although he wasn't sure that he had enough change to pay the vast fee that the footpads at Westminster Council demanded.

He found a parking space opposite The Langham Hotel and inserted coin after coin into the meter until he had filled it up to the period of maximum stay. He retrieved the jacket of his black wool suit from the back seat and, as he walked to the BBC, he saw Billy Vernon smoking at the front door and chatting to two of Taylor's occasional security guards.

'Morning Jack. Don, Billy,' said Peter, nodding at the shivering trio. 'This is a bit fucking early, isn't it?'

'Have you spoken to her?' said Vernon curtly.

'I've left messages. She'll ring me back later. As I said, it's a bit early,' said Peter, evasively.

'Give me her number and I'll call her,' said Vernon.

'She told me she won't talk to you,' Peter lied. 'She thinks you'll get her sectioned.'

'I'll get you fucking sectioned if you don't sort this out.'

'Don't worry, it's fine,' Peter lied again. 'She'll call me when she gets up. Let's get this job out of the way first.'

Peter and the security men swapped banal small-talk as Vernon made a succession of calls on his mobile.

'Who are you calling this early? It's only just gone six.'

'Just checking again that the car's outside his house, we don't want any fuck-ups,' said Vernon gruffly.

'Why have you phoned them twice?'

'I haven't. That last call was to the back-up car. I've got it parked around the corner from his place in case the first one packs up.'

'That's not very likely with brand new Jags.'

'You never know,' said Vernon, who called again to check that the first driver had the mobile number of the second driver in case of 'an emergency'.

'What time's he on-air?' enquired Don Samson, a monolith of a shaven-headed black man.

'Just after the seven thirty news,' said Peter idly. 'He needs to be here by seven fifteen at the latest.'

'Which, of course, he won't be,' said Vernon sourly.

'What's the drill?' continued Samson.

'I'll call the producer in a minute and get him down with the passes...'

'I've got them,' said Vernon smugly. 'The little fucker didn't want to give us them this early but I told him this was Ian fucking Taylor you're dealing with, not some twatting politician.'

'You haven't upset him, have you?' said Peter.

'Course not,' lied Vernon. 'He took one look at Don and handed 'em over.'

Vernon handed Peter a BBC pass in a plastic sheath. The pass had the words 'Please Display Clearly' printed in red on it. Peter put the pass in his pocket; nobody was going to check his credentials when he was walking Ian Taylor into the building.

'Anyway,' said Peter, resuming his briefing of the guards. 'We get him up to the fifth floor...'

'Sixth,' said Vernon.

'We get him up to whatever floor, go to the Green Room, have a cup of coffee, and then they'll take him into the studio, meet the other guest...'

'Who's that?' said Samson.

'A Tory MP called Rees. He slagged off Ian in the papers but he'll be fine; he'll probably ask him for an autograph. They all do.'

'No autographs!' said Vernon.

'Billy! Shut up. He's a fucking MP, it's fine,' said Peter.

'Ian said no autographs,' said Vernon robotically. 'And we don't want anybody else in the Green Room when he's in there.'

'Can we just play it by ear?' said Peter reasonably.

'Your ear?' argued Vernon. 'I'm just telling you what he said.'

'How long will he be on air?' said Samson.

'He wants to do fifteen, but I suspect we'll only get ten. But that'll be enough,' said Peter.

'I told that cunt that we're to get fifteen or I'll fuck him,' said Vernon aggressively.

'What cunt?' said Peter, exasperated.

'That fucking faggot, your mate the producer. I told him fifteen or no fucking show. He's gone off to tell his editor.'

'Billy,' began Peter patiently. 'You've got to be careful with these guys. They judge Ian by how we behave; I don't want them thinking we're going in there like hard nuts because the interviewers will get wind of it.'

'So?' said Vernon sullenly.

'So they'll get their backs up and give Ian a hard time in the interview, and it'll all develop into a row and we'll get fucking told off!'

'The guy's a fucking faggot,' said Vernon. 'He wanted to know if Ian would sign some albums for 'Children in Need'. I told him he ain't signing nothing for nobody.'

'Great,' sighed Peter. 'That'll look good in the *Sun* – millionaire rock star snubs sick kids.'

'Just doing what I'm told,' replied Vernon obdurately.

They stood around bickering and smoking for another thirty minutes until they were interrupted by the arrival of a black Mercedes, which pulled up outside Broadcasting House. A grey-suited chauffeur stepped from the car and opened the rear door.

Out got a balding man of average height in his mid-fifties. Peter recognised the flushed, fat face of Rupert Rees and stepped forward to introduce himself.

'Mr Rees,' he said, extending his hand.

'Are you from the *Today* show?' said the MP curtly.

'No. I work for Ian Taylor. My name's Peter Forth. Ian is on his way. Do you need any help?'

Peter was waiting for a reply when he heard Vernon clearly mutter, 'You're a cunt,' behind him. The MP plainly heard it too and he turned to face his unknown assessor.

'I beg your pardon?' he said in an accent that had been honed at a lesser public school and which was, therefore, foolishly exaggerated.

'Let me take you in. Ah, there's Nigel, the producer,' diverted Peter as he saw the *Today* staffer emerging from the large brass and glass doors to the building. He took the MP by the elbow and gently encouraged him to walk away.

As Peter made the introductions to the harried producer, he heard Vernon say 'cunt', very loudly behind him.

Peter stiffened, not because Billy was playing up but because he knew that Ian had told him to play up. Mr Taylor was obviously coming with an agenda and Peter feared a backfire.

Having deposited the MP with the producer, Peter returned to the pavement and was just about to launch into a tirade of how it would be so much better if Billy did not upset everyone when he spied a large car approaching from Oxford Circus flashing its headlights.

'Here we go,' he instructed, immediately scanning the pavements for fans, photographers or anybody who would need to be shouldered out of the way.

'Where?' said Vernon .

'Down at the lights. The third car. It's him,' said Peter snapping out of his nonchalance. 'Billy, get inside, get onto the *Today* office and tell them to send down another producer or something.'

'Why?' said Vernon, confused.

'Our producer has just taken up that MP. I don't want Ian waiting in reception for him to return. Go get us another guide. Quick!'

Vernon left to relish what he most enjoyed, shouting at people for reasons that he didn't entirely understand, and Peter glanced around to check that Don and Jack had stepped back to ten feet either side of him, thus securing the pavement in the event of anybody running up to the car.

He smiled reassuringly at Samson and deliberately lit a cigarette. The large Jaguar suddenly lurched out of the north-travelling traffic and crossed the road at speed, pulling up within inches of Peter's feet, which he did not move at all. Casually, Peter opened the rear door and a dark-suited Ian Taylor sprang out and walked straight past him without a word or a glance.

'Hi guys,' said Taylor, overtly shaking hands with his security team. He turned to Peter, glaring at him.

'Have you found her?' said Taylor .

'I'm expecting her to call shortly, it's a bit early still,' said Peter, holding his eye.

'You're lying,' said Taylor, brushing past him.

'Hi Billy boy,' continued Taylor, hugging Vernon who had re-appeared with a confused-looking young woman that he had dragooned from the BBC reception desk in order to take them to the studio.

'Lead on, Bill,' said Taylor chirpily before glaring at Peter again. Flanked not only by his own security but also by three BBC stewards, who had now appeared wearing blazers and expressions of heightened alert, Taylor strutted across the foyer of Broadcasting House, Vernon leading the way towards the lifts and waving aside commissionaires' requests that Mr Taylor go through the metal detectors, please.

Peter walked in their wake, watching as Taylor, ever the charmer, threw his arm around the shoulder of the pretty blonde that Vernon had press-ganged from her receptionist duties.

'Sure,' he heard Taylor say to the blonde. 'For your mother? What's her name, luv?'

So much for the autographs ban thought Peter as he heard Taylor yell back, 'Oi, Forth! Give us a pen.'

The elevator arrived and Peter watched as Vernon's body

language dissuaded three BBC staff from entering it with them. Peter was appalled by this display of tribal arrogance that always happened whenever Taylor was in the company of people whose names he did not care to know. He followed the others into the lift, glaring at one of the BBC stewards who attempted to bar his entry until Samson intervened with a firm, 'He's alright.'

During the course of the ride through six floors, during which the elevator was stopped twice by others wanting to enter it and who were told, 'we're full' by the gruff Billy Vernon, Peter learnt that the receptionist was called Sally and that she had read all about 'your naughty rock show.' He also learnt that she giggled a great deal and, he noted, did not appear to mind when Taylor obviously brushed her breast with his hand as he autographed her BBC identity card.

'There's a good role going in my naughty show, actually,' said Taylor.

'Oo, I know,' she flirted. 'Do you think I should audition?'

As he was in the company of three BBC marshals, Taylor just grinned in reply. But Peter saw him nudge Vernon behind him and as the lift doors opened and Taylor got out, he heard Vernon say 'Err, Sally, what's your number? In case we need to check anything later?'

'See you then, Sal,' said Taylor as another posse, this one numbering seven producers, researchers and an editor, emerged to guide him all of the twelve feet into the entrance to the *Today* studios.

As gushing introductions were made by the BBC men and were immediately forgotten by Taylor, Peter darted around the back of the throng to confront the photographer that only he had spied in the corner of the corridor.

'Hello mate,' said Peter extending his hand. 'I'm his PR. You staff?'

The BBC photographer nodded.

'OK, listen. Let him get settled first and ask him before you do anything. Don't just snap anything off. And just take a few. It'll be fine,' he smiled.

'They want a shot of him and the presenters,' said the photographer.

'Sure. No problem. Let's just wait a bit. Don't worry, I'll get it for you.'

'We said no photographers,' said Vernon, looming up aggressively.

'It's fine, it's fine; there's not a problem,' soothed Peter.

'He said no fuc…' Vernon began belligerently, but a voice behind interrupted.

'Hello, old Forth's got the paparazzi 'ere already,' said Taylor. 'Fucking typical.'

Sensing the star's evident displeasure, the *Today* posse confronted the hapless photographer to shoo him away. But Peter stood in front of him, defensively.

'He's just a staff snapper, Ian' he said evenly, ignoring the BBC team and talking directly at Taylor. 'They just want a quick shot after the show.'

'Fine,' said Taylor, smiling but with eyes that were black with fury.

'OK mate,' he said to the photographer. 'We'll do it later. One shot, yeah?'

Taylor and his growing gang of sycophants moved in convoy to the Green Room as Vernon held back and then said to the cameraman, 'One fucking shot, alright? You take two and I'll break your camera.'

'Shut up Billy,' said Peter, hating every minute of this bullying.

Vernon was poised to argue when the sound of Taylor shouting his name sent him scuttling off to piss on another fire. Peter smiled apologetically at the photographer and then followed, wondering what in hell would upset Taylor next.

As he approached the Green Room he saw Taylor standing outside it and Vernon seething, 'Well get him fucking out of there,' at Nigel, their producer.

He glanced beyond the terrified producer and saw that Rupert Rees was sitting in the Green Room drinking coffee and oblivious to the row ensuing outside the door over the demand that Ian Taylor needed to have the room just for himself and his obsequious entourage.

'But he's a Member of Parliament,' squealed Nigel. 'There's nowhere else for him to go.'

Peter watched Taylor look at Vernon and then nod towards his security guards. He heard Vernon opine that the Right Honourable member could wait in the fucking toilet, we agreed no goldfish bowl. Before Vernon and Taylor could cause more upset, Peter pushed past them and entered the Green Room.

'Excuse me, Mr Rees,' he said. 'The BBC photographer would like to get a few pictures of you.'

As the Member gathered his things, Peter turned and winked at Nigel, who scampered off to instruct the cameraman to delay Mr Rees for as long as possible.

As Rupert Rees left and Ian Taylor entered – passing the MP with a 'Wotcha, mate,' that perfectly revealed he hadn't a clue who he was – another leggy young woman arrived and asked if Ian would like tea or coffee or anything.

'Turkish coffee,' snapped Vernon. 'You've already had an e-mail on that.'

'Umm, I'm not sure that we have any Turkish coffee,' said the production assistant.

'Well I'm fucking sure that you should have,' said Vernon, making the girl flush with embarrassment. She looked to Taylor for reassurance, but he ignored her.

'Excuse me, love,' said Peter, indicating she should leave the room with him, 'Sorry. Look, take this. It's what he wants.' Peter unzipped his shoulder bag and took out a thermos flask of Turkish coffee that he had made for this very contingency before leaving home.

'Don't say I gave it to you, take the credit yourself. Just pour it in a cup.'

As the production assistant walked away with what Peter noticed seemed to be a rather suggestive swish of her hips, he saw Nigel enter the corridor looking worried again.

'Problem?' said Peter.

'Sort of,' said Nigel. 'We're getting reports coming in from Kabul. There's been a massive car bomb. Reuters claim there's more than two hundred dead, including a lot of squaddies.'

'Shit,' said Peter.

At that moment Vernon emerged from the Green Room and approached the producer, glaring.

'Where's his fucking coffee?' he demanded. 'I fucking told you he wanted Turkish coffee, I confirmed it by e-mail last night. I bet fucking Sky would have Turkish coffee.'

'They probably would, Billy,' said Peter placidly. 'It's just their total lack of radio station status that made Sky a bit of a drawback when we chose to do a radio interview.'

'What's the matter?' said Vernon, seeing the furrow in Peter's forehead.

'There's a bit of a problem; a bomb's just gone off in Afghanistan killing people, including British soldiers.'

'So?'

'What do you mean, so? Nigel says there's two hundred dead; it's a fucking big bomb, and a lot of our guys are killed.'

'So?' said Vernon again and Peter wanted to punch him. 'That's the gig for squaddies; join the Army, see the world, die. What's it got to do with us?'

'*Today* is going to have to report on it, this is breaking news.'

'So?'

'What the fuck is the matter with you this morning?' said Peter angrily.

'I don't understand the problem. People get killed out there all the time.'

'Don't be a twat,' said Peter. 'Look at the time, it's coming up to Ian's slot. But if a fucking great bomb has just blown up a bunch of British servicemen then obviously the programme has to report on it.'

'So? They can do it in the seven thirty news, before Ian comes on. Ian Taylor is more important than some bomb going off,' said Vernon woodenly.

'No, Billy, he isn't! Ian is a pop star, what he does is put fluff into people's lives; he adds a little glitter. He does it well and he makes many lives more enjoyable. But he is not, and never has been, important in the wider scheme of things. Birth and death, Billy, that's important, selling records just isn't.'

'Do you want to tell him that?' challenged Vernon.

'Sure, but first I need to brief him about this bomb because if he's going live I don't want him sounding like some celebrity. Nigel, can you find out exactly what the situation is? How many dead? Which regiment are they from? I know we're here to sell records under the pretence of our peace banner, but if we're calling for peace we may as well know what the fuck it is that we are talking about. For a change.'

Peter pushed past Vernon and walked into the Green Room without knocking. Taylor was reading the *Independent* and did not look up. Peter noticed that somebody, presumably security, had disabled the speaker in the room so that nobody could listen to the show.

'I had them turn that racket off,' said Taylor seeing Peter looking at the silent speaker. 'Has she called?'

'Ian, there's a problem,' said Peter, using the four words that Taylor least liked to hear.

'Well don't tell me about it, then. Have you found the girl?'

'No, but I'm on it. She'll call me later. Look, a bomb, a big bomb, has gone off in Afghanistan, and apparently there are a lot of British soldiers dead.'

'So?'

Jesus fucking Christ!

'Two things; the programme has to report on this blast and that may cut into time we'd agreed for your interview. And, second, you nee…'

'Why the fuck should it cut into my time? Why don't they just report it after my interview? Cut into somebody else's interview. Why it is always me that gets the shitty deal? Fuck 'em. I'm staying on air for how long we agreed. How long was that?'

'Ten to fifteen minutes,' said Peter patiently. 'The thing is…'

'Who said ten minutes? I never said ten minutes! I want fifteen fucking minutes. Fuck them, man! Fuck you. I've got up at some ungodly fucking hour to do this fucking show for you…'

For me?

'I don't fucking need this shit! You fucking tell them they agreed fifteen! I don't give a fuck about some bomb! There's always fucking bombs going off out there, that's not fucking news! A bomb in Afghanistan is like finding sand in the desert! Fuck 'em!'

'But…'

'You tell them I'm doing fifteen fucking minutes or I'm not doing the show! Who the fuck do they think they are? Fucking thousands more listeners are tuning in 'cos they know I'm on the show. They don't want to hear about fucking bombs! Fucking sort it out.'

Peter briefly considered relaying this verbatim to the editor of the programme but, as he judged that such a communication might be broadcast, expletives deleted, as an on-air explanation for a change to Taylor's advertised appearance he clung to his training of nannying the star.

'Ian, look,' he said with a firm tone that did not betray his fear. 'You are going on this programme to talk about peace…'

'No, I'm not. I'm talking about the show at Westminster Abbey.'

'Sure, but we've pitched it that you are doing this show in order to make a call for peace. That's what the Rose is known for, as a great peace album. If Christ knows how many have just been killed in Kabul then people listening are going to be more sympathetic to your call for peace. This plays into your hands. Use this disaster, go on air and sympathise with the families; don't get heated, just be calm and use this as an example of why you're saying we should try for peace.'

'You know, man,' said Taylor in the controlled voice that he used whenever he was about to become his most threatening, 'I'm really not impressed by the way that you lecture me. I mean, who the fuck do you think you are these days? Fuck you, man. Don't fucking tell me how to think!'

'Jesus, all I am saying is….'

'Fuck off! Get Billy in here. You're fucking fired!'

You Brummie twat, thought Peter as he opened the door and stepped out. He saw Vernon talking to the girl with the Turkish coffee and heard him enthuse at her apparent efficiency.

'Excuse me,' he interrupted. 'Bill, can I have a word?'

They walked away from the woman, who winked at Peter and then walked to the Green Room bearing the coffee.

'What is it?' said Vernon. 'You've gone white.'

'I've been fired, apparently. He wants to commit idiocide on air.' Vernon was prevented from asking what? by the bellow of Billy!' that came from Taylor at the end of the corridor. Peter watched as the flustered manager dashed to the Green Room, dropping his mobile and then his cup of coffee and, in his increasing panic, his mobile again as he hastened to Taylor who was standing in the doorway glaring.

'What's going on?' said Nigel, who had reappeared holding a sheaf of press agency reports on the bombing in Iraq .

'I've been fired,' said Peter evenly. He smiled because with the realisation of his sacking came a unreal feeling of release. His decree absolute had come though and no more would he have to worry about wearing the wrong kind of expression.

'What? Why?' said Nigel, panicking.

'For questioning the divine right of queens,' said Peter with an angrily-deliberate lack of caution.

'What?'

'The Brain of Britain in the Green Room does not agree that his epoch-shaking appearance on your programme should be overshadowed by the marginal matter of an international military disaster.'

'What?'

'He's refusing to have his interview cut. Either he does it for the full fifteen minutes that only *he* appears to be aware of agreeing, or he's out of here in some monstrous strop.'

'But why have you been fired?' said Nigel as he worried about how to explain to his editor that the big guest was unavailable due to a temper tantrum.

'Fuck that, what's the score in Kabul?'

'It's bad. A huge explosion in an army base. It looks like a few of the police swapped sides and blew themselves to Allah and took anything up to two hundred along with them for the trip…'

'Any British dead?'

'Reuters reckon at least a dozen. The earlier reports got confused; they said it was a British base that was blown up, but it seems it was Afghan cops who were kipping in the base, most of the Brits were out on manoeuvres.'

'That's lucky,' said Peter.

'Not if you're the wife of an Afghan policeman,' said the producer.

'Nor if you are the ex-publicist of a very bad tempered rock star whom you have just informed about the arrival of Armageddon.'

'Well, it's not quite a bunch of laughs,' said Nigel. 'Apparently there was a big briefing going on for journalists at the time. It sounds like the blast took out some of the foreign press corps…'

'How many?'

'It's sketchy but it seems that at least seventeen hacks are dead or wounded,' said Nigel, consulting the wire reports. 'We're rescheduling the programme. They're trying to get the deputy prime minister to a radio car. We can't raise our correspondents out there, nobody knows if they're OK or not….'

Peter looked at his watch, the time was approaching seven thirty. 'Do you want to tell Ian to forget it?' he said. 'Scrap the interview, in the circumstances?'

'You'd think so, wouldn't you? But my mob reckons that this latest atrocity actually gives more of a platform to his peace gig…'

'Thought they might.'

'As I said, we're rescheduling. They want him to hang on until after the eight o'clock news and then do his chat.'

'But he's a fucking pop star, his views aren't relevant at a time like this. They certainly won't be informed,' Peter protested.

'I know. But somebody high up has got it into his head that your man is the voice of the ordinary people…'

'Bollocks. He doesn't know any ordinary people.'

'Well, there's also…'

'What?'

'Word has come down from the chairman's office. Apparently your man and our boss are sort of mates and the chairman wants the BBC to get the broadcast rights for your guy's gig.'

'So?' said Peter. 'The Beeb will just have to bid along with everyone else and Ian will sell to the highest bidder.'

'Umm. Yeah. But the thing is that the chairman is planning to pop in and say hello to him in the studio. That's why that snapper was told to hang around. Apparently the chairman wants to invite Ian to his garden party next week, so he can bend his ear there about the gig.'

'Doesn't anybody have any fucking decency around here?' said Peter in astonishment. 'Is the entire world self-serving?'

'C'mon, Pete,' said the producer calmingly. 'Your guy is a big name, having him on our programme or screening his gig on 'One' is good for our ratings. Even public broadcasters have to be popular these days.'

'And what about your listeners who want to hear about the poor buggers in Kabul?'

'There will be other bombs for other bulletins, but there may not be another opportunity for us to talk to Ian Taylor,' said the producer, sighing. 'Fortunately, it looks as though the vast majority of the media dead aren't British.'

'So therefore they don't matter,' said Peter grimly.

They were interrupted by shouting from the Green Room. Peter stood his ground as Vernon marched up, flushed and wild-eyed.

'What are you still doing here?' he demanded. 'And why haven't we been moved to the studio yet? It's gone 7.30. Are we doing this fucking interview or not?'

'Umm... well, because of the explosion...' said Nigel.

'Which has only killed two hundred people...' said Peter.

'...the editor would like to move Ian to...' said Nigel.

'We're not fucking moving anywhere!' snarled Vernon.

'Good call,' said Peter.

'The editor would like to move Ian up to the 8.10 spot,' offered Nigel.

‘That means the big slot,’ said Peter, enjoying this.

‘Fuck off!’ said Vernon.

‘Is that fuck off to the move or fuck off to me interpreting?’ said Peter.

‘I’ll have to ask Ian,’ glared Vernon.

‘You surprise us,’ said Peter as Vernon walked back to the Green Room.

‘Will he do it?’ asked Nigel nervously.

‘Yeah, but he’ll be cross.’

‘Why?’

‘Because he will have presumed that he was already getting the top slot. He can’t bear to think that you might have anybody more important on your show. Who was doing the 8.10?’

‘The Home Secretary.’

‘There you are, then – how many hit albums has he had?’

Peter and the producer kept their eyes on the door of the Green Room. After less than a minute, it opened again and Vernon backed out of the room saying, ‘Yes… of course, boss… absolutely… no, no, I’ve got it… yeah… really good idea, boss.’

‘Oops,’ said Peter.

‘What’s the matter?’ said Nigel.

‘Ian’s had a good idea. That’s going to fuck things up for you.’

They waited for Vernon to address them, which he did after pausing to shout at his least-favourite production assistant to get some more of your shite coffee in that room.

‘Right,’ said Vernon. ‘I’m under instructions only to ask you this once. Do you want your job back?’

‘No,’ said Peter.

‘Are you sure?’

‘That’s twice,’ said Peter.

‘Then you are to leave this building immediately,’ recited Vernon.

‘Piss off,’ said Peter.

‘What?’

‘This is the BBC, Billy. Therefore I presume that Ian does not own it. Tell him I said to fuck off.’

'Hmph,' said Vernon, turning to the producer. 'Right, you…'

'Nigel,' supplied Peter.

'Whatever. You are to take us to a studio now!'

'But they don't need you yet,' said Nigel.

'We don't care if you need us or not. We're taking over a studio. We're staging a sit-in for peace. And if you try to stop us our peaceful security will break your fucking arms.'

'Really good idea,' said Peter. 'Pulitzer-winning PR.'

As the producer walked off towards the Green Room, Peter went back to the elevator. He took it down one floor, where he calculated he could make a call in the corridor without Vernon intervening. Although it was early, he knew that Mike Stone would answer.

'If you're calling to remind me to listen to the bloody radio, I'm already monitoring it,' said the Press Association man.

'I'm sure you are, Michael,' said Peter. 'Listen, get one of your snappers up to Broadcasting House and have the desk send another reporter to doorstep the front entrance…'

'Why?'

'I can't really talk. I'll fill you in later, but world war fucking three has broken out up here. I've been sacked…'

'What?'

'Never mind; Ian has completely fucking lost it and he's occupying the *Today* studio, tooled up with three heavies, as some sort of bizarre sit-in protest for peace…'

'Is he smoking crack?'

'There's more. I'll give you all the details later, but get some of your guys up here – and you probably ought to tip off PA Broadcasting, have them send a TV crew. This is going to get big.'

'It sounds it…'

'Yeah, but it's not over yet. I reckon he's planning to seize the chairman of the BBC as a fucking hostage.'

Peter knew that this last claim was somewhat wild, but he calculated that as the chairman was planning a surprise visit and that by then his VIP guest would have surprisingly taken forced possession of a studio, then anything could be perceived to be the truth in the confusion.

Of course, it would get all cleared up and explained away later, but it was the first impressions that mattered most with publicity and if Peter was getting out of the game, he planned to get out chaotically.

Ian Taylor wanted attention? Fine, then watch this, luv. Even in his dismissal, Peter could not resist making a drama out of it. He took the stairs back to the sixth floor and saw that the corridor was empty; Peter presumed everyone was already barricaded up in their studio sit-in, threatening the authorities with good vibes, man.

He checked his watch again. Taylor's address to the nation would be soon. The corridor was still relatively empty, only a security guard on sentry at the studio door and the coffee girl on another run. The fact that neither senior BBC management, nor a cavalry of security reinforcements had yet arrived indicated to Peter that Ian had not yet announced that he was seizing the studio for his petulant protest. He darted back to the Green Room and reconnected the speaker. He turned up the volume and listened as the second – and least obscene – verse of 'Come to Daddy' aired.

You look much older now the lights have gone dim
In boots and mini with that black leather trim
But are you ready
To be loving my sin?
Come with Daddy

'And there you have it,' said the presenter, James North. 'A world exclusive. And for those of you not entirely familiar with the sounds of the sixties, that was 'Come to, *err* Daddy', a rather controversial song from the universally-acclaimed record by, err, Taylspin, err… Grey Rose, which has never been permitted to be played on radio before. As you may have read, this album, which was first released in 1968, is shortly to be re-issued by the founder member of Taylspin, the British rock legend Ian Taylor. And I'm delighted to say that Ian Taylor is here with us in the studio today. Ian, welcome…'

'Hi, man. Cool.'

‘Yes, err… quite. Now, you are, as I say, re-releasing Grey Rose in order to make a peace protest against the war in Afghanistan and, in particular, against the American involvement in that conflict. But in conjunction with this, you are staging the first live performance of Grey Rose and reports claim that you are seeking to do this inside Westminster Abbey…

‘But there has been some controversy, has there not, surrounding the err… mounting of this concert because, and I am convinced that you will correct me here if I get this wrong, as I understand it your plan is to enact the err… content of the songs and that has upset some people, principally our other guest, Rupert Rees, the Tory MP for Solihull, because one of these songs, in fact the one that we have just heard there, depicts sexual acts between a young woman and a rock star. Am I right?

‘Yer, s’right,’ said Taylor gutturally.

‘Yes, err, quite. Now, I put it to you that this entire venture is simply a publicity stunt, as some have been saying, designed to cause a stir among the media and therefore…’

‘Get me on programmes like this one,’ Taylor interjected.

‘Yes, quite. Well, you’ve obviously got a good publicist. But what…’

‘I’ve just fired him, actually. He’s crap,’ said Taylor.

‘Right. Well, what I must put to you is… why are you doing this concert for the first time in forty years and is all of this sex stuff just a stunt?’

‘Course it is,’ said Taylor.

‘Sorry?’ said North, sounding confused.

‘Of course it’s a stunt. It’s a very cunning stunt…’

‘Well, quite, but…’ blustered North, as the programme editor said in his earpiece that he didn’t like the way this was going.

‘It’s all to get headlines, innit?’ continued Taylor whom, Peter noted, had lurched into his faked man out of it accent that he adopted whenever he felt truly truculent.

‘Look,’ said Taylor, ‘if I just say I’m re-releasing the Rose and I’m going to do it at a gig for the first time, then I might get a few lines about it in *Bizarre* or the *NME*, but you aren’t gonna ’ave me on the *Today* show like this, in like the top slot and stuff. But if I say I'm gonna get on stage and shag some bird…'

'Well, exactly,' said North, interrupting swiftly. 'So, can I get this clear? You are actually intending to do this… err, you do mean to… umm actually have sex, live on stage?'

'Yeah,' said Taylor.

'Well, now Rupert Rees, err… you have a view about this sort of thing, do you not?'

'I 'aven't finished yet.'

Uh-oh, thought Peter, here we go…

'Umm, err… well you'll have plenty of time to explain yourself in a moment. If you would, I just want to bring in Rupert Rees, MP for…'

'I 'aven't friggin' finished.'

Peter burst out laughing. Evidently five seconds did not provide the *Today* team with sufficient delay in which to determine whether frigging was an obscenity. Peter imagined that dozens of listeners were phoning to put them right about that as Ian spoke.

'What I was gonna say was,' Taylor menaced, 'is that the only reason why I am trying to draw attention to this gig, with this sex angle and all that, is because there is a bigger angle to it all. I'm doing this gig to make a stand for the many millions of people who believe that war is wrong. We think America is just as guilty now as it was in Vietnam in the sixties. Like millions of others, I want peace in Afghanistan. Now, people say I'm being obscene planning to shag some bint but my point is, I'm doing this in order to push the fact that what is more obscene is all of the killing that's going on in this war.'

'Right. OK. Fine. Now you've had your say and we'll return to you in a moment, but Rupert Rees, what do you say to this? Is sex more obscene than shooting? Isn't it better to make love, as they used to say, not war?'

'Good morning Jim,' said the MP unctuously. 'Now where I, and I believe where the vast majority of right-thinking listeners also stand on this, is that it is all very well wanting peace, and we all want that, but there are ways and means of going about it. 'My honourable friend the Foreign Secretary, along with our American colleagues, is working very hard behind the scenes to try to effect a truce in the hostilities so that all sides can sit down and discuss a plan for Afghanistan that is satisfactory to all. It does not help this process when somebody like a rock star who, if I may say, strikes me as rather amateur in these matters, intervenes with some crackpot stunt that serves only to enflame tempers and cloud the position.'

'Quite. But I also understood that you had expressed outrage at the sexual aspect of Mr Taylor's production. I believe you called him, did you not, the umm… biggest pervert in pop?' said North.

'Well, I mean, it's a bit off isn't it?' began the MP. 'It's one thing wanting peace, and we all want that, but is there any real need for this sort of thing as a way to achieve it? I mean, yes, I believe it is perverted to organise a display of sexual activity for paying entertainment. I think that's wrong and I believe most of your listeners would agree with me.'

'I agree with you,' said Taylor.

'What?' said North and Rees together.

'I agree with you. I think it's very wrong to deliberately stage some form of sex show just for entertainment. I don't think that's particularly clever or admirable. I don't think it's art either. That's just bollocks. It's just shagging…'

'Err… thank you,' said North quickly. 'If we could just contain the language, I know this is a very passionate debate but…'

'But it is,' Taylor continued. 'Of course we artists say it's art, that's the only way we can disguise the real truth, which is that we know what you want, and you want filth. People are generally pretty disgusting. But if we both pretend that it's art by dressing it up, then neither of us feels guilty about enjoying it. But my point is still that staging Grey Rose in this way is not for entertainment, the actual reason why I'm doing it is to shock the widest possible audience into paying more attention to the main issue – which is that war is wrong and peace is right.'

'Well, he has a point there, Rupert Rees, does he not? Does the end, which in this case is the hoped-for peace, justify this means?'

said North.

'Well, that's a difficult concept that philosophers have argued over for centuries,' dodged the MP. 'But what I think is unjustifiable is Mr Taylor's proposal to present rock and roll as *Oh! Calcutta!* within the hallowed walls of Westminster Abbey.'

'What's wrong with that?' said Taylor.

'Well, it's downright pornographic isn't it? It's a place of holy worship.'

'Yeah, a place of holy worship for a religious order, namely the Church of England, which was formed on the beliefs of Jesus Christ whom, I think you'll find, said sweet F-A about anything being good about war,' said Taylor. 'Your problem is that you've got your head so far up America's arse that you lot are all terrified that people will actually agree with me.'

'There's no need to be insulting,' sniffed Rees.

'There's every bloody need to be insulting. Or shocking. Or bloody anything that will get attention to the fact that you and your government refuse to accept, which is that most people in this country and on the planet do not want war. A bloody child of five could tell you that. I'm not being obscene, you're being obscene for mounting any argument in defence of the needless death of thousands of people.'

'The world situation is far more complicated than that,' replied Rees cuttingly.

'No. Rupert, it's not!' said Taylor and Peter felt proud of his boss's stance, then immediately saddened when he remembered he was not his boss anymore. 'It's very bloody simple, bring the troops home. Stop killing people and they will stop trying to kill you. It's easy!'

'What about the tomb of the unknown soldier?' said Rees, seizing on a new target.

'What about it?' said Taylor.

'Well, don't you feel that your disgusting production in the Abbey will in some way defile the grave of this brave man who died for his country?'

'How do you know that?' Taylor began angrily. 'He's the

unknown soldier, nobody knows anything about him. We don't even know his bloody name! How do you know that he was anti-sex? How do you know he was brave? Who said he died for this country? How do you know he didn't die in abject bloody terror, Rupert, just like how most people die in war, frightened and wishing they were at home? That's obscene, mate, never mind me and my little sex show, you're the bloody pervert to try to press-gang a dead man to your dirty little political cause.'

'Right. OK. Well I'm afraid we're going to have to wrap it up there,' North butted in quickly. 'I'm sure many of you listening will have your own views on the matter and, of course, you can send them to us here at the usual address and we'll be reading your letters on Fri…'

'I'm not going anywhere, mate,' Peter heard Taylor say.

It was generally agreed later by most of those who heard what happened next, that it made their otherwise tedious day. Listening in the Green Room, Peter was especially impressed by Ian Taylor's deft publicity skill and he felt envious, wishing that he was still involved.

'Umm, err, sorry? What do you mean?' Peter heard James North say.

'I'm not going anywhere. Neither are you, Rupert. We're staying here. I'm staging a sit-in, in protest against the war,' said Taylor .

'Umm, err…' said North.

'Right,' cut in his co-presenter Sarah Beaulieu swiftly. 'Now… umm, as we heard earlier this morning… err… teachers' unions are threatening a strike after the latest round of pay talks broke down last night. Earlier today I spoke to union leader Max…'

Both Beaulieu and North heard their programme editor yell, 'Fuck the teachers!' in their earpieces, 'drop the fucking teacher segment, stick with this; Sarah give it back to Jim!'

Peter heard Sarah Beaulieu suddenly halt her introduction of the next scheduled item, and there was the sound of a rustling of paper, microphones banging and voices shouting, 'Get off me, get off!' and 'Fucking sit down and shut it, you!' before North's voice cut in again.

'Right… well, umm… now here's a strange thing. If you've just joined us let me tell you that I'm here with the rock star and umm… peace protestor Ian Taylor and the Conservative MP Rupert Rees. We've been discussing, umm… Mr Taylor's controversial plan to stage a concert in Westminster Abbey as a… umm… protest against the war… and he has defended his decision to include umm… live sex scenes in this concert because, as I understand you, you're saying you… err… want to create a controversy in order to draw attention to… your stand against the war.'

'Everyone's stand against the war, yeah,' said Taylor.

'Right… umm… but now… now you're saying what exactly?'

'I'm saying that if the only way to draw people's attention to the need to end this war is by kicking up a fuss, then I'm going to stay here, in this studio, live on your show, and we're mounting a sit-in, right here, right now and we're not moving until somebody at the BBC backs us and shows some commitment to the peace movement.'

'Fine… and umm… by we you mean yourself and the three gentlemen with you, whom I take to be bodyguards…' said North.

'Yeah.'

'And I suppose ourselves, Sarah Beaulieu and me…'

'Yeah.'

'And… umm… Mr Rees too, I presume.'

'I am not part of this preposterous outra…' began the MP.

'Bloody shut up!' said Taylor.

'Umm,' began North again. 'Mr Taylor… is Mr Rees free to go?'

'No, Mr Rees is not.'

'Why not?'

'He's our hostage.'

'This is outrageous!' bellowed the MP.

'Are you prepared to prevent him from leaving?' said North.

'I'm not. But these guys behind me are,' said Taylor.

In the control room, separated from the studio by thick soundproofed glass, the *Today* editor was shouting into a telephone at the Radio 4 publicity officer, instructing him to alert the BBC newsroom at Television Centre and to get a TV crew sent up to the studio, bloody fast. On another phone, his deputy was calling the office of the BBC chairman to warn his staff that an incident might interfere with his plan to arrive imminently for a photo-op with Ian Taylor.

'No, nobody's hurt. Well, not yet,' said the deputy editor. 'We just think that the chairman should know that his photograph might well not happen… What? Yes, of course we're alerting the police.'

'So,' said James North, 'it appears that we are still live on air and so, gentlemen, I would ask you that whatever you say in what is now umm… a rather… err, heated situation is said with the listeners in mind.'

'You mean no swearing,' said Taylor.

'Quite,' said North, who heard the editor say this is priceless in his earpiece.

'I'll tell you what I'd like to say,' continued Taylor. 'I'd like to ask the honourable member here to tell me what the words are that one should use today to comfort the mothers and wives and children of the, how many is it – twelve soldiers, and the journalists, who have been killed by today's bomb?'

'Possibly seventeen or eighteen dead,' supplied North.

'OK, so, Rupert, why don't you tell the nation what it is that one should say to families of the maybe thirty British men and women who got killed today in the war that you and your pals started? What do we say, Rupe? C'mon, you're a politician, what's the politically right thing to say to the woman who will never see her husband again? C'mon, tell us the secret of how to make it better for a kid who has just learnt that his father has been blown into little bits?'

'Way to go, Ian,' thought Peter.

Rupert Rees just glared at Ian Taylor.

'Mr Rees?' urged North.

'Ladies and gentlemen of the audience,' said Taylor. 'The honourable member from Solihull, from my old neck of the woods, is just sitting here glaring at me. Were it not for the fact that I have with me three very large men, ladies and gentlemen, I would guess from the furious expression on Mr Rees's rather red face that he would like to punch me very hard…'

'You won't get away with this, Taylor,' spat the MP. 'We know your kind. This is not the way that a civilised democracy settles things, you know.'

'We all know how civilised democracies settle things, Rupe. They're so civilised that they settle whatever they want by marching into any place they fancy and blasting everyone to hell simply because we civilised nations don't like countries that have got more oil than us. We stamp our feet and bomb the shit out of them. That's our civilised response, isn't it?'

'I must ask you to watch your language,' said North.

'Sorry,' said Taylor, meaning it.

'It is obviously a tragedy that people have… err… lost their lives, nobody is denying that,' said the MP, gathering himself. 'I express my profound condolences to their families. But, sadly, there are always casualties in war and, although Mr Taylor would like nothing better than to intimidate me into saying I know not what, what I can say is that the families of these… err… casualties can draw comfort from the fact that their loved ones died defending democratic freedoms.'

'Fuck off, you complete twat,' said Taylor .

'Mr Taylor! Please!' yelled North.

'Oh, come on, Jim,' continued Taylor 'He's talking like a fucking idiot!'

'Mr Taylor! Mr Taylor! Must I remind you that we are live on the radio. If you continue to use such profanity my editor will take us off the air.'

'No he won't,' said Taylor evenly. 'This is huge for your ratings. This is going to make your show the talking point of the week. But, ah, sorry; I'm just saying what I believe most of your listeners actually think.'

'So, what would *you* say to the families and loved ones of these men who have died so honourably for their country, then?' challenged Rupert Rees, mistakenly.

There was silence for some moments and in the Green Room Peter thought that BBC management had ordered the programme to be taken off the air. Peter opened the door and looked out. The corridor was full of security guards, police, camera crews and a lot of worried-looking men in grey suits. He was tugged back into the room by the sound of Ian Taylor's voice, sounding gentle now.

'…God, what would I say? I would say… that some wars might be right to fight but this is not one of them and I would say, I would vow… I will vow that in honour of these men and women and all those who have tragically died in this war before them, I promise that I will do everything that I can to try bring this evil, misguided conflict to an end...'

Taylor was almost whispering now.

'John Lennon helped to bring the Vietnam War to an end when a million people marched on the White House singing 'Give Peace a Chance'. I say to you all now… here… that together we can do that again… I'm sorry for your loss… let those of us lucky enough not to have suffered loss, now act to ensure that this shitty little war will end.'

There was silence again. In the studio Billy Vernon and Taylor's bodyguards looked at the floor. James North was made speechless by the moment. The silence continued until Rupert Rees spoke.

'Clever words,' he said spitefully, 'but adding up to nothing.'

The next sound that Peter and the rest of the radio audience heard was a sharp smack followed by a loud yelp and a thump as if a considerable weight had hit the floor. And then the broadcast went dead as the editor, having watched in horror as Ian Taylor punched Rupert Rees hard in the face, ordered that the plug to be pulled.

Billy Vernon was the first to act, punching numbers into his mobile he called Taylor's lawyer.

'Conrad? It's Billy. Yeah… yeah… I'm with him. I know… Yeah… he just hit him… Yeah… out cold. Get up here now.'

Peter stepped back out into the corridor, emerging at the same time as Martin Leslie, Chairman of the Governors of the BBC, stepped out of the lift flanked by aides, one of whom was carrying a small radio.

'What precisely is the situation now?' asked Leslie, directing his question at anybody who could answer.

Police, security guards, managers, production assistants and a television reporter all began to gabble at once. Sounds like someone's been hit, Peter heard above the excited cacophony. The chairman raised his hand and the throng fell quiet.

'You,' he said, pointing at Peter. 'Do you work for Taylor?' Peter felt that this was not the time to argue details and so he nodded.

The chairman walked towards him, waving the entourage back.

'Tell me, what does Ian want?'

'He wants to be taken seriously in his stand against the war,' said Peter.

'Evidently,' said the chairman. 'I was just listening to him. Quite an orator is Mr Taylor.'

'He really needs to make a big noise with this concert,' said Peter. 'The sex thing isn't the issue, that's just a stunt. Ian needs the biggest audience he can get. That way he actually might change things. If he can reach people, he can make a difference. You know what he's like.'

'I do indeed. Tell me, what sized audience is Ian looking for?'

'Global. Millions. He needs a telecast. He needs the BBC behind him, not just some edited highlight on 'Two', he'll want all-channel support. It's not about the Rose, it's not about Ian anymore. Now he's making it about ending the war.'

'Yes, well he made that perfectly clear,' said the chairman. 'Look, apparently we lost three good men in the explosion today, bloody good journalists all of them. Excuse my Greek but fuck this bloody Government. Now it's personal and, besides, I think Ian's right, I think the nation has had enough of this war.'

'Are you going to get behind him, then?' said Peter.

'I think that might be a popular move with the licence fee payers. Of course, this bunch of bloody barrow boys in government will probably crucify us for it when it comes to renewing the terms of our charter but, bugger it, maybe if we make enough noise the elected might actually listen to their electorate…'

'Err…'

'No, I doubt it too,' said the chairman, 'but at least we can try.

Your man's had rather a stirring effect upon a few of us this morning. Let's give it a go. The only problem is, how do we tell him when he's boarded up like Butch Cassidy in there?'

'Just go in and tell him,' said Peter. 'He knows you. Do it on air.'

'I'm afraid they've taken the programme off, as you've probably gathered.'

'Sir,' said Peter politely, 'you are the chairman of the BBC. You can order it back on air. And the nation will hear as you speak to him.'

'Hmph,' said Leslie. 'Let's give it a go, then.'

'But don't swear,' said Peter. 'The BBC doesn't like it.'

The chairman grinned and walked back to his team. The crowd outside the studio door parted as he strode through, entered the control room and spoke to the *Today* editor. Moments later there was a knock at the door of the occupied studio.

'Ian, there's some big old bloke in a suit at the door,' said Samson. 'Looks like he wants to come in.'

James North rose and looked through the round window in the door into the sixty-year-old smiling face of his ultimate master.

'It's Martin Leslie,' he said.

'Ooo,' said Taylor. 'Big guns. Let him in.'

Leslie's large frame made the studio still smaller. The chairman nodded at his presenters and shook Taylor's hand. He glanced at the MP slumped on the floor holding a bloodied handkerchief to his nose.

'No time for the weather, chaps,' said the chairman, waving his hand at the editor through the glass divide. 'Right, we're going back on the air. Jim, Sarah, busk it. Ian, just listen for once.'

Back in the Green Room, Peter heard the emergency Mozart that the continuity department had arranged stop suddenly.

'Right. Well,' said James North, 'if you've just joined us, I'm afraid it's a little difficult to summarise this morning's unusual events. But now we appear to be back on the air and we have been joined in the studio, this rather… err eventful studio, by Martin Leslie, chairman of the governors of the BBC. Mr Leslie, sir, good of you to pop in.'

'Thank you, Jim. Good morning Sarah… gentlemen. Umm, how to start? As we know in recent years the BBC has had more than an occasional clash with Her Majesty's government, who are our *de facto* masters and who also control the means and extent to which the corporation is funded.

'But occasionally we are reminded that it is not the powers of Westminster whom we serve, it is the people of this country, the licence fee payers. They are our ultimate masters. Like many of them, I have been deeply affected by the tragedies of this conflict. It is not for me to decide upon the right or wrong course of political action: that is, rightly, the role of our elected representatives. But it is beholden upon me, as BBC chairman, to ensure that both sides of the political debate are explained cogently to those who elect the elected.

'By whom I mean our audience. Like many who have heard this morning's, as Jim says, unusual, broadcast I have been moved by the words of Ian Taylor. And it strikes me that while, for many years now, we have dutifully provided a platform for the explanations of why we are at war, we have perhaps not given the same platform to those who argue why we should not be. This morning, and after the deaths of three of our finest people in the bombing, I have decided that this will now change.

'Ian Taylor, you will get your BBC broadcast. As chairman, I offer you the extent of coverage on all of our channels and stations for your concert. This may be rash and politically problematic, but I believe that the terms of the BBC charter dictate that as this country's only public broadcaster, we must give the public a choice of voice. Ian, you have your broadcast. We are going to give your peace a chance.'

'Well,' said James North, 'there you have it. Strange days indeed. And now here's Gary, a little late, with the sport.'

Moments later the hijackers of Room 456F emerged into the corridor, straight into the glare of the camera light of the TV crew who filmed until a nod from Vernon directed the security guards to hustle them away. Backs were slapped and more hugs were made as BBC staff congratulated Taylor and his gang of three.

At the end of the corridor, no longer part of the moment nor of the triumph, Peter could only look on, with painful regret tarnishing his admiration and pride.

Peter looked up and saw that Taylor was staring straight at him, unsmiling. Peter held his gaze and shrugged. Taylor smirked. And then a police officer approached the rock singer.

'I'm very sorry, sir, but there has been an incident and I must ask you to accompany me for questioning,' said the cop nervously.

Peter heard Billy Vernon growl and move towards the policeman.

'Billy…' said Taylor, 'it's alright.'

He put out his arms towards the policeman, holding his wrists together.

'Oh, there's no need for that, sir,' said the cop.

'Do us a favour, mate,' said Taylor. 'Cuff me. Go on. It'll look great for the photographers.'

Ten minutes later, flanked by six policemen and accompanied by the smiling figure of Martin Leslie, Ian Taylor stepped out of the lift into the foyer of Broadcasting House.

Tears of pride glistened in his eyes as what appeared to be the entire staff of the BBC's headquarters filled the large room to cheer and applaud him as he walked to the door.

But their cheer was nothing compared to the roar that met Ian Taylor as the doors of Broadcasting House opened and he emerged into a street so packed with photographers, TV crews, police and people, his people, that traffic was at a standstill all around.

As Taylor approached a waiting police car, he held his handcuffed fists aloft and, with his left hand, made a peace sign for the photographers.

CHAPTER 31

In the backseat of the police car, Taylor was listening to the officer in the front passenger seat talking to his wife on his mobile.

'You'll never guess 'oo we've got in the back,' said the cop. 'What? 'Ere, Charlie, Sheila says it's been on the news. What? Well, I don't know, 'e might. OK. To what? And the kids? What? Yeah. Yeah. Look, I said I'll try it. Yeah, see ya.'

Taylor watched as the policeman ended the call and then turned to face him; he knew what was coming next.

''Ere, Ian… Err, Mr Taylor… look, sorry to ask and that and I know you must get sick of it, but do you think you could sign us…'

'To Sheila and the kids, right?' said Taylor, taking a pen from the cop. 'Sure, man; you hold the pad.'

As Taylor wrote a message, the officer continued to express his amazement.

'My wife says you're a national bleeding 'ero. She says you struck a blow for justice, hitting that MP like that. Not that I'm saying you did 'it 'im, course. Anyway, she said to tell you it's the best hit you've ever had.'

'Yeah. You're the hit man, Ian,' said his partner, Charlie.

Taylor smiled and said nothing. But he logged what they had said. The hit man; that was good. The papers would like that one. Nice edge to it. He'll tell Pete to run with that. Then he remembered that Peter Forth had been sacked. He resolved to un-sack him, but not yet. Mr Forth needed to be brought to heel first. Especially now that he was a national bloody hero.

As the squad car arrived at Bow Street police station, Taylor obligingly raised his cuffed hands again and grinned for the platoon of photographers and TV cameramen who were already penned on the pavement. Although the police did not lower the rear windows, he could hear the press yelling his name and cheering. He made an OK sign with his forefinger and thumb as a reporter from GMTV rushed with a microphone to the side of the slow-moving vehicle and shouted, 'How do you feel?'

Following the convoy of police and press cars in Taylor's chauffeured Jaguar, Billy Vernon pointed out the hubbub to Conrad Marks, the expensively-retained lawyer they had picked up en route.

'Look at all that; he'll be bloody loving this,' said Vernon. 'This is it now, he's back at the top.'

'Uh-huh,' said the solicitor.

'The money, the number one album, the critics raving, the magazine covers, it'll all fall into place now,' continued Vernon. 'And anything he's done will be forgiven because of this. Thank God for the British love of violence.'

'Quite. But let's get him off first,' said Marks.

'What do you mean? Are you expecting a problem with that? Come on, Con, Ian only hit the bloke once. It was provocation.'

'It was actual bodily harm, Billy. Punching an MP, unlawful imprisonment, behaviour likely to cause a breach of the peace. And God knows whether seizing the airwaves is still seen as a form of piracy. This could be bad, Billy.'

'Yeah, well sort it out. We pay you enough,' said Vernon grimly. 'I want him doing a press conference in time for the news at six.'

CHAPTER 32

When Billy Vernon next saw his employer more than two hours later it was not the new, smiley Ian Taylor who was shouting at his manager and solicitor inside one of the interview rooms at Bow Street station.

'What the fuck do you mean, remanded?' yelled the star, who had just finished a lengthy session of making his statement and an even lengthier stretch signing more autographs.

'Ian! Ian! Conrad will get you out very shortly. We're calling all the people we know,' soothed Vernon.

'So what's the fucking problem? Why the fuck am I still here?'

'They're not treating this like the average assault, I'm afraid,' said the lawyer. 'Clearly, we've put some important noses out of joint in a rather public way. I'm hearing the Government is very embarrassed by your peace protest.'

'Good,' swiped Taylor.

'Well, perhaps. But not good for our immediate purpose of freeing you. The authorities don't want you shouting for peace to the nation, Ian. They, and I believe their American counterparts, would like you to hush up. Now, if I could give them some sort of assurance that…'

'They can fuck themselves,' spat Taylor.

'If those are your instructions…' said Marks. 'Obviously the authorities will not enjoy the outcry that can be orchestrated to meet your incarceration and we can use their discomfort to our advantage. But…'

'But what?'

'Well, with the Home Office cracking down on loutishness, they cannot easily turn a blind eye against one of their own men being injured…'

'Can't we say he just slipped? I could testify that Ian never touched him and our security would swear blind the same,' suggested Vernon.

'But the *Today* presenters are not so easily forgetful, Billy,' said Marks. 'I am beginning to believe that this has all of the hallmarks of 'setting an example' about it. The government will not tolerate this anti-war campaign. I hear that they are furious with Martin Leslie.'

'Are you saying that I'm going to get sent down?' Taylor demanded.

'No, no. No, that wouldn't wash with your public. And, clearly, they have become your public again. A brief tour of the news bulletins makes it evident that your current detainment is in no way popular.'

'So it's who breaks a fucking butterfly on a wheel all over again, is it? Bloody wonderful,' said Taylor gloomily.

'Conrad thinks we're looking at one or two days inside, three at the absolute most, Ian,' said Vernon. 'The powers won't want a 'Free Ian Taylor' row going on for any longer than that. Don't worry, we can spin this.'

'How are you going to do that when I've sacked Pete?'

'Don't worry about that, Peter will always heed a cry for help,' assured Vernon.

'You sure? OK. Well then, tell him that the cops are calling me 'The Hit Man'. He'll like that, he can run with that.'

'The Hit Man?' queried Vernon.

'Hit as in punch,' explained Taylor wearily. 'And as in number one records. One of the cops coined it; we should nick it.'

'I'll get Pete onto it as soon as I'm outside,' smiled Vernon.

CHAPTER 33

When her friend and confidante, Sandy, had phoned excitedly, Susie had been rearranging her underwear drawer. Now that Jackson had rebuffed her and left only Pete as the only man in her life, she had decided that she would have no more need of the stockings, suspenders and saucy knickers that she had bought recently.

Susie listened with increasing shock as Sandy detailed the morning's events that she'd heard on the radio, adding her own analysis that it had probably been one of Pete's ludicrous stunts.

'What do you mean, he's been fired?' said Susie after Sandy had gleefully revealed that the news was quoting police sources that Taylor would be spending the night in a cell.

'That's why I'm calling, you dork,' said Sandy. 'Pete rang Alex and said that Ian has sacked him. So I'm saying let's have a Pete is free party. Al says we'll host it at our place. I think it's a fab idea.'

'Well who are you planning on inviting?'

'Everyone, darling. Nobody's had a party in ages and this is the perfect excuse. They'll all want to come!'

'I wouldn't bank on it; Pete's not so popular these days, you know. He's upset a lot of people just by being Pete.'

'But he's only upset everyone because that git made him so unhappy,' trilled Sandy. 'Now we can have our old Pete back.'

Susie doubted that the old Pete would make an appearance for a year or so. Until then, she knew she would have to put up with 'I'm So Crap Pete' and 'It's Not Fair Pete'. She couldn't decide which Pete would drive her from their home first.

'Are you still there?' she heard Sandy say.

'Sorry, I was thinking that Pete will be gutted.'

'Yeah, poor lamb. Well, you look after him and leave the rest to us. As I say, we'll do all the invites. It'll be huge fun, sweetie.'

'I'm not sure I know what huge fun is anymore.'

'What do you mean, darling?'

'Pete and fun… I don't know, it just seems like that part of life's deal has passed us by, Sand.'

'Which is why this is a great idea…don't you think?'

Susie did not reply.

'Hello?' said Sandy. 'You still there?'

''Course,' said Susie, sniffing. 'Where else have I got to go?'

'I'm coming over, darling. Stay there. I think Auntie Sandy needs to help you offload. Shan't be a tick.'

The phone to her ear went dead as Susie wondered if Sandy, best friend though she was, really had any idea just how much there was to offload. As she sat at the kitchen table waiting, her mind drifted through her years of unhappiness and she lost where she was in a wave of despair. She gazed at the milk scum on her untouched coffee and thought that's me, congealing.

'Walkies!' trilled Sandy at the door at last. 'Sorry I was so long, sweetie. Had to catch Nelson, he'd gone off after some rabbits.'

Susie rose from the table to fuss her hand over the head of the large flatcoat retriever panting excitedly.

'Hello Nelson. I wish I felt like you, lovey.'

Sandy eyed her friend and recognized the hunch of hopelessness.

'Get your shoes, love,' she said gently.

They walked down the road, Sandy curling her arm in Susie's and saying nothing as they quickly reached a flint path which led them off in single file down a narrow track with rusted railings that ran towards the beech woods. When they could finally walk in-arm again Sandy unleashed the dog to bound off in an frenzy of sniffing. She nudged her pal.

'Come on, out with it.'

Susie brought her head up and looked mournful. She pulled at the tops of the long grass as they followed the dog.

'I don't know what to do Sand. It's all got so awful I think I'm going to have to leave Pete,' she said at last.

'Ah,' said Sandy. 'Why?'

'I can't handle it anymore, I just can't. And it makes me feel so weak and pathetic.'

As she began to sniffle Sandy gave her one of the handful of large tissues which she had taken from her husband's study.

'I mean, it's just too much. Everything's just too much!'

'What is?' said Sandy.

'Bloody Pete! He's too much. Everything is so extreme, there's never a single moment when he's – I don't know. I was going to say 'normal' but that's the last word that anyone would ever use about Pete. I never know which Pete I'll wake up with in the morning – excited or depressed, caring or angry, drunk or sober or stoned or high… I don't have the strength to cope any more with that and to try and make a home that is in some tiny way 'normal' for the boys. And that's so wrong because I know that I should.'

She wiped her eyes with the tissue and handed it back to Sandy without thinking. Sandy pocketed it without demur.

'What's he done now?'

'Oh, nothing… everything. Nothing new, but I just can't cope with it any longer. I had no idea when I married him that he was an addict and that he would always be moving emotional goalposts. It's never ever calm for more than two days. I lie there before he wakes up, praying that he'll be in a good mood.'

'Have you tried a rude awakener? That usually puts Alex in a good mood.'

'Sandy, Alex is normal, predictable. Sometimes that's worked, but sometimes he says his mind's too busy. He always wants it last thing, when I'm shattered from cleaning and ironing and cooking for whenever he deigns to arrive home without calling. By that time I just want to sleep and then he gets cross. But to be honest, I'm just so angry with what he's doing to us that I can hardly even manage a duty fuck these days.'

'Men are such sex pigs,' said Sandy.

'It's not just the sex. It's, it's just all of it. He says he's too busy to take me out – I know he's got a difficult job, but he's always shouting. The boys hate it, and I feel so taken for granted and just… unloved. Sandy this sounds stupid, but I decided it would cheer me up to have an affair.'

'Uhuh,' said Sandy, who'd heard a rumour. 'Anyone I know?'

'It doesn't matter, it was ridiculous. It was just the thrill of being fancied again really, of being noticed. But… men… why does work always come first? He was no better than bloody Pete.'
Susie began to sob and this time Sandy gave her all the tissues.

'It's kick the cat,' said Susie after a while.

'You haven't got a cat.'

'I'm the cat. Something at work pisses Pete off, he over-reacts and starts yelling at me. But I haven't done anything.'

'What about a holiday?'

'We can't afford it. Pete spends like he's Ian Taylor. I keep waiting until he seems to be in a good mood to talk about his credit card bill, but if I make just the tiniest suggestion he explodes. Says I'm always nannying him, won't let him have any fun. And yet if I suggest fun that won't cost anything, like a little picnic or something, he says he hasn't got time.'

'Poor you.'

'But why do I feel so wretched? I feel like I've failed, that I'm not being a good wife. He's the one with the pressures. Maybe I should just watch soaps in silence and wait until he notices that I'm in the room?'

'No,' said Sandy firmly, 'you shouldn't.'

'I mean… is this it? I keep thinking well that's it, that's your life gone now.'

'You're not dying, darling.'

'I feel like I am. I feel like I'm dying inside. Like there's a cancer growing. I can feel it. That's going to be it, I'll get cancer and that was it, my life. Miserable, apart from the boys.'

'You could start again. No, listen to me. You could. You're lovely looking, everybody likes you. Put Peter in the past. It's allowed, Suze.'

'I couldn't. The boys…'

'The boys would be fine. All this shouting you two do really isn't good for them, you know.'

'Pete would kill himself and then I'd feel even more dreadful.'

'Pete's not going to kill himself. He just says that for effect.

He'd get by. And besides, as you said, you're not his carer.'

'Oh I don't know. It just seems so wrong,' said Susie, beginning to whimper again.

'Susie,' said Sandy firmly, 'you've been a saint. Everybody knows that. You've tried and tried. But I'm not going to watch my best mate wither into where you're heading from bloody loyalty. Sweetheart, you've done enough. Give it up, you're not going to change him. God couldn't change Pete, especially now that he's probably thrown the mould away because it was a bad idea.'

Susie dabbed her eyes dry with the corner of a tissue and then blew her nose loudly into it.

'Thanks Sand,' she said, 'I'll think about it.'

CHAPTER 34

Billy Vernon already had a headache before he started to try to cajole Peter back to chair an emergency publicity meeting, but now Peter's resistance was making the pain worse.

'No. Fuck off,' said the former publicist, who sounded like he was on his mobile in a bar.

'Oh come on, Pete; for old times' sake. Ian didn't mean it. Honestly. Come on, the team needs you.'

'What team? There is no team, Billy. There's just the enablers of Ian's opinion, nobody else gets a vote.'

'Yes, well, you know what artists are like, mate. But he wants you back; he wants you to run this. Come on, Pete, you can do this standing on your head.'

'No. Sorry, Billy, but I've had enough servitude. Tell him I said 'thanks but no fucking way'.'

'I can't say that. You know that. Look, I tell you what, come back and just sort out this bloody mess and then we'll call it quits. With no hard feelings and a big cheque. Come on, that's reasonable.'

'I'm not interested in reason, Billy. I'm not interested in Ian. Anyway, who's to say that he'll hate prison? He'll probably love it in the showers,' Peter mocked.

'OK, well there's another thing; if you won't help us spin this, can you at least give me the number of this Catherine person?'

'No.'

'What do you mean? You can't keep that from us,' protested Vernon. 'That's really not fair; she could be his daughter.'

'You mean she could be the key to solving the label's problem with his increasingly-obvious sexuality. She's the golden ticket, isn't she?'

'Can I please have her number?'

'No.'

'Why not?' said Vernon.

'I've lost them. I've lost my mobile. And my contacts book. Nicked from my car.'

'Bollocks, I'm calling you on your mobile.'

'If you say so.'

'Well then can you ring her…'

'I haven't got her number, I told you.'

'OK. But if by some miraculous intervention of God you just happen to remember her number, can you let her know that we want to talk to her? And give her my number?'

'No.'

'You're being very unreasonable, Peter, I'm disappointed.'

'Join the gang, Billy. Anyway, are you coming to my leaving do? I'd ask Ian if I didn't suspect that he'd nick the silver, or whatever it is that these old lags do.'

'It's not funny, Pete. The man is being denied of his liberty and of his right to free speech.'

'Well then he'll know what it's like to work for him, won't he?' said Peter spitefully. 'And stop being pompous, Billy; I've not been sacked for being wrong, remember.'

'When is your do?'

'Next Saturday night at a mate's down here. I've still got some friends Billy. Are you going to come?'

'Don't be ridiculous,' said Vernon, ending the call but making a note in his diary.

CHAPTER 35

As he sat uncomfortably in the back of the Prison Service van that was taking him to Wormwood Scrubs, Ian Taylor was already making notes in his head to use this for his advantage.

There would be a good album in this, he thought, called *Songs from Inside* or something like that. He could dump all his unfinished demos on it; change the lyrics a little, nobody would ever know. Maybe he could launch the album with a prison gig?

Obviously, he pondered, all of this would be great promo for Grey Rose, as the press would go ballistic for interviews when he got out. And it neatly solved the problem of new artwork for the album; simple – just the same as before but with the rose behind four grey bars.

He quite liked this new image of being, what, a peace martyr? And in a fine tradition; Mick, Keith, Macca, him and Oscar Wilde. Well, maybe best not mention Oscar. But he could slip Nelson Mandela's name into any subsequent interview; maybe he could get Billy to organise a message of support from someone like that? This could be great!

He began to whistle 'Jailhouse Rock' but it was a bit fast for him, so he switched to a more sardonic 'Please Release Me' instead.

'What do you think they'll do with me?' he abruptly asked the prison officer who had been assigned to travel in the back with him.

'What do you mean, er... Mr Ta...'

'Call me Ian. I mean do you think I'll be in solitary, or sharing?'

'I can't see why they'd put you in solitary; I mean you're not a nonce or anything are yer?'

'Nonce?'

'You don't shag boys or nothing?'

'God, no!' said Taylor, feeling awkward. 'What about drugs?'

'Oh, you'll be fine for them; there's plenty of drugs available inside.'

'No, I meant do the other co… inmates have issues with drug-taking?'

'Nah. Most of them are too out of their box to notice if you're high.'

'So what's the form, then?' persisted Taylor, eager not to appear too naïve to the other prisoners.

'Form?'

'What's the best way to behave, to survive?'

'I shouldn't worry too much about that; you'll be able to be yourself, seeing as who you are and that. For starters, everybody will know who you are and most of them will know by now what you're in for. By the way, what are you in for?'

'Decking a MP,' said Taylor, grinning.

'Well, you can't get more popular than that. I would have thought they'd have knighted you.'

'Nah, wrong school, mate. I'm too secondary modern for that club,' Taylor smirked. 'So what's the food like? As bad as they say?'

'Well it's a damn sight better than what my missus cooks,' said the guard. 'Mind you, she doesn't tend to gob in our meals. Not that it would make it much worse. Best stick to the stuff they can't mess with, like cheese and fruit.'

'Anyone that I should avoid? Anyone especially dodgy?'

'They're all dodgy, Mr… Ian. That's why they're locked up. But, no, you'll be OK. There's nobody special to bother about.'

The guard thought for a moment about mentioning Clarkey, but then he decided not to. No point in frightening the guy, especially as he did look a bit of a faggot, close up.

CHAPTER 36

After signing for his confiscated effects, Taylor entered the jail proper and, having seen enough prison movies, he was not surprised to hear the whole place making a hell of a racket welcoming him.

As he was used to conducting crowds, he grinned widely and held up his right arm to form a fist salute. The cheers became louder and he loved it.

As he was escorted to his cell, Taylor shook all the hands that were offered to him, which were many, and said, ‘Thanks, man,’ to all the expressions of support and good luck.

When Prisoner 44729 arrived at the cell, he was surprised at the size of it. He had expected something much smaller and smellier. Instead, he was pleased to see that not only was it spotless, but that nobody else appeared to be sharing it. There were none of the glamour girl posters that he had thought to find on the walls. Instead he was delighted to see that they had provided a television.

‘This is fine,’ said Taylor.

‘Good, ‘cos you’ve not got the chance to phone reception and ask for a bigger suite,’ said the guard.

‘What I meant was, I’ve dossed in worse rooms than this. Back when I started out, we used to kip in some well-dodgy places.’

‘I’m sure,’ said the guard. ‘But maybe your neighbours were a little less, ah, confined then.’

‘Am I sharing or on my own?’

‘Apparently not solo,’ said the guard, consulting a clipboard. ‘It says here you’re getting a room-mate later, but he’s not arrived yet.’

‘Ah, a surprise,’ said Taylor.

‘Yeah, you’ll get used to them. Well, make yourself at home; the governor said he’ll be along shortly, to talk you through the ropes. I’ll leave you to it. Shout if you need any help.’

‘Any help with what?’ said Taylor, confused.

'With nothing. I mean help-help. Like if you get attacked.'

The guard grinned and walked away. Alarmed, Taylor looked around the room for anything that might work as a weapon. But there was nothing. Money, he determined, was his best defence. It had always worked before.

He sat on the bottom bunk and winced at its hardness. Then he looked through the small parcel of prison belongings, they had given him for a pencil and pad. He wanted to jot down every moment of this experience, it would be worth a fortune later.

After ten minutes he became aware of another presence. He looked up from his notes and saw a thin young man with beautiful brown eyes smiling at him. Obviously bent, Taylor judged, his gaydar on full alert.

'Hello,' he said, smiling.

'Hello Ian. Dennis. it's been a while…'

'Do I know you?' said Taylor, sensing that he did.

'Well, at least Biblically,' said the young man. 'That party at the Hilton, after you won the *Q* award?'

'Ah,' said Taylor, who sort of remembered the rent boy now. 'Good to see you again.'

'Yeah. The shame is that I'm out tomorrow. Pity, I could have shown you around. Still, I expect your money will soon help you out of here.'

'Hope so,' said Taylor, still smiling.

'Maybe we could meet up on the outside?' ventured the prisoner.

'That would be great, er, Dennis.'

'How?'

'How what?'

'How shall I contact you?'

'Umm, you can call my office. I'll give you the number,' said Taylor looking back at his pad.

'Get real; your office ain't gonna put us in touch.'

'They will,' Taylor lied. 'I'll tell them to.'

'No, they won't. Tell you what, give us your number.'

'My number?'

'Yeah, your mobile.'

'Shit! Do you know, Den, I can never bloody remember it,' Taylor lied again. 'Why don't you give me yours?' Taylor lowered his voice to a whisper. 'As I remember, we had a very nice time together. I'd definitely ring you.'

''Specially now that I've got HIV,' said the tart.

'Have you?'

'Yeah. So I could do with a little money, see.'

'Could you?'

'Yeah. Still, I s'pose the Sundays would cough up a good wedge, to hear how we got to have this reunion, in here of all places. Seeing me old bum chum again and that.'

'Look...' began Taylor, but he never got to conclude the offer that he was about to make. Instead the conversation was brought to an end by the appearance at the cell doorway of a large, white-haired man who looked muscular for his sixties.

'Piss off, you nonce,' said the older man, and the rent boy scuttled away immediately.

'Sorry about that, Mr Taylor,' said the new arrival, smiling and extending his hand. 'Hello. I'm Clarkey.'

'Oh, hello Clarkey,' said Taylor convivially. 'How can I help you?'

'I don't know if you can, old son. I thought I'd just drop in to help you.'

'That's kind of you. How can you help me?'

'Just point you in the direction of what's what, old son. Let you know the lie of the land, as they say.'

For fifteen minutes Taylor listened eagerly as Clarkey itemised the 'house rules' of the Scrubs; whom to trust, whom to not, which screws were OK, which were bullies. Taylor jotted notes; explaining that he had a poor memory but, in truth, was recording details for his press interviews when he got out.

'Tell me,' Clarkey said after a while, 'does the name Georgie Clark mean anything to you?'

'Georgie? No, I don't think so. Is he your son?'

'My only lad.'

'A good lad?' said Taylor, hoping not to sound patronising.

'Yeah,' the old man brooded for a moment. 'Anyway, he used to write to you.'

'Did he?'

'Yeah, he did. He wrote to you for fucking weeks, he did. Pages of shit.'

'Saying what?'

'Oh, he loved his music. Like yourself Mr Taylor. Loved it. He wanted to form a band, just like you did.'

'What and he wanted some cash, like, to help get his band going?' said Taylor, sensing the sound of the usual plot.

'Nah, he wanted your help, old son.'

'What, with his band? Help with song-writing and stuff?'

'Nah, just help. With his job.'

'He needed a job?' said Taylor.

'Sad lad, my Georgie. Not too bright, see.

'Oh.'

'The thing is that, not being bright, he could never get a decent job. Leastways, not till he joined that radio station. He loved that radio station. Loved the music, see. He said it gave him a real sense of worth. Made him their post boy, they did, he loved it.'

'And?' said Taylor.

'Well, he lost the job, didn't he? Him and all the others. Turfed out on their ears when they closed the station down. 'Course some of 'em just went to the BBC, but Georgie, being a bit touched and that, he couldn't find another. Terrible upset he was.'

'Oh dear,' said Taylor sympathetically.

'That's why he wrote to you. Pleading, he was.'

'For money?'

'Nah, we had money. Well, I did. No, he wanted to save the station.'

'How could I save his station?' said Taylor, perplexed.

The old man looked at him without smiling. For the first time, Taylor noticed that there was no light in his eyes.

''Cos you shut it down, Mr Taylor. Don't you remember Radio SWN?'

'Err?'

'The Swindon station you bought and closed just because they were going to play your bloody record, Mr Taylor.'

'Um... look... that was a management thing,' Taylor lied quickly. 'I really didn't know much about it...'

'Sure, sure,' said Clarkey, raising his hand for Taylor to stop. 'Still, funny old world isn't it? I mean if I hadn't been done for murder, I'd probably never have been able to tell you all this.'

'Murder?' said Taylor uneasily.

'Pah! Pinned on me, it was. They fitted me up like a kipper; said I ordered a revenge killing of some Paki who they reckoned had crossed me. I mean, I ask you! Look at me, do I look like a mobster to you?'

'No,' said Taylor quietly.

'Exactly,' said Clarkey, rising to leave. 'Anyway, nice to have met you, Mr Taylor. I like to put a face, as they say.'

'What happened to your son?' said Taylor optimistically. 'Maybe I could help him now?'

'I doubt it. He topped himself, old son. Hanged himself and left a note saying nobody cared. He spelt cared wrong, two 'r's. But he never could spell properly. Still, you'd have known that; having read all his letters and that.'

Again there was an interruption, this time from a guard. Taylor wanted to cheer with relief.

'Alright Clarkey, on your way. Mr Taylor here's got an important visitor. On your feet, Taylor.'

As Taylor rose to follow the guard, Clarkey gave him a last long look.

'I'll see you next time, old son,' he said.

CHAPTER 37

When Taylor entered the small, stark room that his lawyer and manager had obtained as a private area in which to consult him, the first thing that Billy Vernon noted was that his swagger had gone. The room was furnished with just a table and three uncomfortable plastic chairs. A prison officer stood against one wall, watching Taylor with a wry grin.

Neither Vernon nor his companion, Conrad Marks, had any experience of meeting a contrite and frightened Ian Taylor and at first they reacted awkwardly, waiting for things to stabilise to the point at which they would be shouted at again.

'Ian. How's it going? Are you coping?' blustered Vernon, shocked at the shuffle that had replaced Taylor's strut. 'Don't worry, we'll soon have you out of here.'

'How soon?' said Taylor in a soft voice that was so unlike his usual tone that Vernon thought he was unwell.

'We're working on it non-stop,' replied Vernon evasively.

'I can't handle this,' said Taylor, looking at the gouges in the Formica table top and wondering what misery had made them.

'It must be very difficult, you're being very brave.'

'I wouldn't have the courage to make a stand like yours,' Marks chipped in. 'This is earning you huge respect.'

Normally, Taylor would have met a craven compliment with a shrug and saying something like, 'Well, not everybody's got it, man.' But now he just said, 'Oh.'

'Is there anything you need?' said Vernon, trying to be helpful.

'Yeah. Get me out.'

'Everybody's working on that; we've even got the chairman of BPA bending the ears of the Cabinet Office. We'll get you out.'

'When?' said Taylor.

Vernon looked at Marks, abdicating the responsibility of answering.

'Oh. Err… hopefully by the day after tomorrow,' said Marks.

Vernon gave Marks a glare that read, 'Go on,' and Marks added, 'I promise you, soon this will all be just a bad dream.'

'It's a bad dream now,' said Taylor, picking at the Formica.

'I know,' said Marks reassuringly.

'No you don't.'

'Sorry, I mean I've been in prisons before, with clients, it's never easy. But, as Billy says, you're bearing up much better than mo…'

'I've had two visitors in my cell,' Taylor interrupted.

'No threats, I hope. If you've been threatened we can get you in a secure section straight away,' said Marks.

'The first visitor was a ren…er, a boy who knows m… er… our scene,' Taylor lifted his eyes to look into Marks's face with barely-controlled loathing. 'He came to tell me that he has HIV and that when he is released tomorrow he intends to go to the newspapers and sell them the story of meeting me inside.'

'What's his name?' said Marks, picking up his pen.

'Dennis something.'

'OK. Leave that with us. I'll find out who he is and have him picked up when he steps out tomorrow. I take it he wants money, not the publicity?'

'Yeah.'

'Don't worry about him, he's sorted. Who was your other visitor?'

'A bloke called Clarkey.'

As Marks wrote down the name, Vernon noticed that the guard smirked at the mention of it.

'And what's his probl…?' said Marks, who was silenced by a sharp nudge from Vernon 's elbow.

Vernon looked at the guard.

'Who is Clarkey?' he asked with a voice of assumed authority.

'Your Mr Clark, sir, is your Mr Big. A villain of the old school, sir. He runs a lot of things, inside and outside of here. Not a nice man, sir.'

'Thank you,' said Vernon, who had taken the precaution before Taylor arrived of tipping the guard enormously.

'What did Mr Clark have to say, Ian?' said Vernon gently.

'I killed his son,' said Taylor miserably. 'His kid topped himself because of something I did... Billy, you've got to get me fucking out of here, man! I'm not joking. Fuck the album, fuck it all, fuck the bloody peace thing. I just want to get out! It's fucking hideous!'

'Did this... Clarkey threaten you in any way? Were you intimidated?' persisted Marks, still making notes.

'I killed his son,' said Taylor evenly. 'He is a convicted murderer, a gang-lord, and I killed his son. What are you expecting? Grapes?'

'Do you have reason to feel that you are in personal danger?' said Marks.

'What sort of stupid cunt have you suddenly become?' Taylor yelled. 'Of course I'm in fucking danger! I'm shitting myself! I've got nobody around me, I can't hack it on my own.'

'Do you have a cell-mate?' said Vernon.

'Not yet; I'm getting one later, apparently. Knowing my luck it'll be that fucker who eats other convicts' brains with a spoon.'

Vernon forced himself to laugh, a little too obviously.

'That's the spirit, Ian, laugh at the buggers. They're staying in. You're coming out.'

The door opened and a short and very fat, balding man in a cheap suit entered. He was sweating and he removed his horn-rimmed spectacles to wipe his face with a soiled handkerchief.

'Gentlemen, sorry to interrupt. My name's Perkins, I'm the governor here. Good afternoon, Mr Taylor... err, Ian. Is all as it should be?'

'Governor, I'm Conrad Marks, Mr Taylor's solicitor,' said Marks, rising and extending his hand. 'I have a number of grave issues concerning my client whom, I need not remind you, is only on remand. He has been convicted of nothing.'

'Quite,' said Perkins.

'This is William Vernon, Mr Taylor's manager,' said Marks, indicating Vernon. 'We are given to understand that there may be serious security matters concerning the operation of this prison and my client's safety. I would like to discuss these with you in private and come to an immediate arrangement that is satisfactory to all.'

'Of course, of course,' said Perkins, nodding gravely. 'We can talk in my office presently, gentlemen. I just popped in to well… err, introduce myself to Mr Taylor and to say, Ian, how much I respect this brave stand that you are taking on the war. Well done, sir.'

'Thanks,' acknowledged Taylor meekly.

'Good. Right. Gentlemen, if you would care to follow me? Mr Taylor, the guard will take you back to your cell. Very nice to have met you.'

As Perkins led the way to his office, Vernon said, 'Chin up, mate,' with a smile at Taylor. Marks was already in negotiation gear, saying to the governor, 'I recently read that you are experiencing funding issues…' as they left the room.

CHAPTER 38

When Taylor re-entered his cell he saw that a skinny man aged about twenty-five with long, lank hair was stretched out on the bottom bunk that he had wanted for himself, looking at a shabby copy of a cheap porn magazine.

'Bleedin' 'ell, they said I was twinning with you but I thought they was pulling my pisser,' said the young man, jumping up off the bunk and holding his hand out to Taylor.

'Hello,' said Taylor, dully.

'I'm Frankie Cairns,' said the cellmate, still shaking Taylor's hand. 'Fuck me, you came back at the right time. I was just about to have a Jodrell. That could have been embarrassing, could've given you a complex about size for the rest of your stretch.'

Frankie Cairns laughed in a loud cackle. He stood back and looked Taylor up and down.

'You're a bit of a fat fucker on the quiet, aren't ya? Well, more what they'd call podgy, I guess. Still, s'pect they clean up your photos, don't they? To make ya look leaner, like?'

It had been a long time since anyone had told Taylor he was a fat fucker and he did not know how to reply.

'Oo, 'scuse my manners, were you wanting that bunk?' Ave it if you like, I just presumed that you'd be used to being on top. You know, top of the pops, like.'

'It's fine,' said Taylor wearily.

'Do you wanna borrow the Tossing Times?' offered Cairns.

'The what?'

'This crock of shit,' said Cairns, waving the porn magazine. 'There's some right old dogs in it. Still, 'spect you're used to a better class of slapper, ain't'cha?'

'Sort of,' said Taylor, climbing up onto the top bunk as Cairns paced the cell.

''Scuse me buzzing about, I've just 'ad a hit of whizz. Do you fancy any?'

'No. Thank you.'

'Nah, guess not. S'pose coke's more your thing. I've got a bit of green if you want some. It's good gear but it don't half give you the frigging munchies. So, fuck my old boots, Ian fucking Taylor; stroll on! 'Ow long are you in for, Ian? Can I call yer Ian?'

'Please,' said Taylor. 'My solicitor tells me I'll be out in a couple of days.'

'Oh, fucking 'ell!' said Cairns disappointedly. 'That soon? Fuck, I was 'oping to get to know yer, like. Still, beggars can't be bastards, never mind. I'm in for dealing.'

'Speed?' said Taylor, putting two and two together.

'Speed? Fuck me, son, where've you been living? You won't make no wonga off speed. Nah, I got felt with a bunch of 'Es. Middle England's new little 'elper, mate. The beak'll duff me up rotten for dealing to his own sort.'

'What do you mean?' said Taylor.

'Stiffer sentence, like. Reckon I'll get three years. If I was selling on the estates, I'd have got probation. But selling to the nobs, well, they won't stand for that.'

'Where were you caught, then?'

'I was flogging 'em at a posh girls' school.'

'And the parents kicked up?'

'Nah, nothing to do with fucking parents! I was sorting out the staff. Doing alright, too, till some silly twat tripped out and ended up in casualty. Still, I s'pect you can handle yer gear; must've 'ad a bit in yer time.'

'Just a bit,' said Taylor, smiling for the first time.

'Funny them putting us together like this, innit?' continued Cairns. 'Still, s'pose they thought we'd get on; like I'm not gonna rape yer or nothing. 'Ere, you're not a bandit are yer?'

'No. Why do you say that?' asked Taylor, unsettled by the query.

'Nah, nothing, I've just always wondered; that's all.'

'Why?'

'Dunno. Something about the way you cross yer legs on them chat shows; we always thought you looked on the turn. But if you say yer not, fine.'

'Would it matter if I was… a bandit?' T

'Not to me, son. 'Course it'd make yer 'ere. But, nah, it's legal innit? And it's only life newspapers that's got a problem with queers. Pro a toss.'

'Interesting,' said Taylor.

'Listen, seeing as we've not got long, yer brief 'avin you out sharpish and stuff, and seeing as we'll like as not never meet again, can I ask you some things?'

'Some things?' said Taylor, amused. 'Like what?'

'Well, for starters, why did you do that last CD of yours? I thought it was shite, all that disco bollocks. Embarrassing for a man of yer age.'

'You mean 'Let's Go'?' said Taylor, recalling the album that he had told Peter to angle as his nod to the new young turks of club rock.

'Let's Go to the Fucking Shitter, more like,' said Cairns, cackling again, 'What a load of old toss that was. Don't you 'ave producers or nothing? Nobody to say 'ere, that's a crock of crap, mate?'

'Well, yeah,' said Taylor.

'So what, are they fucking deaf or something?'

'It was critically well-received,' said Taylor defensively.

'Yeah, in fucking Chile. Me and my mates thought it was shite. Still, you were top at Reading, though.'

'Thanks.'

'Still, I 'spect that was because you did yer old stuff.'

'Probably.'

'So what's with all this bollocks about Grey Rose, then? You really doing that?'

'You mean the gig? Yeah, I thought it would be sort of cool.'

'Sort of cool? It's fucking shit-hot cool, mate. Coolest fucking thing imaginable. But all that shagging shit, doing the bird on stage and that, which prannet told yer that was a cool idea? 'Cos you should sack the fucker.'

mean?'

oo wants to go and see you shagging? Fucked if I do. I na hear you fucking play, mate. And not in a fucking church, neither. I mean to say, when was the last time you went to a fucking church? Fucking never. So why the fuck do yer think that we'd want to go?'

'It was my publicist's idea.'

'Well you should tell 'im he's a cunt! Fucking publicists, what the fuck do you want with fucking publicists? You're a national fucking 'ero, mate. You don't need fucking publicists to tell us 'oo you are. Winston fucking Churchill never 'ad a publicist and he was known enough.'

Taylor was interested to see that Cairns was now blatantly rolling a joint without any apparent concern for retribution.

'Actually, I will have some of that. If that's OK?' he said.

'Fucking right-on!' said Cairns, grinning. 'Smoking with Ian fucking Taylor. Wait till I tell 'em that.'

'What else do you think about my stuff?' said Taylor. 'I'm interested; people don't tend to tell me this sort of thing.'

'Do ya let 'em?' said Cairns perceptively.

'Hmm,' said Taylor, reflectively.

'Well, seeing as you asked, I tell you what, you should stop trying to get in the papers so much.'

'Come again?'

'It's so fucking obvious that you're trying to sell something,' said Cairns. 'I mean, you don't like talking to reporters, do you?'

'Not really.'

'So do you think that the rest of us are so fucking thick that we're going to buy your album just because we've read how much you like go-karting or how you hated breaking up Taylspin...'

'I...'

''Ang on. There's a classic, you're always going on and fucking on about fucking Taylspin. Great fucking band, no question, but stop fucking talking about 'em and get it together to play with 'em.'

'Err...'

'That's what you're meant to actually fucking do, after all.

You're a musician, so make so fucking music. Don't talk for us; play for us. You wouldn't go into a pub and ask the landlord to talk about pints he's pulled. Do your fucking job!'

'It's not as easy as that,' Taylor protested.

'What's not to be easy about it? 'Ave you forgotten how to play guitar? And here's another thing, pardon my front but why does a bloke like you always bloody bicker about 'oo's best, you or Jack Jackson?'

'What?'

'Give it a fucking rest, for Christ's sake. All we ever fucking hear in your bloody interviews is how you were the bollocks behind Taylor and Jackson. Or if it's a piece on 'im, how he was the business. People are sick to fucking death of you two droning on like a pair of kids about how yer better than each other. I mean, what's it say on the writer credits? It says Taylor and Jackson. Not fucking Taylor or Jackson.'

'Good point,' said Taylor, memorising every word.

'Anyway, 'ere you go. This'll shut you up,' Cairns cackled as he passed Taylor the joint he had lit.

'Sure this is OK?' said Taylor, nervously.

'Yeah, they won't send yer to prison for it,' Cairns roared.

Taylor smoked in silence for some moments, considering the home truths he had learnt. Do ya let 'em? It was a good point.

'Have you done time before, Frankie?'

'This'll be my third stretch. One for burglary, the second for dealing; mind you that was for grass. It's bloody criminal, sending yer down for grass.'

'What would you do if you weren't dealing?'

'What, besides time? Dunno really. Well… don't laugh but at school they used to say I'd make a good manager. They said I was good at getting others to get stuff done an' that. A good motivator, they said.'

'Good managers are as rare as good songs,' said Taylor reflectively.

'Why's that, then?' said the voice from the bottom bunk.

'I'm not sure. I suppose it comes down to honesty.'

‘There’s a lot of that in your game then, is there?’ Cairns was laughing again, ‘’Ere, you bein’ a celebrity an’ that, ’ave you met Clarkey yet?’

‘Yeah, earlier on.’

‘Thought you might. You wanna watch ’im.’

‘Yeah, he looked like he could be a nasty bit of work.’

‘Nah, I don’t mean that,’ said Cairns, accepting the joint back. ‘I mean you wanna really watch him; like study him.’

‘Why?’

‘’Cos ’e reminds me of you. ’E’s from my manor, well, ’e’s the lord of it, really. I remember ’im when I was a kid. Lovely bloke then. Everybody liked ’im.’

‘So what happened?’

‘’E got to be successful, didn’t ’e. Bit like yerself. Not in the same game, mind; Clarkey was a top fence. As I say, it went to his ’ead, ’aving all that money and power an’ that. Started mistrusting everyone. Only ’eeded his own counsel. Then when ’is kid pegged it, well, ’e got to be one of them meg… megla…’

‘Megalomaniacs.’

‘That’s it. Reminded me of a bloke in a play that they dragged us to see at school once, King Gear or something…’

‘Lear.’

‘Yeah, ’im an’ all. You got any kids?’

‘Not that I’ve met,’ said Taylor truthfully.

‘Pity,’ said Cairns. ‘You ’aving all that money an’ that. Shame to share it alone. Can’t be so much fun, buying an’ opening gifts you gave yerself.’

But Taylor was no longer listening; he was daydreaming of playing Earls Court, where the billboards outside said ‘Tonight, for One Night Only – Ian Taylor in King Gear.’

‘After you with the Tossing Times,’ he said, relaxing.

CHAPTER 39

The cannabis had worked its dream-weaving magic and Taylor was in the middle of a slumber in which Billy Vernon appeared as the prison governor, sitting in a court room shouting, 'Silence in court!' and sentencing Taylor to four years in a cell with Clarkey, where he was ordered to build a model of a radio station out of matchsticks, using only rolling papers to fasten them.

'Come on, sleepy 'ead,' he heard a Cockney voice say as Cairns gently shook his arm to wake him.

'What's up?' said Taylor, finally surfacing back into reality.

'Time for tea.'

'What?'

'Teatime. Supper. Grub's up, Ian,' said Cairns, smiling. 'And we'd better go and fill our faces or they'll be thinking we're 'aving a cuddle.'

'I'm actually not really hungry,' said Taylor, turning over to face the brick wall.

'Sorry, not good enough. You're like the main guest for dinner, mate. Everyone's gonna want to take a look at you in yer prison denim. You'll be expected. You can't disappoint 'em.'

Taylor was mildly irritated that even behind bars he had to perform in the goldfish bowl; watched from the corners of the cons' eyes as if he was a freak at a circus. But forty years of the automatic pilot that turned him into *Ian Taylor!* made him get off his bunk for this, the strangest of show times.

'Speak when you're spoken to and keep it nice, look relaxed. They'll be watching you 'ard,' advised Cairns. 'An' keep close to me; any bother, let me talk first. Chin-up mate, it could be worse.'

'How?' said Taylor following him out of the cell and onto an iron grated landing.

'Nobody else in 'ere has got out after only a couple of days,' said Cairns over his shoulder.

No cheering greeted him now. Instead the hundreds of heads that turned were watching him keenly, making their minds up on the evidence of appearances. Taylor remembered what Cairns had said about how he looked on chat shows, so he pulled his shoulders back and pretended that he was walking on at Madison Square Garden.

He was used to scanning a crowd of strangers in search of a face that looked interesting and he applied the stagecraft here. He noticed the rent boy, principally because he was pointing at Taylor and leering as he said something doubtlessly damaging to three others who were sitting with him at a table. He watched the group laughing raucously as the rent boy made a masturbatory gesture.

Still holding a half-smile and keeping his head erect, Taylor looked for Clarkey and after some moments spotted him in hunched conversation with a huge, bald-headed man whose neck was decorated with tattoos and at whom Clarkey was sternly wagging his forefinger.

'Frankie,' said Taylor as they came down the iron stairway into the large canteen, 'who's the Thursday job with Clarkey?'

'Thursday job?' said Frankie, confused.

'Sorry, it's old rockspeak; if he says it's Thursday but it's Friday…'

'…then it's Thursday. Gotcha. Umm… where's Clarkey again? Oh, I see. Oh, fuck, that's Cobbo, Gerry Cobb. Now 'e is a piece of work. But only if Clarkey tells 'im to be: 'e finds solutions for our Mr Clark.'

They reached the canteen floor and joined a line of men waiting to be served by a row of uninterested cooks.

'Let's 'ave a look; bangers, mash and beans or, err... looks like pie and chips… Ask for the pie and chips,' Cairns advised Taylor.

'Can't I have pie and mash?'

'You can but I wouldn't. There's things they can put in mash. Trust us, 'ave the chips. 'Less yer like jizz, of course.'

Taylor decided not to want his own way for once and responded by asking for exactly what Cairns took although, in his cellmate's case, his every request did not have to be punctuated with a handshake. He followed Cairns to a table that was not, as he had expected, far from where most of the men were sitting but was instead in their midst.

'This is Banger,' said Cairns as he indicated a short man of Taylor's age wearing very thick glasses. 'Banger, say 'ello to your betters.'

'Saw you in '67 once, at the old Rainbow,' said Banger, pointing at Taylor with his fork. 'Facking great night, it was. Mind you, I'm a Jack Jackson man meself. I always thought he had the edge on your guitar work.'

'Yeah, I'd say he did too,' said Taylor smiling and offering his hand.

'Bleedin' 'ell, now there's an admission for the tabloids,' chipped in Cairns. 'Christ, Ian, we'll be seeing burning bushes next.'

Banger and Cairns gobbled their food. Taylor attempted to do the same but his eating was frequently interrupted by men coming to the table to pat him on the back, wish him luck and ask for his autograph. He signed for every one without any irritation.

Having cleaned his plate, Cairns took out a plastic pouch of tobacco and rolled the thinnest cigarette that Taylor had ever seen.

'May I? Please?' said Taylor, pointing to the pouch.

'Thought yer didn't smoke; what was that anti-fags ad you did all about, then?' said Cairns, grinning.

'I don't much. But I figure it'll make a good story, telling them where it was that I started,' said the star, smiling and rolling himself a cigarette with Cairns's nodded permission.

'Betcha don't mention us when you do,' said Cairns uncertainly.

'What do you wanna bet?' said Taylor.

'A quid?'

'You're on,' said Taylor, and he spat on the palm of his hand before shaking on the deal with Cairns.

'Aah, very nice, Mr Taylor; good to see you settling in and making mates, old son,' said a voice behind them that both men recognised as Clarkey's.

'Shove up sonny,' Clarkey said to Cairns as he moved to sit next to Taylor.

'Evening Mr Clark,' said Taylor amiably.

'Hmph. Right, this here is Cobbo,' said Clarkey, pointing to the hulk who was standing behind him. 'Cobbo... ah... collects for me, you see. I have a lot of gentlemen in Cobbo's suit size who collect for me, Mr Taylor. Thought I'd introduce you seeing as Cobbo may be paying you a little visit some time soonish.'

'To collect?' said Taylor.

'Possibly. Possibly not. I'll leave the details of the visit to Cobbo; he can fill you in. Ha! Fill you in. Very good, Clarkey,' said the ganglord, amused by his own pun as he rose and walked away.

'Shit, that's not good,' said Banger, 'Clarkey wanting to collect and that. Cobbo's ending his stretch soon too. You wanna watch your back, mate.'

'So I gathered,' said Taylor. 'Let's hope the collection is made outside; I've got people there.'

'Fack people, you'll need facking guns,' said Banger.

'My people have got them as well,' said Taylor. He changed the subject. 'Why do they call you Banger? What are you, some sort of rapist?'

'Rapist? Fack off! I used to do safes. But there's no call for it anymore; all the facking thieving's done by banks over the Internet these days; put blokes like me out of a job. Typical, and shouldn't be allowed.'

Frankie Cairns said that they should return to their cell, so Taylor followed him back, snaking through more men who wanted his signature on small pieces of paper.

'Fancy a spliff?' said Cairns as they took to their bunks again.

'I can roll it, if you like,' said Taylor. 'In fact, why don't I give you some dosh and you can score us a decent supply.'

'I've read about yer decent supplies,' cackled Cairns. 'They say you get through more gear than all of Amsterdam.'

'Not many people in Amsterdam,' said Taylor, smiling, 'I'd say more than Spain would be more accurate.'

He accepted a little tobacco and cannabis from Cairns and began expertly to manufacture a joint. As he did so, he noticed his cellmate studying a hand-written letter.

'Note from home?' said Taylor softly.

'From me bird. Moaning as usual that I never write her. She's got the hump 'cos I promised like. Says if she don't get a letter soon she's off.'

'Bit harsh, isn't it?'

'My fault. I never write her, see.'

'Why not? You've got the time,' smiled Taylor.

'Yeah, but time's fuck-all use when you can't write proper. That's why she's never got a letter. But you don't wanna tell your bird yer thick like.'

'I could write it,' said Taylor evenly.

'Oh, there's loads of 'em in 'ere who could write it for us. But then it's not coming from me, is it? Wouldn't be right.'

'What if I wrote it from me?' suggested Taylor.

'But you don't know 'er.'

'Sure. But I'm getting you know you. I could write her a letter telling her what I, as a… well, as a former-outsider, can pretty much see what you're having to go through. What it's like in here and all of that.'

'Why would yer wanna do that?' said Cairns cagily.

'Because you've helped me.'

'What by pointing out a few dodgy old lags? 'Ardly.'

'No; by more than that, Frankie.'

'Alright, then,' said Cairns, finding a pen and a pad of paper. ''Er name's Janice. But no trying to pull 'er. I know what you fucking rock stars are like.'

'It's all made-up, Frankie. Usually by ourselves when we're out of it. Got a light?'

CHAPTER 40

Taylor was thoroughly enjoying writing the letter the next morning. He had started it the evening before and, after a surprisingly fear-free night, he had woken early to resume the confession he was relating to Frankie's girlfriend.

After enduring thirty years during which saying anything unguarded would earn him mention in the gossip columns, it now felt new and refreshing for him to write what he thought, instead of writing in the style of The Ian Taylor.

He quite liked this other bloke that he'd discovered inside himself and he was just telling all of this to Janice, and crediting Frankie for initiating the excavation, when a guard disturbed him and woke Cairns by nosily unlocking their cell.

'Right Taylor, on your feet and get dressed. The governor wants you.'

Taylor was just at that moment composing an important paragraph that had begun, 'I think what Frankie wants to tell you...' but he left the pad and pen on his bunk and quickly got himself in a state that was presentable enough for the governor.

As with the other time that he had been summoned from his cell, he had no idea what this meeting would be about but he presumed that, because of his celebrity status, Governor Perkins was covering his rear by continually checking that his famous charge was vaguely comfortable.

'Tall latte for me,' muttered Cairns from under his blanket.

'I'll see you in a minute; wait for me for breakfast,' said Taylor as he left the cell.

When Taylor got to the governor's office, he was not very surprised to see Conrad Marks having coffee and biscuits. He was a little surprised, though, to see that his lawyer was smiling.

'Good morning, Governor,' Perkins remonstrated mildly.

'Sorry, sir,' said Taylor.

'You're coming home Ian,' beamed Marks.

'When?' said Taylor.

'Now.'

'Now?'

'Mr Marks has negotiated your immediate release with my superiors and, off the record, I am delighted,' said the governor.

'Where's Billy?' said Taylor.

'Out the front in the car. I believe there's quite a reception committee,' said Marks.

'You mean press,' said Taylor grimly. 'Who told them? Actually, never mind, I can guess.'

'Shall we go then?' said Marks.

'Can't I have breakfast first?' said Taylor, and was annoyed that they both laughed.

'Excellent,' said Marks.

'No. I mean it,' said Taylor. 'I need to go back to my cell first, to sort something.'

'A guard is collecting your things from your cell, Ian,' said the governor. 'They will be returned on your way out, along with the possessions that were taken when you arrived here. It's all in hand.'

'But I want to go back; I need to say goodbye to my cell-mate and quickly finish something up,' Taylor insisted.

'You can write to him, he's not going anywhere,' said Marks, taking him by the arm.

Taylor jerked himself away from his solicitor and faced the governor.

'Sir. I really do need to just say a few things to Fran… inmate Cairns, sir. Please.'

'I'm sorry, Ian, but it's all been arranged by the higher-ups,' said Perkins.

'But just for a minute…'

'Ian. We have to go now,' said Marks looking at his watch anxiously. 'Trust me, there is no choice in this.'

'But surely you can give me a minute…'

'We're running late as it is, I'm afraid,' said Marks.

'Late? Late for what? The fucking eight o'clock news?'

'Language, Taylor,' said the guard, sternly.

They walked to the main exit, retrieved his possessions and ushered him into a small room where he was told to change back into his civvies. Taylor did what he was told sullenly and without saying a word. As he finished changing he opened the door and indicated with a jerk of his head that his solicitor should come into the room.

'What's this all about, Con?' he said evenly. 'Why the rush? It's not a fucking photo-op, is it?'

'It's the Home Office's idea, Ian,' said the lawyer nervously. 'Some of the press has been giving them a bit of stick for jailing you, they want the world to see you released.'

'Live on the breakfast news, I suppose?'

'Billy says it's great publicity, apparently. He says it will do wonders for the housewives' sympathies.'

'He would,' said Taylor, striding out of the room to shake hands with the governor and sign more autographs before the guards finally opened the large front gate and he stepped back into a different form of insanity again.

Taylor was not in the least surprised to see thirty photographers and a dozen television crews. Instead of waving, he ignored them and turned back to the guard who had let him out.

'My cellmate, Frankie Cairns. Can somebody get him a message? Tell him that I said thanks.'

'Anything else, Ian?' said the guard.

'No, except thank you.'

When he turned his back on the Scrubs again, he was Ian Taylor; grinning, peace-signing and affably posing for the photographers.

'How was prison?' gushed a reporter from BBC News.

'Eye-opening,' said Taylor and the press laughed. He saw Billy leaning from the window of a black stretch limo and calling him over. As the sound bite was accomplished, four of his security team suddenly took control, barging a gap for him through the media and, within seconds, he was sitting in the back of the limo, his eyes seeing only stars from the photographers' flashguns.

Inside the stretch there was more commotion; Billy Vernon was opening champagne and letting it gush all over the carpeted floor, a large joint was lit and put in his hand and Vernon was shouting, 'And the coke! Give him the coke!'

'No thanks,' said Taylor.

As his senses became realigned, Taylor saw that Vernon was accompanied by Klive Whicker, the press officer from BPA.

'How was it?' said Vernon grinning.

'Illuminating,' said Taylor. 'Where are we going?'

'To The Savoy.'

'For a free breakfast,' smiled Whicker. 'A free break...'

'Yeah, I get it.'

As they drove across London, Vernon detailed the swell of public calls for his release, the newspapers' support, that it was proposed to move the Westminster Abbey gig to five nights at Earls Court to accommodate demand and how the band were all up for it.

Vernon noticed that Taylor just listened and did not interrupt for a change. He presumed that he must be tired, which was understandable after all he'd been through. As the limo swept up to the riverside entrance to The Savoy, Taylor saw more crowds of media and scores of fans waving banners celebrating his freedom.

'How did that mob know to be here?' said Taylor.

'We had it announced on Capital Radio,' said Whicker.

'Good-oh,' said Taylor, a thin smile disguising his sarcasm.

The limo stopped and a dozen more security heavies pushed the crowd back so that Taylor could enter the hotel unmolested.

'We'll go straight in,' said Vernon, shifting across his seat to open the car door.

'No we won't' said Taylor, getting out of the car and grinning for the cameras again. After posing for some moments, he raised his hands for the press clamour to silence and then methodically issued a long, ad libbed statement that thanked everybody for their support, including 'my new pals at the Scrubs'.

He answered five or six questions on camera, posed for more photographs and then said, 'OK guys, I've got to split and get some breakfast. You've got everything you need, so let's call it a day, yeah?'

The reporters and crews nodded assent, patted his back and let him go unbothered.

'Who's here?' said Taylor as Vernon led the way into the hotel.

'Oh, just friends. People from the office, a few from the label. People who want to congratulate you.'

'On what?'

'On your triumph.'

'What triumph would that be, then?'

'You're the hottest news in showbiz, Ian. Everybody's raving about the war stand you've made. They're calling you the peace-maker on Radio 1; you're a hero and you're going to sell millions!'

'Hmm,' said Taylor.

He was surprised when he entered the Savoy ballroom, as he would never have said that the number of his 'friends' would run into the hundreds of people he saw before him. A big band struck up a version of 'Please Release Me', there was loud cheering and applause and balloons fell from a net attached to the ceiling.

The first person to shake his hand was Justin Abford, the president of BPA. 'Well done, well done. This'll be a number one album all over again, a huge seller,' he said smiling, as Taylor noticed a video crew that he had used before record every moment.

'Congratulations, Ian,' said the associate editor of the *Sun*. 'I've been talking to Klive about a three-day series – 'My Jailhouse Rock' – we'll run it around the album release, of course.'

'Ian, can I introduce Ethan Yintov,' said a beaming Billy Vernon as he pushed the controller of BBC Arts to him. 'Ethan wants to talk to us about a documentary…'

'…charting your struggle,' offered Yintov.

'What struggle?' asked Taylor genuinely but they just laughed and Vernon said something about 'modesty'.

'I love you man,' said a thin and receding man of almost sixty who threw his arms around Taylor in a dramatic hug. 'You're the fucking best, man. The best!' Over his embracer's shoulder, Taylor made a quizzical look at Vernon, who stepped in quickly to say that Roy had flown in from France for the party.

Roy? thought Taylor. My old bassist? He looks fucking dreadful.

He heard a familiar voice say, 'Sweetheart,' and he turned away from Roy Adams to see Eileen Lore standing there beaming with open arms, her decrepitude paying tribute to the skills of whoever was airbrushing her album covers. His face hid his shock but his eyes did not, and Eileen saw it immediately. She, too, hugged him and, as she did, she whispered in his ear, 'We've all aged, darling, but I'm still as hot as ever with the lights off. I'll show you, later.'

Like the Queen on dope, a dazed Taylor uncertainly threaded through a throng of excited congratulators, many of whom, he noticed through a gauze of unreality, seemed to have damp nostrils. A glass was put in his hand and filled with champagne as his mind studied the surreal scene as if he was watching a movie. This must be costing somebody a fortune; me, probably he thought as he half-listened to Des and Les, the TV duo that Taylor called Hiss and Piss, tell him how their mothers were huge fans and how pleased they were to be hosting the broadcast of the Rose gig.

Taylor looked at his watch. It was now more than an hour since he had left Wormwood Scrubs and in that time he had been welcomed by around six or seven hundred people. He noticed that so far nobody had asked him if he was okay in himself.

'Ian! Ian!' he heard his manager cry. 'Can we just get a shot of you with Justin? It's for Billboard.'

'I need a piss,' said Taylor and he walked off in what he recalled was the direction of the toilets.

CHAPTER 41

The gentlemen's lavatories were empty except for an elderly black attendant who smiled a welcome even though it was obvious to Taylor that he didn't know who he was.

Why don't toilet attendants ever come in white? Taylor thought as he saw that the doors to all four cubicles were locked. The tap-tap-tap of plastic on porcelain betrayed the purpose of their occupancy and Taylor bitterly reflected that the cost of that was probably coming off his album's promo budget too.

He was relieving himself at the urinals and hoping that he had a few quid in his pocket for the attendant who was hovering behind him, waiting to brush the dandruff from his shoulders, when he heard another sound from the cubicles; the sound of a camera lens electronically focussing.

He zipped up, washed and dried his hands and finding only five and twenty pound notes in his wallet, he tipped the attendant with two of the former. Then he left the toilet but stood around in the corridor, pretending to be on his mobile. After some moments and an exchange of smiles with guests at his party whom he did not know, the door to the Gents' opened and a short man wearing cheap shoes and a scruffy parka over a badly-cut, worn suit stepped out, looking about anxiously.

His eyes fixed on Taylor seconds before Taylor's right hand shot out to ram him against the wall and hold him by the neck.

''Ere, fuck off, this is assault,' said the paparazzo.

'No, this is assault,' said Taylor as he kneed the photographer hard in the groin and then, as he doubled up, hit him hard with his left fist on the end of his nose, where he knew that punches hurt the most.

'Jesus!' exploded the snapper as blood splattered across the front of his grey shirt.

'Where's your mate?' said Taylor, kneeing him in the testicles again without waiting for his answer.

'Arrghh!' reacted the photographer.

Taylor took the man's bleeding nose between his forefinger and thumb and twisted it violently. The photographer screamed.

'Your mate. You lot work in pairs. Where is he?'

The man was spared from answering by a movement that Taylor caught in the side of his eye. He spun his head and saw he was looking right into the lens of a camera aimed at him by a young woman.

Taylor hurled the bleeding and crumpled body of the first photographer into his companion, knocking her down. Then he kicked the man in the groin again.

'You're gonna fucking get it!' yelled the girl, clambering to her knees and pointing her camera at Taylor again. He kicked the camera hard, jerking it out of her hands and then he kicked again, striking her high in the chest with his foot and catching her in the face. Now she was bleeding too.

'I pose for your fucking pictures! I stand there giving quotes and you fucking scum always have to have more!' seethed Taylor as he tore the cameras from their necks and repeatedly smashed them against the wall.

'You've fucking had it! I'm suing!' shouted the girl, whom Taylor noticed was in her mid-twenties and plain, going on ugly.

'Good! Here's another ten grand,' yelled Taylor as he slapped the girl on the face, smashing her glasses and making her weep with pain.

He was about to hit her again when he was distracted by the arrival of three of the hotel's security team.

'Keep hold of these two, they attacked me. And take their mobiles off them,' ordered Taylor as he strode back into the ballroom, holding the damaged cameras by their straps in his left fist.

Ignoring the simpering well-wishers, he barged through the crowd seeking out Klive Whicker, whom he spotted leaning against a pillar laughing with a glamorous BBC entertainment news presenter.

‘A word, please,’ said Taylor, aware that three of his own security team were now standing beside him.

‘Oh. Hello. Ian… Have you met Cassandra?’

‘No. And I don’t fucking want to,’ said Taylor, holding up the cameras. ‘Do you know anything about these?’

‘Wh… what do you mean?’ said Whicker and Taylor could see his answer in the frightened PR’s eyes.

‘You invited fucking paparazzi to my party?’

‘Umm… no… err… Nobody invited them. They just turned up,’ weaselled Whicker.

‘Fuck off you faggot cunt,’ said Taylor viciously.

‘Dear me,’ said Cassandra.

‘Shut up, you whore,’ said Taylor, turning to Whicker again. ‘Did you know that two snappers were here?’

‘I didn’t invite them.’

‘Did you know that they were here?’

‘Well… yeah, but…’

‘You complete fucking cunt!’ yelled Taylor as he swung the cameras by the straps at Whicker’s head, hitting him on the forehead. The record company’s press officer made no sound as he fell to the floor but Cassandra screamed, activating the security men to intervene and hold their boss back from hitting him again.

‘Ian! What the fuck is happening?’ cried Billy Vernon as he finally arrived at his master’s side. ‘Ian! You can’t do this! You’re on bail!’

‘We’ve been stitched up,’ said Taylor, glowering.

‘Those photographers, was that you?’ said Vernon, panicking wildly.

‘Yes.’

‘You can’t hit photographers!’

‘Why not? It appears to work,’ seethed Taylor.

‘You’re bloody mad!’ howled Cassandra, who was tending on the floor to a badly-bleeding and unconscious Whicker.

‘Really?’ snarled Taylor.

‘I’m telling this to my viewers,’ threatened Cassandra.

‘Tell this to your fucking viewers,’ said Taylor as he spat at her.

'Jesus!' said Vernon in horror and he tried to grab Taylor, but the star shook him off as he pushed through the startled crowd to the stage.

The band was playing but stopped when Taylor climbed onto the stage and took the microphone from the lead singer.

'Ladies and gentlemen,' he said to a room that was immediately silent. 'I don't know who the hell most of you are, so no change there.'

There was a titter of laughter from one corner of the room but most of the faces stayed stony and confused.

'Thank you for coming to my freedom party in the hope of meeting me. Sorry that things have got a little out of hand. I'm leaving early because I can't play this stupid game any more.'

Taylor walked away from the microphone and heard a shocked woman at the front of the stage say, 'What does he mean?'

He walked back to the microphone again.

'And just to fuck-up the damage-limitation department, let me make it clear that I am not drunk, nor on drugs. Thank you for all the years of your salaried friendship.'

He got off the stage and was immediately flanked by his entire security contingent, their jaws jutting and shoulders back.

'Let's get out of here,' said Taylor, walking to the door.

CHAPTER 42

It was slowly dawning on Peter that he was no longer part of the game. When he had first heard the news that Taylor was going to jail he had been thrilled by the PR advantage it afforded but when, seconds later, he realised that none of this was his business any longer, he slumped into a depression that was expressed in the thick clouds of cannabis smoke that were stunting the growth of the dog that sat faithfully in his office passively smoking a much better deal than the beagles got in the cancer labs of Cambridgeshire.

He took another large gulp of the energy drink that he had defiantly adopted as his new coffee, despite its massive caffeine content being far more dangerous to the blood pressure of a heavy-smoker of his age, and he was just about to light another joint in order to balance the buzzing when he noticed a lad standing in the garden outside his shed. The young man was too long-haired to be another reporter and his waistcoat, bangles and elegantly-dishevelled jeans reassured Peter. Ostentatiously still rolling the joint with one hand, with the other Peter opened the shed door and gave the lad a contrived smile.

'Can I help you, mate?' he asked, licking the gummed edge of the Rizla paper.

'Yes,' said the lad, unsmiling.

'How's that, then?' said Peter, more warily now that he was beginning to suspect that the youth was a fan of the singer that Peter had pretentiously started to refer to as 'my ex'.

'I want to be famous and apparently you're the man for that.'

Peter had heard that too many times before and wearily he hung his head to concentrate on finishing building the joint.

'Sorry mate, I'd rather give you the clap.'

'What?' said the lad, whose eyes had not left Peter's face.

'You really don't want to be famous, it's a shit life.'

'How would you know?' said the lad, candy-coating the

challenge with a smile.

'Sorry?' said Peter, a bit winded but attracted by the lack of the usual fan deference.

'Well, you're not famous, you just know people who are famous and...'

'And I also know that they have shit lives.'

'Do they? Or do they just make your life shit?' said the unblinking wannabe.

Refusing to be corrected on the calibration of his own misery, Peter lit the joint and inhaled in silence, his own eyes now not wavering from the lad's intense stare.

'And you are?' he said eventually.

'Steve Little,' said the lad, extending his hand.

In reply, Peter passed him the joint.

'You've obviously got a good dealer, though,' said Little, coughing as he passed it back after a couple of tokes.

'Very important in my game.'

'So you're still in the game, then?'

'To be uncharacteristically honest, no, I'm probably not. And I probably don't want to hear your demo or see your DVD or hear how good some amateur rock critic has claimed you to be in a local newspaper whose opinion does not matter at all.'

'They said you were a rude bastard,' said Little, smiling again.

'Did they also say that I was an alcoholic and a drug addict and that I've lost everything including 'it'?'

'Yes,' said Little. 'And that you're a manic depressive and that you have the petulance of a two-year-old and the morality of Rabelais.'

'I'm impressed, at least that you've heard of Rabelais,' said Peter, truthfully. 'But I still don't think that a bright lad like you plainly are would want to be famous if he knew what it entails.'

'Which is what?'

'Famous people are owned by those they do not know, that's nice for starters,' said Peter sarcastically. 'Fame means no more anonymity, no more crossing the road without being pestered, no more being the judge of your own life, no more anything other than being constantly heckled by utter strangers who demand that you must always be better.'

'And a lot of money,' said Little.

'Yeah. And a good supply of all the treasures and pleasures.'

'Sounds like a fair swap, I'm in.'

'Fame is a suicide of identity that nobody else knows you've committed,' said Peter, thinking that he should write that one down. 'Once you're famous, you have to be who strangers demand you to be. You don't change in yourself, but everybody else changes how they react to you – causing you to become the very lonely expression of their wants rather than of your will.'

'You should write that down,' said Steve.

'Nobody reads what I write,' said Peter flatly. 'And even if they did, even if it was written on the menus at the BAFTA awards, it wouldn't make any difference because I'm history. Which is a drag because once you've tasted fame, you'll want it for the rest of your life and that, that wanting will ruin, or at least rule, the rest of your life. As they say, a glimmer is more addictive than smack.'

'It's curious to hear a drunk like you remonstrating against the evils of addiction,' said Little. 'I'd heard that mad old Peter Forth was up for anything so long as it was dangerous.'

Peter grinned at the cheek, which appealed to him. He continued to smoke the joint, not passing it this time to this determined youth, whose attitude he was already liking.

'Look, it's not a matter of just being in; you don't just volunteer and then you're in the charts with a bird sitting on your face. Are you any good? Will you sing to an audience of three until your throat bleeds? Do you have any songs?

'Yes.'

'OK, come in,' he said and ushered the lad into his shed, indicating that he should sit down next to Peter's stoned dog on the old sofa.

'Let's have a listen then,' he said and Little passed him a CD.

The first two tracks were a big sound and cheerily upbeat; Peter thought Little's band sounded like Lynyrd Skynyrd, chirpy and chippy, but certainly no better than he was expecting from a demo of a band that he presumed he had never heard of. But the third track, a ballad, made him actually bother to look at the CD sleeve to see its title. It was Neil Young-like, layered with a grandeur of clever variations on a simple melody that stuck in his head like he had been hearing it all his life.

'OK, I'm in. You're good,' said Peter impulsively.

'In for what?' said Little.

'Err… I presume you're asking me to do your publicity. Why else would you come knocking at my door?'

'Drugs?' said Little, grinning.

Peter stared him out.

'We don't want you to do our PR, we've got a PR; we want you to manage us.'

'What's the name of your band?' said Peter.

'Tundra Pox,' said Little.

'And what's the name of your PR?'

'Catherine Hornby.'

'Really?' said Peter, smiling. 'Where is Catherine these days?'

'Oh, she moved out of the flat since she got her new bloke.'

'What new bloke's that?' said Peter, too eagerly.

'Umm … well that's not really for me to say. I don't know if it's a secret or not' said Little, rather gallantly for a youth Peter thought.

'Err… does she know that you want me to manage you?' said Peter, warily.

'Oh sure,' said Little. 'It was her suggestion.'

'Excellent. Excellent. Let's set up a meeting with Catherine and the band. By the way, that name Tundra thing, it has to go.'

'Why?'

'Because it's shit, people don't really dig the word Pox.'

'The name stays,' said the lad evenly, staring out Peter. 'The band like it and it's our band.'

'Oh you'll go far, thinking like that,' said Peter, grinning, 'but as a minor precaution against your arrogance, may I have some sort of small signing fee?'

'I guess,' said the boy, smiling. 'Talk to Catherine, she's also doing all our accounts'.

CHAPTER 43

Billy Vernon stood on the kerb of a corner of The Embankment getting increasingly sodden by the London rain and increasingly furious that all the chauffeured cars had been commandeered by security to tail Taylor when he left The Savoy in the limo.

He had been waving at taxis for twenty minutes but all of them had been occupied, and he was resigned to catching the Tube back to the office when his mobile rang again. He ignored it.

Vernon was depressed and weary of telling a stream of callers that yes, there had been an incident and no, he did not see Ian hit anybody and sorry, but as he was not a lawyer he could not comment on whether these new and alleged assaults would affect the terms of Ian's remand, bail or whatever it was that technically precluded Taylor from going about beating up whomever he felt like attacking.

Vernon calculated the tasks that lay ahead of him and considered that it might be less of a problem just to jump off Waterloo Bridge and allow himself to drown.

On the one hand, it appeared relatively straightforward; he only had to organise the comeback concert and its global telecast of a controversial show during which Britain's most-idolised rock star would have some sort of sex onstage with somebody in order to draw world attention to the peace call of the associated album that the concert was designed to promote.

But stacked against this was a collection of setbacks; his artist was charged with assaulting a Member of Parliament and would be sought, at any moment, to help the police with their enquiries into an assault on a BBC presenter, the assault and battery of two photographers and a rap of grievous bodily harm, at least, against an executive of his own record company. Vernon was beginning to appreciate why people took heroin.

And, he recalled ruefully, there were also the minor matters of

Ian living under the threat of being outed for previously-unsuspected homosexual activity by a woman claiming to be his banished love-child. A woman, he reminded himself bitterly as he attempted to reach Peter on the phone for the fiftieth unsuccessful time, of whom only one person knew her whereabouts and that person had been alienated against sharing her location with them by a rash sacking.

Oh and… yes, Vernon considered, let's not forget the fact that every media organisation on the planet was now hunting for Ian Taylor, who had wisely planned for this occasion by firing one of his two PRs and hospitalising the other.

Vernon began to giggle at the surreal nature of his situation. He noticed that people passing by were giving him, the manager of one of rock music's most acclaimed stars, the sort of glances that people always gave to nutters who stood drenched in the rain chortling to themselves.

His mobile rang again; the caller display said that it was Taylor. 'Ian. Where are you?' said Vernon, a little too anxiously.

'Where are you?'

'On The Embankment out the back of the hotel. I'm trying to get a cab.'

'I'll come and get you. Look out for a black Porsche.'

'I thought you were in the stretch?' said Vernon, confused.

'It's a bit too 'look at me' to be safe, under the circumstances. I had the limo drop me at a dealer's on Park Lane and got myself a 911. Wonderful things, credit cards. If you've got the credit.'

'Ian, we have to talk,' urged Vernon.

'Yeah, yeah. I know; everybody's looking for me, especially the press. It's cool, Billy, we just need to get away for a bit. To somewhere they won't think of. You and I are going to take a little trip down to see Jack.'

'Jack?'

'See? Even you're surprised. Stay in the rain, where I can spot you. I'm on The Mall, I'll be there in a tick.'

CHAPTER 44

Peter had been drinking most of the day. He had said he wouldn't but now he was, so fuck it. He had also decided to further aggravate his standing with others by now driving very badly around Dorset in a confused fog of what to do with himself.

Had he been driving a smaller car he would probably have crashed it, but fortunately the Volvo pretty much drove itself and Peter just followed the bends and the hedges as he listened to a BBC Radio 5 Live's idiot hour, or whatever it was that they called their phone-ins.

He was muddling around the back roads when the phone-a-fool show was interrupted by a news bulletin on 'the latest dramatic development in the shock Ian Taylor controversy.'

The effervescing news presenter passed the baton of the report to, 'our man on the spot, outside the record company,' who started babbling away about, 'a reconciliation' that BPA was seeking with the 'fugitive Ian Taylor' who had disappeared to somewhere beyond the media's imagination.

The reporter gushingly revealed that the BBC had been deluged with calls of support for Taylor from the public and that Ladbroke's had made the Grey Rose album five to four favourite to be number one in the charts in its first week of release. A Lib-Dem MP from the West Midlands was apparently launching a campaign to have Taylor knighted for services to humanity, whatever the fuck that meant, and an unidentified record company spokesman said that BPA would be printing up to ten million copies of the reissued album whilst the editor of *Mojo* magazine had opined that Taylor could earn more than three million dollars from broadcast rights of what they now appeared to be calling, 'The Peace Gig'.

The reporter added – a little cuttingly, Peter felt – that Taylor's long-time spokesman was not taking calls, amid unconfirmed reports that the PR has been dismissed for this publicity disaster.

Peter was furious, livid, to be outed in public, scapegoated for what he felt was not his fault. OK, he decided in that moment, two can play silly buggers.

He continued to listen as it was revealed how crowds of girls had apparently spontaneously gathered to hold a vigil for peace outside Taylor's London home, and that the recently bloodied photographers had dropped actions against him following an undisclosed settlement for damages. The reporter then again told the presenter that in the last few minutes there has been a dramatic development.

'Which is what?' said the presenter, speaking for the nation.

'Well, this is unconfirmed, but we have heard that the church synod and the authorities of Westminster Abbey have refused permission for Ian Taylor to stage his peace gig there. We are hearing that they have decided not to allow the concert because of fears over possible problems with crowd control.'

Well there's a fucking surprise.

'But we have also heard that the Bishop of Birmingham has stepped in is offering Ian Taylor the cathedral in his own home town for the concert.'

And there's another.

'Anyway, thank you David, I'm sure we'll be hearing from you again later. And of course *Radio 5 Live* will be bringing you all the developments in this remarkable Ian Taylor story as they happen, including the latest news – in case you just missed it – that church authorities have banned Ian Taylor from Westminster Abbey because of serious fears of a riot. And now, cricket…'

Riot? Nobody mentioned the word riot.

Peter was tempted to pull over at and call up *5 Live* to shout abusive corrections at them. But although he was feeling more sober than he had been, he knew that the whisky would have left anger in his blood and he didn't especially want to make himself even more of a hopeless case by going on the radio ranting.

As the alcohol's surreal effect of acting like gauze between Peter and reality began to wear off, he drove faster. He'd switched off the radio now, preferring to listen to old-style rhythm and blues played at top volume. He had just joined the A30 heading west when his private mobile began to vibrate. It was Susie. He pulled over, wearily, into a lay-by.

'Hello,' he said, flatly.

'How are you doing?'

'Fine, I'm going to go to a meeting.'

'I think that's wise,' said Susie sympathetically.

'I don't know about wise, but it's a bloody necessity,' said Peter, unkindly.

'What are you going to say there?' said Susie, saying the wrong thing and immediately realising it.

'What?'

'I mean… oh, I don't know what I mean… Umm… I mean are you going to tell them you've been fired?'

'It doesn't work like that. It's not a mothers' coffee morning, you're not reporting on what's happened since they last saw you. You don't swap photos of your family holiday at these things or report news. In my experience people tend to say the same fucking thing over and over and over again.

'Well, I think you are very brave for going…'

'There's nothing brave about it, it's not intimidating enough to need courage. It's just a bunch of people sitting around drinking coffee and looking like they got dressed in the dark…'

'Well I think you're brave. And if you come home sober…'

'What do you mean?'

'Never mind… let's just see,' she teased.

His mood brightened immediately and his tone told her so. She was pleased. Offloading to Sandy had somehow cleared her options for her, but her conscience was still nudging her to try to mend things. They talked on for a while about the impending financial disaster that now faced them and she tried to persuade him that it would be fun to be church mice for a while.

Peter had his doubts about that. He could see no fun in not being able to afford to behave as he pleased, but he didn't want yet another argument so he let it go and promised to see her later, sober.

CHAPTER 45

Following the breakdown of relations with Peter, Catherine had immediately adjusted her aim to make Jack Jackson the new target of her seduction. She didn't really want to sleep with anyone in order to get close to Taylor, but her purpose was more pressing than her conscience. So she had slept with Jackson twice during the last three days. He had demanded more sex and only some expert fellatio and the fabricated excuse of her period had kept his interest.

Catherine had been much amused by the recent glut of increasingly bizarre news stories about Taylor's antics, but she was alarmed to learn that he had now started attacking women. To her, that signalled that Taylor was losing it fast, and she feared she couldn't afford to waste any time in getting to him before he pulled that old rock chestnut of asphyxiating on his own vomit. However, she decided to allow herself a little playtime, so she had been intrigued to hear from Jack that they were to attend the 'Pete is Free' party that Sandy McAlpine was organising. Not that she had been invited *per se*, but her double roles as Jack's date and the PR of Tundra Pox, who were booked to play, would legitimise her presence.

Catherine smiled as she imagined the discomfort that her being at the party might cause. All that remained now was for her to cause further unease by arriving at the party in an outfit that would totally piss off every other woman present. Especially Susie.

'Lover, I need to go shopping. Do you want to come?' she said as she turned to face Jackson, who was watching TV on the sofa.

'What, again?' said Jackson, engrossed in MTV.

'I need party shoes,' she explained, smiling as she tousled his hair.

'Do you now? Why? Are you on the pull?' said Jackson dozily.

'Might be,' she teased. 'There's bigger fish than you, you know.'

'Possibly,' grinned Jackson, 'but very few bigger… you know.'

'Don't I just? Do you usually supply wheelchairs for your

girlfriends, lover?'

Jackson laughed, delighted by the compliment.

'How to do you think your friend Ian will have coped with prison?' she delved, having buttered him up.

'Ha!' said Jackson, smiling to himself.

'What?'

'Nothing. Well, nothing that I can tell you about.'

So he knows too, Catherine thought as she continued to beam at him.

'Actually,' considered Jackson, 'he'd probably cry. Maybe, I don't know what he's like now. Although I suspect that Ian wouldn't be thrilled by the challenge to his way of doing things.'

'What do you mean?' said Catherine.

'Taking orders from others. It's not one of Ian's strongest points.'

'What are his strong points?' she pressed.

'Self-preservation, obstinacy, genius… he's a great one for doing what you don't expect. Oh, and he's got a thing about girls in boots.'

Very good to know, thought Catherine.

CHAPTER 46

Although Billy Vernon did not believe in God, he began to pray quite intently as Ian Taylor floored the accelerator of the Porsche and the black car shot out of the gates of his Wiltshire mansion the next morning with such velocity that two of the cabal of waiting photographers missed injury by millimeters. Without hesitating to check whether the car had hit anybody, Taylor sped off in the direction of the Salisbury road as camera flashes burst in their wake and the paps shouted bastard and you fucking prick.

'Bloody idiots,' said Vernon as he wondered whether Taylor permitted people to smoke in his car. 'Somebody's going to get killed one of these days.'

'Probably,' said Taylor, thinking of the paparazzi at the Savoy.

'Actually, it would be good if one of those bastards was killed. It would be better if a whole bunch of them died. It would hugely improve matters,' said Vernon.

'I guess they must make a lot of people feel like that sometimes,' said Taylor, wondering what had got into Billy.

'It would be the best thing that could happen for this country,' added Vernon.

He became more nervous as Taylor took one hand off the steering wheel in order to rummage in his Levi jacket for a small, neatly rolled joint that he then lit with the car's cigarette lighter.

'How do you mean?' said Taylor, who was horrifying Vernon by aiming to get stoned and drive at double the speed limit.

'The paparazzi have done more than anyone in the past ten years to destroy the morality of this country. Somebody ought to begin killing them. You watch, it'll happen,' explained Vernon, wondering what was the matter with Taylor, as he was not saying much.

'I take it you don't agree, Ian?' said Vernon, gratefully receiving the joint simply because it meant that the driver wouldn't be smoking it.

'Err…'

'They've killed the respect for stars. All that hanging around outside clubs to get shots of stars when they're pissed, that's humanised celebrities, it's destroyed the illusion that stars are superior people and it's all the fault of those bastard paparazzi. They should be scared off the streets. Everyone would benefit. You should mention it in your next interview.'

'Seriously?' said Taylor.

'Not really, Ian,' chuckled Vernon, thinking this is odd.

Vernon thought this might be the time to voice his concerns about the repercussions of Taylor's part in the ethic cleansing of the British media but he expected to be told to shut up about all of that. He was not having a great day. Taylor had not bothered to reveal how long they would be staying in Dorset, or even where they would be staying, thus forcing Vernon to cover all bases and book suites for them both at hotels in Lyme Regis and every neighbouring town. Vernon had shouted at the managers of almost every establishment, demanding the best suites for him and his unnamed companion.

'Did you see that poll in the *Telegraph*?' he asked. 'They did a poll of Britain's brainiest people, and eighty per cent of our liberal intellectuals said that they want Britain to go back to the way it used to be, like in the sixties. People want the past to be their future. Do you know why?'

'No,' said Taylor, delighted to be given the opportunity not to have to contribute to the bizarre conversation and wondering whether Billy had been drinking.

'The past is safe, Ian. We know where we are with the past. That's why people enjoy nostalgia; it's not asking you to learn new tricks. People don't want more danger and risk in their world anymore, they want idols who stand for tradition because tradition is valued in a world of fear. People have had too much change, Ian. People in Britain want to go back to when everyone had a place.'

'What, like owning your own house?'

'No, in society. Where people got to be famous because they deserved to be famous, because they had talent, and they'd grafted to get there and they'd learnt how to deal with it…'

'Deal with what?' said Taylor, wishing he had not let Billy smoke his dope.

'With fame. If you're not talented but you become famous then the whole system comes crashing down because it loses all validity, any measure of excellence, if just anybody can attain it. Fame has become too easy, Ian.'

'You're right, it is too easy to be a star now,' he ventured. 'I suppose it does require some training to cope in a world where nobody will ever disagree with you.'

'And that's a power that shouldn't be in the hands of nerds and bimbos,' said Vernon, confused that Taylor was appearing to agree with him. 'TV and technology have made it too easy for the ordinary. I think people want heroes back. It's funny, us lot used to worry that the suits would take over, we didn't think about the anorak threat.'

'Excuse me, Billy,' said Taylor, thinking that his manager was both a suit and an anorak, 'but have you ever thought that people like me become this way by listening to the sort of shit that you've just said?'

'Sorry,' said Vernon, 'I was only saying what Pete used to argue.'

Vernon spoke before his brain shrieked don't say that. He automatically hunched his shoulders and was surprised when Taylor did not fly into a fury at the mention of his former publicist and uneasy as Taylor maintained a total silence for some minutes.

'Have you spoken to Pete?' Taylor asked eventually.

'Not really,' said Vernon defensively.

'What do mean, not really? How can you not really speak to someone? What's not really speaking to them? Ringing them up and putting the phone down when they answer?'

'Err… I spoke to him a while back, when you said to find out if he had any ideas for girls for the 'Come to Daddy' thing,' excused Vernon, relieved that the old, argumentative Taylor was returning.

'What 'Come to Daddy' thing?! What thing is that? The thing? What the fuck is the thing?' said Taylor who, Vernon recalled, was rarely entirely pacified by cannabis.

'Err… the gig. The gig. You said to ask him if he knew of any girls who'd want the part in 'Come to Daddy'.'

'And did he?'

'Err… yeah… Err… he said he had pix of a couple of girls who might be right.'

'Well fucking phone him up. Go on! Phone him and ask him about Catherine. Ask him where her fucking picture is. If she's in Dorset I want to see her. Do you know where she is?'

'Err… only Pete knows that, Ian. I'm afraid I got distracted by the recent events and he hasn't given me her contacts.'

'Well get them off him now,' ordered Taylor. 'I'm not having Pete knowing something we don't. I don't want him having any hold over me.'

Vernon began to scroll through the contacts on his mobile for Peter's number. He knew it was a waste of time because he was expecting him to be difficult. As he rang, Taylor interrupted with more of his obvious instructions.

'And don't tell him you're with me. Pretend I'm not here,' ordered Taylor.

Vernon heard the phone ring twice before a recording of Peter's voice cut in. He rang off.

'Answerphone,' he said.

'Try his mobile,' said Taylor.

Vernon did and got the same result, which he told Taylor.

'His mobile's off too? What is the fucking point of him having a mobile if I can't get through to him? Why's he turned it off when he knows I might want him?' said Taylor, who believed that other people's telephones were devices created entirely for his convenience.

'Maybe he thinks he doesn't need to be on call now that he's been sacked,' suggested Vernon, bravely.

'Who says he's been sacked?' said Taylor, astounded.

'Err… you did. You sacked him at the BBC.'

'Oh for Christ's sake!' Taylor exploded. 'Pete's so fucking sensitive that you can't even sack him without upsetting him. I only said he was fired because he'd pissed me off, it was just a bollocking. I suppose he's bloody sulking now. Does he really think he's been fired?'

'Err… yes,' said Vernon. 'Everybody thought you meant it.'

'Did I tell anybody that I meant it? Did I tell you that I meant it? Have I put it in writing? Why can't I just lose my temper occasionally without everybody taking me so seriously?'

'Are you saying he's not fired?'

'Are you fucking deaf?' shouted Taylor. 'Fucking phone him up and tell him that I'm ordering him to be un-fired. Tell him I'm fucking cross that he's saying he's been fired, he's got no right to do that unless I say so!'

'I'm not sure he'll believe me,' said Vernon nervously.

'Well then fucking find somebody who he will believe and fucking tell them to tell him! Jesus!'

Vernon rang Peter and Susie's home number. The phone rang several times before Susie answered it.

'Oh, hello Susie,' said Vernon in a voice that he forced to sound chirpy. 'It's Billy. How are you?'

'Hello Billy,' said Susie, surprised. 'I didn't expect to be hearing from you again. What can I do for you?'

'What's she saying?' whispered Taylor, confusing Vernon as to whom to answer.

'Err…' said Vernon.

'Don't say I'm here,' hushed Taylor.

'Billy?' said Susie.

'Err… is Pete around?' said Vernon.

'He's upstairs in bed. He's got a headache.'

'What's she saying?' persisted the whispering Taylor.

'Err…' said Vernon.

'What?' said Susie, irritated that partners were forever passed over in the work enquiries that people like Billy Vernon treated as matters of state.

'Err… may I speak to him?'

'Tell her to just bloody get him on the phone,' hissed Taylor.

'Well, no, actually,' said Susie reasonably. 'He's got a headache.

He's trying to sleep it off. Can I get him to ring you when he wakes up?'

'Err… can't he get to the phone? Just for a minute?' tried Vernon.

'Tell her you have to talk to him. Tell her it's urgent,' whispered Taylor.

'Who's that with you?' said Susie.

'Sorry… it's, err…. just the radio,' said Vernon, waving his free hand at Taylor to shush him.

'Hmm,' said Susie. 'Anyway, sorry Billy, but I'm not getting him up. Besides, he doesn't work for you guys any longer. Remember?'

'Err… yeah. That's what I wanted to talk to him about.'

'What? What are you saying? What's she saying?' said Taylor faintly.

'Pete's no longer available. Sorry. But you and your hissing friend there are, of course, welcome to come to his leaving do,' said Susie and she rang off.

'Shit,' said Vernon.'she's gone.'

'What do mean gone? Gone where? Did she hang up on us? Fucking cow! She can't fucking ring off! Who the fuck does she think she is? Who the fuck does she think pays her fucking phone bills anyway? Fuck that! Fucking phone her back! Tell her I want to speak to him! What's the matter with him anyway? Why couldn't you talk to him?' said Taylor, furiously.

'Pete's got a headache and she says he's sleeping. She's not gonna budge.'

'Headache? What's he doing having a fucking headache when I want to speak to him? This is fucking bullshit. What's the point of employing people with headaches? You don't catch me having fucking headaches! Nobody doesn't phone me in case I've got a headache! Do you ever consider that I might have a headache when you ring me?'

'Err…' said Vernon, confused as to what was the correct reply.

'Fucking great!' moaned Taylor. 'I can't even fucking talk to my own team when I feel like it now… This is your fault, you know.'

'Sorry?'

'It's your fucking fault! You're meant to be my manager. You're not fucking hard enough on people. That's why they think they can go around having headaches because you're too soft. Nobody ever had headaches in the sixties…'

Abruptly, Taylor stopped shouting.

'Sorry,' he said.

Vernon said nothing because he feared he was hearing things and now he was waiting for the next hallucination, seeing the bats. Bloody strong weed this, he thought, I just imagined that Ian said, 'Sorry.'

CHAPTER 47

As was usual when Peter woke up still drunk, he didn't realise he was still drunk until several minutes after waking. His initial thoughts were of wonderful wellbeing, feeling happy, optimistic and wanting to be nice. He would roll over towards Susie, smile at her still sleeping and, if her back was facing him, snuggle up to the contours of her body to clip together like a couple of worn spoons. And he loved to lie there like that. He could stay there all day like that, just holding onto her as if she was his life raft in the deep seas of his very complicated life. Which she was. Or at least, he thought she was.

Until Susie spoke he knew that he was quite safe. He could just cuddle up and try to remember what had happened the night before. He knew that as soon as she woke, the tone of her voice or the pulling away from him would tell him what he had done. So when Susie got up out of bed without saying a word, without even acknowledging that he was there, he knew that he was going to be saying'sorry' a great deal.

His mind was a complete blank on whatever it was that he should be apologising for on this morning. Peter thought about it and began to consider the likelihood that he was going insane. Perhaps he actually had been driven mad by the pressures now on him – Susie's affair, the strain of persuading the press and public to adore Ian Taylor with a fervour that Ian Taylor believed he deserved, his own worry that he was drinking too much and taking too many drugs and didn't know how to stop.

He wasn't sure what was happening to him but he knew it wasn't normal. For starters, he felt as if his nerves were not up to the task of getting out of bed; by which he meant that he felt as if he had no longer had any nerves left, as if all of his boldness had gone.

He wondered whether this was the nervous breakdown that people had been warning him against working himself into ever since… well, ever since forever. But what actually was a nervous breakdown? He'd read about enough of them, soap stars citing them all over the place whenever they appeared to be out of work, pop singers blaming breakdowns for collapses actually caused by too much cocaine, but he had no real idea of what the symptoms were.

Peter looked to the foot of the bed, where a bookcase hung on the wall holding a collection of cookery and reference books that he kept for reading on Sunday mornings when he had woken early and was bored with nothing to do, not least because Susie had curled away to indicate that nothing was to be done to her. He reached out and pulled the General Family Medical Encyclopaedia from the shelf. He looked up 'nervous breakdown' and was irritated to discover it wasn't listed: apparently such a hideous condition did not afflict the general family.

He reached to the shelf again and pulled out a dictionary, thumbing through the pages until he read that what he was afraid he had was defined as 'any mental illness not primarily of organic origin, in which the patient ceases to function properly…'

Define 'properly', thought Peter's mind, as he knew it would. 'If I'm to be calibrated by the standards of proper people, I'm fucked.' He read on.

'…often accompanied by severely impaired concentration, anxiety, insomnia and lack of self-esteem; used especially of episodes of depression.'

Peter knew that he was perpetually anxious and he couldn't remember the last time he'd felt self-esteem. Probably it was when he won the relay at the school swimming gala in 1972. Certainly he'd never felt good about himself since then. But then that would mean he'd been having a nervous breakdown for the best part of thirty years, and that couldn't be right.

Insomnia, no, he did not suffer from insomnia, but then who could fail to fall asleep if they went to bed having drunk as much as Peter did most nights? Impaired concentration? Again that came back to 'properly'.

He turned back to the family medical textbook and looked up 'depression'. His doctor had said that he was 'severely depressed' when she had put him on Fluoxetine five years ago. Typically, Peter hadn't bothered at the time to investigate what this meant.

Peter read that apparently there were three sorts of depression. Great, he thought, even if I'm ill I have to sit a fucking test to discover what it is that I'm suffering from.

He learned that Reactive Depression was precipitated by chronic illness or death, 'factors that would sadden anyone'. Fine, count that out then.

Next was Involutional Melancholia, which was something you got in middle or old age but the family encylopaedists didn't say why; just something that happened, apparently, like getting liver spots or getting breathless climbing stairs. OK, so he might have that, but then how come that none of his friends of similar age didn't appear to have it?

Finally there was Endogenous Depression, of which there was no obvious cause although it may run in the family. Again, too vague, how far back up the family tree did you have to climb to look for the culprit who gave you that gene?

Peter was just about to conclude, a little disappointedly, that he was not suffering a nervous breakdown when he read 'there may be pure depression or curious mood swings between despair and elation, the condition known as Manic-depressive Psychosis'. That was it, there you go: pure depression. Peter knew that he could not be suffering from anything diluted.

As with everything in his life, even illness had to be extreme. Pure depression; he liked it, it had an arrogant, elitist ring to it, none of your common or garden reactive depression that everybody got when their entire family drowned on The Titantic. No, this was pure shit, way beyond the normal parameters of feeling perpetually unhappy. This was something really to worry about, Grade A insanity. Having learned that he was grotesquely sick, Peter almost began to feel better. Then he heard Susie shout, 'it's eight thirty, we're going soon' from downstairs and he fell back into feeling sorry for himself again as he realised that not even the children wanted to kiss him goodbye anymore.

Probably they were too embarrassed at the sight of their once-dynamic father still lazing and reeking in bed. And who could blame their little minds for being frightened by that? They were not to understand that their Daddy was quite possibly really ill. They could only see that he was being weird, and they wouldn't want to talk about that weirdness because they loved their Dad and they wouldn't want other kids at school to tease them about him because he had been great, once.

He decided that obviously his righteously furious logic was intact but, from Tommy's point of view, that was not a winner in the playground, so he lay back to look at himself.

For a start he felt like crap because, for the first time in his entire life, he was two stone over the weight he had been throughout adulthood. And what bothered him most about being fat, he could barely believe that he was using the word about himself, was that he didn't care. Ordinarily, he would have been shoving his fingers down his throat after every meal, doing loads of cocaine and quite probably using those rapid-release enemas you could buy at the chemist if you could bear the embarrassment of being sold them by some cutie of the counter. But now, Peter just didn't care. If he felt bad about his weight, he just ate more. He knew it, he saw the surprise in people's eyes, but he didn't care.

What else would make his son Tommy worry about him? That his hair was now perpetually uncut, unkempt and unwashed; he rarely shaved. What else? Unless the phone rang he did not get out of bed until ten and then was lying down again by noon. He was losing interest in sex, he had no drive, no ambition, little seemed to interest him.

He remembered that he seemed afraid of talking to people some days, monitoring his calls so that he answered only the ones he actually had to. He seemed afraid a lot, but he was never certain about what frightened him. He wandered around at home wearing the same jeans and sweater that he had worn for four days without changing anything other than his socks.

Peter concluded that he just didn't care about anything anymore. Nothing at all in his or anybody else's life seemed to matter to him; it was as if he had become emotionally paralysed. He thought that anybody else would have accepted the medication and counselling to deal with that, but even in determining his sickness, Peter could not delegate because he didn't trust anybody to do the job as well as himself. Assuming his new role as psychologist, Peter lay in bed debating whether it was the doctor's pills that were his problem.

He had read that Prozac could make you feel worse. Certainly he had been disappointed that the anti-depressants failed to make him feel any of the elation that he logically took to be the opposite of depression. They should have called them 'Just about OK' pills, he felt, and certainly not 'happy pills'. But, he wondered, maybe this was what other people considered to be a state of happiness and, as usual, he expected so much more.

Peter steered himself to work out the meaning of happiness and thought back to the immediate problem that was making him cower at the thought of leaving his bed. Was it the Prozac? So what was it that had caused him to need Prozac in the first place?

He grimaced at the shining truth. It was his bloody job. He knew that now. Somehow, and he was not clear how it had happened or indeed when, but year after year after year of the relentless stress of being the point man for the world's enquiries about the life of Ian Taylor had caused his nerve endings to collapse. He had no defence against the ordinary pressures of life any longer; the incessant anxiety had broken his neurological immune system.

At that point Peter realised with horror that he had AIDS of the mind.

And just as he felt that he really wanted to tell somebody that, he heard Susie shouting up the stairs again, saying that the hot line in his office was ringing like crazy.

'I know!' Peter shouted back.

'Well, aren't you going to get up, then?'

'I can't, I've got AIDS,' said Peter, not yelling.

'What?'

'I said… I've got AIDS of the mind!' he lobbed back, shouting again.

'Oh. Right,' said Susie wearily and Peter thought he also heard her mutter, 'Good.'

CHAPTER 48

Later that day, Peter hauled himself out of bed to give Catherine another call. At the time, she was intent on deciding whether or not to wear a G-string, a thong or nothing at all beneath the fancy dress that she couldn't wait for Susie fuckwit Forth to see, so she ignored the call, as she had all of his recent attempts to contact her because, right now, how best to present her arse was far more important.

She was surprised when he rang back immediately and again, and a bloody gain after that.

'What do you think of my arse?' she said when she finally answered the seventh indication of his persistence.

'Sorry?' said Peter.

'Never mind,' said Catherine, ending the call because she had just noticed that she had not painted her toenails yet.

The goon rang back.

'You know that jeweller's near the Cobb?' she said this time.

'Yes,' said Peter, ready for her games now.

'Do you think they sell clit rings?'

'I believe that's all they sell,' said Peter, making her chuckle.

'What do you want anyway?'

'You,' said Peter.

'What for?'

'There was a story in the Lyme News saying you've got a great arse.'

She giggled and Peter loved the sound of what it suggested.

'What do you want really?' she said.

'I have been thinking and I'm calling to apologise and ask if your arse is still up for grabs?'

'Bollocks.'

'OK. But it's true, actually. I was also calling to ask you about this Tundra Pox business; are you really their publicist?'

'Yep, I'm their purring PR,' replied Catherine. 'Why? Are you going to take the gig?'

'I might take it,' said Peter. 'I want to meet to discuss it.'

'No you don't,' she said as she turned her torso to the mirror to see how she looked in the black knickers that had FUCK ME emblazoned on the back.

'OK, OK, I'm calling to say….'

'What? Just tell me… Actually, I'm not interested. How's my promise coming along?' she replied.

'What promise?'

'The promise you made when I was playing with your balls. The promise that you'd get me close to my father, remember?'

'Oh, that. Sorry. It's sorted,' he lied.

'Liar.'

'How close do you want to get?

'I want to see him alone, as I've told you,' she said.

'OK, well let's meet up to discuss it, then I'll call Billy and arrange something,' Peter lied again. 'Now… about this arse.'

'It's taken,' she said flatly.

'What?'

'It's now in the hands of another, Pete; you had your chance.'

'Fuck,' said Peter dejectedly.

'Err, not for you I'm afraid, darlin',' she added spitefully.

'Well I need to see you. Where are you? You've disappeared,' said Peter, fishing for the information he needed for his new plan.

'I'm surprised you care,' said Catherine flatly, 'I thought you believed that I was just a money-grabbing, mad, bitch fan.'

'Catherine, I'm sorry about losing it like that. I was under a lot of stress. Of course I care. I'd just like to see you for a chat.'

'You're up to something, I can smell it,' she said.

'No I'm not, why are you being so guarded?'

'Hmm… why the sudden change of interest in me, all these calls? How do I know that you're not going to get me arrested?'

'Because I'm not working for him anymore,' said Peter with attempted sincerity.

'Hmm… something's not sounding right. Let me think and I'll call you,' said Catherine, and she ended the call again.

CHAPTER 49

Peter sat morosely in his office, lighting Marlboros and wondering how long it would be until he could only afford to smoke roll-ups. He knew that without the cushion of the £140,000 that Taylor had paid him to be on hand for press liaison night and day including Christmas Day, he was going have to make cut-backs. He was just calculating those cutbacks when his phone rang.

'Where are you?' said Billy, calling from a roadside café where Taylor had stopped so that his manager could buy them coffee.

'Umm, where do you think you are ringing me, Billy?'

'Look Pete,' said Vernon, sounding stern, 'Ian is very wound up about the girl. Has she made contact? Do you know where we can find her?'

'As I said before, I've lost her details and besides, it's not my gig anymore. I can't help you Billy.'

'So, how's the Jobcentre?'

'What do you want, Billy?'

'Nothing. Nothing. Just phoning up to check that you're alright.'

'You mean Ian told you to check that I haven't sold my story to the *News of the World* yet.'

'What do you mean, yet?' said Vernon, immediately alarmed.

'Joke, Bill. Remember them?'

'Yeah, yeah. Right. Ummm…'

'What does he want?' said Peter, sighing wearily.

'Nothing at all,' said Vernon ironically. 'Everything's good for a man on the run, apart from his bloody daughter business. But otherwise, he's got what he wanted: he's all over the papers and he's on every news bulletin. He could get sent down after the BBC skirmish, but he doesn't think that any jury's gonna want to jail Ian Taylor for hitting a MP. Either way, he'll get great publicity for the album and his anti-war thing. He's calling it the punch of peace.'

'Nicely contradictory,' observed Peter.

'What? Oh yeah. And he's well pleased about the BBC syndicating the gig. All those countries! Have you any idea how many albums that'll sell? I told those fuckers at BPA they'd better start printing more albums…'

'What's happening with the band in all of this,' Peter cut in.

'Yeah, they're all on board.'

'Really? I'm surprised. I thought Jackson hated Ian's guts…'

'They all hate Ian's guts, and he hates their guts, but they're doing the gig because of a little thing called a lot of money. Principles and all that cost, but they're for sale just the same. Plus doing the gig gives 'em all the chance to promote their crappy little solo albums that nobody wants to hear,' said Vernon.

'And the gig's moving to Birmingham Cathedral, is that right?'

'Nah. They offered us it but they wanted some stupid no shagging in church clause, which rather defeats the point of all the publicity that's going on. We've dumped all that church shit, he's gonna do it at Earls Court.'

'But I thought he wanted to do it in a place of peace,' said Peter.

'That was your idea, remember? We only went along with it for the publicity. We don't need no church now he's outraged middle England. Now that we've got everybody's attention we need to put on the show in the place where we can get the most bums on seats. But we're gonna make it look like a church, some shit-hot designer from LA is flying in to build a fucking great cathedral set. Ian wants all the stewards dressed as choristers, in cassocks and all that shit.'

'What about the 'Come to Daddy' thing, have you got a bird for that yet?'

'Ah, yeah. Well… actually, he did want me to talk to you about that,' said Vernon.

Here we go, thought Peter.

'Yeah, well the thing is that since you baled out…'

'Got fired.'

'He didn't mean it. He was just stressed. Anyway, we'll come back to that…'

'No we won't,' Peter insisted calmly. 'As I keep on saying, I'm no longer playing the game. Anyway, is he actually going to go through with that?'

'Sort of,' said Vernon.

'What the fuck does that mean?'

'We're thinking of putting a screen up during the song, so that anything that goes on will be seen only in silhouette. But Ian doesn't want anybody to know that before the gig.'

'So they won't actually have sex?'

'Whether they do or not will be up to the bird on the night. We just don't want a load of fans taking fucking pictures on their mobile phones down in the front row.'

'But as far as the press and the public are concerned, the line is that it's going to be an actual shag show? Amsterdam comes to Earls Court ?'

'Of course,' said Vernon, 'We want mayhem on this one, Pete, maximum chaos and mayhem. It's all for a good cause, apparently.'

'Good or bad, it's not my cause anymore,' said Peter.

'You'll be back. You enjoy the torture.'

'No I don't and I won't. I want to do my own thing.'

'By which you mean getting poor and having Susie leave you?' said Vernon spitefully. 'Because she will, Pete. Without your salary you're not a great catch, you know. Look at yourself; you're getting fat, you're almost-permanently grumpy and you're a drunk. Oh, I'm sure you can handle it now, Pete; it's always easy to handle addiction when you've got money. But take the cash out of your pocket and see what happens then.'

'Give it a rest, Billy,' said Peter in a small voice.

'Why? Because you think you're so hard done by. You think you get a hard time. But you don't know shit! We just humour you; it's easier than dealing with your bloody fits or you flying off the handle and storming out whenever you don't get your own way. But the moment you leave Ian, you just watch how long it'll take for the phones to stop ringing. Nobody's going to call you, because they're going to be calling the next guy who's doing your job. We only kept you around because you did the gig and that's all.'

'Thank you, Billy. Thank you and goodbye,' said Peter and as he put the phone down he could hear Vernon's voice saying, 'Oh, fucking grow up!'

It was unfortunate timing that, as Peter sat slumped from Billy's tirade, Susie opened the door to his office and stepped in wearing a low-buttoned blouse and skin-tight jeans. Peter wondered whether she had those hold-up stockings on again, under her jeans and stared at her thighs suspiciously.

'Are you alright?' she smiled from beneath her carefully-applied make-up.

'Yeah,' he glowered.

'I'm just taking the kids to stay at mum's, then I'll pop into town then I'm going on to Sandy's. Do you want anything?'

'No.'

'No cigarettes or anything?'

'No.'

'Are you sure you're alright?'

'Yeah.'

'Alright,' said Susie, knowing that look and in too good a mood to want the drudgery of listening to one of Pete's tantrums. 'I'll see you later.'

'Great,' muttered Peter, who was barely listening as he was obsessing about what he could do that would make everybody feel really bad. As his mood blackened and the impulse to self-destruct surged through him, he decided to start by picking on Susie.

'Where did you say you were going? To see your boyfriend, I suppose,' he said accusingly.

'What? What do you mean?'

'Have you got stockings on again?'

'Of course not. Anyway you were the one who was always wanting me to wear them,' said Susie defensively as she attempted to sidle away from yet another argument.

'You must really fucking hate me,' he snarled at her.

'I don't hate you at all,' said Susie, who was bone-weary of this reprise of Pete kicking the cat again. 'But I don't like you when you get like this.'

'Like what?' he challenged.

'Like this. I can see what you're doing, Pete. Something has upset you again, and now you're going to take it out on me. You're going to pick me up on what I say or what I wear, or you're going to get all hunched and sorry for yourself. It's such a waste of time, Pete. And it's very unattractive.'

'Great,' he sulked.

'Oh, don't be like this,' Susie tried. 'Come on. Cheer up. We're going to have a party in your honour.'

'No. Fuck it. You go off and have a great time with Sandy, or wherever it is you claim be going. I don't want to go to a fucking party. I don't want to see anyone. I don't give a fuck. My whole life is shit anyway. Everything's shit. I've got no money, I've lost my job and my wife would rather talk, or whatever you want to call it, to some other guy. I don't know anyone who's got a shittier life than me. I tell you what you can get me; you can get me a big bottle of vodka. I'd rather drink that here than go to any stupid party.'

'I don't want to listen to this, you're talking rubbish,' said Susie, moving to the door.

'That's because I am rubbish, apparently. Billy's just bawled me out for being rubbish. Everyone thinks I'm rubbish. You think I'm rubbish. I don't know why I don't just do everybody a favour and fucking hang myself.'

'Well, the rope's in the shed,' said Susie and she left, angry, and partly hoping that he broke his bloody neck.

CHAPTER 50

When Susie finally arrived at Sandy's and attempted to park in the drive of their eight-bedroomed farmhouse she found her usual spot taken by three enormous trucks, beside which Sandy was gesticulating to a clutch of teenagers and gardeners sweating in overalls.

'That goes in the marquee, that goes in the kitchen. Who ordered absinthe? That wasn't on my list. Alex!' she heard Sandy yelling as she parked on the grass, knowing it would annoy Al.

'Hi,' said Susie brightly, determined to shake off the contamination of her latest row with Pete.

'Hi,' said Sandy. 'Careful with that, child, breakages must be paid for. No, Mr Peterson, I said in the marquee. The marquee… the great tent on the lawn. Jesus. Sorry darling, with you in a sec. Alex!'

Susie smiled as the dentist appeared at the front door adopting the hunched position that Susie knew long-term husbands assumed defensively when summoned by a yell.

'Sorry darling,' said Alex instinctively. 'Hi Suze… you're looking gorgeous today.' He dodged Sandy's scowl by greeting Susie with a hug.

'Absinthe, Alex. Did you order absinthe? I didn't.'

'Err…' said Alex.

'You did.'

'I thought that Pete might like a drop?'

'Well, you know… ask Suze. Suze, didn't Pete say he'd got a taste for a little absinthe on that Monaco visit. I'm sure…' said Alex, weasling awkwardly.

'And you ordered some as Pete's little treat?' said Sandy, whom Susie sensed was now circling for a kill.

'Yes. Quite. A little Pete treat. Cheer the chap up and all that.'

'But why did you order a whole case?' said Sandy, scoldingly.

'Err…'

'Have you any idea how much this is costing us?' said Sandy, which Susie sensed was for her benefit.

'But it was your idea,' protested Alex. 'You wanted the party.'

'For friends. I said for friends. Now there's four hundred people coming. We don't have four hundred friends.'

'But you wrote the bloody invitation list.'

'Exactly,' spat Sandy.

'What?' said Alex.

'I wrote the bloody invitations.'

'Yeah?' said Alex, now almost entirely fuddled.

'But not four bloody hundred! How did that happen. Alex?

'Err... Well, I just mentioned it to a few people at the golf club... Suze, darling, tea?'

Susie hesitated and glanced at Sandy.

'What's up darling?' said Sandy. 'Pete not want to come? I told Alex that would happen. Don't worry, he'll succumb. If necessary I'll tell that fool of a husband to tell him about the bloody absinthe.'

A lanky, smiling boy with public school hair approached them, put down the box of glasses that Alex had told him to take just bloody anywhere or ask your blasted mother and ambled over to embrace Susie.

'Auntie Susie, you look fabulous,' said Sandy's seventeen-year-old son cheerily.

'Thank you Jon-Jon,' said Susie affectionately. 'Do you have your outfit for the party? What are you going as?'

'A Blues Brother, the tall one,' said Jon-Jon triumphantly.

'Very novel, darling.'

'Well, Mum, you said I couldn't go as a hostage.' accused Jon-Jon.

'I did not, Jon-Jon. I said, if you'd been listening, that kneeling handcuffed on the floor with a bag over your head was not funny at a masked ball.'

'It is masked!' Jon-Jon continued grumpily.

'It's inappropriate and that's all there is to it; you're not with your clever Boojis crowd now. Anyway, I'm not going to argue with you and nor is your father. It's bad taste and kneeling will make it very difficult for you to circulate and top up people's drinks, and people will fall over you. Come on Susie, I think we need a cup of tea.'

Sandy led the way to her large kitchen, which was almost completely taken over with the caterers' supplies for the party.

'How many people have you really invited, for God's sake?' said Susie as Sandy edged round the crates to find the kettle.

'The whole county's coming, darling. Nobody refused,' said Sandy, dithering over where to hide the Amarone that Alex had ordained that only he and Pete were allowed to drink.

'I didn't know Pete was that popular,' said Susie, a little enviously.

'Oh, I don't think it's Pete that's popular. It's getting pissed and having a grope that's popular. How are things with Pete, by the way?'

'He's as suspicious as hell about my non-starter affair but he can't prove anything,' said Susie, 'but I worry that at some point he'll work it out. Anyway, it was playing second fiddle to fucking Ian again that pissed me off.'

'Well, at least we won't have to see vile him ever again.'

'Who do you mean?' said Susie.

'Horrid Ian, of course. He's not invited. He'd be spat upon if he turned up, by everyone. Possibly even by Jack.'

'Have you invited Jack?'

'Sorry, sweetie, it was going to be a little surprise for you. In case you'd changed your mind and fancied a nibble.'

'Is he going to come?'

'Well, that's in your hands, dear. Although Vera told me this morning that she saw him in The Standard with that Catty Horny woman. Vera claimed that they were looking very lovey-dovey.'

'What?' Susie exploded, spilling her tea.

'Apparently young Ms Horny moved in on him and with him the minute you'd flounced out.'

'Who told you that? And it's Horn-by,' said Susie, petulantly.

'Horny, Hornby, who cares? What's the point of a 'b' in your surname anyway, when it's only short for slapper? Now who told me? Umm… I think it was Vera again. Not that she's one to gossip.

Though she did say that Jack had a hickey on his neck.'

'Ugh! How common. Do you think he's bringing her, then?' said Susie, already re-thinking the outfit she was planning to wear.

'Do you think that might cause a problem for anyone, sweetie?' said Sandy distractedly.

'No, I'm sure that nobody will even notice she's here,' said Susie, thinking 'Bitch!'

Jon-Jon sauntered in and helped himself to a Coke from the fridge.

'I noticed they're setting up a stage in the field,' Susie observed, keen to change the subject. 'Is there a band playing tomorrow, Jon-Jon?'

'Yeah. Tundra Pox. They're mint. I've seen them play at a couple of gigs, that's why we booked them for the party. That's why all my mates are coming. Oh, Mum, I added some extra people to the list... um...' He saw the look on Sandy's face and hastily added, 'Anyway Uncle Pete's going to manage them or something, so they said. It's very cool,' said Jon-Jon keenly. 'And you should see their PR girl, she's hot. I hope she comes.'

'And you invited her too?' said his mother, irritated.

'Mum, she's part of their crew, OK? God, it's just one more person... She's called Catherine Hornby. She's really hot. I told her you're my auntie, Auntie Susie, well, not my auntie... you know, my Mum's oldest friend.'

'Hot. Oldest. Great. Fuck.' thought Susie as her antennae picked up the Tundra Pox conjoining of Pete and Catherine. 'What's been going on there?' she wondered, thinking that the best way to find out would be to float it past Peter and read the lies off his face.

CHAPTER 51

'Where are we now; right now?' demanded Taylor, startling Vernon into frantically looking for road signs of which there were none on the stretch of D-road in isolated Somerset.

'We're almost at Chard or somewhere, I think,' offered Vernon.

'You think. You don't know, of course,' swiped Taylor.

'No, I think I'm right,' insisted Vernon weakly.

'So you think you're right in thinking that we're almost somewhere?'

It had been like this since Vernon had forgotten he was navigating and had accidentally added hours to the trip by not knowing his right from his arse, apparently; the Taylor of old barking questions that he knew Vernon could not reasonably be expected to answer, then berating him for incompetence.

Consequently Vernon was jumpy with nerves and longing more than ever for the cigarette that the now cannabis-incinerating Taylor refused to allow him on the grounds that he didn't like smoke inside his car. But, despite his frequent tellings off, the manager in him knew that his artist needed to be coaxed gently back to commercial reality.

'Err,' said Vernon, flinching as he expected to get hit, 'What's your current thinking on the gig?'

'What about it?'

'Err… the record company's got a bunch of queries.'

'The record company is a bunch of queeries,' joked Taylor, reassuring Vernon immediately.

'Ha. Yeah. Very good. But… they're asking if you want a support band?'

'They might be good and then we'd have to be better, so no, thank you.'

Vernon was so surprised to hear Taylor use the words thank you that for some moments he was silenced. First Ian had uttered the previously-unheard word 'sorry', and now this thank you business. He began to worry that Taylor was not well.

'Is that it?' said Taylor irritably.

'Err… no… they want to know if you want to do a press conference the day before the show, maybe after rehearsals at Earls Court?'

'Not particularly. It's always boring to be asked ven are you coming to Sveden? Besides, in the light of my recent activity I don't think it's a good idea to be put up in front of the press.'

'What about a photo-call?'

'I suppose I could do that. Maybe me with the Come to Daddy bird, whoever she is. But I don't want the band in the shot, some of them look too old. We could have the TV crews there and maybe just a couple of questions…'

'Like about how come you're bigger today than you were in the sixties. OK, I'll organise some plants,' said Vernon.

'Talking of which, get onto to the promoter and make sure that he doesn't do any gardening at the gig.'

'Gardening?' said Vernon, confused again. 'Like flowers for your dressing room?'

'Audience arranging, to make sure there's no uglies in the first few rows.'

'Uglies?'

'Ugly fucking people.'

'I understand,' said Vernon.

'Do you? I bet you fucking don't. I bet you have no idea what a drag it is to perform to fat old housewives when you once played to screaming, highly-fuckable girls. I know some promoters will plant the best-looking chicks down the front…'

'Sounds like a good idea,' interrupted Vernon.

'Maybe. But I'm saying that I don't want to see it happening at my gig.'

'May I ask, why not?'

'I would have thought that was obvious,' said Taylor, looking at Vernon as if he had just trodden in him. 'Because it stinks.'

'But if everybody else is doing it, doesn't it place you at a disadvantage if you don't?'

'I couldn't give a flying fuck,' said Taylor. 'It's a concert, not a race. Make sure it doesn't happen. In fact, fix it so that the front rows are given to simple kids.'

'Simple kids? Umm… sorry, Ian… I don't get what you mean.'

'Well, you're obviously one of them, then. I mean simple as in… well, fucking simple. I hate the word retarded, it's what they called me at school; the bastards. Disadvantaged kids. Give them the first few rows.'

'But then where will the celebs and press sit?'

'In the fucking car park, for all I care; they never pay for their seats anyway. They want to be cool, so let them freeze to death.

'And there's another thing, I don't want any of that green-housing going on.'

'You mean with the ozone layer?' said Vernon, mystified.

'Are you on drugs? Green-housing, turning up the heat in the hall to con the crowd into getting sweaty and artificially thinking they're having a ball.'

'Why wouldn't we want that?'

'Because it's fake. I've gone off fake since my enjoyment of Her Majesty's pleasure. Real people, real feelings, that's what I want from this audience.'

'But if we don't stage-manage it, how can we be certain of getting a good crowd reaction?' said Vernon.

'We'll just have to fucking play good. Anyway, enough of the vaudeville; what else does my esteemed record company require?'

'Umm… well, there is the issue that we may have rubbed the authorities up the wrong way with the peace gig…'

'Which would explain why I got banged up for one little slap,' said Taylor. 'Yeah, I'd worked that out. The powers don't want me making a noise against the war, let alone and God forbid upsetting our American masters, so they'll want to discredit me in the eyes of people who wash. Take me down a peg.'

'So the label was wondering if you could appease the Home Office a bit by endorsing their new Drugs Aren't Cool campaign.'

'No way,' said Taylor firmly.

‘What about getting behind another Make Poverty History sort of thing movement? That’s not a heavy gig, even though everyone pretends that it is.’

‘Bollocks to that,’ said Taylor. ‘I’m sick of fucking celebrities doing the government’s work for them. If governments had any decency whatsoever, we wouldn’t need charities; state aid would look after it. Fuck making poverty history, we should make charity history. As long as celebs keep propping up charities, it takes the responsibility off governments to do so.’

‘Well, what about helping the anti-fur movement?’ Vernon attempted.

‘I already do help it; I don’t fucking wear it. It’s only the rap brigade that’s into fur, and they’re too fucked on their three grand bottles of brandy to see reason. Make Rap History, now I’d do a gig for that.’

‘Ian, look… we could be in a lot of shit. God knows what the powers are going to make of the brawl at the Savoy coming on top of the BBC thing. You’re on bail but you could go down, you know.’

‘I would rather not think about it until it happens. And I certainly will not play ball with the authorities just because they might bang me up for being right. Fuck’em, make me a martyr. That would keep BPA happy. Martyrdom’s an easy way of shifting old stock of shit records, ask the rappers. Anyway, where are we now?’

‘Err…’ said Vernon, ‘almost there, I think.’

CHAPTER 52

Like a number of her other no-longer-nubile friends, Susie had initially been miffed by Sandy's instruction that the party would be fancy dress. Susie loathed fancy dress because there was always such a thin line between looking OK and looking a joke; but the codicil that the party was to be masked fancy dress had almost persuaded her that she could wear the preposterously short nurse's uniform without feeling awkward.

She knew Jack would like her looking tarty but, although she was contemplating leaving Peter, she felt that a public display of his humiliation at what was meant to be his party would be unfair, so she resolved to wear jeans instead and say that nothing had fitted.

As soon as she entered her kitchen and saw Peter, even before he grunted at her, Susie could tell that he was preparing to go to the party and ruin it; one of his nostrils was shining from cocaine and he'd left the Rebel Yell bottle out prominently on the worktop, Pete's version of a danger sign. Confirmation of his intention was signalled by the look that he always dropped into at times of destruction; slit-eyed glaring, as if expecting an attack.

'What?' he said before she had said anything.

'Sorry?'

'You looked at me.'

Susie ignored him, switched on the kettle and began to hum. He lit a cigarette and glowered.

'Sandy's invited about four hundred people, did you know that?' she said gaily over her shoulder.

'Invited them to what?'

Susie continued, ignoring his taunt.

'To your party of course.'

'I bet they'll all be those posh twats.'

'Which posh twats?' said Susie, indifferent to the menace but interested to find out what on earth had wound him up.

'You know, all of those simpering gits who're only coming to get introduced to Jack Jackson. They wouldn't know rock and roll if it fucked them in the arse. Actually I was thinking, and just so you know, I'm going to go fucking mad if any of your mates ask me if I can get them Ian's autograph…'

'My mates aren't interested, Pete; fuck off.'

'Bollocks! I'm always getting hit on for signed fucking albums.'

'And you can say no. You don't have to be rude. Everyone will know that the reason for the party is that you don't work for Ian any more. What's pissed you off?' said Susie, making herself coffee but not bothering to ask if he wanted any.

'Nothing.'

'Something has, I can tell.'

'I know you're up to something with Jack fucking Jackson.'

'Who told you that, your new assistant?' parried Susie, brilliantly, she thought.

'What? I haven't got a fucking assistant! I haven't got a fucking job, let alone a fucking assistant!'

'Your new PR girl for your new bloody band.'

'What?'

'Don't start on me when we all know that you fancy Catherine Hornby.'

'What do you mean, you all know?' yelled Peter. 'Who is all? All your fucking coffee coven?'

'My fucking coven! Fuck you, Pete, just fuck you. These people who are all bending over backwards for you, putting on a bloody party for you, you selfish prick!'

'I don't want a fucking party! I haven't exactly got anything to celebrate, you stupid bitch.'

As soon as he stopped shouting he knew it was a bad idea.

'Tell you what Pete,' said Susie after looking at him for a while, 'we're finished. But I'm not going to talk about it now because I'm going to go upstairs and try on the flirty nurse outfit that I actually didn't really want to wear tomorrow. Ian's right, Pete, you are a bastard. Don't go to your own party and then maybe everyone else can have some fun!'

CHAPTER 53

The manager of the Black Bear hotel in Lyme Regis had spent the best part of twenty years placating difficult and demanding guests. He was vastly experienced in explaining, in conciliatory language, why breakfast was traditionally not served after eleven in the morning and apologising for the fact that yes, it must be very misleading, sir, that one had to go to all the inconvenience of first dialling nine for an outside line to Texas, but he had never dealt with anyone like Billy Vernon before.

'If I may interrupt, sir, may I respectfully ask you to modify your language as there are children staying in this hotel,' he'd said after Vernon had begun yelling what was it that he had to fucking do to find somebody with a fucking brain in this motherfucking yokel backwater.

'Look,' said Vernon, who was sweating quite heavily now, 'all I am saying is when my colleague enters this bloody hotel in a minute I want your fuc… I want your assurance that your staff will not speak to him, they will not stare at him and, under no circumstances whatsoever, will they even fu… think of approaching him at any time for an autograph.'

'I do understand, sir. Whomever your colleague may be, and I quite understand your persistent refusal to identify him, please be assured that we are more than familiar with accommodating guests of distinction. As I have already indicated, this hotel was occupied by a number of the entourage of *The French Lieutenant's Woman*, no less.'

'I am not fucking interested,' said Vernon. 'I just want to make myself clear. No looking. No talking and absolutely no fucking photographs or autographs. Got it?'

'It is crystal clear to me, sir.'

'And another thing, no bloody press! I don't want to see any photographers suddenly appearing on the other side of the street. If

I do, there will be a lot of fucking trouble.'

'Of course, sir.'

'Good,' said Vernon and he passed the manager four fifty-pound notes. 'One other thing, is there an emergency exit to my colleague's suite?'

'Of course, sir, we abide to the highest standards of safety.'

'Good. Well I want to see it and I want you to show me the back entrance to this place. We may want to come in through the kitchens at any time. I'm going to need a key to the back door.'

'Not a problem, sir,' said the manager, wondering if he should hire a defibrillator in case Vernon became more worked up.

'Oh yeah, do you happen to know where a guy called Jack Jackson lives around here?' said Vernon, looking around nervously in case he was overheard.

'The pop person? His shop and studio are just up the road here, but I believe he lives in a cottage on Cobb Road, sir. That's the rather steep and winding road down to the harbour. You can get to it by going up the hill outside, taking the left fork by the cinema. It's on the left at the top, clearly signposted.'

'Do you know what number on this Cobb Hill?'

'I'm afraid I do not, sir. But at the bottom of that road you will find The Cobb Arms. I believe Mr Jackson frequents the place. They can probably help you there, sir. I can telephone the landlord and ask him, if you wish.'

'No,' snapped Vernon. 'No phone calls. I'll find it. Oh and by the way, we're looking for another friend. Do you know a Catherine Hornby?'

The hotel manager looked blank.

'Pretty woman, dark hair, in her thirties? Probably new to the town?' said Vernon encouragingly.

'Are you police?' said the manager.

'Do I look like police?'

'Yes', said the manager, 'you do, actually.'

'Well I'm not. Anyway, do you recognize the description?'

'Sound like police too. Sorry,' said the manager turning away from him.

Vernon pocketed the keys to his and Ian Taylor's adjoining suites and went back out to the main street, continually looking left and right for possible press threats as he prepared to escort Ian from the car and into the building. As he walked to the Porsche he could smell marijuana from thirty feet away.

Vernon sidled up to the car and tapped on the driver's window, but as it was already lowered he succeeded only in knuckling the side of Taylor 's head.

'Ow! What the fuck are you doing?'

'Sorry, sorry. Sorry, boss. Sorry,' said Vernon. 'I thought the window was…'

'Yeah, yeah,' said Taylor dismissively. 'I'm fucking bored. Are you finally ready?'

'Yeah. I've cased the place. We're cool,' said Vernon, picking up all their luggage and noticing that Ian gave no indication of helping him carry it.

CHAPTER 54

Catherine was trying on different outfits very carefully. She had given her hair a henna rinse, which had added a gypsy look that she was pleased with. She had also dyed her pubes, or what was left of them after yet another neat trim and, although it had stung a bit, the end result was nicely racy as it indicated that she was expecting to welcome an audience down there.

After rubbing her body with cocoa butter to add sheen she chose a black, lacy, low-cupped bra, sheer black hold-ups and zipper-front knickers, which she felt would be most appropriate for the final positioning she sought for herself.

Next she tried on her black suede cowboy boots, a thin black cotton Romany blouse with plenty of cut for show and a long black flouncy skirt with a silver and turquoise studded belt borrowed from Jack. Finally she shrugged on an old and battered biker jacket and posed again, jaw jutting and legs apart. Very rock chick, she thought, as she fancied herself in front of the mirror. All she needed now was a dozen silver bangles distributed over both wrists, big silver hoop earrings and the application of a little glycerine to her cleavage to make a gleam that would draw eyes to her breasts. She put on a black cat mask that only revealed her lips and stood back to admire herself in the large mirror next to Jack's unmade bed.

For once in a very long time, Catherine was not dressing to pull. She was dressing to piss off every other woman who would envy her being on the arm of Jack Jackson.

Catherine knew she was playing a potentially calamitous game with Jackson. Although girlfriending him now represented the best way of certain access to Taylor, she could not count on the reunion being a happy one. If Taylor and Jackson still hated each other, her dating Jack would only infuriate Ian. In fact, she decided, if Taylor was to accept her, he wouldn't want his daughter shagging Jack, whether they became best buddies again or not. Damn Pete, she thought, it would have been so much easier using him.

She had a few hits on a little joint of hash, then applied two trial layers of wet-look gloss to her lips, pouted lasciviously and liberally dabbed her neck and breasts with the sex musk. She wanted to sleep in the smell, to make it pore-deep and get Pete drawn back in. She felt that although he may have worn out his usefulness, it would be interesting to reel him in and screw up his precarious mind a little more.

She hoped he wouldn't make a scene, what with her being with Jack and Jack having been with Susie and, hopefully, Catherine winning the Taylor that Peter had lost. But she suspected that a huge row would erupt. She couldn't wait; parties never got properly going until the shrieking and tears began. And it was such fun to watch other women humiliating themselves.

CHAPTER 55

Jack Jackson felt a prat for agreeing to dress up for the party. Even when he had been in Taylspin performing to hordes of self-wetting thousands, he had preferred to go onstage in jeans and an old leather jacket – although it always caused dressing-room rucks with Ian and his ridiculous obsession for the weird and theatrical.

Ordinarily, if anyone had told Jackson he had to wear fancy dress he would have told them to fuck off, but the fact that this dentist and his wife had made it a masked ball appealed to him hugely – behind the mask of Zorro and inside the rest of the poncey black outfit he would be spared the irritation of people asking him if he really was Jack Jackson.

Like almost everyone else who achieved great fame, Jackson craved anonymity but only when he felt like it. Of course, anonymity was bugger-all use when he wanted a good table at an exclusive restaurant or sought to impress a bird, but at a party crammed with gushing hillbillies it was a godsend to be given the chance thoroughly to enjoy not being the person that everybody thought he might be.

Anyway, he was looking forward to making that Susie Forth push the limits of her wantonness: how dare she turn on him merely because he was preoccupied with Taylspin business?

Catherine was cute but predictable; she knew the groupie game and her willingness to play it spoiled the pleasure. But Mrs Forth was proper meat and he would make sure she had a night to remember. It irritated him that Susie so obviously fancied him, or at least his image, and it was a drag that she had delusions that they might share some sort of romance. God forbid. But Jack calculated that a few lies about his commitment plus a few drops from the small bottle he'd carefully placed in his jacket pocket could easily turn Mrs Housewife into a howling whore for the one-night-only performance that was the true extent of his interest in any love gig.

CHAPTER 56

'Whose is the double Jack and Coke? Whose? Lincoln, here, brandy and cider, pass it to Thackwell… err… G and T's mine. Oh, here's another, Roger is that yours? What? I don't fucking know. Well you should have said diet, then. Anybody want Roger's fat fucker tonic? What? Fuck off, you cunt, it's fucking there in front of you. Well try looking. Lincoln, sorry mate, can you pass that Jagermeister, that one there, yeah; give it to Gabriel… right, has everybody got a drink?'

'Yeah, yeah, sit down Kev,' said Roger Morris of the *Sunday Mirror*, pouring a large shot of gin into the half pint glass that already contained three other measures. 'Did you get any receipts?'
'Naturally,' said O'Mara of the *Mirror*, taking from the inside pocket of his expensive Savile Row pinstripe a fat book of blank receipts all printed with the name, address and VAT number of the Cobb Arms, Lyme Regis.

'Pass them round, then,' said Jeremy Thackwell of the *Daily Express*, picking up the receipt book and tearing five blank pages from it before handing it on to the other members of Her Majesty's Press who'd had their weekends ruined by instructions from their news desks to get down to Dorset at top speed to chase a tip-off that Ian Taylor had been sighted.

The round of drinks had cost the *Mirror* almost £50, a figure that each of the journalists would then replicate in their own inspired expenses claims to their respective newspapers.

'Where are our monkeys?' said Nicola Freshfield, show business editor of the *Daily Mail*.

'I told them to fuck off to that pub around the corner or they'd scare the grackles,' said Lincoln Roundhill of the *Daily Star*.

'Grackles? It's grockles, you daft git,' said O'Mara, gulping his gin and tonic.

'What are grockles?' said Carol Stitch, the lip-glossed show business correspondent from AMTV who had bought her own drink at the bar and was now trying to find a spare chair among the pack.

'It's what they call outsiders down here,' informed O'Mara without looking up from his Blackberry. 'So people like you, basically.'

'You love me really, Kevin,' said Stitch, squeezing past him to sit next to Gabriel Thomas, *Bizarre* editor of the *Sun*, and gratuitously crossing her fabulous legs so that her skirt rode up high enough for Roger to look up it curiously.

'Are you drunk?' said O'Mara, characteristically sneering at the pretty blonde.

'Err… my news desk is saying what the fuck with two ks is going on?' said Thomas, reading the curt text from Wapping.

'Yeah, my lot's getting arsey,' concurred Freshfield. 'They want an early piece.'

'Tell them they can have an early piece of my arse,' chuckled O'Mara, finishing his drink already and seeing that so too had the *Independent's* David Moorfield.

'Seriously,' said Thomas, 'we're meant to be splashing on this.'

'OK,' said O'Mara, as ever taking control of the pack who had booked all the best hotel rooms in Lyme. 'Gab's right, let's agree an early line, I think it's 'Scandal-ridden rock star Ian Taylor plunged to a new low last night as he fled to the arms of old pal Jack Jackson amid claims that the Taylspin pin-up is gay'.'

'Explosive claims,' chipped in Thomas.

'Shock explosive smears,' said Thackwell.

'What do you mean, fucking smears?' snorted O'Mara. 'We've got him bang to rights. Don't start introducing fucking smears into the equation, there's no fucking doubt about this.'

'Apart from the fact that nobody's asked him yet,' said Moorfield, giggling.

'Err… if we say he'd fled to the arms of Jackson and the other bit, the gay claims, aren't we inferring that Jackson's his boyfriend?' Nicola Freshfield countered warily.

'So?' said Roundhill, prompting howls of laughter from O'Mara and Thomas.

'What's funny?' said Carol Stitch, who was always on the edge of getting it.

'That Jack Jackson's bent,' said Thomas, grinning widely. 'Bloody hell Carol, you must know that. Or have you started paying money for your stories now?'

'Must know what?' said Stitch, blushing now that all the pack was watching her.

'Oh bollocks!' exploded O'Mara derisively. 'Are you saying you've not had Jack Jackson? Fuck off, Carol…'

'There's your early line,' said Morris, poised over a notebook as there was no space for laptops on the table because of the eclectic collection of variously filled glasses.

'What?' said O'Mara.

'In a shock confession last night Jack Jackson was revealed as the only man in rock not to have an all-access pass to Carol Stitch's magic snatch…' said Morris.

'Fuck off, Roger,' said Stitch. 'I'm telling you, I've never even met the guy. What's he like?'

'Huge, apparently,' informed Thackwell. 'And somebody at Mojo told me he has an unfeasibly long tongue.'

'Really?' said Stitch, leaning forward so that eyes opposite her could be reminded of her expensively-sculpted new cleavage.

'Nick's right,' said O'Mara, taking control again. 'The story is that Ian Taylor's an arse bandit and he's frightened of admitting it.'

'Well then why don't we just do it completely straight?' suggested Roundhill, 'Jailhouse rocker Ian Taylor can't wait to get back in the prison showers again, it was revealed last night…'

'By his mum,' added Thomas, giggling.

'Fuck it, I'm going on that,' said O'Mara.

'On what?' said Thackwell, puzzled.

'That this whole fucking Grey Rose sex stunt is just a cynical ruse to disguise from his legions of female fans that he's gay and he doesn't want to admit it in case it damages his bloody album sales,' summarised O'Mara.

'Has anybody managed to speak to Pete Forth?' suggested David Moorfield.

‘Answerphones,’ said Freshfield. ‘Constantly unobtainable, twat.’

‘Well that means it’s true,’ said Thomas.

‘What do you mean?’ said Stitch.

‘Pete’s trick of confirming something he doesn’t want to deny, let alone confirm, is to disappear, just completely vanish until the story’s run,’ explained Thomas.

‘So if you are incapable of reaching Peter Forth that means any story you’re writing on any of his clients will be true?’ repeated Stitch.

‘Pretty much, and by the way it’s your shout,’ said O’Mara, handing her his empty glass.

‘But how does he know what you’ve got? Is he psychic or something?’ said Stitch, dimly.

‘Clearly,’ said O’Mara, exasperated. ‘You leave a message saying what the fucking story is and if he doesn’t call you back, Pete’s signalling at you.’

‘What if he doesn’t pick up the message?’ said Stitch.

‘Then he’s fucked,’ said Morris. ‘By the way, Carol, have you got any smoke with you?’

‘I was going to ask Kevin the same,’ said Stitch.

‘Don’t look at me, babe, I didn’t have time to pack; fucking news desks sending you off at weekends,’ replied O’Mara.

‘Peter Forth will have smoke,’ said Thackwell musingly.

‘Yeah, well I want a quick shower and a few large Jagers meself before you lot turn into the mad In Crowd,’ announced Lincoln Roundhill firmly. ‘So are we agreed? Everybody files that Taylor ’s a bandit and then we’ll go and talk to Pete? Where is he again?

‘At a party to mark the end of Peter Forth mattering,’ said O’Mara. ‘About five miles from here. Meet back here in an hour. Somebody should go and tell the monkeys that they’re driving us.’

CHAPTER 57

As Nurse Susie left for the party saying that she would see him there, Peter went to the fridge-freezer and took out an almost-frozen bottle of vodka. He poured himself a shot, which he slugged back before sitting at the kitchen table to roll a joint.

As it always had been with Peter and parties, he needed to put himself in the mood and this he accomplished by taking three hits on the joint and another four shots of vodka whilst listening to the stereo play the Stones at volume nine. To add the edge, he then snorted half a wrap of cocaine and put the other six wraps he'd prepared in his shoulder bag, with the grass.

He knew that he was carrying far too many drugs, even for his kamikaze capacity, but he liked to be generous and, besides, he needed the stiffeners if he was going to get the 'first photo' of Catherine which he figured might interest the nationals, if needs necessitated its appearance.

Peter walked the pleasant lane from his house to Alex and Sandy's place in his loose interpretation of fancy dress; old blue jeans, a white collarless shirt with a black waistcoat and a black eye patch. As he arrived at the bottom of their long, gravelled drive, he attempted to ignore the local teenage lad at the gate who was checking invitations.

'Excuse me, sir, are you a guest?' joked the seventeen-year-old.

'Yep, a guest in my own life, son,' said Peter smiling.

The lad grinned. He had heard the stories about Pickled Pete's temper and he could smell that he had already had a few. It looked like Mr Forth was going to realise all the fears that the village had of him, especially as he was the only person so far who had arrived swigging a litre of vodka.

Alex was just enjoying a large brandy under the porch when he spotted Pete swaying up the drive. Until this point, he had been delighted with the turnout; he estimated that at least two hundred and fifty had already arrived and he was pleased that all had heeded the request to come fancy-dressed and masked, but now the bugger of the hour was swaggering towards him with that pirate grin that so unsettled everyone who recognized his face of self-destruction..

'Oh... hello Pete... I see you've brought your own supplies. Excellent.'

'Swig?' said Peter, exaggerating the loutishness just because he knew that it unnerved his conservative host.

'Err... well, actually I'm drinking my own hard stuff. Best not to start mixing it this early,' excused Alex, raising his glass.

'Well then let's toast you, old son,' said Peter, unscrewing the lid of the Absolut again.

Peter clinked the bottle dangerously against Alex's lead crystal glass then slugged the vodka again. From the corner of his one eye, he noticed Alex wincing.

'Take it easy, mate,' said Alex as Peter glugged again. 'It's going to be a long night.'

Peter winked at him and walked by. Then, after deliberating that enough moments had passed for Alex to form the thought 'Pete's going to be trouble', he walked back to the dentist and took a tiny package wrapped in tissue paper from his pocket and slipped it into Alex's hand.

'Thanks, Al. Really. Thanks,' he said and walked away again.

Assuming it to contain drugs that he did not want in his possession, Alex quickly unwrapped the package and discovered instead a solid gold golf tee on which had been minutely inscribed Al – The Best of the Few.

Peter gently eased himself through the bubbling throng, nodding and smiling at everybody whether he recognised them or not. He was heading for the large marquee holding the band on the back lawn where he guessed that Susie would be dancing when a short, bosomy redhead in a Venetian mask blocked his way.

'So they let you in, then?' said the redhead.

'Oh, hello Sal,' said Peter, ostentatiously leaning forward to kiss her and pointing to her chest. 'Good of you to bring the puppies. What do mean, they let me in? This is my gig, apparently.'

'Ooo! Don't say, but I heard that Alex was worried you'd disgrace yourself.'

'You astound me. He's worried about me spliffing up, is he?'

'Oh, you know Alex. Apparently he's read that it's rife, as he puts it, in Dorset and now he's concerned that you'll get all of us out of it.'

'Just like I always do?'

'Exactly. But between you and me I think he's worried that Sandy might like a puff.'

'Well you round up her and anybody else who's interested and we can all creep out to the barn,' said Peter, not giving a toss.

'Ooo, goodee! I told all the girls you'd be bringing some stuff. I'll bring them all over later. But no husbands, though. We don't want to get told off,' said Sally.

'Same as it ever was,' said Peter scanning the crowd for sight of Susie. 'Have you seen my bird?'

'She's in the marquee,' said Sally, 'talking to a rather dashing-looking farmer. I don't know who he is, though.'

'Probably anyone with the right money,' said Peter spitefully. 'Excuse me, Sal; I'll see you later.'

Peter moved off again but was stopped by a tap on his shoulder. He turned round and beamed into Alex's confused face.

'Pete, what's this about?' said Alex holding up the gold tee. 'Look, I say… this is awfully kind of you. I mean… it's completely unnecessary, Sandy and I are pleased to do the party for you.'

'It's not for that, Al. It's for being there when everybody else had another appointment for the past five years. Just keep your head down when you follow through, or else you'll slice your shot as usual and bend that bugger.'

'Quite. Look here, Pete… I don't know quite how to say this but… I think… I mean, well… you might hear that I was a little jumpy earlier on today about you playing up tonight.'

'You mean in case I started sniffing drugs?'

'Well… you know, there has been talk…'

'I'm sure there has, Al. But no, you didn't get me wrong on that; first thought best thought, as Ginsberg used to say.'

'Oh Lord.'

'Al,' said Peter, taking his hand deliberately in an over-intimate gesture, 'don't worry. You know I know what I'm doing.'

'Oh, of course, old chap,' said Alex, retrieving his hand from Peter's clasp. 'It's just… well, you know...'

'It's OK. Really. I'm not going to set up a stall.'

At that moment Sandy arrived at his side and kissed Peter on the cheek.

'Are you winding him up already, dearie?' she pouted.

'Now why would I do that, Sans?'

'Because you're a very naughty man, Peter Forth.'

'You hope,' he grinned.

She returned the knowing look and then became embarrassed as Peter added the shine of wicked intent to his eye.

'Darling,' she said, grinning and she pecked his ear and walked away with a swish.

Peter watched the crowd for a while and was attempting to walk after one of the waitressing village girls bearing a plate of canapés, when his way was blocked again, this time by his hairdresser who was dressed as Queen Victoria. He gave Peter a rather passionate kiss on the lips.

'No tongue, Kevin,' said Peter.

'Spoilsport,' flounced his friend, 'Anyway, what this queen wants to know is… are you carrying the means to get me royally into a state of even more highness?'

'Green, brown or white?' said Peter.

'Oh you fabulous creature!' trilled Kevin gaily. 'How utterly considerate. You are a love.'

'Do you want some now? I've got a lot on me and I can always get more from home.'

'Maybe I should just powder my nose in the little girls' room.'

Peter took one of the grams of cocaine from his pocket and passed it to Kevin.

'Don't have all of that,' he said firmly.

'Just a little sniff of the sherbet, dear. By the way, where's your jailer?'

'Susie?' said Peter. 'I haven't seen her yet; she came ahead of me.'

'Oh women always do, dear, the selfish cows. And talking of which, ooh there she blows...'

They were distracted from their bitching by the sight of Catherine gliding through the crowd with a far more seductive strut than Peter had noticed before.

'My God! What's got into our Miss Hornby?' said Kevin.

'I don't know, but I'm hoping to make it me,' grinned Peter.

'Oh God, don't you get all suburban like the rest of them, Pete,' said Kevin, indicating he was serious by saying Pete and not the usual ,dear', 'love' or 'you tart'.

'What do you mean?'

'Well, look at them all,' said Kevin, indicating the chattering guests. 'Give them all a mask to hide behind and they're all at each others' libidos like bloody stoats.'

Peter looked around, smiling as Kevin continued to bitch.

'They're all jostling for missionary position, Pete. Look at them! Eyeing each other up, sniffing out the chances of groping a bit of midsummer arse. They're like dogs circling each other's bottoms.'

Kevin paused to look at Peter. Then he sounded more serious.

'And you've quite clearly got the means of infamy in your possession, which signifies that you won't just drift over the top, you'll dive over it. Do yourself a favour, Pete, try behave tonight, go easy. And don't pick fights.'

'When have you ever seen me pick a fight?'

'All the bloody time, dear. Not fight fights, I admit. Thank God you're far too tarty to start getting all macho on us. You know what I mean, when you get picky with people and start your sarcasm.'

'Is it that obvious?' said Peter, surprised.

'To a dead bat, dear. All I'm saying is, please don't start being Peter Forth the binge drinker.'

'I'm not; I'm a binge thinker,' said Peter, grinning. 'It's not my fault if my brain works.'

'Fine, fine. But don't get those flirty thoughts because Susie will rip you to shreds if you do, and right now everyone's going to take her side.'

‘What do you mean everyone’s going to take her side?’ said Peter. ‘What the fuck have I done wrong? She’s the one who’s behaving like the biggest slag since Aberfan.’

‘Shush!’ scolded Kevin. ‘Tell you what, let’s go off to the toilet together with this coke and make the rest of them wonder about your sexuality. It would start wonderful gossip, you know. C’mon, give a queen a break.’

‘I’m thinking about writing a book about the danger of gossip,’ said Peter, who had become suddenly depressed.

‘Bor-ing, boring! Don’t want to hear this,’ said Kevin, theatrically covering his ears with his hands.

‘Are you saying my book is boring or that I’m being boring by being anti-gossip?’

‘I’m saying that you are getting boring, dear. You’re so bloody serious these days. What happened to the old Peter who liked fun so much?’

‘Constant scolding killed his capacity to have it, too many of the right people told him he was shit,’ said Peter sourly. ‘Give me the rest of that coke back later.’

‘Suit yourself, Mr Grumpy,’ said Kevin leaving Peter and bustling further into the crowd chanting ‘excuse me love’ and ‘sorry dear’ as he nudged through.

CHAPTER 58

Twenty minutes later, watching from a distance by the side of the barn, Peter was smoking a joint and studying Tundra Pox as the teenage band prepared to sound check on a stage the size of a tennis court that had been rigged undercover in the paddock.

He didn't want to say 'hello lads' to anyone yet because once he had, he thought the band would start being artificial. He wanted to look and learn who was urgent and who wasn't, who was ready last, who was laughing, who dressed well in his street clothes and assess all the other little hints that would help him calculate how to help them make it.

'Admiring your new crèche?' said a familiar, breathy voice close to his ear.

'Hmm,' replied Peter without turning to Catherine. 'Like the look, by the way.'

'My God!' said Catherine.

'What?'

'You flattered me; you just flattered me.'

She was laughing and so were her eyes and Peter glowed at the intimacy.

'What does the kingmaker think?' she asked.

'They haven't played anything yet. Look good, though; all that Lynyrd Skynyrd outlaw thing…'

'Have you ever managed a band before, Pete?'

'Not as such, not with my name on the door as such. But I've had two baby boys; it's the same principle,' said Peter, still scanning the band. 'You know, I think we could make this work.'

'And the band?' she toyed.

'Just the band, Catherine, I've given up on the other games. You're beyond my depth.'

She watched him concentrating on Tundra Pox, his eyes observant and alert, happy to be working again. It was almost a shame to wreck everything.

'My Dad's here,' she murmured.

'Here?'

'Not here; in Lyme, apparently. He checked into The Black Bear with somebody who was asking questions about Jack. The manager tipped off Jack. I expect that'd be Billy Vernon with him,' said Catherine, smiling warily.

'Great,' said Peter, lighting a Marlboro.

'Do you think you could introduce…'

'I said I would and I will,' said Peter, angry and disappointed that he would have to work faster than he expected. 'And you're wrong, he will be here,' said Peter surely. 'He'll be down here to see Jack and Jack's here. Billy will sniff it out. Great.'

'Pete, don't get uptight, they can't just barge in uninvited.'

'You want to bet? I know how they work, Catherine. Bollocks, never mind. Anyway, looks like your dream's coming true.' He turned to face her and smiled fondly.

'You'll forget about me once you become Catherine Taylor.'

'No I won't, I really won't Pete.'

'Yes Catherine, you really will. He will insist upon it. Hmm…. hey, can I have a picture to remember you by?'

He pointed his phone at her and took a photograph before she had time to reply.

'Nice shot,' he said, looking at it. 'Now can I have one without your mask?'

'Sure,' she said, 'just as soon as you keep your promise. I wasn't born yesterday, Pete.'

She kissed him affectionately on the lips and walked away, swaying her hips and knowing that she was leaving him frustrated.

CHAPTER 59

'I fucking knew that you should have told him we were coming,' said Taylor, who hadn't mentioned any such thing.

Once again Taylor and Vernon were driving around lost. After Vernon had been sent out to knock at three wrong doors, eventually they had found Jackson's large thatched cottage on Cobb Road, only to be told by his housekeeper that he was out, at the dentist's apparently. The little old woman, who had eyed Vernon suspiciously, as if he was a burglar, and had demanded proof of identity that Vernon didn't have with him, had only been persuaded to reveal the location of the party after Billy had cajoled the reluctant Taylor out of the car to talk to her.

'Ooh, you are, you're 'im,' said the housekeeper, recognising Ian and at last reconsidering phoning the police about the shifty Vernon. 'You were in our Jack's band, weren't you?'

Billy blanched at this demotion and was surprised that Ian let the comment pass, although once they were back in the car Taylor let rip.

'Our Jack's band! Is that what he fucking tells them, that it was his band? I bet he bloody does!'

'I think she was just old,' said Billy soothingly. 'Old people get like that.'

'Get like what?'

'Get stuff wrong.'

'Hmph,' said Taylor. 'Anyway, what's he doing at the fucking dentist's at this time of night?'

'He's at the dentist's house, not his surgery. She said it's a party,' said Vernon, musing that sometimes Ian wasn't so far removed from senility himself.

'Well you better bloody find it because I have no idea what that daft fucking bat was talking about. Was that English she was speaking?'

‘It’s the Dorset accent,’ said Vernon.

‘Ooh arr,’ said Taylor, steering the Porsche in the direction that Vernon told him he thought the old woman had said.

After another forty minutes of wrong turns, during which Vernon was constantly reminded about his complete and utter incompetence, they arrived at the village and Taylor slowed the car to crawling speed as they looked out for any sign of the Golden Hind pub that they had been told was close to the dentist’s farmhouse.

‘I spy with my little eye something beginning with S,’ said Taylor suddenly. Vernon said nothing.

‘I said ‘I spy with my little eye something beginning with fucking ‘S’!’

‘Oh, sorry,’ said Vernon. ‘I thought you were talking to yourself.’

‘How can I play I fucking Spy with myself?’

‘Sorry… what did you say it began with?’

‘S!’

‘Umm… signpost?’

‘No.’

‘Sheep?’

‘No.’

‘Stallion?’

‘Where?’

‘In that field we just passed.’

‘How do you know it was a stallion? Could you see its balls?’

‘Err… well…’

‘Anyway, no, not that.’

‘Give us a clue,’ said Vernon playfully.

‘Fuck off.’

‘Shed?’

‘No.’

‘Err… spliff?’

‘Outside the fucking car!’

‘Sorry… you didn’t say.’

‘I did!’

'Umm… I don't know,' conceded Vernon, knowing that it was best not to win. 'I give up.'

'Serpent,' said Taylor.

'Serpent? Where? A serpent? Are you sure?'

'Flashback,' said Taylor triumphantly.

'What?'

'It was a flashback. I saw one of those serpents that me and Jack used to see when we were doing a lot of acid, around the time of writing the Rose.'

'Did you really see one?' said Vernon.

'What? Hundreds of the fuckers. There was some shit acid back then.'

'No, I meant just now. Did you really have a flashback?'

'Might have done,' said Taylor evasively. 'Maybe thinking about Jack put it in my head.'

'My turn,' said Vernon.

'I don't want to play anymore,' said Taylor moodily. 'Anyway, there's the pub.'

'Well spotted!' said Vernon, over-enthusiastically.

'Well, fucking hardly,' said Taylor. 'How many other pubs called the Golden Hind have we passed? I guess that's the place over there, the big one. Jesus, look at all the fucking cars around here, how the hell am I meant to park?'

'He must be a popular dentist,' said Vernon.

'Hmm. Do you reckon he'll let us have any novocaine? Ask him later. But don't say it's for me. Tell him you've got a drug problem.'

'Pete will have coke,' said Vernon without thinking.

'Pete who? My fucking publicist? What the fuck will he be doing here? I don't want to see fucking Pete! You'll have to tell him to leave,' said Taylor.

'The party is being thrown for Pete, some form of celebration. God knows what occasion.'

'Fucking wonderful! Great bloody party this is going to be,' said Taylor sulkily. 'I wish we hadn't come now.'

We weren't asked to, thought Billy, but he said nothing as he was calculating how much money it was going to cost to pay for the damages, actual, moral and mental, that he anticipated they were about to cause.

'Fuck this,' said Taylor after failing to find a parking space in the road outside the farmhouse. 'I'm going up that drive. We'll park up there.'

'It says, 'No Entry',' said Vernon nervously.

'It says cigarettes give you cancer on the packets, but that doesn't stop you smoking,' replied Taylor, driving the Porsche straight at the young steward who jumped out of the way at the last minute, shouting, 'Oi! You can't go up there!'.

'He's pissed off,' said Vernon.

'He'll be fine. Tell him I'll do him an autograph later.'

CHAPTER 60

Susie was not happy. It was bad enough that Jack seemed to be deliberately taunting her by looking gorgeously dashing in his Zorro outfit, but her mood was made worse by bloody Catherine swishing about inciting erections with her leather and lace.

She had some more to drink and seethed with frustration, and there she was again, although, hello, she was looking worried now. Good, thought Susie, sweat, bitch.

'I think she must have been a porn star, to move like that,' said Sandy, arriving at Susie's side with a bottle of farmhouse white.

'Yeah, far too cocky,' said Susie holding up her glass for a refill.

'They say that he's rather cocky; enormously cocky, apparently. Still, I expect you already know that, darling.'

'Some bugger's had the cheek to park their bloody Porsche right outside!' stormed Alex as he made a rapid path through his guests to his front door. 'I'm going to have a bloody word with that boy on the gate, I knew he was a half-wit.'

'A Porsche? Who do we know who owns a Porsche?' said Sandy, following him.

'Well that's what the lad claims. He rang my mobile and said a Porsche had just blatantly ignored the sign. I don't care if it's the bloody Popemobile, nobody's parking there. It's just not on, Sandra.'

Sandy hung back, letting him go to his confrontation alone as she had no wish to be embarrassed by one of his hissy fits, but as she was curious as to which guest had arrived in such a flashy way, she kept him in her line of sight.

It had been many years since Ian Taylor had heard anyone address him with the words, 'Who the bloody hell are you?' so it was a few moments before he could reply as the dentist angrily opened the car door to berate him.

'Umm… we're guests. Of Jack Jackson,' said Taylor, wondering whether this actually was a flashback.

'But you're not even dressed for it!' continued Alex. 'It clearly stated fancy dress on the invitation. What the... hang on... you're... you're... bloody hell! I say! Aren't you...?'

'This is my fancy dress,' said Ian, grateful for the recognition, 'I've come as a rock star.'

As Alex turned towards the house and began to shout, 'Sandy, Sandy! Come and see!' Taylor glared at Vernon.

'You should have known about the fucking fancy dress,' he hissed.

'How could I have known?' bleated Billy.

'I don't fucking know. I don't keep a dog to bark myself. It's your job to know these things. Anyway, what are you going as?'

'What do you mean?' said Vernon nervously, as he watched Cat Woman come out of the house to join the angry man, followed by a whole peering crowd of weirdos in masks.

Vernon wanted to say that he'd come as Vincent Van Gogh with his ear chewed off but he knew that Taylor was not in the mood for sarcasm, not least as an audience was plainly gathering for him and that meant that Ian would now be adopting yet another persona as Our Ian. So he said nothing and got out of the car, looking mournful.

'Sandy McAlpine, hostess,' said Cat Woman, offering Vernon a leather-gloved hand. 'I'm sorry, Jack didn't mention that you'd be coming. What a surprise! How fabulous! Do come in and have a drink.'

'Billy Vernon. I'm afraid we didn't know that it was fancy dress...'

'Oh don't worry about it. I'll get you a spare mask. You can be the mystery man,' said Sandy, happily. 'Umm... do you think you could introduce us?'

'I'm sorry,' said Vernon and he walked around the car to where Ian was presenting Alex with a bottle of Cristal that he had quick-wittedly plucked from his emergency stash behind the driving seat. 'Excuse me, Ian,' said Vernon. 'This is... Sandy. She's....'

'Oh yes, do allow me to present my wife,' interjected Alex, who was surprised that Pete had not mentioned this wonderful bonus.

'Your wife?' said Taylor as he took Sandy's hand and held it tenderly between both of his, looking right into the brown eyes that were widening behind her mask.

'You're a lucky man. I'm very pleased to meet you, Sandy.'

Sandy thought that she was going to pass out with pleasure, especially as this very warm and intimate introduction was being conducted in front of scores of their guests, many of whom were saying loudly, 'It's Ian Taylor! It is! Ian Taylor's here!'

As more and more masked people came out of the front door to look, Taylor adopted a bashful face and smiled at everybody. He let Alex take him by the arm as he shooed the crowd to part and let the poor chap through.

Everybody moved aside, grinning, and then followed like the Pied Piper's children as the world's most ecstatic dentist led the way to the marquee.

'What will he want to drink?' Sandy asked Vernon anxiously. 'What do rock stars drink? Does he drink? Does he want to eat? What does he eat? Oh dear, I hope he'll be alright, I'm afraid Alex's going to be all over him. Will he want to go somewhere quiet? Oh God! Look! Anthea's taking a photograph. Some people are so rude. I'm so sorry about this, Mr Vernon. Does he want to use the bathroom? Will he want to lie down or anything?'

'He's fine,' said Vernon. 'He's loving this. One thing though, do you know if Peter Forth's here?'

'Yes, of course,' trilled Sandy. 'The party's actually for Peter. Shall I go and find him? I suppose Mr Taylor will want to see him.'

'Call him Ian, he prefers that,' said Vernon, making Sandy positively fizz with excitement. 'But… err… no, don't get Pete just yet. But, if I could just see him first?'

'Of course! Oh, I'm so delighted you've come. Peter will be too. I'd read in the papers that there had been some, umm, problem between them. Trust the press to get it wrong as usual.'

'Quite,' said Vernon. 'By the way, how is Pete? Have you seen him tonight?'

'Oh, he's fine, quite happy, actually. Well, happy for Pete.

Although I expect he'll be doing his drugs by now. I know that some of the girls were hoping he might share whatever it is he does with them.'

'That might not be a good idea. Peter has slightly more capacity than most other people. How's things between him and Susie?'

'Pretty much the same,' said Sandy. 'In fact, between you and me Mr Vernon, there's talk that she's been seeing somebody else and that somebody is here tonight too. I'm rather hoping that there isn't a scene. Especially now that Mr Tay… Ian's here. I would hate it if anyone ruined the night for Ian.'

Great, thought Vernon. Pete coked-up and pissed, just the combination you wanted: Mr Volatile at a party, his wife shagging somebody else and now Pete's Guilt has turned up wearing an Ian Taylor mask. Great.

'Is Jack Jackson here?' asked Vernon.

'Oh yes, Jack's around. Of course, silly me… Ian will want to see him first, won't he?'

'Actually, it's a surprise. Jack didn't know we were coming.'

'Oh how fabulous! This will be a night to remember. Look, I'm terribly sorry but would you mind dreadfully if I just go and take a peek to make sure that Ian's alright? Alex will monopolise him dreadfully otherwise. If I see Jack, shall I take him over to Ian?'

'That would be very kind,' said Vernon. 'I must just use your toilet. I'll find you in a minute.'

Vernon smiled and politely nodded at the burglar in the striped sweater with the bag marked swag who was waiting for the toilet door to open. As he queued, he listened to the party guests excitedly chatter about what was now the sole topic of conversation.

'He hasn't lost his looks, has he? He's gorgeous!' said a curvy ER surgeon to an SAS man in a balaclava.

'I always preferred The Who myself,' said the SAS man.

'Do you think he's really going to have sex at that Grey Rose concert?' asked a woman in a burka to a thinly-veiled belly dancer.

'Maybe he's here to audition,' said the belly dancer. 'I'm up for it if he is.'

'I'd read he'd sacked Peter,' said a woman in a witch mask, 'and you can hardly blame him, can you? I mean Peter's such an arrogant twat. He always behaves like he's the pop star.'

'Do you think he'll get up and sing with Jack Jackson?' said the belly dancer excitedly.

'Well I'm going to ask him to dance, anyway,' said the ER surgeon. 'Can you imagine! Dancing with Ian Taylor. I used to have posters of him on my wall.'

Vernon reflected that it was always the same. Whether you were with Ian at The White House or in some East End pub, people always bubbled in his presence. The fans, of course, screamed to touch him, but the ordinary people, those who hadn't bought an Ian Taylor album for fifteen years, they were the interesting ones to watch as they acted as if somebody had thrown into their midst a love grenade that had exploded smiles all over them.

For a moment, Vernon felt proud to be serving somebody who had put so much joy into so many different lives, but then he was jolted from the thought as the toilet door opened and the burglar came out saying that the flush had broken.

CHAPTER 61

In the barn behind the paddock at the bottom of the garden, Peter was carefully chopping out cocaine onto the side of a dry brick.

He had already used the same surface to roll up the two strong joints that his dressed-to-tease disciples, the simpering wives of local Rotarians, had smoked between them and now, because Babs was stoned and not thinking properly, he had given in to her pretentious demands for something a little stronger.

Pete had no qualms about upping the ante to Category A. As he figured it, they were all grown women, he wasn't trying to deal, just to give them a brightener and, besides, he knew that if somebody caught them and the shit hit the fan nobody would blame anybody except him.

His experienced hand had formed five decent lines and he was just about to tell Juliet to reach into his waistcoat pocket and roll up the twenty-pound note she would find there when they heard somebody approaching through the grass.

'Don't worry, we're only having an orgy,' said Peter to his suddenly-agitated flock as he carefully hid the brick behind a hay bale and held it there one-handed so that the cocaine didn't spill.

'What's going on down here, then?' they heard Sandy laugh. 'Room for one more?'

'The girls thought you were their straighter halves,' said Peter and he nonchalantly began to chop and divvy up the powder again.

'Do you want some of this?'

'Not for me. I'm having enough excitement for one night.'

'Not for me either,' said Jane. 'It doesn't agree with me if I've been drinking.'

'I don't agree with anybody when I've been drinking,' quipped Peter and they laughed as Juliet, Annie and Babs took turns to bend over the brick with the note as Peter held the block steady. After the women had each taken their turn, Peter swiftly made the remaining

two lines disappear up his nose.
'So. What's the excitement?' he said, wiping his nostrils and sniffing aggressively. 'Is my bird stripping on the dance floor?'

'I don't know where Susie is, actually,' said Sandy. 'I haven't seen her for some while.'

'She's probably shagging Jack Jackson,' swiped Peter, as the drug worked with the alcohol to loosen his grip on his resolve.

Sandy stayed quiet on that subject because she could see that Peter was already well-advanced into a new self-destruction; his hands were quite visibly shaking and there didn't appear to be much vodka left in the bottle that he was swigging from again.

'So?' he said again as he took the bottle away from his mouth, spilling vodka down the front of his waistcoat. 'What's up?'

'Umm... how's things between you and Ian?' said Sandy nervously.

'On a one to ten of mutual friendship I'd say ours is currently knocking around minus infinity,' said Peter defiantly. 'Why? Is he on the phone or something?'

'No, he's here!'

'Here?' shrieked Babs. 'Ian Taylor's here?'

'Here we go,' said Peter moodily. 'Cry havoc and let slip the dogs of whore.'

'Err... there's a chap with him...' ventured Sandy hesitantly as she noticed Peter's eyes beginning to blacken.

'Billy Vernon,' said Peter.

'Err... yes. He says he wants to talk to you.'

'He can fuck off,' said Peter.

'Well I'm going to have a look,' said Jane.

'Me too!' shrieked Juliet. 'I adore Ian Taylor, he's very sexy.'

'He's very old,' said Annie.

'You wouldn't say no,' said Jane and the four women sped away giggling, leaving Peter and Sandy alone.

'I expect Billy wants to ask me to stay out of the way,' said Peter, drinking more vodka. 'I guess they've come down to see Jack. Ian won't want to see me, even though this is my village and was my party. Now it'll be Ian's. Don't let Pete spoil the party, eh?

Especially when he's ruined so many before.'

'Oh, Pete,' said Sandy.

'And I guess you won't want me to ruin what will now be Al's big moment either. It's alright. I understand.'

'No, I'm not saying that. You're our friend, Peter. I hate you feeling that you have to skulk away just because Ian's here. I mean, if anyone here has a right to see Ian Taylor then surely it's you. You're his friend, after all. We don't even know the man.'

'Was, Sandy. Was. No, it's alright. I know what Billy's doing. I'd have done the same, once; make it all appear to be happy and nice, keep anyone who might piss Ian off out of the way. Don't let him step into anything that looks like reality. Look, you go back to the party. Enjoy it; you'll find that Ian will be wonderfully charming. I'll stay out of the way until he's gone.'

Sandy took him in her arms and hugged him. She could feel that his whole body was now shaking with either drugs or fury.

'Thank you, Pete. Oh, poor you, are you sure?' She said as she attempted to cradle his head into her shoulder before he snapped away.

'Par for the course, Sand, the greatest good for the greatest number.'

She was horrified at how pathetic she found him now; an unemployed drunk, scruffy and, frankly, rather useless if he could no longer introduce his friends to the famous. No wonder that Susie found him so unattractive.

'Will you be alright? You do understand, don't you? It would be such a shame to ruin everybody else's night just because this was your night. Oh God, that sounds awful… There'll be other parties, Pete. Maybe he won't stay long…'

'Yeah,' he said sullenly. 'Listen, if you see Susie tell her I've just popped back home, say I'm sleeping off some booze or something. Don't want her worrying.'

CHAPTER 62

When Sandy returned to the marquee she discovered that, unlike before, when people had arranged themselves in various gossiping clumps around the sides of the tent, now they were all crowded down at the far end of it, standing ever-so-obviously around the table where Alex sat with Ian Taylor.

Alex was talking avidly and Taylor appeared to be half-listening whilst signing autographs on paper plates for a bunch of excited matrons who imagined themselves to be yum-mums. As Sandy strode across the dance floor to put an immediate end to what she protectively believed to be an outrageous exploitation of her now-principal guest, she saw her eldest son coming towards her.

'What is your father playing at?' she hissed at the grinning Jon-Jon.

'What do you mean Ma?'

'Doesn't he know that celebrities like to be left alone sometimes? Can't he see that the poor man deserves a night off? This is shocking! Ian hasn't even got a drink, for God's sake! Jon-Jon, go and get a bottle of wine for him. Get it from the cellar, not that muck in the kitchen.'

'I can't Ma,' said her son. 'Dad's got me doing something.'

'What has he got you doing?'

'He wants me to ask the DJ to start playing a selection of Ian's hits.'

'Oh for crying out loud! Does the gauche fool have no sensitivity? You're to do no such thing! Such sycophancy would embarrass the poor man.'

'But Dad said…'

'I do not care what your father said. Let me deal with your father. Go to the cellar and get a bottle of Petrus.'

'The posh stuff?'

'Yes, the bloody posh stuff. Go on! Oh, and Jon-Jon, bring a bottle of good Chablis as well, in case he's a white man. And a cooler. And get those bloody girls to bring out something for him to eat – those canapés – tell them to make sure that they're not cold. Tell them I'll kill them if they're cold.'

'Jesus Ma, he's just an ordinary bloke. I've been talking to him. He's just like the rest of us.'

'Don't be preposterous,' said Sandy. 'When have you ever met an ordinary bloke like Ian Taylor? He's a celebrity and we should show him the appropriate respect.'

'But he's not even been invited to the party. He's just gate-crashed.'

'He has done no such thing! Don't you dare say to anyone that he wasn't invited! If anybody asks, say I invited him along with Jack Jackson.'

'Are you saying he's Jackson's date?' grinned the young man.

'You are not too old to be slapped and sent to bed, my lad. And don't think that I wouldn't. Now go and get that wine and be quick about it!'

Her son sulked off and Sandy looked again at where her husband had established what appeared to be a sideshow. She was alarmed to see that Taylor had now stopped signing plates and was looking straight at her.

Instinctively, she put a hand up to her face and was immediately pleased to remember that nobody could see her blushing as she was masked. She walked over to the centre of attention to attend to him herself. He was still holding her eye.

'Problem?' said Taylor, perceptively.

'No. No. Everything's fine. I just noticed that you haven't got a drink. Sorry about that. I've just sent my son to fetch a couple of bottles of the better wine. Or perhaps you'd like a beer? Or a lager? Anything you want, really.'

'Anything, Sandy?' grinned Taylor wickedly.

'Well… err… well, yes, actually. Anything you like,' she twinkled, enjoying the flirtation.

'Oh for God's sake, Sandy, give the poor chap a bit of peace,' said Alex, who had been proudly showing off the plate on which Ian had perceptively written Thanks and best wishes to mine host – guess who's coming to dinner? Cheers Al, your mate Ian (Taylor).

'Actually, Al, it's me who was bothering Sandy, I'm afraid.'

'Oh, bother away dear chap,' said Alex. 'You bother her as much as you like. We're all here to be bothered as you see fit. Really, it's a privilege. I want you to treat this party as your own. Truly I do.'

'About that drink?' said Sandy, hideously-embarrassed that her husband was obviously tight.

'Wine would be great. Honestly, anything is fine. But what I would really like is a dance.'

'A dance?' said Sandy, not comprehending.

'Yes. Would you do me the honour?'

'A dance with me?'

'With your permission. And with Al's, of course.'

Sandy knew that if Alex had made even the slightest hint at demurring she would have broken a bottle over his head.

'What would you like to dance to?' she asked, trying to ignore the fact that everybody was looking right at her.

'I'll fix that,' said Taylor. 'Shan't be a moment.'

She watched as Taylor walked over to the disc jockey and shook his hand. As he spoke into the DJ's ear, she became aware that her legs seemed to have turned to stone and she couldn't move. Now she wished that she had taken some of Pete's damn cocaine. Oh God, she thought, I hope it's a song that I know. Please God, don't make it a fast one, I don't want to look old.

As Springsteen's Hungry Heart came to an end, the disc jockey spoke into his microphone in a throaty drawl that did not disguise the fact that he came from Weymouth and not Wyoming.

'Okaaaaay. And now we've got a super-special request for a spin from the man that the tales of tonight will all be about,' punned the DJ horribly. 'This is a request for the first lady of the evening, our cat in black. Sandy, this three minutes of magic is just for you…'

Sandy made a mental note to bollock the DJ for that later, but she forgot her irritation as Ian took her hand and led her into the centre of the floor for a samba-smooch to Peter Green's Black Magic Woman.

In her nervousness she stood on his toes during the song's first twelve bars. But after everyone had laughed as Ian theatrically hopped about feigning injury for a few moments, he clasped her to him again. She danced in a state of total disbelief, not only because she was in the arms of a hero of her youth and a damn good dancer, but also because he appeared to be rubbing a heroic erection against her thigh.

She relaxed dreamily into the moment, wondering which of the girls she could tell about this later. She did notice Catherine Hornby watching her closely, but she suspected that was just envy.

CHAPTER 63

Susie had been searching for Pete for what felt like ages but he couldn't be found, and everyone she had asked had said they hadn't seen him either. As a result, she was becoming increasingly irritated by her growing suspicion that Pete was ruining yet another party by hanging out somewhere with the bad influences that were the justifications for his addictions.

She was disgusted, and had said so to Sandy, that Pete's party had been allowed to become Ian's event by the fawning of their friends.

Sandy had replied that Susie was being ridiculous to expect anything else under the circumstances, and Susie had flounced off to find Pete and say, 'Let's go home, we need to talk.' So far she had managed to avoid the risk of any reintroduction to Taylor by leaving the marquee and kitchen every time he had entered them. As she was dressed in a micro nurse's uniform she was able to hide herself from Taylor's glances by pulling the surgical mask up over her face. Now she was back in the entrance hall and was about to give up and go home, when she saw Jackson going up the stairs and, for once, he was not attended by that limpet of a Hornby woman.

Susie knew that she should find Pete, even though she also knew that when she did she would find him in a state of near-collapse. But Catherine's usurping of her place in Jack's arms had stirred her competitiveness, so she followed her heart.

As she climbed the stairs to where Jackson had gone she thought briefly of Peter and pictured his probable intoxication, and that was reason enough for her to shun all thoughts of him and unbutton her nurse's uniform a little more.

'Hello Nursey,' said a chuckling voice that made her glow. 'Have you come to put me to bed now?'

'You bastard,' she grinned up at Jackson. 'The only treatment you deserve is an enema with that bloody cucumber of yours.'

As Susie had shared her marriage for long enough with Peter's friend cocaine, she instantly knew that the dilation of his pupils and the damp in his nose signified that Jackson had been enjoying the same habit; but she still returned his kiss with a frenetic passion. After some moments, they relaxed to exchange smiles and hold hands.

'Did you know that your mate Ian's turned up downstairs?' she said, interested to see his reaction.

'You're having a laugh,' he grinned.

'No, honest. Ian's arrived with Billy. Sandy says they are looking for you.'

'Hmm, he must need somewhere to hide away from the press. Well, I'm not going to go running in with welcomes. He can fucking wait.'

'Yeah,' Susie breathed huskily, 'wait until you've finished fucking…'

She was about to say, 'Me,' but their bubble was burst by the heart-jolting interruption of a woman saying, 'Hello, what's going on here, then?'

Susie jumped away from Jackson with an abruptness that advertised their union. She turned to see Catherine looking icily through the banisters.

'Hello darlin',' blagged Jackson. 'Have you met Susie? She's Peter's wife.'

'Exactly,' said Catherine, still coldly.

'Actually, I must go and find him,' said Susie, blushing with fury. 'I'll catch you later, Jack.'

As she disappeared quickly down the stairs, Catherine glared at Jackson.

'What?' he said with a nervous laugh.

Catherine saw an opportunity that Jack might embrace, if only to change the subject, so she took it.

'I was looking for you because you promised that you'd introduce me to Ian,' she said with coy eyes and a wide smile.

'Oh yeah, yeah. Susie just came to tell me he was here. Some surprise eh?'

'So will you introduce me?'

'Sure, babe, sure. In a minute, OK? I've just got to get myself together; you know, powder my nose and all that,' said Jackson.

'Ohh, you promised,' she kept on.

'Yeah. Alright. In a minute. I haven't seen him for years, remember? Just hang on while I sort my shit.'

'I'll make it worth your while,' she purred.

Jackson had spent too many years playing Taylor's second fiddle to be seduced by an offer that he felt should be his in his own right and offered unconditionally. He had also spent so long in stardom that such an offer was in no way extraordinary.

'Oi, cool it, alright? I've got to go to the loo first.'

Panicking that she might run out of time, that Taylor might leave and her chance be gone, Catherine misread his indifference. She leaned back from him against the stairway and then lifted her skirt to reveal what was libidinously-packaged beneath it.

'Well, I'm going in there,' said Catherine, indicating an adjacent bedroom. 'I'll wait for you to come in and do whatever you like.'

Suddenly and with cocaine clarity, Jackson realised the perfect way to solve all his problems with Catherine's clinginess and her irritating obsession with meeting another rock star who was apparently far more bloody interesting that he was.

It was, the drugs convinced him, the ideal solution; freeing him up to play around with the obviously on-heat Susie and enabling him to provide the sort of welcome present that would keep Ian in a good mood.

'I'll bring you a drink,' said Jackson.

'Great; champagne if there is any,' said Catherine as Jackson went down to the kitchen.

Smiling and nodding his way through the now universally drunk guests, he took a bottle of fizzy Spanish wine from the table. He poured two glasses and went back up, pausing on the stairs briefly to fiddle in his pocket for the small bottle of Soho Lust that he had brought to try out on Susie. He went into the bedroom and found Catherine preparing to undress.

'Here,' he said, passing her the glass.

She took a gulp.

'Ooh, bitter,' she said.

'Well they only had the Spanish stuff, cheap gits,' excused Jackson as he put an arm around her waist and kissed her. 'I'm just going to see a man about a runny nose and, when I get back, we'll get to the bottom of everything you want.'

'Hmm, I'll wait for you lover,' said Catherine dreamily.

CHAPTER 64

In searching all over the house for Peter, Billy Vernon had been a landing above Jackson and had looked down to witness Susie and a sexy-looking rock chick both clearly competing to pull Jack. Now Vernon returned to the marquee to inform Ian that he had found Jackson, but the tent was deserted.

He rushed back to the house and, as he neared it, heard a piano playing and Taylor's distinct voice singing 'Bridge Over Troubled Water'. He walked in and saw a wall of people's backs in front of him. Looking over their shoulders, Vernon could see Ian sitting at an upright piano, thumping the keys as he led the crowd in a raucous chorus of 'I will ease your mi-iiii-ind"

As the song finished, there was loud cheering and whistling and Vernon saw Ian rise to his feet and bow, grinning widely.

'Ladies and gentlemen!' Sandy called above the dying applause, 'I'm sure you'll agree that our guest of honour has more than earned a rest for a while. Let's all go back to the dance floor!'

Vernon casually wound his way to the piano and waited until he had heard the last of twenty people thank Taylor for what they each proclaimed to be the best night of their lives. Only when he saw his employer acknowledge his presence with the very slightest of winks did Vernon butt in on the farmer who was beseeching Taylor to open the village fête.

Politely, Vernon asked if Ian could be excused for a moment to take a telephone call.

'This is fucking great!' beamed Taylor as Vernon led him away from the swarm of adoration. 'Who's on the phone?'

'Nobody,' said Vernon. 'I just figured you needed a breather.'

'Yeah, thanks, man. This is brilliant! I've always said ordinary people were more fun than stars. Nobody's too cool to enjoy themselves. We should do more of this, I fucking love it!'

'So do they,' Vernon observed.

'Yeah. Talking of people who are too cool, where's Jack?'

'Upstairs,' said Vernon.

'And where's Pete?' said Taylor feeling all magnanimous now. 'You know we should see Pete, say hi and stuff.'

'Pete's disappeared.'

'What do you mean?' said Taylor, looking serious as he picked up on the hint of worry on Vernon's face.

'He's nowhere around. I've looked.'

'Oh, he's probably just crept off for a shag somewhere. You know Pete,' said Taylor jovially.

'Umm… there's another thing.'

'What? Tell me, Billy.'

Vernon sighed and looked his most lugubrious.

'I saw his bird, Susie, upstairs… err… playing.'

'With another guy?'

'With Jack…' said Vernon.

'Fuck,' said Taylor, thinking quickly. 'OK, I'll talk to Jack. But as we know, he can get a bit lively at times and I don't know yet if him and me still have issues. So make a call to security and get some guys down here. In fact, get a team down here anyway; this crowd's alright but they're getting a little excited.'

'I can't get a team here for a few hours, it's a long drive,' said Vernon.

'Tell them to get a chopper. That way I've got a get-out as well. And find Pete; he may have gone home. I don't want him to hurt himself, Billy. I'm going for a piss, I'll catch you back at the marquee.'

As Taylor walked away, forcing a smile back onto his face and taking the arm of the hovering Sandy, Vernon poked the buttons on his mobile and, without explanation, told the head of Taylor's security that he didn't care that it was a bit last minute, he wanted six men, in a chopper, delivered now to some middle of nowhere place in bloody Dorset. Then he took grabbed a handful of food from a waitress's tray and munched it as he strolled down the lane to Pete's place.

CHAPTER 65

'I thought I'd find you here and I thought I'd find you doing that,' said Vernon, walking uninvited into the kitchen at Peter's house and pointing at the cocaine that was already in four lines on the oak table at which Peter was sitting and not looking up.

'Do you win a prize from yourself, then?' said Peter, lighting a Marlboro between clenched teeth and now eyeing the manager with very large pupils.

'Can we talk?' continued Vernon, pulling himself a chair and pausing to look hard at Pete. 'Well, can we?'

'Do you know what I absolutely fucking hate?' replied Peter as he played with a large ratchet knife that he had abruptly pulled from his boot.

Vernon looked blank; he was considering the knife, which Peter was now stabbing into the table top with the repetition of a metronome.

'I fucking hate people who expect you to listen just because they want to talk; I think that is very ill-mannered and…'

'Look, Pete…' began Vernon, nervous now.

'I haven't finished and I believe that in my own kitchen, at the very fucking least, I should be allowed to finish addressing intruders whom I haven't invited either in or to sit. Even, under the circumstances, if they don't want to listen.'

Vernon shut up; he was trying to remember how he was once taught to parry someone attacking you with a knife.

'However,' Peter grinned, 'I have done rather a great deal of cocaine and therefore will quite probably enjoy an increasing need to talk… So, although I was going to say, 'What is even more fucking hateful and bloody bad-mannered is people who want to talk to you, but can't be arsed to make the gigantic fucking effort of actually speaking, so they send somebody else to say it for them,' instead I shall say, 'Billy, how nice to see you. Would you like a drink and some rather superior Brazilian blend?"

'Can… may I have a line?' replied Vernon, not wanting to appear impolite to a man with a knife.

'Please,' said Peter as he unscrewed the lid on another bottle of near-frozen vodka and poured two glasses.

'Ian wants to see you,' said Vernon, sniffing hard and wiping his nose.

'I'd gathered that. Why?'

'He wants to talk to you. I think he's going to ask you back,' said Vernon, smiling now. 'I think you will find that if you just roll on your back and apologise, then it'll all be OK.'

'Sorry?'

'He's feeling very generous. Getting him out to meet normal people at the party has been very good for him,' continued Vernon, who hadn't noticed that Peter had stopped stabbing his table and was now holding his knife by the tip of the blade, assessing its balance.

'What other opinions of your own has he allowed you to make?'

'Oh don't be like that,' said Vernon pleasantly.

'Or else what?' said Peter evenly.

'Why did you leave your party?' said Vernon, changing tack and aware now that Peter was weighing the knife as if he meant to throw it.

'It ceased to be for me,' said Peter simply. 'As you very well know, Ian's presence at anything makes it Ian's gig. I was nudged to leave by the friend who was throwing it for me; the same friend who didn't invite you or Ian and who now will doubtless suck Ian's cock if he asks her to.'

'That's a bit unfair; we didn't ask her to say that, to ask you to leave. We wouldn't do that; c'mon Pete, we're not that bad.'

'Yes we are,' said Peter, his huge eyes narrowing a bit. 'We are very bad, Billy, we are appallingly rude to others and we are allowed to be so because we are so famous. Stars are the new feudal kings, Billy, it's medieval how we let them behave to us.'

'You're such a fucking socialist,' said Vernon, taking care to grin widely.

'And proud to be so, mate. Remember where you're from, not where you've been.'

'We're getting a bit deep, Pete,' said Vernon, keen to divert Peter away from an ethics competition.

'The coke,' explained Peter, smiling. 'Please help yourself to another line. Anyway, listen, Billy, you're a lovely bloke… no, I mean it, you're good-hearted and you care, and so's Ian; he's a sweetheart, I love him to death in himself; one of the genuinely nicest human beings I have ever met…'

'So come back…'

'No, fuck off; Ian, you, you're all lovely in yourselves, Billy. Musos, showbizzies, you'll all fascinating, electric company, great, great fun, as people. But once you go to work, then you are a bunch of cunts,' said Peter, smiling. 'Nobody has any fucking idea what massive bullies you guys are.'

'I'm not a bully,' said Vernon, his defences downed by the drug.

'You bully the record company,' said Peter flatly.

'Yeah, but they deserve it.'

'There you go!' 'But they're the record company,' said Vernon, laughing now.

'No human being deserves to be bullied, Billy, it's just wrong.'

'You bully Susie,' said Vernon carefully.

'And that's fucking wrong! I'm fucking wrong to bully Susie, it's appalling. I'm sure that's why she's shagging Jack, my bullying pushed her away, or at least put her off. How many bullies do you want to shag?'

'What do you mean she's shagging Jack? Susie?' asked Vernon, convincingly.

'Do you know what really pisses me off, Billy?' began Peter, taking the circuitous route to answering that cocaine always sent him down. 'It pisses me off with Susie and it pisses me off with Ian. I don't care, I don't mind, if people think I'm a bastard. I don't mind if people think I'm a drama queen or a meddler, or an egotist or too aggressive, I really don't care. But what I cannot fucking stand is when people think I'm an idiot. Don't try to pull a stroke on me when I wrote the bloody book. Of course she's fucking Jack. I do have eyes, I do have ears, I do have instincts and intuition. I can recognize human behaviour. People try to deceive me as if their deception is completely untransparent to me. Anyway… fuck, I'm whizzing on this… Thanks Billy, but I'm not coming back and I'll tell you why, I've seen through the illusion. It's not just that I won't come back, I can't come back because I now get it, I know now that it is all just insubstantial bollocks. Seriously, fame is one of the most absurd concepts ever created by society because it is the fucking antithesis of the greatest good. Fame is a fucking reward for self-centredness, and that's pure madness.'

'Why is it absurd? Because you're not famous? You're just jealous, Pete. I think you're scared. You must know that nobody will touch you with a bargepole if you walk away. C'mon, it's not like we're not going to put the word around that you're a junkie or an alkie or a know-all, argumentative pain in the arse. Fucking hell Pete, your name will be made shit and people will believe you're shit because the whole world will know about your shitness and only you will know about ours.'

'I might write my biography, then they'd know,' said Peter moodily as he sought out more cocaine to shore up himself.

'We'd stop it getting published,' said Vernon bluntly.

'I could publish it myself,' countered Peter.

'But Pete… Pete, for fuck's sake, you know you can't win. We could get your book savaged by the critics, dropped from shelves, we can close down your every attempt at publicity. For Christ's sake, you of all fucking people know that Fleet Street will dance at any fucking speed we want if there's an Ian Taylor exclusive in it for them. In exchange for a three-parter with new photos, I could probably have you shot. Your fucking mates in the media are no more interested in your fucking integrity than we are, not if it means losing a chance of an exclusive chat in Ian's dressing room. People don't want to know truth, Pete.

'Has it ever occurred to you that you might be wrong?' said Peter sullenly.

'No, Pete, no. You're mad. I don't know whether it's because you're ill, or too out of it, or what. But, irritating though it is, for some reason Ian wants you back, maybe as his conscience.'

Vernon could see that Peter had weakened now. He'd closed the knife and was pushing around the remaining cocaine with a credit card, staring at it intensely as he made spirals in the cream powder.

'You know what, Billy?' he said, suddenly looking up and grinning again. 'It's not the morality or what's right, we know it's all horrible self-serving shit; I've always known that, and it goes with the gig. It's like joining the Army; don't whine if you get shot at. No, the reason I've had enough is because it's not fun any more; rock and roll is too straight for me. It's too earnest and sober and serious. It's computer-calculated, sing x and y will happen; there's no dash and daring, it's fucking tea with the President. We shouldn't be having tea with the President, we should be looting The White House cellars and copping blow jobs off the First Lady's girlfriends. It's fucking sanitised, there's no rebellion, no rule-breaking. It's suits and nice fingernails, it's clean shirts and X-Factored schlock, it's all about formatted comfort zones, nothing is rocked or rolled or made uncomfortable in the fucking slightest.

Fucking hell, Martha fucking Stewart's done more time than your average rock star. We've now got the punkest of rockers advertising fucking butter? What the fuck is that about? Never mind your fucking granny not liking it, we've all become fucking grannies now; rock and roll is the new bowling, Billy, and it bores the fuck out of me.'

'So I can tell Ian that you're considering it?' said Vernon, helping himself to another line and downing the vodka that he hadn't wanted, 'Seeing as you're just talking coke crap?'

'Fuck off.'

'And I don't suppose there's any risk of you helping us find Catherine?'

'Fuck off with that too,' said Peter.

CHAPTER 66

Too much cocaine was making Peter brood, so he finished the last of the vodka after Billy had left. Now that all the pennies had dropped he realized how tawdry and worthless his last years had been – a time during which he had believed he was doing something worthwhile, but which had now come crashing down in rubble around him. Someone had once told him that he didn't deal with loss very well, he remembered.

'But too many years of achieving C+ in humanity gnarled me against expecting anything better,' he said out-loud to himself.

He lit a Marlboro and went to the window. He breathed in the hay-scented air and, although he thought he did not understand which moves he had made wrongly, he grinned sardonically at himself.

'Fuck it, at least we had a laugh.'

He wished now that he had not confidentially emailed the Ian Gaylor blowjob shot to various newspapers' news editors that morning, even if it was the one he had carefully faked so that it could be denied later, and he knew that, if he hadn't still been drunk from the night before he would not have committed such a betrayal. He felt all the more ashamed of his disloyalty because Taylor now wanted him back; he was offering him his two hundredth and second chance within hours of him having shopped Taylor to the press for silver. Albeit rather a lot of silver.

He considered himself deeply. He saw that he, not Taylor, had wrecked his loving marriage by choosing the work over family because it was more exciting. He, not Taylor, had trashed his job by choosing to be bolshy and evangelistic about integrity. He, and nobody else, had pushed Susie away by choosing to ignore her need for affection in preference to his urgency for sex. He had chosen to do Class A drugs when he knew the effects they had on those who could only wait in horrified anxiety for him to come down. All of his problems had been the results of his choices, he accepted, and although he had long blamed others for everything, he saw now that it all had been his fault, his choosing.

'And the biggest problem,' he concluded, 'is that I don't give a flying fuck.'

He returned to the kitchen table, snorted more cocaine, inhaled hard on the Marlboro and waited for the whap force of the coke to hit him like a train in his chest. Then he stood on a chair and put around his neck the rope that he had tied to a large hook in one of the old beams.

There were no tears in his eyes; but his face was creased in sadness as he took one last drag on his cigarette, thinking how much he liked the taste of smoke.

He exhaled and, with a little hop, he kicked the chair over and fell in the same second that he realised he'd forgotten the bloody death note.

CHAPTER 67

Ian Taylor had slipped away from Sandy's guard as he needed another piss, but as he didn't want to queue and be hit on for more autographs he thought that nobody would really mind if he took a slash in the garden, around the back of some sheds.

He unzipped as he approached the sheds and was aching to let go when out of bloody nowhere came a woman in a short nurse's outfit, bumping into him.

'Aarrghh!' yelled the nurse. 'Shit. Sorry… oh, hello Ian.'

'Shit! Fuck! Susie, oh thank Christ for that. Hang on darling… excuse me, sorry… I'm breaking my neck here,' explained Ian, unable to hang on any longer and spraying the side of the shed.

'Oh godddd… ahhhh… sorry Suze, I was fucking desperate…'

As Taylor slowed to a dribble and at last looked up from guiding his penis away from dripping on his shoes, he saw that Susie was staring at it. He grinned at her.

'Don't worry Suze, I'm not going to ask you to shake it dry… unless you especially want to.'

'Bugger off Ian, I've had enough of your arrogant assumptions for one night,' she said as she began to walk away from him.

'Hey! Hey, what do you mean? What arrogance? Susie?'

She turned to face him, furious that he should be so relaxed.

'What do you mean by just turning up here? It's Pete's party, not yours. You do know that he's been sent away, out of sight in case he causes a scene now you're here? At his own bloody party. How could you do that Ian?'

'I didn't know any of that and I didn't ask him to leave. I told Billy to find him, I wanted to talk to him,' said Taylor defensively. 'I swear it. And if you don't mind me saying so, from my experience this is just Pete bloody over-reacting again. I'm sorry, Susie, but right now I can't deal with another one of Pete's problems. He's been doing my head in…'

'Actually, Ian, I do mind you saying so. Not because I'm defending Pete, but to be honest you just piss me off. You're a self-centred fucking bully!'

Susie immediately worried that she had gone too far. She watched his face darken with anger, but she held his glare.

'I'd be careful what you say if I were you,' began Taylor, scowling. 'I can make things very difficult for Pete...'

'Difficult! Fucking difficult? You don't know what the word means. Don't you think working for you has been difficult? Don't you think it's difficult bringing up kids without their father because he's always at your endless bloody beck and call? Don't you think it's difficult never knowing if an evening or a weekend or fucking Christmas will be ruined by you phoning to demand attention on some pathetic whim?'

'You're not the only ones who have it tough,' protested Taylor. 'I have difficulties...'

'Piss off! There's no difficulty in your pampered bloody life, Ian, because every time your shit hits your fan you send somebody else to clear up the mess you make...'

'You watch your mouth...' began Taylor, but Susie was beyond caring now.

'Or else what, Mr bloody Past It? What will you do, set Billy on me? Bloody Billy who's been made into a cowering mouse by all your shouting and tantrums and blame?'

'I'm warning you Susie,' said Taylor, lowering his voice as he could see that her yelling was attracting the attention of other guests out on the lawn.

'Warning me? Warning me what? To stop telling the truth, that you're a bad-tempered spoilt and petulant twat? Shut up, I haven't finished. You swan in here, knowing that it's not OK, you just bloody take over as usual and you expect people to say nothing and just live with it because you're such a big fucking star!'

'Have you finished?' seethed Taylor, his eyes repeatedly darting from her face to the shocked looks of the growing numbers watching them now.

'I've finished with you, you... you... has been! How fucking dare you piss on Pete's parade like this? You're such a bastard, Ian, and the tragedy is you've been one for so long you no longer even recognize it.'

Susie spun around and strode off but was stopped by Taylor's mocking retort.

'Off to give Jack a good seeing-to are you, Mrs Forth?'

She turned again, glaring.

'What's the matter Ian? Jealous?'

'You fucking…'

Taylor lunged towards her but was stopped by the sharp slap of her hand across his face.

'That's for all the people you've trampled over,' Susie snapped as she stormed off down the path, passing Sandy who had rushed up shouting what the bloody hell are you doing?

'Oh piss off Sandy,' said Susie, starting to cry as she headed back to the house, 'I'm off. Enjoy the rest of your fucking party.'

CHAPTER 68

As Peter pulled pieces of wood and plaster out of his hair he thought that it was just fucking typical that the beam which those bloody builders had insisted would 'hold anything, Mr Forth' of course did no such fucking thing.

He was sure he had broken his ankle in the fall that had torn out half the ceiling and left him on the floor, and not swinging as a grotesque welcome home for Susie. He was resolving to sue the plasterer, and was already forming the complex logic to argue that preventing his suicide was not a legitimate defence for shoddy work.

He was gutted to see that in his botched attempt he had knocked over the other bottle of vodka and he was already expecting seven bells of hell from Susie for the mess and for making the kitchen reek of booze. Fuck.

Peter reached out to the table and pulled himself up off the floor, grabbing for the chair he had kicked away and wondering whether he could explain away the mess if he told Susie that he'd just been having a quick drink when, a propos bugger all, honest, the ceiling had just caved in.

He removed the rope that was still around his neck and looked in a mirror at the red welt. He thought of trying to pass it off as a love bite until he realized that such an excuse would start her ranting about how the hell had that happened.

He also noticed that he wasn't feeling very well. Besides the ankle pain and a bloody sore elbow, he was also contending with the heart-revving effect of the coke. The racing and panic was a very bad sign, and Peter knew that the only way to counter it was to lose the speediness through the depressant effects of alcohol.

He pushed himself painfully from the chair, limped to the freezer and extracted his last bottle of Absolut. He tried to glug it from the bottle but on top of the coke rush, which was feeling more unpleasant by the minute, swallowing the spirit just made him vomit immediately.

This is good, he thought as he wiped his mouth on his sleeve; plaster, vodka and sick on the floor now, Susie will be pleased. He wondered how she would react if he told her that he'd found the kitchen like this and that there had clearly been a break-in but he knew that Susie would just look at him with contempt and disbelief. For a moment he thought of his boys. What would they think of their Dad like this? But then, as he always did, he squeezed their faces out of his mind because he suspected that dwelling even for a second on his sons' disappointment at his wretchedness really would cause his heart to break. Best not to go there, he reasoned, best to just shut down any valves of conscience that might explain his pain to their little, confused faces.

Peter was surprised that, on this occasion, it was a struggle to close out the thoughts of his family when he usually blocked them with ease, so he forced down some more vodka when the phone rang. Dutifully, he answered it.

'Pete? Pete, it's Kevin,' said the voice of O'Mara of the *Mirror*.

'Why aren't you at your party?'

'Wort?' grunted Peter, his speech handicapped by the full-facial numbing of the cocaine.

'Doesn't matter. Listen, we're coming over, the whole fucking pack... don't worry, none of this has come from you, but the fucking desks are saying we've all got to kipper your man,' said O'Mara.

'Oh,' said Peter.

'Are you gonna be around? Like I said, we'll keep you out of it but a few of the lads were wondering if you had any smoke on you? Maybe we could pop by your place first?'

'Suar,' said Peter.

'What?' said O'Mara.

'Yesh,' said Peter.

'Top man,' said O'Mara. 'We'll be over shortly and we can talk you through what we think the story ought to be.'

CHAPTER 69

Catherine was lying in the middle of a wide brass bed in the dim, candle-lit guest room wondering what she had drunk, and whether it was her imagination that made her think that the room had become distinctly scented by the pungency of her moist excitement.

Something, she knew, had been added to her drink but she didn't care as, whatever it was, was pulling sensual stunts and she felt euphoric, a little bit dizzy but hypnotically randy as her heart banged with the excited anticipation of Jack entering the room to do whatever he wanted to her.

She was confused as to why Jack was taking such a long time to arrive and begin her gorgeous impalement, and she was half tempted to go out onto the landing to call and hurry him up. But as she had removed all her clothes except for her mask and underwear she decided to wait and enjoy the drowsy warmth that had been rolling over her since drinking the final drops of the spiked fizz.

Languidly, she stroked her fingers up her stockings to the top of her thighs and was surprised at her melting wantonness. Delicately she touched herself but after some seconds she had to stop, as it felt far too good to endure without the risk of drenching the Victorian eiderdown beneath her.

The urgent compulsion to meet Ian and reveal herself as his child had vanished from her mind as the involuntary lubricity took over and she began imaginings.

She was beginning to feel that it wouldn't matter if Pete or any of the farmers from downstairs came in and took her now, she just wanted to feel full and filthy, when she was jolted to awareness by the sound of someone outside the bedroom door.

Catherine wriggled her bottom, delicious anticipation wetting her more, as she waited for the door to open.

I'm going to come in seconds she thought and she started to giggle softly as her dancing mind added and maybe in thirds...

CHAPTER 70

Taylor needed the toilet again; not to urinate but to chop himself some cocaine and keep out of the way of that cow Susie, whom he was going to tell Peter he'd be better off without. As he required privacy, he ran upstairs and tried the door of the bathroom just as Jackson stepped out.

'Oh, sorry mate,' said Taylor instinctively, before recognizing who was standing before him.

'Fucking hell, you've aged!' said Taylor, grabbing his old friend and pulling him into a hug.

'Gimp,' said Jackson into his shoulder.

They pulled back and stood there grinning at each other.

'Fuck me, it feels like being back at those student parties in Harborne,' said Taylor.

'Yeah, well this time let's not nick all their coats,' said Jackson. 'Really good to see you, man.'

'You too, mate. Though you do look fucking old,' said Jackson.

They sat on the stairs together catching up, playfully teasing and sharing a joint. They glared in aggressive unison at anyone who came near, and quickly the landing emptied of guests.

'Here's a photo for the papers,' said Taylor euphorically, affectionately punching Jackson on the arm.

'Yeah; just like on the stairs at my old Mum's place in Aston,' said Jackson, planning his set-up, 'but with a lot more birds knocking about and all of them up for a knocking from you, mate.'

'How d'you know that?' said Taylor, grinning eagerly.

'Trust me,' said Jackson tapping his nose and then pointing at the bedroom where Catherine was waiting. 'In fact, as we speak in there is a bird who's just dying to meet you. She's been bending my ear over it all night; she'll give you a warm welcome.'

'Ooh, you shouldn't have' said Taylor, campily and giggling as the cannabis took hold. 'Reminds me of the old days; what's mine is yours. But if she's your bird…'

'Nah, go ahead, mate. Have one on me. Tell you the truth, she's been pissing me off whining about wanting to meet you, so you take her.'

Taylor grinned and rose unsteadily. He winked at Jackson and walked to the door until a thought came to him. Abruptly, he turned and stared curiously at his old lead guitarist.

'Hang about, it's not Susie fucking Forth is it?'

'What?' said Jackson, startled by his vehemence.

'Your bird in there, it's not the slutty wife of my PR, is it? 'Cos you can fuck off if it is.'

'What?' said Jackson.

'I was told,' said Taylor in a schoolmaster's tone that had always irritated the hell out of Jackson, 'that you were seen poking her earlier.'

'Bollocks,' said Jackson dismissively. 'She snogged me, that's all, like a fucking fan for fuck's sake. Jesus Ian, what the fuck business of yours is it anyway?'

Taylor looked at him stonily.

'Go and have a look if you don't believe me,' said Jackson, 'then, you can apologise.'

Taylor relaxed.

'Sorry mate, fucking Billy Vernon's been winding me up with his usual panicky imaginings. Actually, fuck it, I don't really fancy it now, shall we get a beer?'

'Why? Can't you get it up for the birds anymore?' said Jackson sarcastically. 'Fucking hell Ian, I wouldn't let that story get out.'

Spurred by Jackson's reminder of his wider predicament, Taylor grinned back at him with the bravado that had always fuelled their competitiveness.

'Bastard,' he said as he walked towards the bedroom again. 'And seeing as it's your bird Jack, I'll make her howl her fucking ass off.'

'I look forward to listening, mate. Fucking get on with it and we can get out of this bloody goldfish bowl,' said Jackson, leering.

Taylor opened the door and entered the darkened room. As he

closed the door behind him Taylor could make out a masked woman lying spread-eagled on the double bed.

'Hello Cleveland,' said Taylor softly as he crossed the room.

Catherine made a guttural moan and raised her hips, invitingly.

'Hi, baby,' said Taylor, assessing the presentation. He sat on the edge of the bed, his hand touching her left leg above the knee.

Fucking hell thought Catherine when she saw him.

'Jack said you wanna get to know me; well I'd like that too,' he said, stroking her leg with practised fingers.

Catherine felt paralysed, incapable of refusing anything but still thinking 'fucking hell!'.

'Come to Daddy, baby,' said Taylor, his fingers making gentle, tiny circles.

'Fucking hell,' said Catherine.

'Exactly,' said Taylor, misunderstanding her.

Oh my God! He's taking off his shirt.

'Jack's cool, darling…'

Deep in the pit of her, up against the weird curiosity of her chemically altered libido, Catherine felt herself yell *'NO!'* but her protest made no sound as Taylor lay beside her and began stroking her hair.

Fuck, she thought, fucking, fucking, fucking hell!

CHAPTER 71

Susie was feeling relieved at last. She'd run into Billy as he'd got back to the party and he'd assured her, with professional sincerity, that everything was cool, he'd seen Pete, he was going to be getting his job back and not to worry because he was quite safe at home, happily taking drugs and drinking vodka.

'Thank Christ for that,' Susie said, as she accepted his light for her desperate cigarette.

'Getting his job back?' said Vernon.

'No, getting out of it,' she said grimly, blowing smoke through her nostrils. 'He'll fall over unconscious in a minute and then we can all bloody relax. Talking of which, excuse me Billy I need to have a pee.'

Susie made her way through the mob of masks who were now clumped in the hall at the foot of the stairs and walked past them, wiggling her bottom with pantomime sauciness as she went up.

'I don't think we're meant to be up there, darling' called Sandy behind her. 'Jack and Ian are having a quiet chat on the landing; everybody's giving them space.'

'Oh, they'll be fine with me,' replied Susie, relishing her exclusivity and without looking back. 'I'm not exactly a fan.'

When she reached the landing the pair of them had disappeared. She saw that the toilet was engaged and with her ear to the door she could hear a telltale tapping from behind it, so she went to use the en suite in the guest bedroom instead.

'Fucking hell!' said Catherine as somebody opened the bedroom door and the light from the landing filled the room, silhouetting a woman in a short skirt standing in the doorway.

Just barge in why don't you, thought Catherine, thank God!

'Fucking hell,' said Taylor, turning to the door, exasperated. 'What the hell is it now?'

'Oops. Sorreee,' said Susie sarcastically as she shut the door, muttering 'slag' loud enough for Catherine to hear her.

Taylor got up quickly and angrily from beside Catherine and was getting dressed again.

'I fucking hate that,' he murmured as he pulled on his shirt. 'Sorry luv, your big moment's been blown.'

Taylor arranged himself rapidly and without looking back he left the room, huffily walking straight past Susie outside the door and ignoring her knowing grin as he pelted down the stairs yelling for Vernon.

Catherine thought that it was probably not the right time to call, 'Dad,' after him. She slumped back onto the bed but then began to battle a sudden drowsiness by forcing herself to get up and stumble to the bathroom to run an icy shower.

Taylor's shout alerted Jackson that his set up was not going merrily and he shot out of the toilet and into Susie's astonished face.

'What the hell was all that about?' she said.

'Oh, hello again, Nursey. All what about?'

'That. Ian's pissed off in a fury.'

'Well that's not unusual. What's the problem?' Jack said, acting coy and wiping his nose.

'Search me. I walked in on him with some slapper and he just lost it.'

'Whoops.'

'Why are you grinning?'

'Umm...'

'You've done something, haven't you? What are you up to?'

'It's just a little reunion present from me to him.'

'The girl? The bitch only had her undies and mask on, I couldn't really see. Is she a hooker or something?'

'Er... not exactly. I just thought it might make a good picture to amuse the band, when we start rehearsals. Look, wanna see it?'

Jackson took a phone from a pocket of his Zorro outfit and showed her a snap of two figures on a bed.

'It's a bit dim, I can't make it out. Who is she? How did you get it?' said Susie.

'Just a little quick peak around the door. It sounds like I was a bit quieter than you were. Actually, it is a bit dark, but I can brighten it up on the computer. Anyway, anything I can do to brighten you up?'

Susie grinned at the lurid suggestion written all over his face.

'Not here,' she said.

'Why not?'

'Too much commotion now. Listen, somebody's coming. We'll meet up later.'

'Is that a promise?'

She pulled down her surgical mask, leaned forward and quickly kissed him lasciviously.

'I promise,' she said as she masked up again and left him to rejoin the party.

CHAPTER 72

Peter had reached enough of a balance to make a reasonable job of clearing up the vomit, vodka and ceiling plaster, so that only a reek of alcohol and the hole in the kitchen ceiling remained by the time that the press pack arrived at his back door, sarcastically chanting, 'Peter For-orth walks on water la la la la la, lala la la.'

There were twenty in the pack, the original gang of reporters now joined by Carly Stock from the *News of the World* and the BBC's arts editor, Jill Campbell, plus their photographers and cameramen, making so large a crowd that Kevin O'Mara had taken control again and instructed the snappers to wait outside and not to ask to use Peter's toilet.

'Come in guys,' said Peter, more at home and more trusting in the company of drunk and raucous newsmen than he had ever been among the ambitious sand-shifters of the music business.

The reporters shuffled into the kitchen and Peter greeted them all with a hug or a handshake or a kiss. He had already prepared by placing bottles of beer, wine, whisky, vodka, gin and grappa on the table along with mixers, a champagne bucket of ice, a dozen glasses of assorted size, two packets of Marlboro and a large wooden bowl of cheese niblets.

'Sit down, help yourselves, I'll get a couple more chairs,' said Peter, waving the pack towards the refreshments. When he returned from the sitting room and O'Mara had told everyone to budge up so that Carol Stitch and the *Independent's* David Moorfield could sit around the table, he smiled and said, 'So what's up?'

'What happened to your ceiling?' said O'Mara.

'It's an old house,' said Peter.

'OK,' said O'Mara, acting as spokesman. 'First up, we're not here, Pete. We haven't seen you and this is all completely off the record.'

'Cool,' said Peter, who was propping himself up by the sink with his hands in his pockets, pretending to be calm.

'Pass those cheesey things,' said Gabriel Thomas, nudging Stitch, who was crossing her short-skirted legs at Peter, 'and put your twat away, you're not on your bloody TV sofa now.'

'Have you filed?' said Peter, getting to the point.

'An early piece,' replied O'Mara.

'Saying?' said Peter, lighting a cigarette.

'Everybody's splashing on your man being a knob-gobbler, Pete,' said Thomas, waiting for the *Star's* Lincoln Freshfield to finish with the tonic water.

'That's an old yarn,' said Peter, stalling pleasantly. 'He'll just deny it. And he's my ex-man.'

'Will he sue?' said Jeremy Thackwell of the *Express*, curtly.

'Probably, you know Ian,' said Peter, calmly preparing a joint from a jar of home-grown skunk on a worktop by the oven.

'We're saying that this whole 'Come to Daddy' auditioning bollocks is just a ruse to cover his arse and he's as bent as a nine-bob bit,' said O'Mara, eyeing Peter and suspicious of his nonchalance.

'So?' said Peter, adding more grass to the king-size Rizla paper. 'Why are you telling me? You know I'm not going to say anything.'

'Will to do a piece to camera saying that?' said Stitch, crossing her legs again.

'Are you fucking deaf?' roared O'Mara as he helped himself to an open bottle of Beaujolais. 'The deal is that nobody's quoting Pete.'

'I just thought…' said Stitch defensively.

'Shut it,' said O'Mara, turning to Peter again. 'The thing is, somebody's leaked a picture…'

'The one of Ian with a cock in his mouth?' said Peter coolly. 'I've seen it. I had it tested, it's a fake.'

'Not according to our picture desks,' countered Freshfield. 'Their testers reckon it's legit.'

'So run it,' said Peter.

'Well fucking hardly,' said O'Mara, laughing. 'C'mon Pete, we need a steer here.'

Peter lit the joint, took three hits and knowingly passed it to Thomas, who said that he had given up.

'I haven't,' said O'Mara, taking the joint. 'So what do you reckon, no comment and then fucking legals all round?'

'Are you still working for Ian, Pete? What's the deal? I thought you'd been fired,' said Thackwell.

'Anybody want any gear for later?' said Peter, ignoring the probing and taking a four-finger pinch from the cannabis jar and placing it on the table.

'Told you,' said O'Mara, 'I'll look after it,' and he wrapped the grass in a paper handkerchief. .

'We'll pay you for this mate,' said O'Mara.

'The Bob Hope or the info?' said Peter, grinning.

'Both,' said O'Mara. 'What's the info?'

'Hmmm,' said Peter, sipping now at a glass of neat vodka. 'OK, I don't know if he's a secret bender; he's never bent it with me and I've never seen him try it with anyone else. God's truth…'

'That doesn't mean he isn't,' said Stitch.

'I'm just telling you…' said Peter.

'Let him fucking talk,' commanded O'Mara.

'So I don't know about that,' Peter continued, 'but I have just discovered he's a secret father.'

'Bollocks,' said Carly Stock.

'Completely true, Carly,' said Peter, deadpan. 'She's turned up tonight at my party to meet him…'

'But he's never married,' said Stitch.

'Twat,' said O'Mara dismissively. 'What are you saying, Pete?'

'I'm saying nothing, mate; it's not my shout anymore. As Thacky said, I've been fired. But, knowing Ian's mob, if you lot run that he's been in the closet then he'll come back by doing a one-to-one with someone, probably the Beeb, with his long-lost-love-child gorgeous daughter beside him, to argue that he's not. He'll shift the story and unless anyone can front-page a gobbling shot past the Obscene Publications Squad these days, it'll be difficult to make that line stronger than the rumour that's long been around and never stood up.'

'How old is this daughter?' said Freshfield, who, like Thomas, had begun making notes.

'Thirties,' said Peter, drinking more vodka.

'Is she gorgeous?' said Freshfield.

'A fucking cracker,' said Peter. 'Dark, sexy, dresses like a right little rock chick. I'd give her one.'

'Said a spokesman,' chuckled O'Mara and everybody laughed.

'What's her name?' Freshfield continued. 'How were they reunited?'

'Catherine,' said Peter, wondering whether to sugar the pot, then adding decisively. 'Apparently Jack Jackson's brought her to the party tonight.'

'What? Is he shagging her? That's good,' said Thomas.

'I don't know, Gab. Ask them, don't ask me. As I say, not my shout.'

'Er, how come you're not at this party?' said O'Mara. 'We heard it was thrown in your honour.'

'I left when Ian turned up; I didn't fancy a scene.'

'Is he trying to get you back?' O'Mara persisted.

'I'm not going.'

'Going back to this Catherine,' said Freshfield, who was now beginning to worry about whether to alert her newsdesk to this new development. 'Who's her mother? Where did she come from? What does she do?'

'Like I say, Nic, I don't know anything much about her. I know she's completely skint, but she doesn't seem on the make.'

'But Ian's acknowledged that she is his kid, right?' said O'Mara, who was also writing in his notebook now.

'Apparently,' said Peter, lighting another cigarette.

'We need a shot of the two of them together,' said Freshfield to the pack.

'A happy shot,' said Thomas.

'Well they're just up the road,' said Peter. 'You can leg it. Tell the guys on the gate you're Peter Forth's plus ones, for the craic.'

'Fucking hell, I'd better warn my desk,' said O'Mara, swigging back the remains of his gin and tonic and getting to his feet.

‘Thanks Pete, we’ll keep you out of this. I might need to call you later with some checks.’

‘Sure,’ said Peter. ‘I’m not going anywhere.’

He watched as the pack piled out of the kitchen, some of them already talking excitedly on their mobiles. When he saw that the last of them had rallied their photographers and driven off, Peter rang Billy Vernon.

‘Billy, it’s Pete… I’m just ringing to warn you that a couple of dozen of Her Majesty’s Press are on their way down there… What? Because I just do… What?... Any second now… Billy! Billy! Hang on, before you do that, tell Alex… Alex, the bloke who owns the house… Shut up, you haven’t got time, tell Alex because he’s got a load of rugby blokes doing security. Tell him to get them on the gate. What?... No, I’m fucking not, I told you… I don’t care… Well tell him I said that he can fuck off… yeah, well never mind that, just tell fucking Alex to get on it and then call me back.’

He rang off, relit the joint that the reporters had left on the table. It felt good to be playing God again.

CHAPTER 73

Until Peter had crudely interrupted him with the phone call that he felt was a bit too bloody autocratic for his liking, Billy Vernon had been rather enjoying the way that the evening was swinging. Despite his blustering protests, Vernon was certain that Peter would return to the inner fold as he hadn't much choice. Ian and Jackson had reunited and chummily made up without the fist fight that Vernon had expected and, more important than anything, Ian was in a good mood and therefore was unlikely to bellow at him.

He had just been telling Sandy how heartening it was to work for the crown jewel of the national treasures because he was such an ordinary guy, quite placid really, when the subject of his sermon came storming across the lawn at him, smoothing his hair and announcing, 'This party is fucking shit and I want to go now!'

'Oh no!' cried Sandy, devastated that scores of her other nearby loitering guests had heard Taylor's furious assessment. 'Oh no, whatever's happened? This is dreadful.'

Thinking quickly and knowing not to argue, Vernon said, 'Of course,' and that he would just go and get their car, leaving Taylor to fume about 'bloody fucking rubberneckers' at Sandy as Vernon ran across the lawn to accost her husband who was now showing off his inscribed paper plate to two men in rugby shirts at the bottom of the drive.

'We have a very big problem and Ian says that he urgently needs your help,' said Vernon, knowing that his calculated wording would achieve any assistance from Alex.

'The press are coming,' Vernon continued. 'I have received information that they will be here at any minute.They are persecuting Ian and it is imperative that we keep them out. Al, mate, could you muster your rugger boys and tell them to make sure that the hacks don't have any access to the party? I've got our own security squad flying in by helicopter but until then I must ask if we can depend on you and your boys.'

Fired by the excitement of being addressed as 'Al mate', Alex rallied his pretensions as a former major in the Territorial Army and immediately imagined himself taking control of some sort of glorious last stand.

'You heard our friend, man the gate! Keep the rats at bay!' he instructed, shoving the rugby players in the direction of the lane. 'Get the rest of your squad down there now! None shall pass!'

Vernon watched with pleasure as Alex snatched up a cricket bat and sped across the lawn, waving it above his head, lunging up the drive, shouting enemy at the gate!

'What the fuck's all that about? What enemy? Where's the car?' said Taylor, who had been watching the peculiar call to arms, when Vernon arrived back at his side, red-faced and puffing heavily.

'Can I have a quick word?' replied Vernon, leading him away from the startled Sandy.

'Where's the fucking car, I told you to get the fucking car!' said Taylor, angrily shaking off Vernon's hand on his arm. 'And what's up with that mad bastard Alan?'

'Alex,' corrected Vernon.

'I don't fucking care what he's fucking called, what the fuck is going on?'

Patiently Vernon relayed an edited version of Peter's warning that a large pack of press was expected, including TV crews.

'There's nothing to worry about,' soothed Vernon. 'Our own boys will be here very soon and then we'll do a runner.'

'Where the fuck is Pete? He does press, he should be fucking dealing with this,' ranted Taylor. 'Why is everybody getting so wound up about a few hacks?'

From their vantage at the top of the drive, Vernon saw a fleet of cars and a van with the logo AMTV pull up in the lane outside the house.

'Shit, they're here,' he said. 'C'mon, let's go inside.'

'Why?' demanded Taylor.

'Long lenses,' said Vernon, taking his arm.

'So fucking what?' said Taylor, angrily shrugging him off. 'Why am I a fugitive all of a fucking sudden?'

Vernon was saved from an awkward explanation of why it might be a good idea for Ian to stay out of the papers for once by the sight of Peter clambering over a fence, having taken a back route across the fields to the other side of the lawn.

As Peter approached them, Taylor shouted, 'What the fuck is going on?'

'Can I have a word?' said Peter, immediately irritating Taylor by smiling in the eye of confusion. 'You too, Billy.'

'This had better be fucking good,' muttered Taylor grumpily as Peter led them behind the shed, screening them from the lane.

'Do you want the good news or the bad news first?' said Peter with relish.

'Do you want a punch in the mouth?' replied Taylor.

'OK, sorry. Right, the press are here because someone, and I suspect it's one of your great mates at the record company, has leaked the story of that photograph of you er...'

'Gobbling,' said Taylor. 'Spit it out.'

Peter grinned.

'Yeah, well the press have got hold of it. Obviously they can't run such a shot in their so-called family newspapers, so they want to challenge you about it. Clearly, Billy can tell them it's a fake, but they're going to want words from you. There's a lot of them, Ian, the whole pack, and on a story like this they are going to chase you wherever you go. Unless…'

'Unless fucking what?'

'Unless you can knock it down with a better story,' reasoned Peter calmly.

'And you have one of those, do you?' demanded Vernon.

Peter ignored him and looked straight into Taylor's furious eyes. 'Ian, I'm not doing the job anymore. I've told Billy but he won't believe me; so I'm telling you to your face. But there's a couple of important things…'

'Which are what?' said Taylor, angrily.

'Your Catherine, I've found her. I've got her here, at the party,' replied Peter.

Taylor looked over at the crowd of guests who had now all congregated on the lawn some yards away, staring at them and wondering what was going on.

'Which one is she?' he said, scanning the masked crowd.

'Could you go and wait in the house for a moment while I find her? Sandy and Al's bedroom is on the first floor at the end of the corridor, go in there, I won't be long,' said Peter, hoping that Catherine had not already left or, worse, that she might be cuddling up with Jackson.

As he left them, Peter heard Taylor say that he bet fucking Pete had fucking tipped off the fucking press, but he ignored it; he no longer cared what Ian Taylor said about him now.

CHAPTER 74

After a lot of darting in and out of rooms, looking sternly purposeful and saying to people, over his shoulder, that he couldn't talk now, Peter found Catherine sitting alone on a hay bale in the barn where, a lifetime ago, he had been happily sharing his drugs with the party girls. She looked pale and vacant, her elbows resting on her knees and her head in her hands as she stared at circles that she was scratching in the dirt with a stick.

She looked up briefly as he approached and gave the thin smile of the over-indulged.

Peter sat down on the bale beside her and put his hand unthreateningly on her knee.

'You're on,' he said gently. 'Showtime.'

'God I feel rough,' she muttered.

'What've you taken?' said Peter, suspecting Es.

'Somebody spiked my drink,' she explained.

'Ah.'

'It feels like it was GHB,' added Catherine knowledgably. 'Jack did it, the bastard.'

'Strange that he felt that he needed to,' said Peter clumsily.

She glared at him.

'Thanks very much,' she said. 'May I return the compliment by noting that you look like shit yourself. And you stink of drink. And wipe your nose, you bloody cokehead.'

Peter smiled to defuse her.

'I've told Ian that you're here and he wants to see you,' he said gently.

'What?'

'I've told him.'

'Told him what?'

'I've told that you're his daughter.'

'Really?'

'Yeah.'

'Did you really say that? Or did you say there's some bird who's turned up claiming to be your daughter?'

Peter looked back at her fondly as her eyes flitted between his, searching him for signs of sincerity. He realised that he should tell her the truth now, not least because he didn't trust Taylor to give her the full version.

'OK. Listen. Ian has pretty much accepted that you probably are his daughter and,' he began but stopped when her face ignited in delight and she shrieked.

'Oh my God! Really? Honestly?'

'Catherine, he accepted it weeks ago, he is thrilled! Honestly.'

'Really? Oh, fucking hell,' she said softly, beaming and then looking puzzled. 'What do you mean weeks ago? Why didn't you tell me? You've known for weeks? You bastard!'

'I wasn't in the mood for doing him any favours, he pissed me off.'

'But what about me? You could have done me a favour and told me!'

'Don't fucking start,' Peter said wearily. 'Jesus, you're exactly like your bloody father. Anyway, fuck all this, I need to bring you up to speed and I'm going to ask you for a favour. The story of your fucking photograph of Ian has somehow been leaked to the press. So anyhow, now I've got the world's press down at the gate, just over there.' He pointed in the direction of the drive and narrowed his eyes.

'I'm taking you now to meet Ian. As I say, he knows, he's admitted it to Billy; who your mother was, who the guy was, the whole deal. Just a tip, but I'd play it that you know he knows, so play up the delight bit when you meet him. Don't get all polite and respectful, just go for the whole Daddy thing.'

'I will know how to greet my own father, thanks,' she said, offended.

'Because if you're not actually his daughter,' continued Peter, ignoring her, 'but you act like you are around him, like you're meeting him at the airport after having been in Australia for a year, listen to me, this is good advice; if you're not his daughter but you love him like you were, then he will believe that you are.'

She smiled warmly at what he was trying to say and kissed him affectionately on the side of the mouth.

'Thank you, Pete. You believe me though, don't you?'

'How do I fucking know?' he said, smiling. 'For all I know you could just be an überfan. This may all be a huge scam for you to stab him or something, but that's not my problem.'

'You do though, don't you?' she grinned. 'That's why you're stand-offish with me but not vile. I know you believe me because of how you kissed me when we screwed.'

'By the way, Ian doesn't know that, I wouldn't mention that,' said Peter, lying in horror. 'Seriously, I wouldn't because it's the sort of thing that would make him deny you, if he thought that I'd… fucking hell, he'd go mental!'

'I shan't,' she promised, 'and thank you, it is good advice. You always give good advice.'

'Fuck off,' he grinned, lighting a cigarette.

'And I really appreciate you doing this for me.'

'I'm not doing it for you,' he said, grinning, 'I'm doing it for him. I think you'll be a good influence on him, stop him being such an arsehole star and bring out the ordinary bloke that he is when he's not feeling threatened.'

'Threatened?'

'By indifference; he hates that.'

'But I really feel like shit. I'm knackered, I just want to lie down,' said Catherine.

Peter produced yet another packet of cocaine from his waistcoat pocket, opened the wrap and offered it to her.

'This'll sort you out. Do it.' he instructed.

Catherine got up, took a pinch of coke, put it on the back of her hand and snorted.

'You said you wanted a favour?' she asked as wiped her nose and began tidying her hair and rearranging her blouse to reduce her cleavage.

'The press want to nail Ian about the photograph, which we've said is a fake. They want to out him and say he's been hiding in the closet in order to protect his commercial image. They may still do that but I want to tilt the story a bit by revealing you.'

'What?' said Catherine in surprise as they began to walk back to the house.

'The press want to talk to Ian about being gay. I want you and Ian to walk down to where they are, by the gate, and just do a quick photo call. Not a whole fucking interview, just stand there hugging like father and daughter and looking delighted. They'll shout questions at you and I don't mind if you reply, but keep it how chuffed you are, all that 'best day of your life' shit.'

'It's not shit. It is,' she corrected. 'Are you going to tell the press before we do the pictures?'

'No,' said Peter, 'I'm going to tell Billy to tell the press that the reason Ian is down here is for a reunion with you that was only arranged yesterday by Jack after he finished checking out that you weren't out to con his best mate. And that's why Ian fled London, not on the run but speeding down to meet you for the first time etcetera…'

'That almost sounds true,' she smiled. 'You've started caring, Mr Forth.'

'Bullshit'

'Do you think the papers will still run the gay story?'

'Yeah, well I'm hoping that Ian may take a hand in that. We'll see but, I've got a little hunch.'

'Tell me. You said I should know everything.'

'Fuck off, you greedy cow,' he said as they entered the house and approached the stairs.

Catherine stopped at the foot of the stairs. She took his hand in hers and gave it a small squeeze.

'Hey, really, why are you doing this?'

'It's a great scam,' said Peter, lighting a cigarette and nodding her up to where Billy was waiting for her. She took two steps and then turned back to face him.

'And Peter, thank you. Really.'

CHAPTER 75

As Catherine and Billy Vernon walked the towards the bedroom where Ian was waiting, she felt, for the second time that evening, as if she was looking down upon herself; that this, too, was not happening. It seemed to be taking place in slow and utterly surreal motion. Her principal fear was that Taylor would recognise her as the masked woman of the bedroom, so she had changed from groupie to country hippie by popping into the toilet to dump the mask, stockings and cowboy boots, tie up her hair and put a white rose in her cleavage before padding barefoot behind Vernon, nervously wanting to run the other way. They reached the bedroom and Vernon held his breath before opening the door.

'Ah, Ian, this is your… um, this is Catherine Hornby,' he said as he pushed her gently into the bedroom.

'Have you frisked her?' said Taylor, who was standing in the centre of the brightly-lit room dominating it with a scowl because he had been kept waiting for twenty minutes with nothing to do except go through Sandy's underwear drawer, smelling her knickers and varying the speeds of her large black vibrator.

'Frisked her?' said Vernon, blinking in astonishment at this sudden change in Taylor's laidback lifetime security protocol.

'She could have a knife,' said Taylor, regarding Catherine coolly. 'You might be a mad fan, young lady. Sorry to be suss.'

Catherine sensed that he had not sussed her properly, and the stab of hurt was quickly overtaken by outraged indignation and fury.

'Oh for fuck's sake! I don't need this bollocks,' she flared.

She turned away from Taylor and went to leave the room but the confused Vernon now blocked the doorway, nervously wondering if frisking meant feeling around the tits.

'Come back,' ordered Taylor curtly.

'You're a bastard,' said Catherine deliberately as she turned her back on Taylor and raised her arms, inviting Vernon to search her.

'I don't think that I hold the exclusive on that one, miss, and that's not the best way to address your father,' said Taylor.

'Git!' she spat, widening her stance to allow Vernon to pat rapidly up her legs. 'You better go higher,' she said with bitter sarcasm. 'I might have a grenade up my arse.'

'That will do Billy, thank you,' Taylor said quickly to avoid more ridicule. 'Wait outside.'

Catherine stood still, glaring at him but still searching for any moment of curious recognition.

Taylor sighed. 'Catherine. Would you please shut the door and come and sit down. I'm new to this game.'

She shut the door but stood by it, regarding him.'You look a lot older than you do in your pictures, but I think gnarled suits you,' she said with a thin smile. 'It certainly suits you better than airbrushing yourself all the time.'

'I don't do it myself, speak to my publicist.'

'Well I know that he hates it,' she snapped.

'How well, exactly, do you know him?'

'You could learn a lot from Peter Forth if you ever listened.'

'Like what?'

'Ooo, let's see; humanity, generosity, fun…'

'Generosity? He's never given me anything in his fucking life!' said Taylor indignantly.

'Except his fucking life,' she said swinging round to face him suddenly and remembering all her mother had gone through.

'So tell me, Dad, why are you such a bastard?'

'Meaning?' he replied irritably.

'Well, you're vain to the point of insanity; you are possibly the most pig-rude person on the planet and you behave brutally to your staff. I'm not even sure that I want you as my father.'

'Fuck off then,' he said stroppily. 'Look, do you want to be my daughter or not?'

'I've told you, I'm not sure yet. There are some things I want to know first.'

'Such as?'

'Such as why did you never reply to any of the letters my mother wrote to you? Why did you ignore my letters too? Why did you put me through all of those nights of fucking agonising confusion? What did I do to you that was so bloody wrong?' She was close to tears now, her head bowed. After some moments she looked up with wet eyes and saw that something she had said had hit home. He had sat down on the bed and was looking guilty.

'Look, if it's true, if you're true, I'm sorry,' he said softly, biting his thumbnail. 'I didn't intend to hurt you. I read the letters. But for fuck's sake it happens in this game. There must be hundreds of fan-children out there. But if you want the truth, I kind of believe you because I don't remember your mother as the sort who would lie. And…'

'You remember her? How come?'

'That picture took me back.'

'You said 'and',' said Catherine. 'You were about to say there's another reason why you believe me.'

'Ah, that,' said Taylor, smiling. 'I can recognize your mother's resemblance – I'm not sure about mine. But you're clearly her daughter and that'll do for me, for now.' He rose from the bed, took her hand in his and kissed her on the forehead.

'And right at this moment I kind of need a daughter. I don't know if you are or you're not; but I'm in the shit so let's wing it.'

He took her into his arms and hugged her, noting that she smelled strangely familiar.

'It's gone very quiet,' said Vernon, his ear to the oak door as Peter stood sentinel on the landing.

'I'd come away if I were you,' advised Peter.

'There was a load of shouting but now nobody's talking. What if she did have a knife? I mean, I wasn't going to search the knickers of the daughter of Ian bloody Taylor.'

The door opened and Vernon almost fell over. Recovering his balance, he crouched and pretended to be looking for something on the floor as Ian and Catherine stood in the doorway holding hands.

'Told you,' said Peter, noting that he had never seen Taylor's eyes glitter before.

CHAPTER 76

'My desk just said that if I don't file official confirmation of the daughter line in the next ten minutes I can fuck off and get a job on Pullman's. What's Pullman's?' said Nicola Freshfield, the Mail's now-anxious girl on the spot, as she and the rest of the press pack huddled in anticipointment as every figure who approached the gate was just another rugby lad sent to re-enforce the muscular line of unsmiling faces which Alex had been positioning and re-positioning for nearly an hour.

'Pullman's Weekly News,' muttered O'Mara as he wrote another imploring text to Peter. 'It used to be the local rag down here. Come on Forth you wanker, take some bloody calls.'

'My lot say they're not taking Forth's word for it either,' complained Roundhill of the *Star*. 'They reckon it could be Pete lying to protect Taylor again.'

'Give it another five and I'll take a snapper in over a fence,' said O'Mara. 'There's got to be dozens of other ways into this place and it might have to be a snatch shot. But on the other hand, hello… aha, OK look sharp lads, here comes the manager.'

The dozen photographers aimed long lenses at the shape of Billy Vernon, unclearly lit by the lamps of the drive, walking quickly towards them flanked by two more rugby players. As he came into range of their powerful flashguns, a battery of light bursts blinded him, as the photographers let rip with their impatience.

Despite losing his sight and depending on the rugby boys to steer him out of the rhododendrons, Vernon was rather enjoying the attention. He had his brief statement and he was just clearing his throat in preparation to read it stolidly to camera to probably the planet when O'Mara yelled at him to get out of the fucking way!

'What? Who? Do you mean me?' blustered Vernon. 'Why? I've got a statement!'

'Fuck your statement,' came a call back from the pack. 'Get out of the bloody way! Look behind you!'

Turning to see what he meant, Vernon saw the unmistakable face of Ian Taylor grinning at the pack as he free-wheeled down the drive on an old bicycle, with Catherine before him, her arm around his shoulders as she balanced precariously on the cross-bar.

'Sorry Billy, it's a better shot!' yelled Taylor as they sped past.

The photographers went berserk, firing off flashes as they shouted pointless instructions of 'Ian! Ian! Over here! Ian, to me! This way, luv!' at the riders who had no need to be asked to smile.

Taylor braked the bike and Catherine took a little leap off the cross-bar, causing another flashburst as the photographers attempted to get a shot up her flouncy skirt.

'Ok, o-kay, cool it. No flashes,' ordered O'Mara knowledgably, keen to avoid upsetting the quarry.

'Oh for fuck's sake!' he added as the AMTV cameraman turned on his even-more-blinding top light.

'Hello boys,' said Taylor, smiling despite the glare. 'And what brings you lot out to the sticks?'

The reporters laughed and then took notes feverishly as Taylor confirmed that yes, this little lady was his long-missed daughter Katie and yes, it was the most fabulous day of his life and yes, it was all thanks to Jack and yes, it was a bloody miracle and yes, if you say so Gab, it did feel better than Live Aid.

The questions and Taylor's perky sound-bites continued for five more minutes. Father and daughter then posed for more pictures, Catherine cannily refusing the snappers' leading calls for just one on your own, luv, until Taylor raised a hand of command and the frenzy stopped.

'Right then boys, I think you've got enough,' he said, still smiling. 'But, as the last time I said that I ended up decking a couple of you lot, can we agree that that is enough? Fair dos, eh? No hiding in the bushes? You're not going to top this yarn tonight. Run along and file and tell your desks that Uncle Ian says goodnight.'

Fucking pro thought Vernon, listening out of shot as he continued to wipe dirt off his trousers. But then his stomach lurched.

'There is one last point, Ian,' said Carol Stitch, thrusting her mike with its AMTV blob at him. 'What do you, as a newly happy father, have to say to all these stories that you are secretly gay?'

'Oh, come on Carol, give us a break,' said Taylor, blinking in the stark camera light. 'Not tonight, eh luv?'

'A break? What sort of break do you mean, Ian?' demanded Stitch, pushing her microphone closer to him.

Taylor smiled at her and shook his head.

'Are you ashamed, Ian? Ashamed to be gay in this day and age?'

'Hmm, in this day and enlightened age, that's a good one Carol. OK, I'll answer your question,' said Taylor, still smiling as the cameraman captured the Stitch exclusive. The rock star put his arm around Catherine and pulled her tight into shot.

'Ready? OK, cool… Carol, I've fucked some guys, I've fucked some girls, I've fucked many more fucking girls than I've fucked guys but I have fucked them all just the fucking same. But on the night that this little lady was conceived I was loving her mother. Other than that, I'll just fuck anything that fucking moves, basically. I'll fuck you now, if you like, Carol. Otherwise, good night.'

With a smile and blowing a kiss to the camera, Taylor abruptly turned and took Catherine by the hand to walk back up the drive, flanked by six of the rugby players.

'You twat,' said O'Mara, as Stitch excitedly prepared for her to-camera world exclusive.

'Shut up Kevin, you're jealous,' she pouted.

'He has fucked *you*,' chuckled O'Mara. 'The only bit of that you can properly use is when he's talking about his daughter, which, by the way, is the fucking story now. Check it back, I'm right. Other than that, for network news he's just a series of bleeped expletives.'

'But I reckon your scoop will run wild on YouTube,' said Thackwell, 'which your boss will like.'

'Which of course is why he's done it, with an album coming out,' said O'Mara, 'The crafty bugger probably planned all this all along. They always said he's the master. You know, I think we may have been shafted.'

CHAPTER 77

In the days after the party Sandy would tell her closest friends that frankly she did not know where to look when it had all happened. She had been standing in the marquee on the edge of the dance-floor, appalled at the idiot that Alex was making of himself by jerking epileptically to 'Free Bird' and all of a sudden somebody pinched her bum!

She was astounded to discover that it was Jack. Of course she hadn't really minded that, after all nobody would not believe what she'd felt being rubbed against her when she and Ian had been dancing together, but probably all rock stars were like that. But it was, she confided to the gossip ring, what he'd said next that began all the fuss that then followed.

'Fancy a feline fiddle, pussygirl? I bet you're a wildcat on the quiet,' said Jackson, who had been made psychotically randy by the cocaine and his thoughts of skewering Susie.

Sandy was so surprised by this character assessment that she said nothing and just looked at him blankly.

'I expect you've got a lovely snatch, Sandy; you'd make one hell of a groupie.'

Even though Alex had objected to her Cat Woman costume, she had not felt that it was that tight around the crutch. Suggestive, admittedly, but surely not so much so that it would prompt people to make that sort of remark. She presumed that he must be a little tipsy, so she just smiled it away.

'I tell you what, you could suck my dick anytime,' Jackson continued.

Sandy was not a fan of fellatio as her occasional forays to nod away down for Alex had always made her gag, and she did feel that such an intimate matter should only be between man and wife. It was certainly not, she felt, a suitable subject for party small talk.

'I beg your pardon, Jack?'

C'mon Sandy, I can tell you're a slut at heart.'

Very few people actually saw her slap his face because most were dancing at the time, but Alex did and he marched over to the astonished Jackson.

'I say, what the hell is going on?' Alex demanded.

'Fuck off,' said Jackson. 'Your bloody wife's being a cock-teaser.'

'I think you should apologise and leave,' said Alex.

'Fuck off, you uptight prick. You can have her back when I've finished.'

So, not knowing what else to do, Alex punched Jackson on the jaw.

And if Billy Vernon had not been so angry with bloody Peter for making him look a prick with his better bloody idea, he might have been in less of a foul mood than he was in when he saw Alex appear to lay Jackson out with a hell of a punch.

Had he been in better humour, Vernon might also have thought twice before rushing at Alex to defend Jackson by body-charging the dentist into a pair of the rugby boys who, until that moment, had been chatting up a couple of the girls from the riding stables.

Unfortunately, one of the stable girls had red wine spilled all over her when Vernon had barged violently into them and it was more in opportunist protection of her honour, than in anger, that the rugby players set about punching Vernon hard.

And had Vernon not been so dogmatic and tense when he had telephoned the head of Taylor's security team earlier, the security director might not have been given the impression that there was some sort of massive problem brewing at this barn dance that Ian was inexplicably attending, so he might not have called up friends who worked as bouncers at an Exeter night club and asked them to get over there fast before the chopper back-up arrived.

But he had and they did. So when, already edgy by the sight of the lurking press outside, they walked into the marquee they went into automatic pilot as they assessed what appeared to be a huge punch-up, which had already floored 'Ian Taylor's guitar bloke'.

Which was why the six bouncers pitched into the rugby players, pulling one of them off Vernon and throwing him across the room so that he fell into a waitress carrying a full tray of drinks.

It was the detonation of the contents of the tray smashing on the disco floor that alerted the other rugby players outside that something was wrong. They piled into the marquee and, seeing their friends under attack by a bunch of burly skinheads in cheap dark suits, understandably waded in to the rescue.

By the time that Taylor entered the marquee hand-in-hand with Catherine, at least twenty men were now fighting. Most of the women were screaming, with the exception of Sandy, who was dividing her time between nursing her bloodied husband, throwing wine bottles and screaming 'Bastards' at Taylor's henchmen.

Taylor watched in amazement as Jackson crawled across the floor in an attempt to reach the disc jockey's microphone and take control of the situation by making an announcement that would inevitably involve the phrase cool it.

Regrettably, the DJ mistook Jackson's attempt to snatch the microphone from him as a threatened assault, so he punched his palm into Jackson's already-injured nose, making Jackson shriek with pain and fall again to the floor.

Taylor continued to watch astounded as Jackson struggled woozily to his feet, only to be decked yet again as one of Sandy's lobbed bottles missed the bouncers and clipped him on the side of the head.

'Time for Elvis to leave the building,' muttered Taylor as he strode over to where Jackson lay motionless, hauled him up with the help of the rugby boys and pulled him onto his shoulder in a fireman's lift.

Pushing and barging people away from him, Taylor staggered to the entrance of the marquee.

'Hello, mate,' moaned Jackson as he came round. 'Who started playing 'Sympathy for the Devil'?'

'Let's get you to my car,' Taylor said.

As he walked to the Porsche, Taylor could see photographers' flashes capturing the unorthodox reunion shot from the bottom of the drive. Slightly behind him walked Catherine, worrying and willing Jack not to open his big leery mouth to ruin everything.

'Katie, can you squeeze into the back, darling? We'll never fit Jack in there, but it's not very comfortable, I'm afraid.'

'That's OK,' she made herself say brightly. 'Hey, have you got a cushion?'

'Err, no. Sorry,' said Taylor.

'There's some in the marquee, I'll just go and get one. I want to rest my head, it's been a bit of a day.'

'I'll go and get one for you,' said Taylor as she had prayed that he would. 'You stay here and keep an eye on this pisshead.'

Taylor open the passenger door and dumped the now-sleeping Jack in the bucket seat.

'Won't be a sec,' he said as he walked back to the marquee, his rugby guards automatically following him.

Catherine knelt down beside Jack and woke him by grabbing his testicles through his trousers and twisting them violently. He came to with a shriek.

'Listen to me, you bastard,' hissed Catherine icily as she maintained her painful grip. 'Ian believes that I'm his lovechild from your Taylspin days and I am. Don't argue, listen. If I tell him what you did to me, setting me up with him like that, he will have you killed; and you, Jack, know that he's capable of that.

She twisted his testes again, making him yelp, and ignored his cries as she applied more pressure.

'I'd keep quiet about us shagging too, because you know he wouldn't like that either, but if you ever, and I mean ever, say a word about it being me in that bedroom, I will cut you up, starting with these!'

She crushed his balls with such ferocity that Jackson screamed.

'Don't doubt me Jack, I'm not his daughter for nothing. Capiche?'

'Okay! Okay! Deal!' whined Jackson.

She released him. As she stood, she saw Taylor returning with a purple satin cushion.

'Is he alright?' said Taylor as he reached her side. 'I thought I heard him yelling.'

'He's fine,' said Catherine, coolly. 'He just needed a hand.'

CHAPTER 78

It was past eleven the next morning before Susie woke in a spare bedroom at Sandy's place. She had not gone home because she feared a confrontation with Peter, which she knew she would not be ready for until the foul mood of his hangover had left his system. So she showered, crept in and borrowed some clothes from the room in which Sandy was still asleep and gingerly descended to the kitchen which the caterers' clean-up team had already made tidy.

She poured herself a large glass of water and took it out into the garden, where Alex was striding around shouting bastards as the cleaners, thinking he meant them, nervously hurried across the lawn with black sacks, picking up plastic cups, cans, cigarette butts, discarded masks and crusts of food.

'Oh, hello Suze. Well this is a fine and bloody, bloody mess,' he said, surveying the detritus and the trampled flowerbeds.

'Tell me about it.'

'I won't tell you what I found behind the sheds: condoms, joints; and a pair of somebody's knickers. Red ones… not yours, I suppose?'

'Thank you Alex. No, I managed to keep mine on, I'm sorry to say.'

'What? Oh. Quite. Sandy said something about that. In my opinion Suze, you'd be better off staying clear of that bastard.'

'Pete?'

'No, not Pete. Pete behaved rather gallantly, compared to the rest of his bloody lot. Bastards. No, I meant that Jackson bounder. Bastard.'

'How's your hand? You must have quite a punch to have broken his nose like that.'

'What? Broken is it? Bloody good show, I say. Ha!'

Immensely cheered by Jackson's injury, he took her arm and they walked towards the marquee.

'Don't take this the wrong way, Susie, but do you think that it's altogether wise to carry on with that creep? I mean, look at this mess. We've had parties before, as you know, and there's never been anything like this and it's all their doing.'

'Who's they?' said Susie, knowing the answer but asking because she knew Alex wanted to rant.

'That bloody rock crowd. Bastards. They're animals, every man Jack of them. They come here uninvited, drink all your best wine and then try to rape your women. Bastards. If you ask me, Pete's better off completely out of that world.'

'Probably,' Susie said to placate him.

'I mean to say, look at this. Just look at it. Bastards,' said Alex as they reached the marquee, which now resembled a bomb scene; chairs and tables turned over and smashed and broken glass everywhere.

'I'll help you clear up,' said Susie, disengaging herself from his arm and starting to stack the chairs that had not been smashed.

'Huh. Another bugger's lost his phone. That's the seventh we've found this morning,' said Alex as he picked up a Nokia. 'God knows how we're meant to return them.'

'Look at the messages,' she suggested.

'What?'

'Go into their messages and see who's sent them. It'll give you a clue whose mobile it is.'

'Good idea,' said Alex and he began to select and scroll as Susie collected empty wine bottles.

'Hello,' he said, 'There's quite of lot of messages from you here, Suze.'

'What?'

'The Inbox. There's a lot saying Susie.'

She took the phone from him quickly and immediately recognised her texts to Jackson.

'It's Jack's. He wanted directions yesterday. I texted him.' She shoved the phone into her pocket. 'I'll get it back to him.'

'Looks like he needed an awful lot of directions,' said Alex, watching her discomfort.

‘Let’s go and get some coffee, Al,’ she said, changing the subject, as she took his arm again and walked him to the kitchen, talking about the fight and saying how he would be considered such a hero up at the golf club.

They found Sandy in the kitchen, still in her dressing gown and looking 100 years old.

‘Christ,’ said Sandy, putting her head in her hands at the table, ‘what a disaster that was.’

‘There’s not too much damage, the caterers are cleaning up wonderfully,’ said Susie, with feigned brightness.

‘My roses are ruined,’ muttered Alex.

‘Sod your roses; what about our reputations?’ said Sandy, getting up to look for painkillers.

‘Well…’ began Susie.

‘There’s cocaine all over the bathrooms, cigarette burns in the carpets and now half of Dorset believes that we’re best friends with hoodlums. Who were all those skinheads?’ said Sandy.

‘Ian’s security,’ said Susie.

‘Disgusting people.’

‘Did you say cocaine? Bloody hell, I don’t want the cleaners seeing that,’ said Alex as he fetched cleaning cloths and rubber gloves from beneath the sink.

‘No. And not the police either. They just rang to say they’re coming back this afternoon for more statements,’ said Sandy as he left the kitchen muttering. She eyed Susie with a malicious stare.

‘So?’

‘So what?’ said Susie.

‘So you and Jackson? Did you? And before you answer do you know what that bastard said to me?’

‘I can imagine, he was out of it. And no, nothing happened. The war started before anything could.’

‘And what about poor Peter? How’s he going to react to you leaving him now? Make me a coffee, dearie.’

‘I don’t know what to do about Pete. I must go back in a minute and see how he is,’ Susie said as she filled the kettle, ‘I fear that he’s having a nervous breakdown.’

'Which you've greatly assisted.'

'Come on Sandy, you know I've tried. I've got to think of the boys, what's best for them now.'

'And?'

'And if he is having a breakdown he'll need looking after. Which I can't do if I'm having to get a job to look after the boys.'

'Why will you need a job?'

'Sandy, we have no money. Pete's crap with money, he hasn't got a pension. He clearly can't work, he's a bloody mess. But I don't think I can just leave him while he's so fragile.'

'Oh, it's all bollocks,' Sandy exploded, relieved at Susie's change of heart and giving her a hug. 'Bloody rock stars, bloody fame, it's all bollocks. Bugger the coffee, let's have a Bloody Mary. Don't worry, darling, he's probably already mowing the lawn in a state of cow-eyed contrition.'

CHAPTER 79

Three weeks later Billy Vernon was facing Ian Taylor in his London office, bravely arguing against what he couldn't believe he was hearing.

It had been an unnerving time for Vernon in his attempts to clean up his employer's image for the album launch. Although the press had reported the discovery of Taylor's daughter favourably, they had been more gleefully ballistic in their competition to describe the fight at the farmhouse, with the *Mirror's* TAYLOR NOW IN YOKEL RIOT vying against the *Sun's* HENHOUSE ROCKER SPARKS PUNCH-UP NO 3.

Fortunately for Vernon's agenda, the deputy of the slowly-recovering Klive Whicker had spun the story so that the media had believed that Taylor was the hero of the hour, carrying his friend to safety after farm yobs crazed on scrumpy attacked the aging rock idols.

But still Vernon was edgy, not least because he was sick of both Ian's and the label's lawyers asking how many more fights did Taylor feel he had to start before he was happy with his headlines? And now this.

'Sorry, Ian, this is madness; I don't understand.'

'It's not difficult, Billy,' said Taylor who had disarmed his manager by neglecting to swear yet. 'I'm cancelling the Earls Court gig.'

'But you'll be losing millions in publicity for the album.'

'No, you'll be losing millions; you, the label and all the rest who only smile at me for the money. I already have millions. Pete was right, I don't need the grief. And anyway, I may have a better idea. I'm thinking about it.'

'Pete? Pete's a fucking alcoholic junkie! You can't go by what Pete says.'

'Ah, but *in vino veritas*, Billy; *in narcos veritas* too. Anyway, this is not a matter for discussion; the gig isn't happening and I'm not going to do any other promo for the album. No interviews, nothing. I've had it with being a whore.'

'But… but… what about the peace protest?'

'Billy, 'Blowing in the Wind' never stopped soldiers shooting heads off. Dylan might just as well have called it 'Pissing in the Wind'. I've made my point and if people are too thick to see its wisdom, well, let us all die stupid.'

'But you don't even have to really do anything for the album, Ian; it's only repackaging songs that are already out there.'

'Precisely,' said Taylor grimly. 'And how fucked is that? I started out with an urge to write new songs. I'm a musician, not a fucking used-car dealer. Anyway, that's that – and Catherine agrees.'

'Umm… have you had the test yet? I mean she might not even be…'

'I know,' Taylor stopped him icily, 'but I would prefer to believe that she is. No, I've not had the test and I'm not going to. After all, nobody tested you lot to see if you were ever telling me the truth.'

'The label will not be happy, Ian, you do know that.'

'The label hasn't been happy since the repeal of slavery. By the way, on that subject I want you to start looking around for another deal. The contract with BPA runs out next year and I don't fancy renewing it. See if you can find me a groovy little independent.'

'But why?'

'For starters their day is done, it's like having a contract with a dinosaur, mate. But mainly because I want to work with people who know about music, or at least prefer rock and roll to opera. I want to work with people who don't know what a spreadsheet is.'

'But…'

'There's too many fucking financiers in the business these days, Billy. I didn't start a band in Birmingham all those years ago to end up working for rejects from 'The Office'.'

'It's not a good time to switch labels, Ian. Can we talk about it?' said Vernon as Taylor walked to the door.

'We just did.'

CHAPTER 80

Peter quite liked his new life in the rented attic flat of the large wooden chalet off Cobb Road, where he been for a month since he was discharged from hospital. He could gaze at the beauty of Lyme Bay and sip a small beer which was all he allowed himself after his exit from the music business meant he had no more need of drugs to get numb.

Best of all, he could stay up all night writing the book that he believed might just fund the cost of divorcing Susie, and not just be separated, as they had agreed in the shared awareness that she had changed beyond the point of return.

He had considered an immediate divorce, citing and shaming Jackson but dismissed it not only because he was weary of scandal but weary, too, of Susie accurately prefacing her every angry excuse with the swipe that it was the years of his own vile behaviour that were to blame for everything.

As it was nearing the last of the summer's sunny days he walked out to enjoy it, watching the boats and squinting against the warm glare as gulls cried above him and children excitedly asked for ice creams. He was just passing the Marine Aquarium, relishing the salted air, when his mobile rang.

'Is that the news desk?' said a voice that he had not expected ever to hear again.

'Hello Ian,' said Peter, immediately cheering a little.

'How's it going?'

'Oh, pretty shit. Well, some days are pretty shit and others are just...shit. It's the depression, the old black dog. But apparently it lifts after a thousand years.'

'Sorry to hear that. I heard that you almost got sectioned.'

'Ish,' said Peter, lighting a cigarette. 'It was a serious consideration, apparently. But I'd have done a runner before they could have managed the ECT.'

'Yeah, you'd have fancied flying over the cuckoo's nest, Pete. Although they'd probably have asked for Nicholson back after a couple of days of you.'

'Huh.'

'So what gear have they got you on?'

'Oh, the usual shit… catering-sized packs of downers, prozac, some other thing that's blue…'

'That's for your knob, mate.'

'I fucking wish… Actually, I don't fucking wish. Poor old Susie. I have no wish. You don't wish on this gear, you just feel like all the highs and lows have gone. Everything's flat. Like some fucking carpenter's just planed your life.'

'Jesus.'

'No, I don't think it was him.'

Taylor laughed enthusiastically and the sound made Peter smile; a rare event, since an emergency course of lithium was the first prescription made by the psychiatrist the day after the party, when he had been taken, near-catatonic in nervous collapse, to the nearest mental hospital.

'Are you allowed to drink?' said Taylor.

'I'm not meant to, or else the trank doesn't work. Or so they claimed. I got around it.'

'How?'

'If I fancy a drink I take more pills to compensate for those nixed by the beer.'

'That's really fucking stupid,' Taylor said.

Peter recognised the tone and automatically hunched.

'Seriously. I hope that is one of your crap jokes'.

Peter wanted to say that he didn't make jokes any more because he felt that every atom of his usefulness at work, as a husband, let alone as a father, all of it had completely and utterly vanished and there was nothing funny about any of it. He wanted to say that he felt bloody hollow inside at the alarming awareness that there might, actually, be no prospect of absolutely any hope; that fate, as he had also told Alex, was not a law of fucking physics, it's just bad fucking luck. No work, no money, no girl anymore. He wanted to say that he had never felt so unbelonging.

'Yeah, of course,' he said instead.

'Pete, you know I can't take you back now? Not like this. It would be madness!.'

'As it were.'

'You've got to rest. You burnt out. It's OK. Fucking hell, you're not exactly the first in this game.'

'Yeah,' said Peter.

'Look,' Taylor lowered his voice, 'I'm going to sort you out, OK? I can afford it. We've had some laughs. But I want that to be between you and me, alright?'

'What do you mean?'

'I don't want Susie to know and I don't want Catherine to know.'

'Why?'

'Well, for starters Susie really pissed me off. I know it's been tougher for you there, but, Jesus, she laid into me like fucking Hitler. Sorry, but…'

'It's alright. We're in separate places now.'

'Yeah. Well…'

'And Catherine?'

'Well, to tell you the truth I'm still not sure about her, you know, if she's telling me the truth.'

'So have the test done,' said Peter.

'Yeah, well I might, between you and me. I mean, if she is, great. And if she's not, she's kind of served her purpose. She's a nice kid, I like her a lot and I really do hope she's my kid. But, as we know, other people have got scammed before.'

'True.'

'So I don't want her knowing I'm going to bung you because I don't want her getting any bright ideas about my largesse. I've given her a bloody fortune already.'

'What?' said Peter, 'She's an 'in the will' job?'

'Bugger off. Test first, will later. No, I felt a bit bad about us using her for publicity like that so I paid her a generous fee for her impromptu role. It's only fair.'

'She was very convincing.'

'Whatever. The point is, outing her made the other… ah, thing, go away for a bit. Now she's the big new thing with the magazines and I can get on with my stuff. Did you hear I cancelled Earls Court? We're gonna play the gig at Wormwood Scrubs instead.'

'Cool.'

'Yeah, I figured it'd probably actually get more publicity for the album. We'll just do most of the the Rose set and a bit of rocking out at the end.'

'Most of it?'

'Well, I'm not doing 'Come to Daddy' in there! Fuck that… hello vicar, dropped your soap? And the tabloids would have another fucking field day if I did, what with Catherine and all that…'

'It's good that you paid her,' said Peter, earnestly. 'You've got a clear conscience either way.'

'Yeah, well she's got a bloody fortune to see her over. She'll be OK, so long as she doesn't blow it on any daft projects. Anyway, look man I've gotta split. You look after yourself. Take it easy, yeah? Oh, I hear you're writing a book.'

'Yeah, a kind of pop pulp fiction. It's pretty crap.'

'Am I in it?'

'Of course not.'

'Well if I am, just make sure that Doris Day plays me in the movie, dear. Cheers.'

Peter walked slowly back to his little flat, planning another dinner from the chip shop again. He went to the fridge and opened a beer, lit a cigarette and looked out at Golden Cap, wondering at its majesty and then realizing that it would soon be time for his lie down to meditate. His mobile rang again.

'Are you coming out to play?' said the slow voice that he had not expected ever to hear purr at him again.

'Hello,' he said affectionately. 'How are you?'

'I'm moving on. Time to. Thought I'd call before I went,' said Catherine.

'I hate goodbyes,' said Peter, 'Especially those that come so quickly after hello.'

'It's not a goodbye.'

'Explain.'

'I'm taking our band on the road.'

'Which one's our band?'

'Tundra Pox, darling.'

'What did you just call me?' said Peter, beaming.

'I'm learning PR-speak.'

'Well, I'll miss you,' said Peter. 'Where are you taking them?'

'We're taking them to Swindon. Darling.'

Peter heard her giggle.

'Why Swindon?'

'Ian fixed it. As a kind of present. He owns a radio station there which he's starting up again. The band is gigging in their car park as part of the re-opening. You've got to talk to a bloke called Frankie Cairns.'

'Who's he?'

'The new manager at Radio Georgie. I'll give you his number on the bus.'

'I've got to talk? What bus? Radio what?'

'The Tundra Pox tour bus. Keep up. I've hired it.'

'Ian's money?'

'My fee, actually,' she said playfully.

'Ah,' said Peter.

'So are you coming?'

'What?'

'Are you coming on the road?'

'No. No, I've had enough of all that,' said Peter.

'You haven't had enough of me.'

Peter started to laugh.

'Believe me, I've had more than enough of you.'

'No you haven't. I can tell.'

'Oh, don't fucking start that all over again,' said Peter.'

'I can tell.'

'Fuck off.'

'Come on,' she said, 'it'll be a laugh. Remember what I told you? Live a little.'

'No, really.'

'Remember the car park after the AA meeting?'

'What about it?'

'The first time you turned me down.'

'Yeah..' said Peter, cautiously.

'I thought I looked quite nice.'

'You looked very nice, Catherine. Somewhat lacking in clothing but, yes, very nice. But that won't work either.'

'Come on, this band's good. We need to plan them a future and you can do that.'

'As soon as you say plan, I think, 'Oh God, bloody meetings again. Meetings, targets and bollockings.' I like spontaneity, I don't do planning. I wing it. But too often I hit a wall.'

'So wing it, come fly with me,' said Catherine as Peter heard a knock at his front door. He ignored it.

'Catherine.'

'Darling.'

'Seriously, I also fall in love very easily.'

'I'd never have guessed that, Pete.'

He heard another knock at his door.

'And I like a lot of sex.'

'Which would be a such problem for a sex addict.'

'Hang on a minute, there's someone at the door,' said Peter, going through the flat to open it.

'Any other riders to your contract, boss?'

'Yes, I don't like surprises,' he said unlatching the front door and then fell silent, grinning.

In front of the chalet was a black tour bus with the slogan Top of the Pox Tour in large red letters along its side. And there, on his doorstep, stood Catherine, holding her mobile to her ear.

'Really?' she said.

'Oh for fuck's sake,' said Peter, laughing.

'I've had more charming acceptances,' said Catherine, smiling as she kissed him.

RAGABOND PRESS

With its entire team of two, Ragabond Press is one of the new wave of super-micropublishers to emerge in the early part of the 21st century, taking advantage of the technological and artistic liberation from the techniques of the old publishing industry.

Following the global market introduced by the Internet, the original micropublishing trend developed when writers addressed a limited, niche market, too small to be of commercial interest to conventional publishers, and reached this reduced readership through online publishing companies such as CafePress or Lulu.com.

Super-micropublishers took the DIY ethic further by addressing a non-niche market but by taking on almost every aspect of the publishing themselves. Ragbond Press came into being from the pooling of the skills of its two partners, whose combined experience includes writing, editing, proofing, typesetting, layout, design, photography, audience-sampling, e-publishing, distribution, marketing and PR.

The Ragabond Two are Jill Newton and Geoff Baker, ex-journalists who, between them, have more than 50 years' experience of the communications industries. Jill Newton has a writing and production background initially established at *The Economist* and IPC Magazines and later developed editing and producing corporate publications. Geoff Baker is a former 'scuzzy hack' who ran the showbusiness department of the *Daily Star* before becoming head of press and PR to Paul McCartney.

Newton and Baker began their partnership in 2009 and, just over a year later, finished Rock Bottom, which is their first novel and one of a number of books in production from Ragabond Press.

info@ragabondpress.com